THE WICKED TWISTED ROAD

BY

DS HAMILTON

Ryan,
Thanks for the great blurb!
Keep up the fantastic work &
sell a million books.
- *[signature]*

From

Dark Owl Publishing, LLC

Arizona

Cover image by Jason J. McCuiston.
Cover design by Dark Owl Publishing.

Visit us on our website at:
www.darkowlpublishing.com

ALSO FROM
DARK OWL PUBLISHING

Novels
The Keeper of Tales
An epic fantasy adventure by Jonathon Mast

Just About Anyone
High fantasy comedy from the twisted mind of Carl R. Jennings

The Black Garden
The beginning of the dark mysteries within the town of Ste. Odile
by John S. McFarland

The Malakiad
A hilarious mythological misadventure by Gustavo Bondoni

Carnivore Keepers
Sci-fi adventure where humans and dinosaurs collide
by Kevin M. Folliard

Anthologies
A Celebration of Storytelling
The anthological festival of tales

Something Wicked This Way Rides
Where genre fiction meets the Wild West

Collections
The Dark Walk Forward
A harrowing collection of frightful stories from John S. McFarland

The Last Star Warden:
Tales of Adventure and Mystery from Frontier Space, Volume I
The first in the series of the Star Warden's adventures
from Jason J. McCuiston

The Last Star Warden Volume II:
The Un Quan Saga
More chronicles of the Last Star Warden
by Jason J. McCuiston

No Lesser Angels, No Greater Devils
Beautiful and haunting stories collected from Laura J. Campbell

Tension of A Coming Storm
Horror and terror within a dark mass of short stories by Adrian Ludens
Coming September 2022

Young Readers
Grayson North, Frost-Keeper of the Windy City
A totally cool urban fantasy adventure by Kevin M. Folliard

Dragons of the Ashfall
Book One of the War of Leaves and Scales
Steampunk fantasy adventure from Jonathon Mast

Annette: A Big, Hairy Mom
A touching story of a boy and his motherly friend, a Sasquatch
both written and illustrated by John S. McFarland
Coming 2022

Shivers, Scares, and Goosebumps
Short tales to chill you to your bones both written and illustrated by
Vonnie Winslow Crist
Coming 2022

Available on Vella
The Last Star Warden: The Phantom World
Eight episodes of nail-biting sci-fi action from Jason J. McCuiston

Buy the books for Kindle and in paperback
www.darkowlpublishing/the-bookstore
www.darkowlpublishing/the-yr-bookstore

More titles are planned for 2022 and beyond!

For my brother.

1
WAYFARING STRANGER

Idegen gnashed her teeth, braced for the collision. The virtual control panel lit up with multiple system warnings. The tang of smoke filled the artificial atmosphere. Her hands flew across the instruments, giving counter commands. Her eyes, hidden behind the flight mask, assessed the situation with several lifetimes of training and experience. With so many malfunctions, she could not maintain orbit. Worse, she might not be able to contact Fleet Command to inform them of her situation.

She had to make planet-fall ahead of schedule. Without the benefit of a stealth shield, as it was one of the damaged systems. She swore. All the cycles of extensive planning and multitudes of intricate calculations thrown into the hazard by a simple, unpredicted bit of space flotsam.

Switching the flight controls to manual, Idegen Videshee, cell commander and scout pilot for the Logonijy Empire, guided her small, injured craft into the blue planet's swirling atmosphere. She seethed at the imperfect intelligence she had received before leaving the command ships at the far distant edge of this galaxy's spiral arm. At that time, long-range sensors had not detected any artificial satellites or debris fields around her target, so she had placed the craft on autopilot and entered her cryostasis for the long journey into this star system's interior.

But the blue planet had made over a hundred revolutions around the white sun since she had gone to sleep. And much had changed in that time. Her brain's neural web, linked to the ship's computer, had been fed a constant data stream of new orders from Fleet Command, updated intel and signal broadcasts from the planet, facts about her ship's auto-corrections to maintain its stealthy approach to the target world, as well as ancillary discoveries and intelligence gleaned along the way. In those informational dreams, Idegen had learned that the dominant lifeforms on this particular planet—indeed in the entire system and even the parts of this galaxy thus far explored—had developed technology at a frighteningly rapid pace since nearly driving themselves to extinction in two globe-spanning wars.

Unfortunately, she had not been revived from the preprogrammed slumber in time to prevent her ship from blundering into the field of satellites and clutter that had grown up around the planet over the past fifty revolutions. The collision with the near-undetectable detritus was all but inevitable under autopilot, the minuscule debris somehow penetrating the shields without so much as reducing inertia.

Idegen used the yoke to push her small, flat ship toward the planet's horizon, hoping to find a safe place to land under the cover of darkness. She broke the atmosphere above a great expanse of blue water near the equator, attempting to reduce the chances of the resulting fireball being witnessed. Warnings from her still-functioning sensors asserted the futility of this attempt.

Three primitive aircraft, slightly larger than her own, streaked up into the darkening sky on an intercept course.

Her communications array spat out garbled signals. It, too, had not survived the orbital collision intact. Not that it mattered in this situation. She was not authorized to make first contact with the planet's inhabitants. Her mission was simply to observe and report.

A mission, Idegen realized, she had already failed as soon as the three jet propulsion craft came within visual range. Her sensors detailed a list of offensive weapons on the interceptors, most of which were more than capable of bringing down her injured craft with a direct hit now that she was inside the atmosphere. The intense heat generated by her ship's deep-space engines, if they were fired, would ignite this atmosphere, reducing the planet to a burnt-out husk in a matter of minutes, so she was reduced to using only anti-gravitational propulsion.

The enemy craft were designed for high-speed combat maneuvers within their planet's skies. Her ship simply was not. "If only I were in a Sabrefang." But Idegen was in a long-range recon Outrider, not one of the Empire's elite fighters, and she would simply have to make do with its limited combat capabilities.

Try as she might, she could not shake all three interceptors. Eventually, they tired of the game and her refusal to respond to their inscrutable communications. The lead fighter released a warhead that streaked straight for her ship. Idegen launched countermeasures, using all her skill to pull away from the formation. The projectile exploded in the cloud of released metal fragments, rocking her craft with the shockwave. She did not have permission to engage in hostilities, but neither did she wish to be killed by a primitive species in a meaningless skirmish on a backward planet.

Idegen powered up the flechette railgun's electromagnets. If she was going down, she would go down fighting.

Another missile careened past before exploding into a second cloud of jettisoned chaff. She pulled back on the yoke, hit the gravitational stabilizer. The ship froze in midair, her pursuers rocketing past at supersonic speeds.

Dropping the nose of her craft, she locked onto one enemy vehicle and fired. A small burst, not intended to be lethal, just enough to weaken the target's shields and let them know she was not easy prey. The superheated barrage of fast-moving metal shredded the offending craft. It exploded in a fireball that lit the night sky like a setting sun.

"Hm. No shields."

The other two broke off instantly, returning the way they had come. Idegen sighed with relief. She had not meant to become involved in such an engagement—and certainly had not meant to destroy a native—not that she had any qualms about fighting or killing an enemy. She just hadn't been told by Fleet Command that the planet's inhabitants *were* the enemy. At least not yet.

However, since the encounter had been forced upon her, she was glad she had emerged as the victor.

The elation was brief. A warning signal flashed across her visor before she saw the three surface-to-air warheads on the display. Idegen hit the countermeasures trigger and tried to climb as fast as the Outrider could. But again, the shortcomings of the ship's design displayed themselves. The missiles climbed much faster.

"Damn." She activated the eject protocol. Her flight harness went rigid, trapping her inside the force bubble that materialized around the command chair. The release charges triggered, hurling her from the Outrider moments before the first missile struck the ship.

Falling from the star-filled sky, she had a clear view of the impact. The ship's shield shimmered like a glass ball against the exploding projectile, the craft losing deflector panels and rocking sideways from the concussion. The second missile completely shattered the shield and scorched the rear fuselage. The third clipped the right wing, shearing it off in a blinding conflagration. The burning Outrider rolled, careened, and fluttered to the dark waters below like a crippled avian before disappearing beneath the moon-touched waves in a hissing geyser.

Idegen wondered if the automated self-destruct sequence would initiate. There were so many system failures before the encounter… She hoped it did. The Empire could not afford its technology falling into the hands of a potential enemy. And yet, if the ship was gone, then she was trapped and alone on this alien world of several billion apparently warlike beings.

Under the power of low-gravity generators, Idegen's command chair came to rest in a swampy region covered by tall, brittle grass, shallow rills of reeking water, and tall spindly trees of a stark and grim countenance. Extracting herself quickly, she activated the distress beacon on the chair, then set the smaller self-destruct sequence in motion. All she could do was hope that her signal reached the fleet or one of her comrades assigned to the other systems of this galaxy's arm.

"Vodie," she whispered as she hurried from the site of her landing, "I wish you were here." But, as the command chair ignited behind her, Idegen understood that she was completely alone for the first time in her very long life.

***

She was alone for three planetary rotations. During that time, she explored this strange, new world—or this tiny corner of it. Preliminary intel had revealed a wide range of climates and ecosystems. Idegen found herself in a stiflingly hot, humid marshland that stretched as far as the eye could see in any direction (and she could see very, very far). But there was a rugged, savage beauty to the place of deep waters and tall trees, evidence of lovely and dangerous life. The sky was a deep cerulean blue during the sun-bright days and so dark at night despite the moon and stars that her rarely used nocturnal hunting lenses slid over her pupils.

Great, white-headed and dark-winged raptors swooped and soared in the blue sky above the treetops before diving to claim silvery-scaled life from the dark waters. Tiny biting and stinging winged and crawling insectoids proliferated in the shallows and among the dense vegetation, only to give their lives as nourishment to slick-skinned, dull-colored, hopping amphibians—these being wonderfully musical at night. Multi-colored, slithering limbless serpents, in turn, fed on these nocturnal singers. Other, smaller avians preyed on the insects, the amphibians, and the serpents alike, and in turn, were food for larger, feral predators of both mammalian and reptilian natures.

Sadly, only the fiercest and largest of these—the wily, dust-colored felines and the long and low reptiles, covered in green-grey armor and sporting an array of fangs that put Idegen's to shame—held barely enough of the life-giving energy to provide her with sustenance. And this they did not surrender easily.

On the fourth day, weakened by lack of nourishment and exposure to the unfamiliar environs, she was surrounded and captured by a score of uniformly armored natives. They were armed with primitive hand-held, chemical-projectile weapons as well as non-lethal electrical and gas devices. Lacking a personal sidearm as her mission dictated, she still tried to fight and escape.

But there were too many of them, and she was simply too weak.

Before they brought her down with electrical charges, Idegen gave them a blood-drenched smile. The natives were hostile, well-organized, and adept at using their primitive technologies and rudimentary tactics. But, after killing two of her captors in battle, she understood something else about them.

They were also an excellent source of food.

2
SLEEPING ON THE BLACKTOP

Jon splashed his face with water in the surprisingly clean men's room and ran wet hands through his greasy dark hair. He knew he needed a shower—needed a good night's sleep even more. But he only had a few hours to make it to Tunica in time to register for the qualifying satellite tournament. Smiling at the hazel-eyed wraith in the black Social Distortion t-shirt staring out of the mirror, Jon French acknowledged that he was just that close to his long-held dream: competing in the World Series of Poker.

Freedom and a fresh start. His New Year's Resolution was finally beginning on the first Wednesday morning in September, but better late than never, right?

In the deserted convenience store of the Love's Travel Center, a Muzak version of "Arthur's Theme" played on the overhead speakers, and the adjoining McDonald's filled the air with the mouthwatering scent of baking biscuits and frying sausage and bacon. Disdaining these belly-bloating delicacies, Jon picked up a big cup of hours-old coffee, a pack of caffeine pills, and a king-size NutRageous bar. He figured that'd be enough of a bump to get him through the other side of Memphis, onto Highway 61, and all the way to the casinos in Mississippi.

After registering, he'd grab a couple hours' sleep in the parking lot until his room was ready. Then the games could begin. He would give himself absolutely no chance to blow the two thousand dollar buy-in he'd just gotten his hands on. He had let himself down too many times before. Usually when things looked like they were just about to turn his way.

Like right now.

At the register, a tired, heavyset lady with a tightly curled white afro watched CNN, something about a fighter plane going down in Florida during a training exercise last week. Shaking her head as she rang him up, she said, "Don't know why we even need fighter planes no more. Not like terrorists have warplanes. Just use our airliners for whatever they want."

Jon shrugged. "They gotta spend our tax dollars someplace, I reckon." Not that he'd filed a tax return in nearly a decade.

"Sure ain't on helping us poor folks." The granny-lady snorted and handed him his bag of socially accepted stimulants and his change before turning back to the news.

Jon walked out into the predawn morning, across the vacant asphalt lit by the harsh white overheads, to the nondescript, Bondo-and-primer, last-century Corolla with Hamilton County tags parked beside the dumpster. He planned on abandoning it in Tunica, having swiped it from an apartment complex in Lookout Valley on his way out of Chattanooga about five hours before.

Life lesson number thirty-four learned inside the Davidson County Correctional Development Center: *No matter how bad it looks or how old it is, nine times out of ten, a Toyota is a safe bet in a pinch.*

The moths still burned the midnight oil, and the mosquitos were just getting out of bed. Jon breathed in the cool air, the scent of fresh-cut grass mingled with those of garbage from the dumpster, car exhaust, and diesel fuel. But at least it wasn't swamp-ass hot just yet. Not like it would be in about an hour or so.

Jon suddenly didn't look forward to sleeping in the stolen Corolla in a parking lot while the Mississippi sun turned him into the brownie of an Easy-Bake Oven. He took a sip of the black coffee and winced at the bitterness, deciding the pending discomfort would be a small price to pay to finally get his life back on track. Just one more round of dues.

If he could place in the tournament, get close to the ten grand buy-in for the Main Event, maybe get some TV time and win some fans, then he could get sponsorship and go pro. He knew he was a good enough player, and with a shave and a shampoo, he was even decent-looking enough to go on camera. He still had his athlete's build. No pot belly or extra chins just yet, which put him head and shoulders above most of the WSOP players.

Getting back into the car, Jon saw his phone on the passenger seat, and his stomach filled with heavy rocks. There was a text message from an Unknown Caller. All the message contained was a Nashville area code phone number. He knew what that meant and had a pretty good idea who had sent it. Worse, he knew he probably wouldn't be making it to Tunica, to the tournament, and not into the World Series of Poker. Not this time. Maybe never.

Jon took the thin red stirrer from his coffee, folded it twice, jammed it into his mouth, and started chewing.

Feeling like someone had let the air out of all the tires on his soul, he sat in the dinged-up '99 Corolla in an I-40 gas station just east of Memphis, Tennessee, and dialed the number on the text. Listening to the dull ring-back, he cursed himself, the cruel twists of fate in his miserable life, and all the bad decisions he'd ever made.

"Duster's." A woman's gravelly voice answered the call. Hank Senior sang about the Lost Highway in the background. "We're closed and don't open again 'til two p.m."

"Is Joey Green there?" Jon knew he was.

After a pause, Joey said, "Hey, Frog-boy, that you?"

Jon closed his eyes and rubbed the bridge of his nose. Joey was the only person still using the jailhouse nickname Jon had picked up a decade ago. He could tell by Joey's frantically sluggish voice that he was tiptoeing the balance beam between drunk on beer and whiskey and high on meth and pills. "Yeah, Joey, it's me. *Jon.* I got your text."

"Where you at, Froggy?"

"Memphis. On my way to Tunica."

Joey laughed like a dull razor blade across an old scar. "Still dreaming of that big score in the World Series, huh? How'd you ever get the buy-in?"

Jon thought about the hefty pot he'd dragged against the Hamilton County Mountie and the THP in the Chatt-town private game a few hours before. Fortunately, the deputy had remembered Jon's days as a tailback at Rhea County High School just up the road. Unfortunately, the state trooper had been an undergrad at MTSU when Jon French, All-Conference defensive back, had been booted off the team and incarcerated for being busted in just such an illegal big stakes game. He was a sore loser who kept raising the question of whether or not Jon was a cheat.

When he had cashed out with most of their money, Jon didn't know if he'd even make it to the door, much less to the parking lot and out of town. In a stolen car. "I managed. It wasn't easy, but I did it. What you need, Joey?"

Joey inhaled sharply, telling Jon he'd been a little too brusque in his tone. "What I need, Frog-boy, is for you to put your little fantasy on the backburner and heel-fucking-to. I gotta remind you who kept you from becoming a white-boy sex toy for Folk Nation back in county?"

Jon winced. That had been almost ten years ago, and he still woke in a cold sweat from nightmares about it. "No, Joey. I remember, and I'm grateful. What can I do for you?"

Joey took a loud swallow of something and belched into the phone. "That's better, *Jon*. I need you to pick up a car at the airport and take it to K-town."

Jon rolled his eyes. He had absolutely no desire to go anywhere near Knoxville, and not just because it was on the other side of the whole damn state. "The Memphis airport?"

"What? No, no, no. The *Nashville* airport."

Jon blinked, didn't know what to say.

"Froggy, you still there?"

"Yeah... don't you have somebody in town or close by who can do this, Joey? I mean, I've been up for almost twenty-four hours, and it'll take me another three to get there... Plus, I'm in a *borrowed* car."

"Naw, Jon. That ain't how this shit works. I ain't concerned about how convenient this is for you. You need to be concerned about how convenient it is for me. And for Craig Byce."

"Shit."

"Yeah, shit." Joey clinked a Zippo on the other end of the line, maybe lighting a joint to take the edge off. "There's something shaking loose in the organization, Froggy, and this job looks to be big. Orders came straight out o' Angola, and you know what that means."

Jon closed his eyes tight and fought down the rising urge to vomit. "Yes. I know what that means. So they... uh... they specifically asked for me?"

Joey gave a wheezing chuckle. "Fuck, no. They just said they wanted the best courier I got. That'd be you as of right now. I got two other guys on runs to Cincy and the ATL. Nobody else got the skills you do, Jon. That's why you're on the hook. Now, how soon can you get to the airport?"

Jon started the car. "I'm on my way as we speak."

"Good. I'll text you the info. And, Froggy, don't get pinched for that loaner."

The line went dead, and Jon tossed his phone onto the passenger seat. For a moment, he thought about getting on I-40 westbound and trying to outrun them. Maybe they didn't have contacts in Vegas or Reno, maybe even L.A. He thought about Mexico, but he didn't speak Spanish worth a damn, and Canada was out of the question. From what he'd heard, the Canucks were tougher on illegal immigration than the GOP.

But his gut told him there was nowhere to run. If there was one thing he knew for sure about the organization, what everybody knew, it was that once you were in, you stayed in as long as they wanted you. Or you suddenly came down with a slight case of death.

Up until now, he'd only been an errand boy and a messenger. A nobody. But Joey had said, "This job looks to be big." Whether he wanted it or not, this run had the makings of his promotion to the major leagues, which meant that he would forever be officially in. Which, by definition, meant he would never get out.

As he pulled the Corolla onto I-40 headed east, Jon tried to ignore the road signs that gave the number of miles to the exits headed for Tunica. He tried not to think about just how close he had come to getting out from under the Dixie Mafia.

3
AMERICAN BLOOD

Dr. Martin Helbourne hadn't slept in two days. Not since they had flown him in from Colorado Springs, sworn him to absolute secrecy, and finally showed him the subject. With very little in the way of specifics, he was told by the hard-faced men in uniform that he was to examine her and find out everything he could—without engaging in communication—before they moved her to a more secure location. He had gotten to work immediately and hadn't stopped in the past thirty-odd hours. But he wasn't tired. He was riding a wave of euphoria, adrenaline, and validation that he'd been seeking his entire life. Or at least the last twenty-five professional years of it.

It had not taken very long to come to the private conclusion that the subject was not of terrestrial origin. The test results proving this to the skeptics and higher-ups would take a little longer.

With PhDs in astronomy and biology, and Master's degrees in engineering and applied physics, Dr. Helbourne had dreamed of being a part of space exploration and discovering extraterrestrial life ever since he had read Bradbury's *The Martian Chronicles* as a boy. Poor eyesight and an assiduous aversion to physical exercise had kept him from becoming an astronaut.

But his inquisitive mind, formidable memory, and workaholic nature had helped him gain positions in both the SETI program and at NASA before landing him a conciliatory teaching job at the Air Force Academy—after being booted from the Breakthrough Listen Program last year for "personal differences." Now, after decades of watching his beloved agencies be defunded, downsized, pushed to the bottom pages of bloated national budgets, and overrun by politics and bureaucracy, he was finally witnessing the fulfillment of his lifelong dreams.

The last tests run, Dr. Helbourne stood at the triple-paned safety glass window, looking past his own unimpressive reflection. Watching the subject, waiting for the results. He was deep beneath the surface of the launch center at Cape Canaveral, hundreds of feet beneath the guided tours and the day-to-day operations. Apparently, this section had been built during the Cold War as a safe haven in case of a Soviet nuclear strike on American space interests. Probably a priority in the wake of the Cuban Missile Crisis. Unlike a majority of the government agencies he'd worked with, the military had shown incredible efficiency in refurbishing the place and transforming it into a fully-secure medical laboratory and holding facility. Apparently, all within twelve hours of capturing the subject on the previous Friday.

"She's beautiful," Helbourne said to himself for not the first time, sipping his cold coffee laced with bourbon. And though she did appear disarmingly beautiful, even desirable, by human standards, he meant that her mere existence and all that it portended was the most beautiful thing he could possibly imagine. *We are not alone in the universe. There are other sentient beings. And how like us they are!*

Of course, those similarities were, in essence, only skin deep. X-rays and thermal imaging had revealed several physiological differences, as had the blood and tissue samples. He couldn't get her into an MRI without killing her, the CT scans disclosing that her body was laced with some kind of metallic implants. Not only was she an alien and a beguiling specimen of feminine beauty, but she was also a cyborg: the pulp-fiction trifecta.

The intercom buzzed, causing him to spill his coffee down the front of his rumpled lab coat. "Dammit."

"Dr. Helbourne," an Air Force MP's voice came through the speaker. "The colonel is here and en route to the lab."

"Yes. Thank you." Helbourne tried to make himself as presentable as possible. He'd hoped to have time enough to take a shower and change into his nicer suit, maybe even shave and brush his teeth before meeting whatever square-jawed and steely-eyed ideal of American military glory they sent to take over this operation. The much-needed ablations would have given him confidence in the coming confrontation. With more hair in his ears and nostrils than on his head and possessing a broader waist than shoulders, Helbourne knew he was not an imposing figure. He also knew he would need to stand up to this jack-booted wall of medals if he wanted to keep control of the subject. No doubt the military had a dissection table ready for her somewhere in Area 51.

The security lock on the lab door clicked and a pair of crew-cut men in crisp, black BDUs stepped in. A tall, athletically toned woman with cool brown skin and short, dark hair shot with silver walked in behind them. She wore a faded grey U.S. Army t-shirt, khaki shorts with a wadded-up Boonie hat peeking out of the left hip pocket, and a pair of Nike cross-trainers. The armed men took up positions on either side of the door as she entered and glanced around the room.

"Dr. Helbourne," the woman said with a husky voice, extending her hand with a polite smile. "I'm Colonel Emily Sharpe. Pleased to meet you."

Helbourne blinked. He returned the smile and shook hands, noting the strong grip. "You're not regular Army." He had expected Richard Crenna from Rambo, not Pam Grier playing Demi Moore in *G.I. Jane*.

Sharpe turned her attention to the main attraction on the other side of the safety glass. "Not anymore. Let's just say I fill a niche between the military and the intelligence community. So, what have we got here, and why the hell is she naked?"

Helbourne flushed. "Well, I was studying her..." He felt blood rush into his ears. "Not like that! No, it's just that... well, she *looks* like us, but she's not like us. I wanted to see if she displayed any more differences in anatomy, physiology, or behavior by the way she moves and acts."

Colonel Sharpe folded her arms and raised an eyebrow. "And?"

"Nothing yet, but—"

"Then let's get her some clothes, Doctor." She gave him a condescending smile that deepened the crow's feet around her dark brown eyes. "We've got a lot of lonely soldiers down here, and I don't need any of them seeing something that might make them forget that she has the blood of three of their brothers-in-arms on her pretty, white hands."

"Four." Helbourne pushed the call button on his desk. "She woke up during one of the procedures, broke her restraints and killed an Air Force medic before we could get her sedated again."

"Hm." The colonel looked back at the subject. "So, what have these procedures and tests revealed about her, Doctor? Is she an enemy super soldier, a secret corporate experiment, a Marvel superhero, or an Amazon woman from the Moon? Has she made any attempt to initiate or respond to verbal communications?"

The security lock clicked, and an orderly appeared. He nervously eyed the two men in black who coolly eyed him back. "Doctor?"

"Please procure some clothes for the subject." Helbourne waved the young man out of the room.

The door closed again, and Colonel Sharpe prompted, "Well? What do we have here, Doctor? Who or what is she? And does she represent a threat to this nation?"

Helbourne frowned at her phraseology. Sharpe did not appear to care about the rest of the planet, just the patches of real estate that flew under the Stars and Stripes. "Per my instructions, we have not attempted to engage her in verbal communication, and thus far, she has returned the favor. We're still waiting on the DNA results, but I have been able to make a list of characteristics that are substantially different from normal *Homo sapiens* physicality." He picked up a clipboard with his findings and held it out to her.

Sharpe waved a dismissive hand. "I didn't come down here to read your thesis, Doctor. Just give me the highlights."

Helbourne scowled and cleared his throat. "Well, let's see... She shows a growth range that is approximately eight to ten percent larger than that of most human females—"

"Are we, in fact, certain that she is a female, Doctor? Surgeons can do remarkable things these days, you know."

"Yes. X-rays show a pelvic structure nearly identical to that of a human female, and our thermal scans reveal organs approximating those of the uterus and ovaries in the expected places. Whatever she is, she appears to reproduce just like us."

Sharpe glanced at her men. "None of this leaves this room."

"Yes, ma'am."

"Please continue, Doctor."

Helbourne ran a hand over his wispy hair and found his place. "...Uh, okay, her muscular and skeletal systems look to be between twenty and thirty percent stronger than human tissue. However, this has been augmented even further by what appears to be biomechanical implants."

Sharpe turned and raised an eyebrow. "That sounds like something our boys at DARPA would love to get their hands on. Any chance of extracting one or two for study?"

Helbourne shook his head. "Not without risking extreme harm to the subject. Each implant looks to be fully integrated into her entire system. It's not like in the sci-fi movies where a mechanical arm is just a mechanical arm that can be ripped off, then bolted back on. The metal and circuitry are as much a part of her as her own bones and muscle fibers. Nanotech doesn't come close to describing it."

Sharpe frowned, looking back at the subject and motioning him to continue.

"As of right now, it's my personal and professional opinion that she's not from around here."

"That's the running theory upstairs, apparently." Sharpe's tone implied she did not necessarily subscribe to it. "Otherwise, you wouldn't be the go-to guy on this. So, did she come with any artifacts or accessories that might support that theory? Any lightsabers or Klingon war weapons?"

"She was wearing a flight suit and boots, very similar to what our own high-altitude pilots might wear. I gave the materials a cursory glance under the microscope and didn't see anything more advanced than a synthetic microfiber. But I ordered a detailed chemical analysis. The results should come back in a day or two.

"They also found a burnt heap of metallic slag not too far from where they captured her. I postulate that it was her command module, but she had used a self-destruct device on it. Again, nothing definitive, and still waiting on the labs."

Sharpe digested this. "What else?"

"And then there's this." Helbourne stepped to the panel beside the window and pushed a button.

The subject's chamber went completely dark. A moment later, the window polarized, giving a green night-vision view. The subject covered her ears, threw her head back, and howled like a caged wolf. Her incisors extended to become two-inch fangs and her eyes glowed white like those of an animal caught in headlights.

Helbourne hit the switch, and the lights came back up. The subject relaxed but gave them a baleful look through the glass. Her eyes reverted to their normal blue-grey hue, and her fangs retracted.

"What the hell was that?" Colonel Sharpe demanded.

"Subsonic frequency. Like a dog whistle, only more intense. As you can see, she doesn't like it very much. Also, in the absence of light, she has a second set of lenses that covers her eyes to give her low-light vision. Obviously, she is descended from some sort of nocturnal predator, whereas we are descended from daytime hunter-gatherers. Her senses are much sharper than ours, capable of operating within a greater range of both sound and light frequencies. I can only speculate that her olfactory capabilities are just as enhanced. I'm working on a series of tests to verify this hypothesis..."

Colonel Sharpe smiled. "Well, whatever she is, we now know her weakness. And that's a start. Especially when it comes time to find out who she works for and why they sent her."

Helbourne scowled. "You don't mean to torture her? If she is, in fact, a visitor from another world, you could severely damage Earth's chances of ever becoming part of a spacefaring community."

Colonel Sharpe returned his look. "You seem to be under the impression, Doctor, that I give a damn about any of that. Right now, all I care about is the fact that she is believed to be the pilot of an unknown craft which shot down an F-22, killing a veteran Air Force pilot, and that we are certain that she killed three of our enlisted men. *Bare-handed.*

"My job is clear: debrief the subject and assess the threat she poses to these United States of America. And, if you're right and she's not a native of this planet, then I reckon the Geneva Convention doesn't exactly apply to her. Or should I say to *it?*"

When Helbourne didn't respond with anything other than a glare, Colonel Sharpe stepped closer to him, emphasizing her height and physicality. "Nothing else to add, Doctor? Good. I'll expect your full report within the next two hours. I'll use it to decide on the best way to transport the subject."

"To Area 51?" Helbourne blurted. "For vivisection, Colonel?"

Sharpe laughed, more good-naturedly than he'd expected. "You watch too many movies, Dr. Helbourne. Why take her across the country to an airbase where there's nothing but crazy test pilots, crazier engineers, and bored security guards when we have the best scientific laboratories in the world just up I-75?"

Helbourne blinked, thinking of his father's wartime contributions. "Oak Ridge?"

Sharpe put a finger to her lips and smiled. "Keep that under your hat, Doctor. Now, get me that report ASAP. Oh, and start drawing up some plans for a portable subsonic generator. Just in case." With that, she turned and led her Stormtroopers from the room.

A dull clank from the subject's room drew Helbourne's attention. The orderly had just slid a box containing medical scrubs and slippers through the tray slot. The subject eyed the articles suspiciously before tentatively feeling them and eventually sliding them on.

"It, indeed," Helbourne muttered as he watched her dress. He caught himself before putting any more thoughts into words. He knew the room had to be bugged.

He smiled at the subject. *You may be more right than you know, Colonel.* He was glad Sharpe's initial inquiry had not touched upon the subject's diet and nutrition.

Helbourne had noted the subject's sorry state when he had first arrived on Monday. Early signs of starvation, dehydration, and exposure, in addition to the minor wounds she had sustained in the brief skirmish during her capture. He had also noted how much healthier and more resilient she had appeared after killing the Air Force medic. On a hunch, he had reexamined the bodies of all three of the soldiers she had killed and had made an alarming discovery. They had all died of fatal *bite* wounds to the throat, and the tissue surrounding those wounds showed signs of accelerated decay. The affected cells appeared to be as much as a decade older than the rest of the body.

Helbourne stared through the glass at the now-dressed subject. The sexy vampire cyborg from outer space. *She really does look like a Frazetta woman come to life.*

So, Vampirella, he thought with a grin. *Do you hail from the planet Drakulon, or what?*

The subject smiled back. Helbourne blinked and took a step away from the glass when strange words formed in his mind: *Idegen Videshee. Logonijy.* He thought he had imagined the meaningless syllables until a question sounded inside his head: *What is a Frazetta woman?*

4
IN HELL, I'LL BE IN GOOD COMPANY

Unknown Caller: *Why did mhmm in lt parking. Gas $ in glances. Drop @ Hopper's pl in ol city by 6pm.*

Jon looked at Joey's sloppy text message again. Shaking his head, he finally decoded the autocorrect after twenty minutes. *White Dodge Magnum in long-term parking. Gas money in glovebox. Drop at Hopper's parking lot in the Old City by six.*

I wonder just how many white Dodge Magnums will be in long-term, and I suppose it would have been too much for the meth-head bastard to tell me which section, A or B. Less than eight hours to find the damn car and get it to Knoxville. Definitely doable, provided absolutely nothing else goes wrong, like me falling asleep at the wheel or getting pulled over or the car breaking down or...

"And when in your life has everything gone exactly right, Jonny-Boy? But hey, maybe I'm due for a cake-walk..."

He ditched the hot Corolla at the Nashville West Shopping Center just as rush hour got into full swing, grabbed the big army-surplus backpack that contained his collected net worth, and called a cab. After a crazy ride through stop-and-go traffic, it was almost nine a.m. central time by the time he made it to the busy terminal at Nashville International. Paying the wild-eyed single mom cabbie forty bucks out of his Tunica stash, Jon hurried into the airport and made straight for the men's room at a trot. The candy bar and caffeine stew in his gut had gone south in a bad way.

He left the airport at a leisurely pace and took a roundabout route to the nearer of the two long-term parking lots, keeping his bloodshot eyes open for any sign of a sting. If this was indeed a big-time job as Joey suspected, there was a very good chance it was already on the TBI and FBI watchlists. Depending on what was inside the car, several other members of the alphabet soup could be involved. The DEA and the BATFE, for starters.

Relieved that he didn't see so much as a parked Metro cruiser anywhere near long-term, Jon set out to find the Dodge Magnum— assuming his translation was correct. Fortunately, it was easy to spot in the crowded Long Term A lot. The big, ugly thing looked like a dirty old hearse and stood out like a turd in a punchbowl among the brightly colored, late model subcompacts and silver and black SUVs. Jon knelt behind the car and pretended to tie his shoelaces, making sure the tags were valid—Davidson County, good through April of next year—and verifying there wasn't anything obviously wrong with the undercarriage. Not seeing anything, he checked the tires while searching the wheel wells for the magnetic key box that was standard procedure on this kind of job.

Opening the driver's door, he almost gagged. He didn't know how long the car had been sitting in the lot, baking in the Nashville sunshine, but the interior smelled like an old microwave that had been used to reheat Taco Bell farts. Wiping his eyes, Jon slid into the cracked leather seat and tried the ignition. It didn't turn over on the first attempt. *Please,* please *don't have a dead battery...* But eventually, the starter's grinding caused the engine to cough to life, and the dash lit up with its 2005 "hi-tech" bells and whistles, including all the warning lights and the low-fuel symbol.

"Just shit."

Rolling down the windows, Jon popped the hood and went around to take a look. He'd just lifted the hood all the way up when he heard a voice from behind the car: "Hey, need some help?"

Jon's heart stopped. He chewed on his inner jaw, looking for the straw he had spit out somewhere near Dixon. Peeking around the hood, he saw an older airport security guard leaning out the window of a small Ford SUV patroller, its blue light bar flashing. The guy looked tired, like he'd been up all night doing absolutely nothing but driving around and waiting for something interesting to happen. Just Jon's luck: he was that something interesting.

Jon forced a smile. "Naw. I got her running now. She's just been sitting cold for a couple days while I was out of town."

The guard smiled. "Yeah, I know how them Mopars can be. My wife had one of the original Magnums back in the eighties. Can't understand why they'd bring the damn things back. As a station wagon, no less!"

Jon's heartbeat thumped in his ears. "Yeah." He grinned like an idiot. "This one's my old lady's... needed something to haul all her damn kids around in, I reckon." From experience, he knew the best way to hurry an unwanted conversation with a stranger to its end was to share too much uncomfortable information. "I'm about to go pick her up at her mama's so we can get down to the courthouse. Gotta file a restraining order on one of her deadbeat baby daddies. Bastard showed up while I was on the road and blacked her eyes and broke her wrist."

The old guy's face went limp, and he glanced at his wristwatch. "Well, hey, I hope it all works out for you. My shift's just about over, but I can send the next guy out here with some cables and a gallon of gas if you want."

"Naw... Thank you, though. She's good."

"All right, then. You have a blessed day, now." The guard waved as he pulled away.

"That would be nice." Jon sighed before going back under the hood.

After making sure all the wires and cables were secure on the engine and checking the dipsticks, Jon hopped back in, paid the twenty-five bucks to get out of the lot, and made straight for the nearest gas station. It took the rest of the hundred bucks Joey had put in the glovebox to fill up the hungry beast. Jon figured he'd have to dip into his own funds to make it to K-town the way the Dodge was belching and coughing. The car needed a tune-up like a dead man needed a coffin. That or a reservation at the nearest scrap yard.

While the tank filled, he looked out over the station's retaining wall at the busy Nashville interstate system and thought about taking I-24 into Murfreesboro to see if he could patch things up with Kelly, the Toot's waitress he had broken up with a couple weeks ago. The redhead was a wildcat in the sack, but even so, as tired as he was, he doubted the make-up sex would be worth the inevitable drama of breaking it off with her again. Or worth the wrath of Joey Green and, heaven forbid, Craig Byce, should he fail to get the Magnum to the Old City on time.

Then again, if this gnawing feeling in my gut is more than just exhaustion and disappointment, maybe I ought to gather some hay while I can... If this all blows up in my face today, it may be a long time before I get another chance to get laid...

Leaving the station with a bag full of Red Bulls and Clif Bars and a mug full of fresh black coffee, Jon popped a plastic straw into his jaw and hopped on I-24. He was so tired that he felt like he was playing a video game of his life. He had control of his actions and could see and hear what was going on around him, but there was definitely a sense of being disconnected from the reality of the situation.

He picked up his phone and found Kelly's number. Before he thought too much on it, he hit the call button...

***

"Want another beer, sugar?" Jenny Q asked over Waylon singing about drinking and dreaming on the old juke. Her meth-mouth smile glowed in the neon bar lights. "That one too warm for ya?"

Craig Byce looked up from the still-full Budweiser bottle like it was the barrel of a gun and tried to return the smile. The twisting bloat somewhere deep in his gut made it harder than usual. Even if Jenny did have teeth like a horror show, she was still a sweet kid. "Naw, J-girl. I think I'm'a call it a day and head back to the house. I might come back out later tonight after I get some work done."

Jenny Q tossed her blonde ponytail and winked at him like she probably did to all the boys when she was a cheerleader for Central High back in the nineties. "You'd better, boss man. I'll be waitin' for ya."

Craig chuckled and tossed a couple twenties on the bar. "Here's the advance. See you tonight, darlin'." He bit down the unexpected hurt that wanted to twist his face into a snarl when he dismounted the barstool. The shards of broken glass digging around in his belly and butthole made him want to cry, but he soldiered on and made for the door.

Huland Elliot left off talking to the old-war-story crew sitting in the shadows beside the jukebox. The big, shaggy-headed bruiser hurried to join Craig on his way out of Stick's Social Club on Heiskell Avenue.

"You okay, boss?" Huland asked when they were in the empty gravel lot bathed in the hot Knoxville sunshine. His dull blue eyes squinted beneath the faded camo bandanna he wore every damn day of his life. "You look kinda, I dunno, kinda shot. Ya know?"

Yeah, I fucking know!

Craig sighed as the pain subsided, swallowed down the angry comment before he spit it out. It wasn't Huland's fault that he was a dimwit whose mommy had drunk Wild Turkey and smoked grass right up until she went into labor with the boy. Nor was it his fault that Craig Byce, one-time VP of the Knoxville chapter of the Outlaws MC, one-time Big Man on the Brushy Mountain State Pen Campus, and now primary regional operator for the Dixie Mafia had just been diagnosed with colon cancer.

"I'm fine, Hu." Craig rubbed the faded tattoos of flaming skulls, thorny roses, and smoking six-shooters that covered his spindly arms, trying to regain a little warmth. He remembered when those arms hadn't been so spindly. Each one could carry a buxom babe or a full keg of beer up a flight of stairs. Two or more if he was on PCP or something stronger... *Were the seventies that fucking long ago?*

"Just old with too many miles on my soul. That's all. Get me home, and we can finish the job. I'll take a nap, then be right as rain come sundown."

"You got it, boss." Huland unlocked the blacked-out Cadillac Escalade. As Craig hauled himself into the passenger seat, Huland asked, "You want Johnny on the radio?"

"Sure." Craig didn't really care. But he did feel a bit better when he heard "Sunday Morning Coming Down" on the high-dollar sound system. Somewhere between Dutch Valley and Powell, he dozed off.

When Huland woke him, there was a brand-new white Maserati Gran Turismo with Florida tags parked crosswise in his driveway, blocking the attached two-car garage. "You think it's the Feds, boss?"

Craig yawned and shook his head with annoyance. "No, you dingleberry. Too flashy and too small. No backseat to shove a perp into." He knew who it was, and he knew it was much, much worse than the Feds.

Craig eased out of the air-conditioned Escalade's leather seat and into the late summer heat and humidity. His fancy new brick-and-stone house sat in the middle of a sixty-acre plot, surrounded by soybeans to the left and right, and corn to the rear. Screened off by a thick stand of pines and cedars all the way 'round. Good for seclusion, but also good for breeding mosquitos, bees, and snakes.

As he and Huland approached the Maserati, the driver cut the engine and stepped out to meet them. The man was tall and slender with broad shoulders and wiry muscles, a blond crew cut above a tanned face. Mirrored Ray-Bans concealed his eyes and black tribal tattoos peaked above the collar and beneath the sleeves of his blue Burberry polo. In his pressed khakis and boat shoes, he looked like a sleazeball realtor from the Sunshine State or a hitman for the CIA.

"Mr. Byce," he said with a smile, extending his right hand. "I'm Jesse Sneed."

Craig forced a half-smile and returned the handshake, cutting it short because he couldn't match the younger fellow's grip. "Call me Craig. I know who you are, Jesse. Been expecting you. Come on in the house, and we can talk."

"Nice place you got here," the Florida pretty boy said as they entered the air-conditioned foyer. The house was immaculate and professionally decorated, more like a spread in *Better Homes and Gardens* than the lair of a lifelong criminal.

"Thanks. I'd have preferred an old Victorian or a restored farmhouse." Craig knew his house was nice. It was the nicest thing he'd ever gotten out of this hard life, and it pissed him off to no end that he wouldn't be around to enjoy it for very long. "But those oldies don't have much in the way of basements, and I like to spread out when I'm working."

He led them into the living room and waved at the huge white leather sectional facing the sixty-inch plasma mounted above the stone fireplace. "Have a seat, Jesse. Can I offer you something to drink? You hungry?"

"Thanks, I'm fine." After they were seated and facing each other on opposite ends of the sofa, Huland standing protectively behind Craig, Sneed said, "Since you know who I am, you know why I'm here."

"Yep, to take over my business." Craig narrowed his eyes and dug his fingers into the knees of his jeans, willing the pain in his bowels to go away.

Sneed laughed. "I wouldn't say that. I'm here to help you get things running as smooth as possible again. Think of me as an apprentice, a protégé. An heir to your throne, so to speak."

"One chosen by the boss in Florida." Craig clenched his teeth. "Not me."

Sneed leaned forward, still wearing those damned mirror sunglasses. "Come on, Craig, you've got to admit, things are not as strong as they could be around here. You've got high school kids making meth in the woods and pimps running whorehouses out of the local trailer parks. Weed is being grown, harvested, bought, and sold from Clinton to Lenoir City like the shit was legal here. And you're getting, what—six or eight percent of that action?"

Craig didn't reply.

"And that's just the *local* shit. In the past decade, you've let Folk Nation get a foothold in Chattanooga—they were making open war on the cops for a while, for crying out loud! Are you gonna let it get as bad as Atlanta? You know if they take control of the intersection of 24 and 75, they cut our throats. We can't let that happen."

"Well, Jesse, the first thing you need to know about my *throne* is that I sit on it at the whim of not one, but three bosses, and that is one hell of a balancing act, let me tell you. I got Cincinnati telling me how to run my drugs and guns. I got your boss in Orlando telling me how to run my whores and gambling. And I got Angola telling me how and when to whack the folks who get out of line—which reminds me of something..."

Sneed continued to smile like a used car salesman as Craig got up and headed for the hallway and the door leading down to the basement. "And I can help you with all that, Craig. That's what I'm here to do."

Craig unlocked the basement door with a snort, flicked on the lights. "Right, and how's it gonna go over when the Ohio and Louisiana crowds decide you're really here to make sure Orlando gets the biggest piece of cheese?"

Sneed started to answer but trailed off as they descended the steps into the unfinished basement. A naked young man hung from a rusty logging chain by his ragged wrists. His toes rested in a blue kiddy pool covered with bright yellow ducks and green frogs. The pool was filled with a mixture of water, blood, urine, and feces. The young man's narrow, tattooed torso was covered in a pattern of black and purple bruises and several cuts trickling tiny scarlet rivulets down his pale skin. His head was covered with a black blindfold, an S&M ball gag, and a pair of pink Winchester shooting earmuffs.

Craig picked up a canister of Febreze and sprayed the stuffy air, covering the stink of human misery with a tropical-flower scent. "He's shit himself again, Hue. Hose him down: I'm too old to get hepatitis."

Craig stepped over to the workbench to look at his toys. There was a stun gun, an old-school blackjack, a pair of needle-nose pliers, a rubber mallet, a ball-peen hammer, a pair of vice grips, an ice pick, several types of knives, garden shears, an acetylene hand torch, and a fully charged cattle prod.

"Who's this?" The way Sneed asked it made Craig pause and look at him. The Florida pretty boy had taken off his sunglasses and was staring at the kid in the pool like he was famished and admiring a fresh-grilled porterhouse. "What did he do?"

"Name's Josh something-or-other," Craig grunted while Huland sprayed the squirming, whimpering kid down with the garden hose. "He's a low-level runner and messenger boy. Apparently, he was telling trade secrets down at the Sapphire Club the other night, trying to impress some coke whore of a dancer. This here's an object lesson."

Sneed smiled in appreciation, looked at Craig with bright blue eyes like he was meeting his new best friend for life. "That's why the sensory deprivation. See no evil, hear no evil, speak no evil..."

Craig returned the smile. "Something like that. This way he can focus on what he feels. Care to give it a shot?" He held out a pair of pliers.

Sneed licked his lips and reached for them with a shaking hand.

Craig pulled the pliers back. "Just remember, he's being punished, not killed. We can still use him if he ain't permanently crippled."

Sneed's face rippled but he gave a curt nod and took the pliers. "Right."

***

The impromptu hookup in Murfreesboro had been good. Too good, in fact. Jon had been at Kelly's almost three hours. His window of opportunity for getting to Hopper's in Knoxville on time was getting smaller. And Craig Byce wasn't known for his patience. When he reached Lascassas Pike, Jon relaxed just a bit and headed out of town. He'd take Highway 96 through Auburntown, then cut through Smithville on 56 and jump on I-40 just this side of Cookeville, and maybe, just maybe, he'd make up some of the time he'd lost while between the sheets with the curvy redhead. "If not, we'll chalk it up to just one more bad decision…"

Doesn't matter so long as I can keep this behemoth moving east and between the lines. And if I do happen to doze off as I cross Center Hill Lake or the Cumberland Plateau, then maybe all my problems will be over before I wake up.

But Jon's problems were just getting started, and they caught up with him at a Pilot Travel Center in Crossville about an hour and a half later. He stopped to top off the Magnum's tank and recycle his coffee. When he slid back into the driver's seat, washing down a mouthful of chewable Tums with a bottle of water, he failed to notice the three unmarked cars that followed him back onto Genesis Road. Until they kicked on their lights and forced him into the near-empty parking lot of the winery across the street.

The three cars surrounded the Magnum. Six armed men in cheap suits jumped out behind their doors. Jon already had his hands on the steering wheel in the eleven and one positions before a megaphone voice told him, "Put your hands where we can see them!"

Not having a straw to chew, he bit the inside of his cheek.

Jon was pulled out of the car, patted down and Mirandized, handcuffed, then led over to where a bald-headed bulldog of a man in a tawny-colored suit opened the Magnum's trunk. He wore black latex gloves, and Jon noted the shiny badge on the chain around his thick neck: Tennessee Bureau of Investigation.

The world seemed to swim around the crowd of men and cars with their flashing lights like a black whirlwind, pushing every little detail in this tiny part of Creation into sharp relief. As if he were watching a movie unfold on an HDTV for the very first time, Jon found himself hypnotized by the little things: the spot on the bald man's neck just above his collar where he'd cut himself shaving while completely missing two long, curly hairs half an inch away, or the Subway sandwich paper stained with dark, dried mustard stuck beneath the Magnum's rear tire, or the smell of car exhaust mixing with the nicotine gum on the guy's breath behind him, or the sound of Led

Zeppelin singing "The Immigrant Song" coming from the radio of one of the unmarked cruisers.

When the TBI guys flipped the Magnum's trunk carpet up and checked the spare tire compartment, Jon's distantly acute focus was washed away by the sudden rush of blood in his ears and temples. His eyes bugged out of his head, and his throat filled with bile. The agent holding his cuffs whistled over his shoulder and laughed when the bull-necked guy said, "I ain't seen this much blow and firepower in one place since the last time I watched Pacino in *Scarface!*"

Where the spare tire and jack should have been, the little pocket had been expanded to hold half a dozen good-sized bags of fine white powder and several disassembled AR-15s. Jon closed his eyes and just wanted to die. Without even looking, he knew the guns had their serial numbers removed and were probably full-auto models, maybe even military M4s stolen from a National Guard Armory. It didn't matter if the powder was heroin or coke or something entirely new; it had to be just as illegal as the rifles.

I am going away for a very, very long time.

5
I NEED NEVER GET OLD

Idegen was alone again.

The observation chamber was empty, but she knew mechanical devices still cataloged her every move. The primitive natives, the *humans*, may have her captive, but they still feared her. She almost smiled at that. If she had been stronger and more comfortable in her isolation, she would have smiled. But she was tired, weak, and alone. She had nothing and no one from which to draw strength.

Vodie, she thought for the thousandth time. *If only you were here, I know we could find our way out of this together. You were always the smarter and stronger one, always more practical. You are the one who made me better. You should have been the one they chose.*

But they had not. The Empire's elite cadre had singled Idegen out for the Black Star and all it entailed, forever separating her from her lifelong companion and placing her firmly on the path that had led her to this isolation in this hole in the ground of this distant world, prisoner of this barbaric race. But deep down, she knew the Empire was not to blame. It had been her own unquenchable thirst to be the best, to outdo her rivals and peers—including and especially Vodie—which had drawn the cadre's attention and that of the hierarchy of the Order of the Black Star Worlds.

Idegen had never been truly alone in her entire long life, and now that she was, she found she hated it.

Perhaps if I had not driven myself to excel at the training and exercises, I might have been allowed a normal life on Logonijy. I could have been appointed a mate and become the matriarch of a family unit. Perhaps I could have been happy in such a domestic role, shaping the lives of my offspring and the offspring of my offspring. Perhaps that was what I was meant to do.

Idegen licked her right fang and finally smiled at the absurdity of this particular self-pitying fantasy. As if she could ever be anything less than what she was, a warrior for the Empire and a member of the Order—a taker of lives and a devourer of souls. These barbarians may have the advantage for now, but she was their superior in every conceivable way. She would escape. And when she did, there would be much lamentation among their kind. The Empire may not have labeled this an enemy world just yet, but she, Idegen Videshee, certainly had.

Thinking of her glorious escape and the epic bloodletting it would entail, Idegen laughed. Alone in her cell. *Even if I fail and perish in the attempt, the Empire will avenge me. They will rain cosmic death from the fiery heavens, and this insignificant little world will become my funeral pyre, burning for all eternity.*

***

Colonel Emily Sharpe carried her pack down the corridor to her private quarters. She and her escort were staying in the security complex one floor above the subject and thirty floors beneath Cape Canaveral. Her men were newly assigned to her, and she hadn't yet learned their names. In her head, they were Race and Brock—two square-jawed and taciturn white-guy cartoon characters with the sole purpose of keeping her safe.

Reaching the door to her quarters, she stopped and told Race and Brock, "I want one of you two guarding the subject's chamber at all times unless I relieve you myself. Make the appropriate arrangements with the locals."

"Yes, ma'am," one of them said.

I really need to learn their names. "Whoever's not on guard duty, keep an eye on Dr. Helbourne. I want to know if he does anything fishy."

"Yes, ma'am," the other one said. "Anything else?"

"If there's any word of the craft's recovery from the Gulf, I want to know ASAP. No matter when that word comes in. And I want the DNA and other lab reports as soon as Helbourne gets his hands on them." Sharpe felt the familiar tingle of pain in her lower back. "And have some ice sent to me."

"Yes, ma'am," they said together before she left them in the hallway.

Locking the door, Sharpe turned on the overhead fluorescent and scanned the small, spartan room. "The finest furnishings the Cold War government could provide." Everything looked like it had come out of a 1965 motel room: cheap pinewood furniture, goldenrod carpet, dated pictures of the Cape hanging on the pale blue cinderblock walls. "Can't wait to see what a fifty-year-old mattress is going to do to my back."

She tossed her pack onto the bed, half-expecting to see a Hiroshima-like cloud of dust erupt from the multi-colored geometric designs on the comforter. Happily disappointed there was none, Sharpe unpacked. After putting her few clothes in the small dresser and the narrow closet, she opened the "secret compartment" at the bottom of the duffle bag and pulled out a six-pack of Miller Lite, her bottle of Vicodin, and her vibrator. These went into the nightstand drawer.

"Home sweet home," she muttered before stepping into the small bathroom with her toiletry kit.

The pain hit her without warning, almost completely dropping her to the green-tiled floor. The cosmetics bag skidded into the corner of the tiny room. She grabbed the doorknob and the sink so hard her knuckles turned white, gnashed her teeth until her jaws hurt. Her legs went numb from the hips down, her pelvis on fire. Lightning bolts arced up her spine to scorch her brain.

"Motherfucker." She breathed, riding out the first and worst wave. "Motherfucker."

She pulled herself back to a standing position, turned on the cold water, and splashed her face with trembling hands. Muscle tremors ran up her calves and quads, then back down her hamstrings and Achilles. Her toes wanted to cramp up into little talons, but she wouldn't let them. As the cold water calmed her, she breathed deeper, forcing her body to obey.

When she felt like she was back in control, she looked at the old woman in the mirror. "Just remember," she said to the haggard reflection. "You're the lucky one. You got out in one piece."

There was a knock at the outer door. "Colonel Sharpe?"

She toweled off her face and limped out of the bathroom. "Yes?"

"You asked for ice, Colonel?"

Sharpe opened the door and fixed a scowl on the chubby airman on the other side. The smile on his pale face vanished as he held the bag of crushed ice out to her. "Would you like me to put this in your sink, ma'am?"

"No, thank you." She grabbed the bag. "You're dismissed."

He snapped to attention and started a salute, but she'd already closed the door.

Picking up the heavy-duty aluminum wastebasket, Sharpe moved it to the nightstand and began making an ice bath for the six-pack. When she opened the nightstand drawer to retrieve the beer, her hand hovered over the orange bottle of painkillers.

"No," she whispered to the burning need climbing its way up her ribs like the rungs of a ladder. "No. Not yet. I can wait."

But can you, really? the pain asked.

***

Helbourne was no fool. He knew as soon as Sharpe had shown up that she was going to try and shoulder him out of position. He also knew his nominal control over the investigation had been entirely at the military's discretion, and that control was never meant to be permanent. But he also knew he was the only one who understood the full truth about the subject—about Idegen Videshee—and what she could mean to the future of mankind.

All Sharpe and the mouth breathers at the Pentagon cared about was whether or not she represented yet another threat to "National Security," the Holy Grail of current budgetary concerns in D.C., or whether she could be taken apart and studied to improve the U.S.'s already overblown ability to make war. No doubt the Joint Chiefs of Staff were drawing up a budget proposal, dreaming up Michael Bay-like weapons to fight off imagined alien invasions, zombie hordes, or city-trashing *kaiju*.

Knowing all this, Helbourne had made arrangements with the labs ahead of time so that the test results were emailed straight to him using outside servers and without going through proper channels. That's why he sat in his room, sipping a glass of Knob Creek as he pored over the data displayed on his laptop. "Amazing," he whispered, reminding himself that his room was probably just as bugged as the lab.

Not only is she telepathic, but she's practically immortal! With this genetic and biomechanical technology, we could eradicate human frailty for all time! If we could just make friends with these beings, let them know that we mean them no harm—that we want to cooperate with them, we could usher in a new golden age for the human race. The fulfillment of all mankind's religious and philosophical dreams. A true Utopian heaven on earth resulting from the end of death, pestilence, and want.

Helbourne finished the glass and poured himself another two fingers. *All I've got to do is figure out a way to get Sharpe under my thumb. Everybody has a pressure point; I just need to find hers. As*

Archimedes said, "Give me a lever long enough and a fulcrum on which to place it, and I shall move the world."

I don't think I need all that long a lever to move you, Colonel Emily Sharpe. You may be taller, tougher, and meaner, but I am ever so much smarter. And smart always wins in the end.

6
THE GALLOWS POLE

"Well, this is the cherry on top of the shit sundae that is today." Jon gnashed his teeth, carefully maneuvering the massive Dodge Magnum out of the full, cramped, Hopper's parking lot. The plastic straw in his jaw was almost a chemical pulp at this point.

His unexpected detention and visit to the Cumberland County Sheriff's Office had led to his not arriving in Knox County until the height of afternoon rush hour. Which meant it took him almost as long to get from West Knoxville to the warehouse-like old brick taproom and pizzeria as it did to get from Crossville to Knoxville. Which meant that his six o'clock deadline was looming large.

The college crowd had finished afternoon classes at UT and had poured into the Old City's eclectic mix of antique architecture and new eateries, watering holes, and nightspots for their required midweek drafts, joining the suit-and-tie crowd from the downtown banks, law firms, city and county offices, and the local network affiliates.

"Why in the blue hell did they want the damn thing here, anyway?" He pulled back onto Jackson Avenue and eyed the pay lot across the street. "Why not someplace nice and secluded out west, like the back parking lot of West Town Mall? Or any place in Farragut, Oak Ridge, or Lenoir City? Why all the way into downtown?"

Not that it matters. Shunning the pay lot, he drove down and pulled the gasping clunker into the gravel lot beneath the Hall of Fame Drive overpass. "I'm a dead man as soon as the shit hits the fan, anyway."

Putting the car in park, he cracked the windows and turned off the engine. The Magnum was running on fumes as it was, and there was no sense in keeping the AC going in the shade. Jon pulled out his phone and prepared to text his message, *I'm here*, to Joey's Unknown Caller number. He looked at the time displayed on the phone: 5:52 p.m. *Eight minutes. I can put it off for eight minutes. Maybe I can come up with a way out of this mess in that time.*

And maybe Angela White will hop in the passenger seat with a briefcase full of thousand-dollar bills and a bottle of Viagra...

The time between being placed in the backseat of the TBI cruiser and being escorted into a stuffy little interrogation room at the local sheriff's office had been a blur. Jon's exhaustion and total surprise at the sudden turn of events had robbed him of the ability to think much more than *This can't be happening*, over and over again.

They had left him in the room, handcuffed and alone, for almost half an hour, judging by the clock on the wall. He dozed off a couple times, but no longer than six or seven minutes at a go before the big, bull-necked agent and his partner, the thin guy with the Clark Kent specs and the nicotine-gum habit, came in and un-cuffed him.

"Jon," the bull-necked guy said, "I'm Special Agent Hicks, and this is Special Agent Arnison of the Drug Investigation Division. We're assigned to the Appalachia High Intensity Drug Trafficking Area, and you, young man, have just walked into our little domain." He took some of the sting out of this revelation by placing a bottle of Dasani on the table.

Jon swallowed hard, realizing just how thirsty he was, watching the two men settle easily into the chairs on the other side of the table. He reached out and took the bottle with a shaking hand and under their expressionless observation, drained the sixteen ounces at a gulp. Taking a deep breath and screwing the cap back on the empty bottle, he said, "I stole the car from the Nashville Airport this morning. I had no idea what was in it."

Arnison opened a thick folder and pulled out an evidence bag. It had Jon's phone in it. "Not according to this, Jon. Two things: you might want to delete texts chronicling criminal activity from your personal phone on a regular basis, no matter how cryptic they are. And you really ought to consider a better security code than your birthday."

The water he'd just consumed flushed straight to his bladder. *Son of a bitch...*

"Look..." Hicks leaned in and laced his sausage-like fingers on the table. "We don't want you, Jon. You're small potatoes with a relatively clean record—relative to the real bad guys, at any rate. But the bottom line is, nobody's getting any TV time, commendations, raises, or promotions for putting you away. We want your bosses, Jon. You play ball with us, and you can go on your merry way. No muss, no fuss."

Jon swallowed hard, his throat already dry. *So this is how it ends. Nobody, but nobody, rolls on the Dixie Mafia and lives to see his next birthday.*

Seeing Jon's hesitance, Hicks leaned back and nodded at Arnison, who pulled a pair of black-and-white surveillance photos from the folder. "Do you recognize these men, Jon?"

Jon looked at the photos. One was of Craig Byce, the nominal head-honcho of the region between Memphis and Asheville and everything from Frankfort to Atlanta. Jon had only seen him once, after dropping a package at one of the old man's Knoxville watering holes. The other picture was, of course, his old pal Joey Green.

He said nothing, kept his face neutral. He might not be playing for big money in Tunica, but this was still high-stakes poker. *So long as I've got a chip and chair, there's still a chance to win. I've got to believe that.*

Hicks frowned and sighed in frustration. When he spoke, there was a dangerous edge to his voice. "Look, Jon, we're not fooling around here. We know you spent time in Davidson County with Joey Green about nine years ago, and we know you've been doing odd jobs for him ever since. Including this little coke run. Or, as we in the law-enforcement community like to call it, *felony drug trafficking...* Then there's the issue of the full-auto ARs. That's not going to make you any new friends on Twitter these days."

Jon narrowed his eyes at the big man. "Then why are you asking me questions you already know the answer to? You've got me where you want me. What do you want? And when do I get to see a lawyer? I haven't even been booked yet."

Arnison smiled as Hicks pushed away from the table and began to pace the small room, making it feel even smaller. "We can hold you for a full twenty-four hours before officially charging you, Jon. And thanks to our good friend the Patriot Act and the presence of automatic weapons in the car, we can hold you for up to fourteen days if we want to tack on terrorism as a charge. The current administration has a hard-on for white-boy domestic stuff, you know."

"Now, based on the text on your phone, that will make you miss your scheduled delivery. And just suppose we keep the blow and the ARs and cut you loose tomorrow morning. How's that going to look to these two gentlemen?" Hicks tapped the photos for emphasis.

Jon felt like he'd just lost his last chip. "Like I cut a deal." *And like a one-way ticket to Craig Byce's infamous basement dungeon.*

"Correct-amundo," Hicks said, leaning over Jon, his garlicky sweat overpowering his Walmart-brand cologne. "But let's cut the horse shit here, Jon. All we want is a place at the table, and you're our invitation to the party."

Jon looked up at the big man. "What are you talking about?"

Arnison tapped Joey's photo. "It might interest you to know that Mr. Green here is playing ball with the FBI and the DEA in exchange for immunity and a place in witness protection. You see, there's a big federal case intent on bringing down Mr. Byce and the regional infrastructure of his organization. If the Feds pull it off without our involvement, well, it's not going to look too good for the home team in the morning papers. You know, budgetary concerns, re-elections, committee appointments, and all that sort of thing."

Jon fought to keep from smiling. He'd gone all-in with a pocket two-seven off-suit and somehow flopped three sevens. "So how does this work...?"

Jon stared at his phone. The clock said 5:57 p.m. He sent his message to Joey and looked at the Hopper's logo in the rearview mirror. He wanted a drink worse than he could ever remember, and he hated himself for it. *I'm not my dad*, he told himself. *I can have a beer or two and not lose my head... not hurt anybody...*

Joey's text came back: *Hav a drink & wate fr a guy in a camp headband.*

"What the hell's a 'camp headband?'" Jon sighed, put the phone away, grabbed his backpack, and got out of the car. *I suppose if tonight's to be when I get offed, I might as well have a decent buzz going when it happens.*

"I just hope I don't get so drunk I feel the urge to call Angie before things go south," he muttered on his way to the bar. *Better yet, I hope I don't need to call her after they do.*

***

Craig Byce and Jesse Sneed sat in the basement, smoking some high-dollar medical-grade reefer Jesse had brought up from Florida. After Josh something-or-other's object lesson, they'd hosed the battered and unconscious kid off and rolled him in a flannel blanket. Huland had tossed him in the backseat of the Escalade to haul up to Norris Dam, where Josh something-or-other would be dumped in the middle of the woods to spend the night.

"So, you think my presence will really ruffle feathers in Ohio and Louisiana?" Jesse asked, handing the joint back to Craig.

"Don't you? What would your boss in Orlando think if Cincinnati had sent me an heir apparent?" He gave the dope one more good pull, thankful that it dulled the pain in his guts, then gave the butt end to Sneed to finish.

Jesse looked at the cherry-red glow of the joint, licked his finger and thumb. Crushing it out to save for later, he said, "I don't know. I'm a soldier, Craig. I go where I'm told and do what I'm told when I get there. Same here as it was in Afghanistan." He smiled as he breathed out the last of the smoke. "Only safer and with better perks."

Craig had seen that same crazy gleam in the bloodshot eyes of guys who had come back from 'Nam. Guys who had gotten used to killing and even developed a taste for it. *Just my luck, they sent a psycho to help me run things.*

"Look here, Jesse." Craig leaned forward to emphasize his point. "I don't want you to get the wrong idea about what we just did down here. I'm not some sadistic maniac, and I sure don't get off on it. I've gotten good at... *discipline* in the past thirty or forty-odd years, but I'd rather not have to use it on any of my people, or even the people we do business with. What we did to that boy, as far as I'm concerned, is a necessary evil of the job. A tool. He needed to learn a lesson, and I could use him to teach a lesson to everybody else in the organization. That's all."

Jesse scowled like Craig had just called his mama a filthy whore. Then his face split into an evil grin. "I get it, Craig. You think I'm another burned-out, kill-crazy vet with PTSD. Well, that's just the line I used to beat the rap. I'm solid, my friend. Just ask the boss. I'll call him myself, right now, if you want."

Craig shook his head. He'd heard about Jesse's rap, how he had come back from serving two tours overseas to find his fiancée playing house with another man and had promptly used a sledgehammer to turn said man into human guacamole. Pleading PTSD and touting a bronze star for valor, his charge was reduced to manslaughter, and he'd served eight years in Raiford. That's where the organization had recruited him. He'd become the Orlando boss's golden boy ever since, and now here he was, big as life in Craig's basement.

"No. That's not necessary, Jesse. I just wanted to get things out in the open before we get started. You know, clear the air."

Jesse smiled, this time not so mean. "Then you're going to accept the deal?"

Craig raised his hands. "Let's not get ahead of ourselves. Like I said, I have people to answer to on just about everything I do. So, let's say we give this a trial run and see if it raises any stink. If Cincy and Angola hold their water, then we'll keep rolling. If not, we'll sit down to the table with those boys and decide from there."

Jesse beamed like he was a high-school kid landing his first lay. For a moment, Craig wondered what Knoxville and the rest of the region would look like in another ten or twelve years with Jesse Sneed pulling the strings. He was sort of glad he wouldn't be around to see it.

Craig's burner chirped in his shirt pocket. He held it out at near arm's length to read the text message from the Unknown Caller: *The ego has lands.*

"Dammit, Joey." He closed the text message and pulled up the contact directory. "Learn how to spell or don't use autocorrect, you skunk-head bastard."

"Something wrong?" Jesse asked.

"No. Just got confirmation of a delivery. I need to get down to the Old City and pick it up." Holding the phone to his ear, he said, "I'll have Huland hurry back and get me down there. You can hang out here if you want."

"I'll drive you. Have Huland meet us there."

Craig thought about it, decided he might like to ride in a brand-new Maserati, even if it would be a literal pain in the ass getting in and out. Besides, as far as he knew, nobody in Knoxville was looking for Sneed's ride, and it might do him some good to go incognito for a bit. "Okay, then."

***

Jon sat at the downstairs bar with the hipsters, the neo-hippies, and a handful of yuppies listening to John Prine on the overhead speakers. Upstairs, the good ol' boys, the jocks, and the party girls played pool, darts, and Golden Tee to Shooter Jennings or Hank III. He finished his second pint of Lowenbrau, ordered a third, and checked the time on his phone. It read 6:21.

After all that worry about being here by six!

At least the beer had mellowed him some. It was also causing him to fixate on the one person he knew he shouldn't. "Screw it."

He pulled up the internet on his phone and typed Angie Lawman into the search engine. When the top results came back, including Lawman—Attorney at Law, Knoxville, Tennessee, he hit the image button.

Taking a big gulp of cold beer, he stared at the lovely dark-haired woman with the piercing black eyes. What he saw was the equally lovely dark-haired girl with the warm brown eyes he had known most of his life. Known and loved more fiercely than he'd ever loved anyone or anything. Or so he'd thought at the time. In the end, he had discovered that he loved the nonexistent gold at the end of the rainbow even more.

I should have married you, but I was too young and too stupid. Too proud and reckless. Now you're a successful lawyer with a husband and a kid, and I'm... I'm the good-for-nothing lowlife you said I'd become if I didn't straighten up. I bet if I called you right now, you'd still have too much class to say, I told you so.

The phone buzzed and Angie's professional picture was replaced by the notification of a text message from a Knoxville area code: *I'm here. Joey said you were looking for me.*

Jon's belly filled with warm water, and he wasn't sure if he needed to puke or piss first. He took another long gulp of beer until the sensation went away. Placing the empty glass on the bar, he turned and looked at the entrance. Beyond the crowd of diners and drinkers, he saw a colossal guy that made the Incredible Hulk look like a soy-boy snowflake.

The huge guy was wearing a *camo* bandana as a headband.

Jon paid his tab, picked up his backpack, and crossed the big room. "I'm Jon," he said, hoping like hell that his voice didn't give anything away. "If you've got something for me, I've got keys for you."

The bruiser looked at him without expression. "Outside." He turned and shouldered his way past the newcomers filing in the double doors, heading down the steps to the sidewalk. Jon followed.

Sunlight fading, the streetlamps came slowly to life. The day's heat and humidity had lost their edge. Little packs and couples of college-age kids roamed up and down Jackson Avenue, looking for the evening's good time. Cars crept along the street looking for parking or for someone familiar, or maybe someone unfamiliar but interesting and willing. Jon envied them and the insignificant little dramas of their lives. He vaguely remembered when he had been just like them—before the night he had gone into that basement off of West End to play an illegal game of high stakes poker.

Jon cleared his throat. "So, uh, where's the boss man? Joey said I was to meet with him tonight." Joey had not, in fact, said anything of the sort, but Special Agents Hicks and Arnison had told him to throw it out there and see where it landed.

"Stuck in traffic. He let an out-of-towner drive, but he's on his way," the big guy said. "With your money. I'm Hue, and I take care of things for him. Where's the car?"

Jon smiled. "This way." He led Hue along the sidewalk past the parking lots and away from the bars and restaurants. "The lot was full when I got here. Had to park under the overpass."

Hue grunted.

"So, uh... Joey didn't tell me how much this gig paid. You got any idea?"

"Nope."

They reached the car, now surrounded by other parked vehicles. Jon waited until a gaggle of giggling girls in club gear disembarked their shiny new red Sentra and made for the sidewalk. One of the blondes smiled at him and the others made her pay for it with a keening cacophony. He would have smiled back if he weren't about to be trapped in the middle of a multi-agency sting with Lurch's stunt double.

"Here she is." Jon tossed the keys to Hue. "She's all yours."

The big guy caught the keys. "You don't want to wait for your pay?"

Jon swallowed, realizing his goof. "You said the big man was on his way. I don't reckon he'll come all the way out here and not bring the dough. And if he does, what the hell can I do about it?"

Hue grinned. "Damn skippy." He stepped to the driver's side door. As soon as he unlocked and opened it, the trap was sprung.

Sirens and blue lights exploded out of nowhere. Tires squealed as black vans rolled up from Patton Street behind them, disgorging over a dozen masked men in black with submachine guns. Red lasers flashed from the rooftops of Hopper's and the vacant NV nightclub across the street. "Hands in the air! On your knees! Now!"

His mind moving in slow motion, Jon found himself pressed face-first into the hard white dust of the gravel lot, a knee jammed into his back as a zip tie was cranked down hard on his wrists behind him. He blinked, saw Hue staring back at him with murder in his narrow blue eyes. Above the din of the raid, he plainly heard the big guy whisper, "You're a dead man."

In short order, the parking area was cordoned off by men in windbreakers marked FBI, DEA, and BATFE. Jon found himself alone in the backseat of another unmarked car. Hue was someplace else, thank goodness. The adrenaline had sobered him up almost instantly, but it had also turned Jon's guts into liquid dog food. He strained his neck, looking out the windows against the flashing lights and the growing darkness to see if he could spot the two TBI agents who had promised him the world in exchange for getting them a seat at the table.

Instead, he saw the grizzled face of Craig Byce staring at him from the passenger seat of a white Maserati parked under a light down the street. The old man chewed his lips like he wanted to use his teeth to tear Jon apart. The driver wore mirror-tinted shades even though dusk was all but over. Those glasses made Jon think of The Man with No Eyes in *Cool Hand Luke*.

Jon bit down on the inside of his cheek so hard he tasted blood.

The door opened beside him, and he almost loosed his bowels.

"You screwed the pooch, kid." Special Agent Hicks pulled a pocketknife from his jacket. "You were supposed to get us Byce. But at least the Feds have agreed to cut us in, so I suppose a deal's a deal. You can walk, but don't go too far. We—"

"Take me in," Jon gasped. "If you let me go tonight, I won't see the sun rise. And there's better than even odds you'll never find my body."

Hicks's broad face split into a grin. "What do you know, kid? You see the boogeyman out here or something?" He looked around at the controlled chaos enveloping Jackson Avenue.

"Or something," Jon said. "So help me, you get me out of this car and cut this zip tie, I'll slug you and you'll have to take me in for assaulting an officer, obstruction of justice, or some other damn thing. Just take me in. And soon, *please*, before I shit myself."

Hicks broke into a surprisingly high-pitched laugh as he slammed the door. A few minutes later, a pair of FBI agents piled in and started up the car. "Next stop," the driver said, "Knox County Jail."

7
A GOOD LOOK

Idegen's consciousness slid from her self-induced torpor, coiled into alertness, aware of another presence. She was still tired, weak, and hungry. Still filled with seething rage at her captors. Still battling despondency over her isolation. Though they had given her foodstuffs three times each planetary rotation, she had taken no real sustenance since killing the science technician. She meditated to conserve her energy but could feel her body breaking down, and she feared her mind would soon follow. She had a few tricks yet, but could only hope for the opportunity to play them. Preferably before she was so weak that the sonic "torture" the humans had prescribed actually had a deleterious effect upon her.

Her cell was dark, as was the connecting chamber behind the observation panel. Idegen knew that if she were at full strength, she could have smashed through the clear partition in a few blows, but at present, it would only exhaust what little reserves she had and leave her vulnerable to more violence from her captors. She had resigned herself to waiting for an ideal opportunity or for rescue. In her present condition, she feared both were equally unlikely to happen before it was too late.

The other room was dark, but it was not empty. Idegen's nocturnal lenses slid into place, and she could see someone standing in front of the glass, watching her.

It was the tall, dark-skinned female she had seen earlier—the warrior. Idly rubbing at a smudge on the glass, the woman did not speak. But Idegen could hear her thoughts, faint and indistinct at first, sometimes confusing—the unorthodox language's idioms were still a barrier—but there was something also familiar about the internal monologue. She rose from her bunk and stepped to the glass.

Idegen was pleasantly surprised when the woman did not step back, but instead smiled. She kept her attention on the smudge, rubbing it with a finger, then scratching at it with her nail. Idegen realized the smudge represented something to this woman, some kind of distraction.

"So, you're awake." The woman's words opened a channel into her thoughts surprisingly easily. Idegen surmised this human must have some level of latent psychic ability, though apparently an underdeveloped one at best. Her name was Emily Sharpe, and like Idegen, she was a pilot, a soldier, and a leader. Unlike her, this woman was an anomaly in her chosen field; the militaries of this world were dominated by the males of the species. And this woman's military was led by the light-skinned variety. Apparently, this mattered to her for some reason.

Idegen returned Emily's smile and touched the glass on the opposite side of the smudge with her open palm.

The woman on the other side frowned, looked from Idegen's hand to her face and back again. She paused, then took a long drink from a metallic container before mimicking the gesture. Idegen closed her eyes and focused...

Sharpe felt a tingle in her palm and a tightening in her chest. Forgetting the smudge she'd been fixated on, she took a deep breath and stepped away from the night-vision glass. She felt something strange as well, a sense of *closeness* to the subject. Shaking her head, she walked back to the rolling office chair, taking another swig of Miller Lite. *Just the Vicodin and the beer making me feel the fool that I am. I shouldn't be here right now, doing this.*

She had already disabled the lab's surveillance and audio recorders, so she rolled herself close to the glass to speak her "confession." Maybe it would feel better now that the subject was actually awake, almost like talking to a real person. A superhuman, homicidal person, probably from another world, but a real person all the same. A confidante was a confidante after all, and sometimes the best ones were complete strangers.

"So, what's your story, Ms. Universe?" She killed the last few drops of warm beer and crushed the can. The painkiller had completely worn off, and she was trying to dovetail its effects with a beer buzz before her next prescribed dose. "You here to warn us of our pending self-destruction, or are you the harbinger of a full-on alien invasion? Or is it something else entirely?" Just like word about the downed craft, the DNA results still hadn't come back, and Sharpe secretly prayed they would offer a perfectly logical and terrestrial explanation.

That I can handle... I'm beginning to wonder if this whole thing isn't some big stupid joke the good ol' boys upstairs have cooked up to make fun of the "new colored gal." Sharpe affected the Foghorn-Leghorn voice of a stereotypical Old South Dixie-crat: "I say there, sugah, go down to Florida and check out that theah UFO and ET, and make sure you do a good job, and look pretty doin' it, ya heah?"

The subject tilted her head, letting her long dark hair fall across her shoulder in a very human way. She gracefully sat cross-legged on the floor in front of Sharpe as if listening. The hairs on the back of Sharpe's neck stood at attention. *Maybe she is listening? But can she understand me?*

"All right, fuck it," she said. "Maybe you can hear me through this glass, and maybe you can understand me. And maybe it's the pain killers or the total mental, physical, and emotional exhaustion, but I don't care at this point. I got some shit to get off my chest, and right now you are the only person in the whole world I've got to say it to."

The subject did not move. Only blinked her eerily glowing eyes.

"Well," Sharpe said, "you may find this as hard to believe as I do, but you are, in fact, my very first assignment in this new position. That's right, eighteen months ago, I was a chopper jockey flying Longbows and Guardians in an 'undisclosed hotspot.' But after my bird took an RPG from local fighters, I limped her back to base and had one hell of a hard landing. I made it out. My gunner didn't.

"Got some medals, a promotion, a shit-ton of bad dreams and a bad back for that. Then I got grounded and reassigned to a desk in Germany.

"But after all the shit I had to do to get into West Point, graduate at the top of my class, and then push for a combat assignment, there was no way I was letting the Army put me out to pasture while I still had gas in the tank. I'd sacrificed the so-called normal life for my dreams, and they weren't taking them away from me."

Sharpe licked her lips and wished she'd brought the rest of the six-pack with her. There were still two more cans resting in the ice bath beside her bunk in her quarters. "So, I put in for a transfer to anywhere there might be action: armor, engineering, even infantry. I was still two paygrades from my first star.

"I raised such a stink, I guess, that the big brass finally offered me command of a National Guard battalion if I'd just transition from active duty." The familiar pain clawed its way out of her pelvis and sent feelers up her spine and into her ribcage. She got up just to be moving and looked through the desks and filing cabinets of the lab. *Maybe Helbourne is a closet drinker. Maybe I won't go into cardiac arrest.* "I almost took it, too. But that's when the spooks stepped in and offered me a new job. This job."

She found a near-empty pint of Knob Creek bourbon in the bottom of Helbourne's desk drawer. "Bingo."

Taking a swig and giving an appreciative sigh, she checked her breathing and continued, "They called it 'Military Liaison to the Department of Homeland Security,' which apparently means that I help the big guys in Washington figure out when to use military assets in dealing with domestic events. Yay for me. After spending half my life fighting for Truth, Justice, the American Way, Freedom, Liberty, the Constitution, and all the other John Wayne bullshit they feed us, I get to be the person who tells the Government it's okay to make war on its own people... Fascism, anyone?"

Sharpe killed the remainder of the pint, promising herself to buy the good doctor a fifth later. "But hey, at least I'm still in the game, right? I've got birds on my shoulders now, and if I play my cards right, I just might become a general. And one of the very few non-white women to do so.

"Like I said, I know how you must feel. I've been on display for men my whole life. Under inspection, every single one of them just waiting for me to screw up. Either so they could run to my rescue and be the big strong hero, or so they could look down their nose at me as an example of 'feminine inferiority' or just so they could feel better about having a little dick... Whatever."

"So here we are." Sharpe rolled the empty bottle around in her hands. "Whether you're Putin's newest toy soldier, the secret love child of Elon Musk and Big Pharmaceutical, or the Herald of Galactus, you're my problem now. And mine alone. If I call in a senior agent, I might as well go back to that desk in Germany and buy a headstone for my dreams. They'll say I can't hack the job and it'll be a cold day in Miami before they even consider giving it to someone with ovaries again..."

Idegen had to concentrate hard to get the gist of the woman's thoughts. The haze of intoxication obscured some of the conscious details and idioms, but it made her emotions clearer. This Emily Sharpe was conflicted, feeling out of her depth and unsure of the righteousness of her path, but dedicated to fulfilling her assigned role to the absolute best of her abilities. A troubled yet worthy adversary.

Idegen could relate. After all, her devotion to the Empire and its military had led her to volunteer for the elite advanced recon program, and her success there had resulted in her induction into the Order of the Black Star Worlds. The traumatic training and transformative rituals of the Order had bestowed upon her the physical and mental abilities to become a member of the Deep Space Exploration Fleet, but that career path had also separated her from her beloved Vodie. How long had it been since they had seen one another...?

"Thanks for listening." Sharpe stood and pushed the chair back to its place. Picking up the empty can and bottle, she said, "Whatever happens next, I want you to know it's not personal. It's just the job."

When the woman left, Idegen rose from the floor and returned to her bunk. Sharpe's thoughts at the end were filled with ominous feelings of dread and danger. "Whatever happens next," Idegen repeated the words aloud. She got the distinct feeling that it would not be good.

She needed a plan, and she needed it now.

***

"Very interesting." Dr. Helbourne ran a hand through his thinning hair. He stared at the black-and-white CCTV feed coming from the secret camera he had placed in his lab the morning after reexamining the dead soldiers. If he were to be killed by the subject, he didn't want his death being swept under the rug by the Powers That Be. If he didn't enter a code every twenty-four hours, the computer was programmed to email the footage and audio to a colleague, and journalists at MSNBC, FOX News, and the BBC.

Helbourne had almost panicked when Sharpe began searching the office equipment. She had come very close to spotting the microphone hidden under his desk before finding the bourbon. Instead, he was elated to know that he now had yet another card to play. He had his leverage on the woman martinet.

Not only had he not yet divulged the telepathic nature of the subject, but Helbourne was also still holding the DNA test results until tomorrow morning. They revealed that the subject had an additional pair of chromosomes, giving her a total of forty-eight. But remarkably, this last pair appeared to be artificially *grafted* onto her genetic code, meaning that she was originally essentially human.

Except that she clearly wasn't. Not only did the DNA show the strange mutation or alteration, but it also showed traces of radiation not normally found in this solar system—or even in this part of the Milky Way. And it revealed her age to be an impossible nine hundred and fifty-odd Earth years. She had been born about the same time as the Battle of Hastings had been fought. Given this information, along with the newfound discovery of Colonel Sharpe's personal foibles, Helbourne felt pretty solid in not only his position, but also in his future funding and his place in the pantheon of Nobel Prize-winning scientists.

"Let's just see you try and take me off this case now, my dear Emily," he said with a smile. "You won't do it if you really want to see those stars on your shoulders. And if you try to cross me, I'll bury you."

8
BRINGIN' HOME THE RAIN

Jon cringed when he saw the aluminum toilet in the holding cell. One or more of the thirty or so other men in the cage had pissed all over the seat. But the dogfight in his guts couldn't wait any longer. He'd held it for over three hours during the laborious booking process. Even through the indignity of the strip search.

He *had* to go.

Grabbing a wad of the flimsy toilet paper, he mopped up the offending urine as quickly as he could before turning and dropping trou under the gaze of drunken men, men with bruised faces and busted knuckles, and men he was sure would just as soon kill him as look at him. There were also men who looked like scared college students, men who looked the way he must have his first time in a county lockup.

Thanks to what was coming out of his backside sounding like liquid thunder and smelling like death and chocolate-flavored sushi, his cellmates all had better things to do as far from him as possible. When he was done and his insides almost felt human again, all he could do was scrub his hands in the sink and pray that he hadn't caught crabs or something worse.

I've never wanted a Silkwood *shower more in my entire life.*

Jon took a seat on the far end of a low bench and pushed the back of his head against the cinderblock wall, hoping to portray a sense of confident relaxation. Inside he was reliving his worst nightmare, the night he had been arrested in Nashville and watched his future get flushed down another aluminum toilet. He chewed on the painfully swollen inside of his cheek and pretended to close his eyes, still watching the other men from under his lashes.

Might as well get a little rest before I go before the judge...

"French," a deputy called, startling him awake. "Your lawyer's here."

Jon blinked and tried to breathe deeply. He coughed against the stench of the toilet and body odor in the cell. Sitting up, he stared at the cop on the other side of the bars. "Lawyer? I didn't call a lawyer." Panic started to rise up his throat like boiling water. *Byce. He must want to post my bail so he can whack me. Or worse, take me to his dungeon out in the woods.*

"She's here nonetheless," the cop said. "You want to see her or not?"

"She?" Jon felt the panic collapse in a wave of self-loathing and guilt. For a moment, he considered saying no, but the desire to be out of the cage, even for a little while, was overpowering. And, if the lawyer was who he thought she was, he would at least get one last chance to see and speak to the one great love of his life.

Even if he did look and smell like hell. "Yeah. I'll see her."

After being cuffed, he followed the deputy through a maze of brightly lit corridors and buzzing security doors before finally being led into a gloomy, gunmetal-grey interrogation room furnished with one metal table and three uncomfortable-looking plastic chairs. Angie stood in the corner, beneath the harsh overhead neon, waiting for him.

She didn't wear a sexy power suit or even anything remotely professional-looking like he'd imagined. As his cuffs were removed, Jon drank the sight of her in. Taller than he remembered. Dark hair tucked under a black NRA ball cap. MILF-like curves beneath a grey Lincoln Memorial University School of Law sweatshirt. She did fill out her faded jeans just like he remembered. Maybe even better.

She wasn't wearing makeup, and the hard intensity of her dark eyes wasn't diminished by the glasses riding low on her upturned nose. It had been almost eleven years since he'd seen that look of disgust and loathing. How he'd missed it.

"Hi, Angie." He forced a smile. "What brings you here?"

She inhaled sharply and dismissed the deputy. "It's after three in the morning, Jon. I've been here almost as long as you have, and I'm ready to go home."

Stepping to the table between them, she jabbed a finger at an official-looking document in an opened manila folder. "You need to sign this. Right now."

Jon stepped over to read the document. "What is it?"

"A statement. Exonerating you of all charges in exchange for cooperating with the TBI investigation and an agreement to testify when the case goes to trial."

Jon gave a tired, bitter laugh. "I know you hate me, Ange, but it would be more merciful just to borrow a gun from one of the cops and blow my brains out. Do you even know who these people are?"

Angie took a deep breath and rubbed her eyes under her glasses. "Of course I do, Jon. I've been practicing law in this city for six years. The names have come up a time or two. But you really don't have much of a choice here."

Jon walked over to the big wall-length mirror and stared at whoever might be on the other side. "If I walk, if I talk, I'm dead, Angie. And not in a good way. It's just that simple."

"You know they've got people in County, too, Jon," she said. "If you get processed into the Detention Center, there's a better chance they can get to you in there than on the outside."

Jon turned. "Talk to the TBI guys. You can get me a better deal from them. Maybe witness protection or something. They need me."

"Do you *hear* yourself, Jon?" Angie gave a short, hollow laugh and shook her head at the ceiling. "I've already talked to Hicks and Arnison. They may have needed you this morning, but now they're tight with the Feds on this one. Between what they've got going with Joseph Green in Nashville and what they've already got on this Huland Elliot, they think it's a slam dunk. He's known to be Craig Byce's 'handyman' in addition to running prostitutes and pills out of a couple local trailer parks. If they can get him to slip up during an interrogation, or maybe even roll, they'll have enough to indict Byce and bring the whole Knoxville branch of the Dixie Mafia down in one fell swoop.

"Not only do the cops not need you, Jon, they don't *want* you. You're just a meaningless detail that comes with too much paperwork and too many tax dollars."

Jon felt weak. Chewing on his sore cheek, he pulled the chair out and sat at the table to stare at the document. Without looking up, he asked, "So why are you here, Angie? Is there a chance...? Do you still—?"

"Oh no, Jon." Her voice was hard and husky. "Do not *even* delude yourself of that possibility for one solitary second. That ship sailed eleven years ago when I caught you in bed with a cheerleader. I'm here because I saw your dumb ass on the news coverage of the sting. I'm here for what we adults call closure. Now sign the damn paper."

He looked up and saw her leaning against the wall, her arms folded across her chest, dark eyes shooting daggers at him, jaw clenched. He knew she was reliving that terrible morning so long ago. She had worked a double shift at her Circuit City job in Chattanooga, then driven half the night, across Monteagle Mountain in a thunderstorm, to surprise him after MTSU had beaten Maryland, partially on the strength of his two game-saving interceptions in the fourth quarter.

Jon touched the tiny scar on the cheekbone under his left eye, where the engagement ring had hit him so hard it could have blinded him if it had been a quarter-inch higher. That's when she'd called him white trash and told him what was going to happen to him if he didn't change his ways. Then she turned, walked back to her car, and drove away.

He'd tried to call her for months after, but she'd never answer. He'd even tried to go see her a couple times, but she'd moved, and her friends wouldn't tell him where. He completely lost track of her, the first, best love of his life, until he'd seen an ad for her law firm on TV about a year ago.

"I guess we're both a long way away from those two poor kids growing up in that trailer park in Graysville."

"Not both of us, Jon," she replied. "Whether you want to believe it or not, you're still there. And you're just like your daddy."

Those words were the absolute worst thing to happen to him in the past twenty-four miserable hours. They hollowed him out like an ice-cream scooper to the soul.

"Now just sign the paper and let me have my good deed."

Jon picked up the pen and thought of those samurai movies where the guy would pick up a knife to open his own belly. The physical equivalent of his current emotional state of being. "Death before dishonor."

***

The Vicodin did double duty on this Thursday morning and did it well. Sharpe hardly felt the hangover or the excruciating hash the old bunk had made of her back. The painkiller did absolutely nothing for her mood, however. She was pissed.

"Good morning, Doctor," she said when Race brought the rumpled Helbourne into the lab where she sat at his desk, decked out in her crisp black BDUs and spit-shined combat boots, holstered sidearm strapped to her thigh—the baddest bitch she knew he'd ever seen. "Where are we on that portable sonic generator?"

Helbourne blinked, looked from her to the two stone-faced guardians, then cast a glance at the pale woman-thing on the other side of the glass. "I've worked out the frequency range; we just need to load it onto a suitable device. One of those nonlethal crowd-control things should work. We could have one here by end of day if we—"

"I've got one on its way now from the local PD. Should be here in about an hour. Same time as we leave for Patrick Air Force Base to board a C-130. Leave the frequency on your computer and we'll download it later." Rising, she offered him her hand. "It's been a pleasure working with you, Dr. Helbourne. Your country thanks you for your service. Enjoy your trip back to Colorado Springs."

His bleary face went rigid and red with startled rage. "What?"

Sharpe gave him a mean smile. "You're done with the subject, Doctor. We're taking over from here. I know you dragged your feet on getting me those DNA results, and I strongly suspect you're holding something else back. But not to worry, once we get her to Oak Ridge, there'll be plenty of bookworms and lab coats falling all over each other for a chance to help out their good old Uncle Sam on this one."

Surprisingly, Helbourne returned her smile. "Colonel, if I might have a private word?"

Sharpe sensed a threat. Helbourne's tone seemed... ominous for some reason. "So you can tell me why you're playing at treason, Doctor?"

"So I can help you see the *stars*, Colonel."

She went taut, and a spasm worked its way up her back and past the Vicodin veil. "All right. Give us the room, gentlemen." When Race and Brock had left them alone in the secured lab, she growled, "What do you want, Helbourne?"

The doctor gave her a wicked smile, smoothed his balding pate, and walked over to the desktop at his workstation. "The same thing as you, *Sharpe*: recognition for a job well done and all the accolades that go with it." He tapped a few keys, moved the mouse, and stepped back as an invitation for her to take a look.

Staring at the monitor, she saw a black-and-white feed of the lab. She glanced at the digital timestamp in the lower right corner and knew what she was seeing before she watched herself walk into the room, Miller Lite in hand.

"Would you like to hear the audio, Colonel? It's quite... enlightening."

Sharpe glared at the dumpy little man, then glanced up at the corner where the concealed camera sat behind an emergency light fixture. Taking a deep breath, she whispered again, "What do you want, Helbourne?"

"I stay on this case with full access to the subject." He wore a victorious smile. "I'm beginning to understand her, Sharpe, and when the time comes, I'll be indispensable in the negotiations with her people. You'll get your stars, and you'll be recognized as the leading military expert on these new beings. We both win."

She stood straight and rubbed her eyes with the heels of her hands. "And if I say no? Turn you in for blackmail and hindering a matter of national security? Charge you with treason?"

Helbourne waved at the monitor. "Then we both fry. And the proof that aliens not only exist but are already here goes viral. And the federal government takes one hell of a black eye from the administration all the way down. Not like they're in any condition to take any more bad PR, right?"

Sharpe looked up from the computer to see the subject staring at them through her glass cage with inscrutable intent. This whole thing had been a no-win nightmare situation from the beginning, and it just kept getting worse. "All right, Doctor. We'll play it your way, but I want to be cut in on all your findings *immediately* from now on." She didn't add a threat because she didn't have one. Not yet.

Helbourne smiled and held out his hand. "It's a deal, Colonel. You know, this could be the beginning of a beautiful friendship that sees me become a Nobel winner, and you get a seat on the Joint Chiefs of Staff."

Sharpe shook his hand. Briefly. "Friendship may be too strong a word, Doctor."

***

"Something wrong?" the flab-faced deputy behind the mesh window asked. He wore a shit-eating grin, like a rube who just flopped an ace-high straight flush.

Jon gnawed the swollen inside of his cheek, debating whether or not to raise a stink. A thousand dollars was missing from his wallet, leaving him just under eight hundred. He looked at the receipt for his belongings, noted that it was not the one he'd signed. He could see where someone—probably the bloated and aging cop smiling at him right now—had used carbon paper to copy his signature onto the page.

"I got a complaint form somewhere 'round here, if you want to fill one out." The cop was still smiling through the safety glass. "Might take a while to get it filed, though."

Jon smiled back. "Why don't you see if you can find it, then go ahead and wad it up and throw it in the trash? It'll save me the time of actually filling it out." He knew he wasn't the first in-and-out perp to be shaken down for what this pension rider and his cronies thought was an entirely just and fair tax on what they felt to be "lucky breaks." Besides, he still had enough cash to pursue the only option left to him at this point. It remained to be seen whether he actually had the time. Or the courage. "Can you at least call me a cab?"

The Cheshire cop pointed at the box with the rest of Jon's belongings. "Your phone's in there, tough guy. Call one yourself."

Jon sighed as he gathered up his things. *They don't even need it for evidence. I guess Angie was right. Like a cheap hooker at a stag party, they only needed me for the space of a few hours. Which is probably about all I've got left to live...*

On the first Thursday of September, Jon French stepped out of the jail and into the early morning air a free man. The sun was hidden by a bank of black and grey clouds that spread across the silvery sky like ink in water, the scent of imminent rain heavy in the cool air. He used what little battery was left on his phone to call a cab.

The car arrived about the same time as the first slow, fat drops of chill rain. Jon hopped in the backseat that smelled of menthols and dirty feet, and said, "Any liquor stores open this early?"

The cabbie knew a place on Cherry Street, and twenty minutes later, Jon was back in the cab heading west with a fifth of Jack Daniels' Old No. 7 and a two-liter of Coke stuffed into his backpack. He had used the dinosaur pay phone in front of the rundown little market to call a seldom-used contact. The conversation had been brief and to the point:

Jon: "I need something with pop for less than five hundred and I need it now."

Reply: "Waffle House. Lovell Road. Twenty minutes. Bring cash."

Morning rush hour in Knoxville is always a beast, and doubly so on days when the weather is less than ideal. Fortunately, the cabbie not only knew where to score outside-hours hooch, but also the best backways to dodge the work crowd and the ever-present, ass-hauling eighteen-wheelers. Knowing he wouldn't need it anytime soon, Jon gave the guy a fifty out of his dwindling funds before heading into the Waffle House on Lovell. His stomach growled and his mouth filled with water at the smells of bacon and sausage frying, coffee brewing, and maple syrup warming.

As expected for a Thursday morning at this hour, it was busy but not crowded. Jon spotted his acquaintance in the booth farthest from the door. Back to the corner, eyes on the whole joint. Jon crossed the tiny dining room and slid in opposite him, meaning that *his* back was exposed to the door, which was more than a little uncomfortable given his current situation.

"Frank," he said to the short, stocky older man in the black VIETNAM VETERAN ball cap, camo jacket, and dark aviator glasses.

"Jon." The man swallowed a mouthful of food and took a sip of coffee. He wiped egg juice from his salt-and-pepper beard. "Have some breakfast. You're buying."

"Least I can do for getting you out this early."

The bright-eyed, heavyset waitress in too much makeup stepped over with a coffee pot to freshen Frank's beverage. She had a spare mug. "Morning, sugar, want some coffee?"

"Sure," Jon said. "And a pecan waffle with hash browns all the way. Oh, and a glass of water, please."

"You got it, sugar." Without turning, she shouted his order to the skinny black guy working the grill as she filled Jon's mug. "I'll be right back with that water."

"Look like you've had a shitty night, amigo." Frank cut into his steak and moved the piece around in runny yellow eggs. "I reckon that's why you called me, huh?"

Jon swallowed the hot coffee, winced at the sting of his inner cheek. "Anybody ever call you when they've had a *good* night, Frank?"

The old vet laughed, chewed his food, and looked out the steamed-up window at the slow-moving traffic on Lovell. "No, I guess not. Hate to ask, but you did bring the dough, right?"

Jon smiled as the waitress, Pamela by her name tag, brought his water and dropped off a saucer with creamer pods and a paper-wrapped plastic straw. When she was safely on the other side of the restaurant, he said, "In my wallet. You got what I need? *Loaded?*"

Frank tilted his scruffy chin down at his right leg. "In a paper bag beside me. When she brings the check, you give me the money—an even five should cover it, including breakfast—and I'll go and pay the bill on my way out. You hang back, leave the tip, and pick up the bag. Wait until my truck is out of the parking lot."

Jon nodded as his food arrived. He stared at the nutty waffle and the gut-busting hash browns, breathing in the sweet and savory smells. *Hell of a last meal.* His appetite nearly died at the thought, but he ate anyway.

***

"She looks like Hannibal Lecter!" Helbourne said as the squad of fully armed and armored Air Force Security troops wheeled the subject up the ramp and into the belly of the C-130 Hercules. Idegen Videshee wore a reinforced, olive-drab straitjacket around her body and a black, sensory-depriving, metal-studded mask over her face. She was bound to the wheeled platform by heavy leather straps and old-school iron chains.

"That's because she acts like him," Sharpe countered as she finished sending an email on her phone. Looking up as the troops secured the subject to the cargo bay floor of the big plane, she added, "That little recipe you came up with for the gas sedative must have been off by a smidgen here or there, Doctor. She took a chunk out of another one of our men when we went in to get her this morning. Fortunately, this one will survive. He won't win any beauty contests anytime soon, but he'll have one hell of a barroom story once all this shit gets declassified."

Helbourne shook his head. He wanted to get close to the subject, inspect her and make sure she was all right, but Sharpe's two black-suited Stormtroopers flanked her—one wielding the sound gun, both with a pair of Tasers on their belts—and the eight airmen were strapping in, carbines at the ready, four to either side.

"We're going to have a shitload of bad manners to explain when her people come calling, Colonel." Helbourne slipped into his seat across from Sharpe. One of the Hercules crew members came over to help secure his safety harness before briefing him on how to use the headphones to communicate, the location of the parachutes, and what the emergency procedures were. The plane's big engines roared to life before he'd finished, filling the world with rumbling thunder and the smell of aviation exhaust and oil.

Sharpe's voice crackled over the bulky earphones. "Seems like they're the ones got the explaining to do, Doctor. We didn't go to their house and let *our* attack dog off its chain."

Helbourne looked at the subject, dehumanized in her bonds. *"Dehumanized." Interesting word choice. But isn't she, more or less? I mean, the differences that separate her from one of us are as negligible as the differences between a modern software executive and a headhunter from Borneo. In many ways, the similarities are even greater and more profound.*

He glanced back at Sharpe, who was probably already composing another official communique on her phone. *And what would you do, Colonel, if you were stranded on* her *planet? How long would it take her people to label* you *the attack dog?*

Even through the earphones, Helbourne heard the thunderous roar as the plane taxied out of the hangar and onto the runway. When all four props fired into powerful whirling life, he could feel the thrum of those monstrous engines reverberating through the floor and the seat and into his body. Then he felt the gradual acceleration grow stronger and more rapid until that fleeting moment of weightlessness was achieved. They were airborne.

Helbourne leaned back into his rigid, uncomfortable chair and closed his eyes. He knew he wouldn't be able to sleep, but at least he could order his thoughts and look forward to the next leg of this adventure. Once they reached Oak Ridge National Laboratory, he would be

THE WICKED TWISTED ROAD

surrounded by peers of the scientific community. They would be in his element, not Sharpe's. She might still have a few of her mouth-breathing gestapo at her beck and call, but he would be the one calling the shots from now on. The thought made him smile.

His eyes flew open, and his heart raced at the words he heard in his head: *And what will you do with your Frazetta Woman when you get her into your laboratory this time, Doctor?*

"Something wrong?" Sharpe asked over the intercom, her dark eyes studying him. "You need an airsickness bag?"

Helbourne licked his lips and shook his head. He didn't bother to glance at the subject. Even with her face concealed, he somehow knew that Idegen Videshee was smiling, and it scared the hell out of him.

***

After Frank left, Jon took his spot in the booth, sliding the heavy brown paper sack into his backpack, between the bottles of whiskey and Coke, just before Pamela came by to check on him. "Anything else I can get for you, sugar? Some more coffee?"

Jon shook his head. "Maybe some more water. To go." When she brought him the paper cup filled with ice water and a fresh straw, he thanked her and continued to sit as she cleared away the dishes. He was working up his courage and watching the Shell station across the street. After about half an hour, he pulled the straw from its paper sleeve, folded it, and popped it into his mouth. The familiar sensation relaxed him despite the sudden irritation it brought to his inflamed inner cheek.

Leaving two twenties on the table, Jon hauled on his backpack and headed out into the intermittent drizzle falling on Knoxville. Crossing at the light, he walked casually into the Shell's parking lot and over to the dingy gold 2001 Toyota 4Runner that had been parked there since his arrival. He pulled his keyring out of his pocket. The Toyota master key had cost him a grand three years ago, but even though it only worked on pre-chipped models, it had more than paid for itself since. And—like everything else he owned—it appeared to be totally legit, so there was no reason for the Cheshire cop or his buddies to confiscate it while he was in jail.

Ten minutes later, Jon was on Pellissippi Parkway in a stolen vehicle that smelled of nicotine and mildew despite the Superman air freshener hanging from the rearview. He was heading toward Alcoa and Maryville, but he wasn't going that far. He didn't know how long the Shell station attendant's shift was or when he or she might take out the trash and realize that the 4Runner was gone, so he had to find someplace off the grid and quick. Fortunately, he knew of such a place, and with the weather pissing the way it was, it was very likely to be abandoned as long as the rain held out.

At a few minutes before ten a.m., Jon French pulled the old SUV onto an unmarked gravel road and crept along until he was sitting on a grassy bank just above the rain-swollen Tennessee River, not very far from Keller Bend Park. Cutting the engine, he closed his eyes, took a deep breath, and listened to the rain beat on the roof. He heard a low, growling peal of distant thunder. The storm was coming in and it was moving slow.

"Good." He opened his backpack and pulled out his morning's purchases. After draining the paper cup of its waxy-tasting water in a gulp, he poured a large quantity of the Jack into the remaining ice cubes and topped it off with Coke from the two-liter. Drinking this down as fast as he could, he set the empty cup in the console holder on top of a bed of sticky pennies and nickels. He could already feel the buzz creeping up on him.

He rubbed the sweat off his palms before he opened the bag he'd gotten from Frank.

Inside was a banged-up Taurus Judge revolver and a box of .45 Colt shells. The blued finish of the gun had been knocked off on the front sight and in places on the cylinder, revealing the dull metal beneath. Of course, the serial number had been intentionally filed away. Jon thumbed the catch, releasing the cylinder to see that Frank had filled the weapon with five of the big rounds.

"I'll only need one."

Slamming the cylinder back into place and setting the gun in his lap, Jon poured himself another stout drink. *Damn, I never thought I'd go out like Kevin... I guess the old man was right. I guess they all were...*

Jon had been eleven on that sunny October Saturday morning. His mom had just finished making breakfast, Cream of Wheat and toast, and told him to go get his older brother before it got cold. His dad was still in bed, sleeping one off.

Kevin had already left the trailer that morning before Jon got up. Presumably he was out in the shed that he had turned into his personal gym. Though Kevin didn't tend to work out that long on Saturdays, Jon hadn't thought much of it as he settled into the college pregame shows.

Griping about missing the preview for the UT-Bama game, Jon had stormed out of the single-wide, hollering for Kevin as he ran down the ramshackle porch and the overgrown cinderblock paving stones that ran beside the exposed wheels of the trailer, toward the rust-blotched shanty at the back of the lot where it butted up against the woods.

"Kevin, you dingus! Breakfast's ready!" Jon lowered his voice as he passed his parents' room. The only thing worse than cold Cream of Wheat and missing anything football-related this morning would be to get the belt from his hungover father.

Or so he had thought.

Jon had opened the groaning metal door to the shed to find his fifteen-year-old brother's naked, muscular body hanging from the tin roof. An old pulley-and-rope contraption wound its red-and-white coils around his twisted neck like a candy-cane snake. The other end was firmly secured over a cart axle Kevin had hauled from a scrapyard to use as a makeshift barbell. Kevin's collection of dog-eared bodybuilder magazines was spread all over the floor and on the second-hand bench beneath his dangling feet, opened to the center spreads of oiled-up and smiling champions.

Kevin's face was purple. His hazel eyes bugged out like those of a cartoon character. His black tongue lolled from blue lips, the tail of some alien thing that had died trying to climb down his throat. Piss and shit ran down his suntanned legs, dripping onto the bench and the concrete floor. Jon would never forget that smell of sweaty death, bodily waste, and bug-bomb residue...

He closed his eyes tight and wiped tears away with knotted fists. He couldn't remember exactly what had happened after that. He remembered his mother screaming and crying like a madwoman, her bleached blonde hair flying wild along with her red-nailed hands. He remembered his father thundering down the trailer's narrow hallway in his tighty-whities and a belt in his fist, not knowing what the hell was going on, only shouting that somebody had to pay for it.

Jon did remember that he was the first person his father had seen, and thus it was his COD. And he remembered the belt. Surprisingly, he didn't remember the pain from the blows, only the words: "This is your fault, Jon! Why can't you be like your big brother? Why did you do this? Why? It's all your fault! It should have been *you!*"

If Angie and her mom hadn't come over after the cops had taken his parents to follow behind the ambulance, Jon thought he might have walked into that shed himself and never come back out. Angie's mom had brought them milkshakes from Sonic, and he remembered chewing that long red straw into pulp so that he wouldn't cry.

But that had been almost twenty years ago, and now Angie was the one saying it was his fault. This time, Jon knew she was right. It had taken him years to accept that Kevin's death wasn't on him, just like he had spent years not accepting that the things that happened in his own life were. "This one *is* my fault. All my fault."

Jon drained the Waffle House cup and poured another drink.

The world was getting a little foggy around the edges and drifting away. He looked at the revolver in his lap, still felt a cold-iron fear in his gut for the oblivion it promised. Glancing at the half-empty bottle of Jack, he hoped there was enough liquid courage in there to help him pull the trigger. "It'll be a hell of a lot easier than anything Byce will do if he finds me."

9
HOLD ON

Idegen waited.

In her cocoon of soundless, sightless confinement, she waited and gathered her energy. She reached out with her mind. First to the fat old male, the one who held her in some perverse fascination. Sliding her consciousness into his, she looked through his eyes, saw what he saw, and made her plans.

But not before rattling *his* cage for a change.

Once she had gathered all she could from him, she sent a psychic filament out to the warrior woman. She was distracted by her small electronic device and heavily medicated... her defenses down. It was easy to slip into her mind like a thief into an empty house. Idegen stole the knowledge she needed from this commander and moved on to the other targets in the aircraft.

All of them. In each mind, she whispered lulling thoughts of peace, serenity, and contentment.

It took some time, but that's all she had now. Time and just a little bit of energy, thanks to the overeager soldier she had nearly killed this morning. She hoped that it would be enough of both but resigned herself to making the effort even if her resources were insufficient. *Death is preferable to further captivity, and I cannot allow them to learn any of the Empire's secrets from me. Secrets that may be used as weapons when my sisters and brothers come...*

When sometime later the craft shuddered, Idegen knew her opportunity had arrived. Listening to the nervous thoughts of the fat old scientist, she heard the pilot's announcement of atmospheric disturbance. A storm very near their destination. Through his eyes, she saw the interior lights flicker, saw the strobes of lightning through the small windows along the fuselage. She felt his insides tighten as the aircraft descended for a lower landing approach, apparently in hopes of avoiding the worst of the electrical discharges.

Summoning all her strength, Idegen commanded the biomechanical implants to do their work. Her body galvanized with self-consuming energy; her limbs became as strong as those of a rampaging *oxilelker*. Taking one deep breath, she shredded the fetters that held her in place as if they were no more than gossamer cloth. The cowl was still attached, but she didn't need her own senses for her plan.

Through the eyes and ears of her victims, she witnessed her right hand, now tipped with diamond-hard talons, rip the throat from the black-clad man to her left before he could think to use his lightning gun. The arterial spray from his near-decapitated body blinded the seated warriors to his other side.

Again, the cabin lights flickered. Lightning flashed outside.

The man to her right raised his sonic weapon and squeezed the trigger. Idegen felt the waves cascade over and through her. Deep thrumming in her ears.

She smiled behind her mask. As she had hoped, as her training had predicted, her earlier performances had convinced her captors that the subsonic pulses were a weakness.

Turning, she kicked the man in the chest. His ribcage collapsed around her foot like brittle avian bones. His body hurtled into the fuselage with such force that the windows around him shattered. Air and rain whipped through the compartment in a maelstrom.

Before the man died, she saw through his eyes. The spastic interior lights went red as the other armed warriors tried to raise their projectile weapons from their seated positions.

Their moves were sluggish. They had been lulled into complacency by her apparent weakness and by her psychic whispers during the monotonous flight.

Moving with the speed of the lightning now flashing outside, Idegen grabbed the bench to which she had been tethered, wrenching it from the floor. Swinging it back and forth in a low arc, she pulverized the helmed skulls of the eight seated men. Only one got off a roaring burst of fire. The projectiles raked the already breached fuselage, filling the craft with more rushing air and stinging rain.

Idegen ripped the hood from her face.

Sudden, searing pain tore through her side. A pair of quick explosions overpowered the cacophony of the storm and the monstrous growl of the struggling aircraft engines. Idegen turned to see the warrior woman facing her, still secured in her seat, a smoking sidearm in her hand. Her dark fingers tensed on the weapon's handle.

Idegen's fangs extended, and she took a single step toward the woman, ready to eviscerate her and feed upon her corpse.

The floor disappeared from beneath her feet.

Just before she was sucked from the opened tail section, she saw a wide-eyed crewman clasping a control panel mounted to the cabin's wall.

She fell into the storm.

***

"This is bad, Craig."

"No shit, Sherlock," Craig snorted. He sat on a barstool in his kitchen, one hand drumming the granite countertop, the other spinning a warm bottle of Bud between his thumb and forefinger. "Why hasn't Joey called back?"

Jesse Sneed leaned against the island on the other side of the counter, his muscular arms folded, chin resting on his chest in thought. He shrugged. "Maybe the Feds snatched him too?"

Craig looked over his shoulder and shouted into the living room, where his gathered troops were watching a porno on the big screen. "Will you guys turn that shit down?" When the overly zealous grunts and moans retreated in volume, he shook his head. "There weren't supposed to be any guns in that shipment. And certainly no automatics. This feels like a setup."

Sneed rubbed his square jaw. "What do you know about this French character? You think he's a stooge for the Feds?"

Craig closed his eyes and gnashed his teeth at the roiling storm in his lower gut, clenched as a sharp pain shot through his butthole and vanished. "He's small potatoes. Been working for Joey for almost ten years since he found him in county lockup in Nashville. A good runner, but his heart's never been in it. So, I don't know. Yeah, maybe. Maybe he got pinched for some nickel-and-dime bullshit and decided to roll to save his own sorry ass."

"What about your boy Hue?"

Craig shot Sneed a dirty look. "Hue's true blue. He won't roll; you can count on that."

Sneed cracked his knuckles one at a time as he worked through the words. "Then we need to know what this French kid knows, what he's said, and who he's said it to."

"I've got my slicker trying to get to him as we speak."

His phone rang. Craig pulled it from his shirt pocket and saw the lawyer's number on the caller ID. "Speak of the devil... Hello?"

Craig listened to the report, the pain in his gut growing cold and hard with every sentence. He could see Sneed's fingers fidgeting, anxious for the news. When the attorney had finished, Craig grunted and hung up.

"What is it?" Sneed asked.

"French is in the wind. Seems one of Knoxville's best and brightest sprung him before dawn this morning. No charges filed."

Sneed stood up straight, a wolfish grin on his face. "Well, there's your answer. I'm guessing if we find him and make him disappear in a most unpleasant manner, it'll go a long way in getting the Angola crowd's approval for our new arrangement. Show them that you're still king of the hill. *Their* king of the hill."

Craig narrowed his eyes, trying to hide the fact that *he* still did not approve of it. "I'm glad you can look at the big picture, hoss. Right now, it's my ass in the sling if they can link Huland and that load of smack and guns to me. I'm too fucking old to go back inside."

He didn't add that he was dying and had no intention of spending his final days behind bars.

"All the more reason to get French. We find out what he knows, what he's blabbed, before we take him apart. That'll help your shyster build a case against whatever they try to spring on you."

Craig suddenly felt tired and weak. Every inch the sick old man. "All right." Turning to yell back into the X-rated theater of his living room, he shouted, "You sonsabitches zip up and mount up. We've got a snitch to hunt down!"

***

Jon dropped the empty whiskey bottle onto the passenger side floorboard. The rain cascaded in sheets down the windshield. He forced himself to swallow the last of the warm concoction that was almost a hundred percent Jack Daniels from the deteriorating paper cup. His vision was blurry, and he wanted to puke.

But he had finally reached the point where he wanted to die even more.

Tossing the soggy cup onto the floorboard with the empty bottles, Jon reached over and picked up the Taurus Judge from the swaying passenger seat. Tears welled up in his eyes. His face twisted into a contorted sob as soon as he touched the metal. He chewed on the pulped straw in his mouth to try and hold it together.

He put the big revolver's snub-nose barrel to his temple.

And pulled it away, his hands shaking. He took a deep breath.

"Come on, you can do this." His voice was deep and slurred. "You've got to do this. It's better this way."

He put the gun back to his head. *No chip. No chair...*

He cocked the hammer. Now all he had to do was squeeze the trigger. No way to miss. And it would all be over.

But what about the owner of this car? They sure don't deserve to have my brains splattered all over it, probably the most expensive thing they've got. Bad enough I stole it. No reason I should ruin it for good...

Jon put the gun down and shook his head, making his eyes roll and his stomach uneasy. "You're just making this harder on yourself. If you start to sober up, you'll never have the guts to do it."

He opened the door, picked up the revolver, and staggered into the rain. "Fine... I'll do it out here. Maybe fall into the river... be carried away, and they'll never find me... I'll just vanish from the face of the earth..."

He took a step away from the car, lost his balance, slipped in the mud, almost fell, caught himself on a tree stump.

The gun went off.

A bright flash, a deafening crash of thunder. A spray of wet earth as the round buried itself in the ground a few inches from his right foot.

Shaking uncontrollably, his ears rang, and his nose filled with that burnt fireworks stench. Jon bent at the waist and let his insides rush up and out his mouth, taking the pulped straw with them. He vomited for what seemed like days until he knelt in the mud, clinging to the soggy bark of the pine stump with torn fingernails. He shuddered, his guts in a wet knot and hot bile filling his nostrils and throat. But he was almost completely sober.

"So help me..." He spit bitter chunks from between his teeth. "I'll never eat another waffle or hashbrown or chili again..."

That's when he saw the woman in the water.

Jon blinked, wiped tears and rain from his eyes. *Yes, it's a woman. She's not moving!*

Hauling himself to his feet, Jon ran two steps and dove into the Tennessee River. Lightning flashed overhead, and the heavy rain continued to fall. He swam against the current, the cold water cutting through the last foggy residue of Jack Daniels. "Hold on!" He spit out river water. "Hold on! I'm coming!"

He reached her just as she rolled over and started to go under. Her limbs were limp, and she didn't thrash or fight to stay afloat. She was completely unconscious. Jon grabbed her around the neck to keep her face above the water and fought hard with his legs and free arm to get them both back to the shore. She was heavier than he'd expected, and the swollen current was stronger. He was running on adrenaline and fumes. It occurred to him that he was just as likely to die as she was.

The thought made him laugh. *Well, that's what I came here to do, wasn't it?*

But he didn't die, and neither did she. Exhausted beyond comprehension, Jon dragged the dark-haired woman up onto the rocky, overgrown shore, and as soon as they were well away from the surging waterline, he collapsed. Seeing that she was still breathing, he closed his eyes and let oblivion take him.

***

Sharpe held the phone to her ear in the cold rain. She stood on the hardtop as the National Guardsmen went in and out of the grounded Hercules, gathering evidence, making notes on their clipboards. Blue lights from the MPs' jeeps flashed, contrasting with the yellow and red lights on the civilian ambulances. Thunder rolled in the distance, mingling with the sound of jets coming and going from the civilian part of McGhee Tyson airport.

"Totally screwed the pooch on this one, didn't you, Sharpe?" The voice on the other end of the line was deep and gravelly. She held the phone with one shaking hand, feeding the cigarette into her mouth with the other. But her eyes were fixed on the row of eight black body bags stretched out on the wet tarmac behind the C-130.

"Yes, sir," she said automatically. She counted the bags for the hundredth time. She knew there were two bags—two bodies—missing. Race and Brock had been sucked out of the plane along with the subject when the panicked crew chief had opened the cargo hatch. *And I never bothered to learn their real names.* "I'm sorry, sir."

"Well then, I guess that makes it all right." The tone from Mr. White, her handler, was mocking. "Don't be sorry, Sharpe! Be busy recovering that subject before this whole thing blows up in our faces! I want it back ASAP. Dead or alive. Don't make me regret sending a girl to do a *man's* job! Am I clear?"

Sharpe snapped into focus, clenched her teeth. "Yes, sir."

"Good. Don't fuck up again." The line went dead.

"Son of a bitch," she whispered, tossing the butt to the wet pavement. *The only reason he's not on a plane headed this way right now is because he doesn't want to be the one holding the bag when the dog shit inside catches fire. Plausible deniability and CYA. He just made me the official scapegoat for this whole mess. Win or lose, it's all on me now.*

"That bad?" Helbourne offered her half his umbrella and a sheepish smile.

Sharpe frowned at him. "What do you think? I just lost ten men and a superhuman soldier from another planet. Did you think they wanted to invite me to the fucking White House?"

"Sorry."

Sharpe shook her head and rubbed at the pain in the small of her back. She needed another Vicodin, but she also needed to stay focused. Finding the sweet spot between being high and being in agony was a bitch of a circus act. "Forget about it. So, why didn't the sonic work?"

Helbourne grimaced, obviously dreading the question. "Best guess? She was faking her response to it in the lab. Sort of like in *The Seven Samurai*, she showed us an apparent weakness so we wouldn't probe for more. Suckered us into a trap… I'm sorry. I… I should have been more thorough."

Sharpe pinched the bridge of her nose and closed her eyes, trying to focus. *Maybe if you hadn't been so busy hiding cameras and microphones in the lab, you could have done more tests…* "Not like anybody's done this sort of thing before, and not like you had a hell of a lot of time to do it. But we know that she bleeds. And if she bleeds, we can kill her."

"Kill her?" Helbourne sputtered. "But Colonel—"

Sharpe cut him off with a scowl. She tilted her head in the direction of the body bags being loaded onto the ambulances. "We came within a frog's hair of winding up in that line, Doctor. If not for one scared crew chief, you and I would both be dead as Elvis. They'll court martial his ass for what he did, even though I think he deserves a medal or two.

"Now, what I *think* doesn't carry water, but what I *know* tends to. And what I know is that your sexy pet alien bitch has racked up one hell of a body count among Uncle Sam's favorite nephews. And now, if she's still vertical, she's out in our world among the civilian populace.

"She's a wounded wolf among the sheep, Doctor."

Helbourne looked at the water pooling around his feet. "Or a dead one, Colonel. Nothing could survive a fall from that altitude."

Sharpe smiled at that. "Let's hope so. But I put two nine-millimeter slugs in her at point-blank range and she looked at me like I had just flipped her off and called her mama a whore. And let's not forget the confetti she made of all those reinforced restraints."

She pulled up another number on her phone. "I think it's safe to assume that your initial assessments of the subject were far from exhaustive. Until I have a confirmed kill, I think I'll err on the side of extreme caution from now on."

Putting the phone back to her ear, she added, "And since I've got nothing left to lose, don't think we won't be revisiting our little arrangement in the very near future. But look on the bright side... you wanted to stay on the case. Well, you're on it to the bitter end now, bucko."

"Who are you calling?"

"You ever heard of Seal Team Six, Doctor? Well, these guys make them look like the Cub Scouts."

***

Jon awoke feeling like a gut with the shit slung out of it. He was cold, wet, and sore all over. At first, he thought he had a hangover or the flu, then he remembered where he was and what had just happened.

He sat up and looked over to see the woman curled up in a ball on the wet grass. She was shivering too, which meant she was still alive. He pulled himself to his feet, every limb feeling stiff and brittle, and stepped over to her. "Hey," he whispered, leaning close. "Hey, you're okay. You're safe." He reached out a hand to shake her.

The woman's pale face turned up to him, her ghost-green eyes flew wide, and she hissed like a frightened cat. Jon tumbled over onto his ass with a startled scream.

For a second, he thought she had fangs.

Jon blinked, and they sat staring at each other for a long time. Then he burst out laughing. He wasn't sure why—only that it felt good, and he needed it after all the shit he'd gone through in the past twenty-four hours. Sitting in the mud, in a thunderstorm, hiding from gangsters, and narrowly avoiding suicide. After saving a strange woman from drowning and then thinking for just an instant that said woman was a vampire or a werewolf was the most absurd thing he could imagine. It struck him as funny.

The woman blinked, apparently surprised as he was at the hysterical laughter. She sat up, pushed her long wet hair from her smudged face, and frowned. "Why do you laugh?" Her voice was low, weak, and tinged with an odd accent.

Jon wiped tears from his eyes and caught his breath. He shook his head and again climbed stiffly to his feet. "Because it's better than crying." Again, he held his hand out to her. "And Lord knows, I've done far too much of that already this morning."

She eyed his hand suspiciously, then reached up and took it. Her grip was surprisingly strong considering the ordeal she had just survived. When she stood, Jon saw a map of dark stains and streaks on her OD jumpsuit. Most of them didn't seem to have anything to do with the two neat holes in her left side.

"Good grief!" His eyes widened. "How bad are you hurt?"

The woman looked down at herself. "Bad."

She reached out for him, and he caught her.

"Let me get you to a hospital," he said. She squeezed him tight, buried her face in his shoulder. Then he remembered that hospitals have to report gunshot victims, and he'd be dragged in for questioning, and Craig Byce would find him that much sooner. *Maybe I can pull up to an ER and dump her... Maybe she's military, and they're already looking for her...*

"No." Her breath was hot on his neck. "No hospitals." She pulled her face back and stared at him with bloodshot eyes. "No military."

Jon wondered if he had spoken aloud. *Probably. I'm half out of my skull right now. Probably still a little drunk.*

He shook his head to clear his thoughts. "Okay then. I guess we're both on the run from somebody. And judging by your condition, I'm guessing your somebody is just as mean and dangerous as mine. Here, let's get back to the car and try to get warmed up, huh?"

Jon helped the woman along the bank until they came back to his secret spot. The river's current had carried them several hundred yards, and by the time they reached the stolen 4Runner, they were both completely exhausted and breathing hard. Jon got her into the passenger seat, started the ignition, and fired up the heater. It made the car smell even worse, but at least it was warm.

Then he went to find the Taurus Judge, knowing he'd need it.

He stood in the rain, wiping mud from the revolver and looking at the woman resting inside the car. He turned his eyes to the weeping sky. *I should get her someplace populated, ditch her and the hot ride, and make haste for anywhere but here... But she's in a bad way. What if she dies before someone else finds her? I just saved her life. Hell, maybe she just saved mine... I can't let her bleed out now... Shit.*

Climbing back into the driver's seat, Jon forced a smile. "Well, if I'm about to risk life and limb by driving back across Dixie Mafia Central in a stolen vehicle and harboring a fugitive from the military, we might as well become acquainted. My name's Jon. Jon French." He held out his hand.

The woman squinted her eerie grey-green eyes, looked from his face to his hand for a moment, then accepted the gesture with a solid grip. "I am Idegen Videshee. Well met, Jon French."

Jon raised his chin and let the smile widen. "*Id*-uh-gen *Vid*-uh-she. Well, that's a mouthful. I reckon you ain't from around here... Hope you're no Russian spy or a terrorist or something. I've got enough troubles without adding Homeland Security and treason to the mix."

"No." She turned her face to the window. "Nothing like that."

"Good." Jon put the car in reverse and eased back up the trail. "You just rest easy for now. I know a guy in Clinton might be able to patch you up."

"I'm hungry, Jon French," she said without looking at him. "So hungry."

"We'll stop on the way. I'll need to give him a call and let him know we're coming, and you can grab a bite to eat... And just call me Jon."

"That sounds good, Jon. Yes, a bite to eat sounds very good."

10
S.O.B.

Idegen shivered and held her hands close to the little vent on the disgusting ground vehicle's console. She was soaking wet, but at least a little warmth was settling back into her limbs. Of course, this only revived the grinding aches hidden therein. Her escape from the aircraft had completely depleted her reserves. She was weaker than she'd ever been in her entire long life. She was starving, and her biomechanical implants were on the verge of feeding on her own organic matter in order to keep themselves "alive."

First, they will take the muscle tissue, then the fats and the softer organs, including the skin. Then the skeleton. And finally, the neural web will liquefy my brain for ingestion. In the end, all that will remain is the mechanical part of the being that was once Idegen Videshee. A soulless record of her existence, ready to be disassembled, downloaded, and eventually integrated into another inductee of the Black Star.

It had taken more willpower than she knew she could ever possess not to feed on this human, this Jon French. Her fangs had been so very close to opening his throat and sucking out the precious life essence within, but then her mind had raked through his thoughts, and she'd seen him risking himself to save her from the river. Idegen and her people were ruthless warriors, and the members of the Order of the Black Star Worlds were apex predators, but they also held personal honor above all else. She could not, in good conscience, kill the one who had just saved her life. A debt was owed.

Besides, I do not know how to operate this craft, nor how to blend into their primitive culture. Not yet. I need him a little longer if I am to elude their military hunters.

Still, these were not comforting thoughts when her body was quite literally devouring itself. She shook with another spasm as the aches in her thighs and forearms turned sharp and jagged as digging knives.

"Hey, just hang in there, okay?" Jon French said beside her. "I've got to take us the long way 'round. Through Hardin Valley, into Oak Ridge. Sorry, but this car may already be reported stolen, and most of the KPD and THP will be on the interstates this morning."

Oak Ridge? That is where the other ones were taking me...

He spared her what she took to be a reassuring smile. "But we'll get you fixed right up. I'm a universal donor in the blood department. So, whatever you're low, I think I can spare." He chuckled. "Course, I did just chug a fifth of whiskey, so you might get a little buzz to go with it."

Idegen returned the smile, struggling to keep her fangs retracted. Until she had fully recovered, she must pretend to be a human. Especially if they were so close to this place her enemies had intended to take her. "Thank you. I will... hang in there."

Jon French smiled, returning his eyes to the road. "Just don't go to sleep... Why don't we listen to some music? The antenna's shot on this old clunker, but maybe the CD player works." He fished down into the door beside him and came up with a circular black case. "Here, see if there's anything in there you might like."

She took the case and scanned it for a moment before understanding the rudimentary sealing mechanism that made use of two strips of flexible, interlocking metal teeth. Unzipping the case, she found an assortment of shiny discs in synthetic sheaves. Her sluggish neural web took a moment to process the information and correlate it to the myriad of broadcasts her ship had received during her cryogenic stasis.

"Music."

Selecting a disc at random, she slid it into the horizontal slot in the center of the dusty console, as the neural web instructed her. There was a mechanical whir, then an upbeat assemblage of sounds accompanied by a man's deep voice flowed from the cabin speakers. Idegen sensed there was some subtle yet indelible meaning in the mingling of sounds and the odd words—but could not decipher it.

"Nice," Jon said. "A little CCR. My dad used to love them when I was a kid."

Idegen studied him. She could feel some of his tension and worry diminish as he listened to the music. Though it had no effect on her, she tried to understand it through this Jon French. Taking a deep breath, she sent out a dwindling psychic filament and brushed his thoughts. As weak as she was, there was no in-depth coherence. Just a splash of images and impressions: sights, sounds, smells. Feelings...

A thick woman with impossibly yellow hair and bright red lips smiling down at him. She had eyes like his and smelled of flowers. A sense of comfort and... something else. The word, *Mom*. The same song playing in the background. A tall, lean man, a metallic can in one hand and a tiny, smoking white stick in the other that smelled like the inside of this vehicle. A sense of fear mixed with that same unfamiliar feeling. The word, *Dad*. A young male, not Jon but similar, brother, *Kevin*, laughing. Brightly colored paper in tatters. A clear bag of tiny plastic green men. An oblong brown object with white stitches along its back. A... cake with fire on it. The smell of sucrose and smoke. *A birthday cake.* "Happy birthday, Jonny!"

"You okay?" Jon asked, shaking her from the connection. "You're crying."

Idegen frowned. "No. I never..." She touched her cheek, felt the warm track of a tear.

She looked at the moisture on her finger, then at Jon French. "I never cry."

***

Craig stood in front of the big bay window, watching the rain fall outside his beautiful house, turning his flowerbeds into a muddy quagmire. He had his hands crossed behind his back, the way he'd seen big bosses in movies do while they made their lessers squirm during these sorts of meetings. Jesse Sneed sat on the arm of the sectional, and a couple of the lower-ranking bruisers stood behind the recliner that contained Frank Gill, a local gun hustler. The rest of his crew was still out on the hunt.

When Craig turned back to face the room, he was disappointed to see the bored look on Gill's face. The grizzled vet didn't look like he'd ever squirmed a day in his life. "Okay, Frank," Craig said with a sigh. "Let's hear it again."

Gill pulled his wet VIETNAM VETERAN ball cap off and ran a hand through his thinning salt-and-pepper hair. "Craig, how many times you want to hear it? I've already told you twice. I met the kid at the Awful Waffle down on Lovell, sold him a dead man's heater, ate breakfast, and went home. I had no idea he was on the outs with you or the outfit."

Craig chewed on this, wishing he wasn't so damn tired. "And he didn't say where he was going? What he was planning to do with the piece?"

Gill pulled his cap back on and shook his head. "Nope. But if you're asking my opinion on the matter, I think he was planning on eating it."

Craig exchanged a quick glance with Jesse. *We can't have that...*
Angola will not be happy...

"What was he driving?" Jesse asked.

"Nothing. Came in a cab. I guess he boosted something or hitched,
but I wasn't around to see it if he did."

Craig's phone rang.

"We 'bout done here, Craig?" Gill asked with a yawn. Craig looked
at his phone, saw his oncologist's number. "That kid got me out of bed
at the ass-crack of dawn, and this is some prime napping weather I'm
missing."

"Just another minute or two, Frank. Let me take this." Craig waved
Jesse off as he answered the phone and stepped into his study, closing
the door behind him. "Yes?"

"Craig," the doctor said. "Your latest tests are back. I was hoping you
could come by the office today and we could discuss them."

Craig removed his glasses and rubbed his eyes. "Not today, Doc. Too
much on my plate. Just tell me what we're looking at."

"I'd rather not do this over—"

"I'm a big boy. And I've already figured it ain't good news, so spill it."

After a deep sigh, the words came. The words he'd dreaded, had
expected. "It doesn't look like you're responding to the radiation, Craig.
I know what you've said before, but I think that surgery is our best bet
at this point." He didn't add that because of Craig's shitty liver, chemo
was off the table.

Craig almost sat down, then remembered that sitting on his fat ass
had been one of the main reasons he was in this situation. "Nope. I told
you; I ain't spending my last days on Earth strapped to a bag of my
own shit."

"It doesn't have to be permanent. If we can get all the cancer in one
go, and if the damage isn't too extensive, then we might be able to go
back in and reconnect the remaining healthy tissue. Once you've
recovered from the original surgery. Two or three months, tops."

Craig balled his fist up and wanted so badly to punch something.
But he was surrounded by his precious things in his pretty house.
"That's two *ifs* and a *might*, Doc. I ain't that degenerate a gambler. So,
no. No more rootin' around in my tooter."

Another long sigh. "Well then, I guess we need to have a discussion
about palliative care and how to maintain your quality of life."

Craig grunted. "Quality of life... So how long we lookin' at?"

Hesitation. "I'd hate to hazard a guess at this stage... but maybe a
year or two. Possibly longer if you *really* try to take care of yourself,
Craig."

Craig almost laughed. "I'm over seventy years old with a gut full of cancer. A little late in the game to start taking care of myself, don't you think?"

"Craig, I—"

"Thanks for calling, Doc. I'll talk to you later."

Craig stood in the quiet, empty room and stared at the phone for a few seconds. Putting it away, he looked around at the bookcases filled with the books he'd never have the time to read, at the computer on the desk he'd never use to write his memoirs or start a legit eBay business, at the Les Paul propped in the corner he had promised himself he'd eventually learn to play.

"Shit."

He walked back into the living room where Frank Gill and Jesse Sneed were entertaining the two big gomers by swapping war stories. Frank stopped in midsentence, something about a whorehouse in Da Nang. "You okay, Craig?"

"I'm fine, Frank." He looked at the two big guys and said, "Get him downstairs. We're about to find out what he's not telling us."

When the color drained out of Frank Gill's wrinkled face like Kool-Aid from a busted pitcher, Craig smiled. *Now you look like somebody about to squirm, you son of a bitch.*

***

Jon listened to the classic rock and watched the grey road and the greyer rain on the other side of the windshield. He was cold and wet and physically miserable. But for some reason, he didn't feel as absolutely hopeless as he had just an hour ago. He glanced at the mysterious, beautiful woman beside him. And she was beautiful, even if she did look like she'd just crawled through six miles of hell on her belly.

She's not just beautiful because of the way she looks. It's because of what she did for me. She gave me a chance to think and act for someone other than myself, for a change. Just when I needed it most, I reckon. She saved me.

The amber gas light lit up on the dash. "Shit."

"What? What shit?" Idegen's big grey eyes flashed nervously at him.

Jon chuckled at the way she said it, like a kid using the swear word for the first time. "Nothing major. Just have to stop for gas. Probably a good thing, anyway. If you're feeling strong enough, you could go into the restroom and get cleaned up a bit while I pump the gas. Maybe you can swap my old *Star Wars* shirt out for some clean paper towels until we can get you a real bandage. And I can grab us some hot coffee and something to eat."

Her eyes narrowed, and her lower lip crawled into her teeth like she was chewing the meaning of his words. "Yes. Something to eat…"

Jon pulled the 4Runner into the RaceTrac in Solway, thankful the place was empty but for two vehicles this late in the morning—and doubly thankful there were no patrol cars in the lot. Of course, if one showed up while he was stranded pumping gas, it would be much worse. *Oh well, just a chance we'll have to take.*

"Hold up," he said as Idegen started to open the door. He reached into the backseat and dragged his backpack into the front. "You go in there looking like something out of a horror movie and we'll have cops on us like flies on shit. Here, put my Doctor coat on."

"No. No doctor." She pushed herself against the door and eyed the backpack like it was a bomb.

Jon frowned. "No, it's not—I just call it that. I saw this guy wear one like it on a sci-fi show a while back and I really liked it. He was called the Doctor. Really, it's what U-boat captains wore in World War II. I found it in a mail-order surplus catalog. Here."

He pulled the crumpled, black leather *Kriegsmarine* jacket out of the pack and handed it to her. She took it with tentative fingers, then looked at him before pulling it on. "Doctor coat," she said.

Jon laughed. "Yeah. Now go get cleaned up and I'll get us back on the road as soon as possible, okay?" He walked her into the empty convenience store and showed her where the restrooms were before giving the clerk a twenty for the gas and heading back out into the cool, rainy morning.

As he stood at the pump, he wondered where things were headed. How they'd end up. *If Craig Byce gets his hands on me, I'm dead. And chances are, anybody who's with me is just as dead. I can't put that on her. But at the same time, she's obviously got somebody after her who's just as bad. And chances are, if they catch us, I'm dead too. So, the question is, are we better off facing our separate dooms alone or working together against both of them? Would she even consider that option?*

She must be some kind of soldier or spy, maybe a female Jason Bourne of some kind. And she's tough, that's for damn sure. Shot and nearly drowned, and she's still upright and talking…

The pump clicked off. He shook his head and returned the nozzle to its place. *Why the hell am I even considering that as an option? I'd never, ever thought of something like that before… Before this morning. Before I had a loaded gun to my head with my finger on the trigger. Before I saved another human being's life. Before I... what, became a hero?*

"You're an asshole, Jonny-Boy, you know that? A certified chicken-shit asshole," he told himself as he went in for the coffee and snacks. "You sure ain't no hero."

He borrowed the phone to call Dr. Kirby, the veterinarian in Clinton. The guy was a tough-luck gambler who owed a lot of money to the Dixie Mafia, but they kept him vertical because he provided ER treatment from time to time, and he could prescribe meds without raising too much suspicion.

And Jon happened to know for a fact that he was scared shitless of Craig Byce and avoided him like the plague. Apparently, Byce had tuned Kirby up with a rubber mallet a while back over a day at the races.

When Jon got back to the car, carrying two large coffees, a bag full of junk food, a bottle of orange juice (that's what they gave you when you donated blood, right?), and a new plastic straw stuffed into his jaw, Idegen was already in the passenger seat.

"Well, you sure look better." He settled his purchases into the cramped interior. And she did, though "better" was a relative term for someone who had been shot and dumped in a river. Her skin was not quite so pale, and her eyes seemed to shine a bit brighter, as did her long, dark hair. She was younger than he'd first thought, maybe even a few years younger than himself. "If I didn't know any better, I'd say you don't even need to get patched up. But I do know better. How's those bullet holes doing? You still leaking?"

Idegen nodded. "I am fine. We should go."

"Okay. We're going." He started the 4Runner and put it in gear. "Have a Little Debbie and some orange juice. It'll pep you up. And the coffee is fresh and hot."

Idegen frowned and looked at the road rations. "I am not so hungry now. Perhaps later."

***

Dr. Helbourne paced back and forth in the little office, occasionally stopping to look through the window blinds at the rain continuing to fall on the air base or to take a sip of cooling coffee from the Styrofoam cup on the absent CO's desk.

This may be the commanding officer's office, but it may as well be a jail cell. Sharpe has locked me in here to wait while she "puts things in order." I was so damn close to having the winning hand and running the show! And now what? I'm being dragged into her downward spiral by the scruff of my neck! Maybe I should have taken the out she offered me this morning before getting on that damned plane...

Helbourne stopped pacing, closed his eyes, pinched the bridge of his nose, and took a deep breath. "Get a grip, old man," he whispered. "You've still got your trump card. No matter who or what she brings in on this, you're still the smartest person in the room and you know the most about the subject."

The door opened and Sharpe stepped in, looking like the cat who'd eaten the canary. "Well, paperwork's done. For the foreseeable future, I'm the effective CO of McGhee Tyson Air National Guard Base, including the units that call it home.

"Got to say, Doc, for all the other shit we've been through, we have lucked out in where we landed. Not only do we have access to all the fuel and mechanics we need to get us airborne in a moment's notice, we got the 119th Command and Control Squadron right here, along with the 1st Squadron of the 230th Armored Cav's Kiowa choppers. We got just about everything we need to track down our subject."

Helbourne gave her a grin. "Command and Control? That's satellites, right? You can actually requisition the DOD's satellites for this operation?"

"Can and have." Sharpe eased into the government-issue chair behind the ousted Colonel Vernon Hill's desk. For the briefest of seconds, Helbourne saw pain on her face, something she had probably managed to keep completely hidden until now. "I've also got orders for those Kiowa pilots to report in ASAP and get in the air. They might not be able to see squat in this rain, but then again, maybe they will."

"Have you heard anything from the Gulf yet? Any word on whether or not they've found her craft?"

Sharpe shook her head, the smile vanishing as she rubbed her lower back. "No. Seems we're not the only ones getting bad weather. There's a tropical storm acting like it wants to become a hurricane down there. But Alpha Squad should be here in—" she glanced at her watch— "well, any minute now. So we'll let the Navy look for the ship, and we'll look for the pilot."

As if on cue, the sound of jet engines rumbled through the building. A plane was coming in for a landing. The smile returned to Sharpe's face, highlighting the crow's feet around her tired eyes. "There's my boys."

An aide knocked at the door before sticking his head in. "Colonel Sharpe? You said you wanted notification as soon as anything strange came in on the local police bands... Well, looks like Knox County just found a murder victim at a convenience store in Solway. Just on the other end of Pellissippi Parkway, here."

Sharpe sprang to her feet, another rictus-like smile covering a grimace of pain. "Come along, Doctor. It's time to meet the hounds, and I need you to help put them on the fox's scent."

Helbourne looked at his watch. It was just after noon, not yet three hours after nearly dying in the stormy skies above Tennessee. "I need a drink."

11
KEEP THE WOLVES AWAY

"**D**r. Kirby." Jon gave the hefty older man a smile. It wasn't easy, as the veterinarian peered at him through the narrow gap of the chained front door. Jon and Idegen stood on the big house's small porch, drenched to the bone like a pair of dedicated Jehovah's Witnesses. "I've got a patient for you."

Kirby wiggled his thin mustache and cut his eyes past them, looking at the parking lot of his offices just down the hill. Jon had ditched the 4Runner in a gravel lot behind the Weigel's convenience store a block away. "Anybody else with you, Jon? Byce, maybe?"

Jon ran a hand through his wet hair and shook his head. "Nobody here but us chickens, Doc. Come on, let us in, huh? We're both soaked."

Kirby grunted. He closed the door so he could undo the chain, then hurried them in before resecuring the locks and resetting the alarm. "So, who's this, then? You and your girlfriend have a lovers' spat and decide to exchange gunfire?"

Jon forced a laugh. "No... well, you probably wouldn't believe me if I told you. It's a long story, anyhow. So..."

The veterinarian eyed Idegen up and down with suspicion. "I don't understand, Jon. You hinted on the phone that she had been shot. Doesn't look that bad to me."

Jon glanced at Idegen, who wore his leather coat over his LEBOWSKI FOR PRESIDENT (This Aggression Will Not Stand, Man) t-shirt and had added his tattered Nashville Predators ballcap to the ensemble. Her pale face showed no expression as her green-grey eyes scanned the posh, if dusty, interior of the vet's house. He had to admit Kirby was right, she didn't look all that poorly. "Idegen, can you show the doc?"

She looked at him, then at Kirby. After a moment, she opened the jacket and raised the bloody t-shirt to reveal a wad of brown paper towels held against her taught abdomen by a bright red bloodstain in the shape of a figure eight.

"She's tough, Doc. I think the bullets went in and out. Must'a missed the vitals. But you probably still ought to take a look at her. If she needs blood, I'm a universal donor."

Kirby licked his lips. His eyes roamed over Idegen's six-pack abs like he was at a strip club. He whispered, "Don't worry. I've got plenty of blood in the fridge."

Jon stepped between the leering doctor and Idegen. "Just her side, Doc. No need for a full exam."

Kirby was clearly disappointed, but he motioned them into his garage. Flicking on the lights, he revealed a small exam room with locked medicine cabinets, cardboard boxes of medical supplies and drug samples, and a fully stocked emergency surgery. Just a few feet separated the ad hoc clinic from a brand-new black Land Rover Discovery Sport parked in front of the automatic rollup doors.

"Welcome to Dixie Mafia General's ER," the stocky vet grunted. "This is where I extract bullets, sew up split scalps, and reattach severed fingers, ears, and toes for the organization's grunts. I've also been known to treat the occasional case of the clap and the drip, which has enriched my life to no end, I can assure you. Now, before I get to work, let's talk dollars and cents."

Jon sighed. "I ain't got much, Doc, and that's the truth. The Knox County Sheriff's office shook me down for a grand this morning, and I've pretty much gone through what I had left to get here. Any way you can do this as a favor, and I can owe you one?"

Kirby sighed, his shoulders sagging. "Jon, I cancelled an appointment for this. I could have gotten at least three bills out of that fourteen-year-old German Shepherd. So, unless you got at least that much, I think this is where I ask you and your gunshot stripper to kindly get the fuck out of my house."

Jon scowled at the man and dug out his wallet. He made a quick inventory of the twenties, tens, and fives peeking out at him. "I've got a little less than two hundred, Doc."

Kirby looked back at Idegen with that dirty-old-man grin. "Maybe... something in trade?"

Jon chomped down on the coffee-flavored straw in his jaw. "Forget it. We'll just go to Walmart and buy some bandages and alcohol."

He made it to the door before Kirby said, "That's probably all she needs... Unless it's already infected. Then, good luck without antibiotics. Ever heard of blood poisoning?"

Jon turned, gave him a go-to-hell look. "I thought you doctors took an oath that said something about doing no harm. She could die."

Kirby laughed. "I'm a veterinarian, Jon. Our oath is more like, 'Don't get attached.'"

Jon took Idegen by the shoulder and led her back into the house. "Let's go. We'll find help elsewhere."

Kirby hurried after them. "Mind the alarm, Jon. I'll just let you out."

They were halfway across the rain-soaked front yard when Idegen started coughing. Jon looked to see that she was shivering, pulling the coat's collar tight around her neck. "Dammit." He turned back to the house. "Come on, we've got to work something out with this son of a bitch... Don't worry, I'm not gonna pimp you out or anything. But there's got to be something else he wants. Something I can give him."

He rang the bell again. The door opened a crack. Kirby hadn't yet reset the chain or the alarm, judging by the green light on the wall console. "Change your mind? I'm old and lonely. It won't take long, and she'll be right as rain by morning."

Jon was about to launch into his best sales pitch on card tips when he noticed the phone in Kirby's hand. He could see Byce's name on the screen. The vet had already hit send.

Jon saw the call timer ticking off the seconds.

He kicked the door as hard as he could. "You piece of shit!"

He followed Kirby into the foyer. He was on his feet, whereas the crooked veterinarian skidded across the floor on his fat ass. The phone went careening into the hallway.

Kirby's beady eyes went wide, and his mouth gaped. Probably because the Taurus Judge had somehow found its way into Jon's hand. "Please!" he blubbered. "I-I wasn't—"

"You knew I was on the outs with the operation, didn't you?" Jon kneeled to shove the barrel of the pistol against Kirby's face. His heart pounded against his ribs, and he could feel his pulse in his temples. Blood raged like a river in his ears.

"Y-yes! Everybody knows! Word's out, Jon! They're coming for you and there's nowhere you can run. Please don't take me down with you."

Jon bit through the straw in his mouth. "Let me get this straight, Doc. You were going to shake us down for everything you could get out of us and then rat me out to Byce anyway? You knew the whole time?"

"Look..." Kirby whimpered, tears welling up in his eyes. "You know how deep I'm into their pocket. This was a chance to climb out, even just a little bit. That's all it is. Just business. Nothing personal, Jon. I *like* you—"

Jon thought about what Kirby had said about working something out in trade and the way he had ogled Idegen. He gnashed his teeth so hard it hurt. "You wanted to…"

He hit Kirby across the face with the butt of the revolver. He felt the cartilage of the man's nose go as blood splattered the eggshell walls and faux marble tile floor. He gnawed on the severed ends of the straw in a desperate effort to keep control. He was his father's son, after all, and at this moment all he could see was red.

"You couldn't even do a simple favor…" Jon's throat was tight, his lungs tighter. "Not without getting your filth all over somebody you don't even know." He hit Kirby again, this time on the forehead. Hard.

Jon watched as Kirby's eyes rolled back into his head and his jaw went completely slack, his tongue lolling out like that of a smitten cartoon character.

Jon was terrified that he had killed the man, but also filled with the fervent desire to hit him again until he was indeed dead. He shook with the conflicting emotions, and stood up, backing against the wall. Gasping for air.

He wasn't in the posh foyer of a shady vet's big house in Clinton anymore. He was in the tiny, faux wood-paneled bedroom he shared with his brother in their single-wide trailer in Graysville. He and Kevin sat on their hand-me-down bunkbeds while their father towered over them, ranting and raving about how stupid they were, about how they were never going to amount to anything, about how they couldn't do anything right, about everything always being their fault.

The world turned red, and Jon flew around the room like a demented mosquito until he landed on his father's back and sank his teeth into the man's throat. Hot blood splashed his face, filled his mouth, rushed down his throat, and his father died screaming. Jon, now the size of an action figure, zipped up onto the highest bookshelf in the room and perched there like a gore-streaked gargoyle.

Jon shuddered, wiped the sweat from his eyes. He hadn't thought about that childhood nightmare in years. But he had lived in absolute terror of it, and of his temper, every single day since he'd had it twenty-odd years ago.

Fighting to catch his breath, he watched Kirby's prostrate body until he was sure the man's chest rose and fell in a steady rhythm.

Putting the gun back into his waistband, Jon glanced at the wall table in the foyer. He saw the dish filled with spare change and matchbooks, and beside it was a set of keys with a Land Rover logo emblazoned on the keychain. "In for a penny, in for a pound." He snatched up the keys, then kicked Kirby over to rifle through his pockets until he came away with his wallet. "Two hundred and thirty-two." He grunted, pocketing the cash and tossing the billfold.

Jon looked up to see Idegen standing in the doorway, silhouetted against the dull silvery sky outside. She watched him with an inscrutable look on her face. Her eyes glowed in the dim light and her jaw was set, impassive and fierce. For a moment, he thought she was deciding whether or not to kill Kirby herself.

"He's not worth it." Jon took her by the hand and headed for the garage. "C'mon, we'll raid his supplies and take his ride. But we've got to get a move on in a hurry."

Byce is on his way.

***

Sharpe frowned, staring at the convenience store for the first time but feeling like she'd been here before. She shrugged the sensation of déjà vu away and exited the car. She showed her military ID to the state trooper and led Helbourne and Master Sergeant Dick "Honcho" Conrad through the police cordon around the Solway RaceTrac.

Conrad was Alpha Squad's leader, and the big, corn-fed Army Ranger looked like he'd just stepped off a G.I. Joe action figure's blister card—blond flattop, cheek scar, and all. Like the rest of his team, he had been in civvies when Sharpe and Helbourne had met them on the rain-swept tarmac. She had corralled him and made for the requisitioned Yukon Denali while the rest of the eight-man team settled in at McGhee Tyson.

She and Helbourne had briefed Honcho on the way. She had tried to study his reactions while she drove, but the big soldier had remained all but impassive as she and the doctor explained that they were hunting a cybernetic vampire woman from outer space. Hearing herself say it out loud, she had wondered why he hadn't tried to call the MPs to bring straitjackets for the two of them. Instead, he had only asked tactical questions: What were her physical capabilities, her comparable level of training, her situational intellect, and, most importantly, was she bulletproof?

"Don't know what the Army's got to do with this," the bulky THP said, his Smoky the Bear hat covered in a shower cap, rain pouring from its brim onto his dark brown slicker. "But since you want it, you can have it. Retirement's too damn close to start hunting a psycho killer."

Under the strobing blue lights, he led them past the array of idle Knox County Sheriff's deputies and EMTs. They stood around holding coffee cups, clipboards, and notepads, trying to look useful. There was already a news van from one of the local affiliates parked outside the cordon, and a pretty, young brunette in a raincoat was making a grim-faced prologue into a brightly lit camera. A couple of newspaper reporters tried to snap photos over the heads of the cops posted at the yellow tape and sawhorses.

"As long as the press doesn't know who we are, I don't care what anybody thinks this is," Sharpe told the trooper. She was glad her grey raincoat concealed her black BDUs, and that Helbourne and Honcho were both in civvies. "Have your people make sure it stays that way. In fact, you might mention within earshot of one of those newshounds that we're FBI. Let them draw their own conclusions."

Leaving the highway patrolman at the door, they entered the convenience store. Sharpe could smell the faint scent of blood above that of tobacco, cleaning supplies, hot coffee, and automotive chemicals in the conditioned air. A pair of deputies stood beside the checkout counter, hovering over a haggard young woman with bleach-blonde hair and an array of unfortunate tattoos on her skinny arms. She wore a red RaceTrac smock over her acid-washed jeans and dingy blouse.

An empty gurney sat beside the entrance to the restrooms near the back. The women's room door was propped open, allowing the flash-and-whine of a CSI camera to escape.

Sharpe turned to Helbourne. "You and Honcho go inspect the body. I'll talk to the witness and join you in a minute."

The two deputies parted as soon as she flashed her ID. The young woman looked up with bloodshot eyes that were too old for her face and surrounded by smeared mascara. Her hands shook around a large cup, half filled with hot, milky coffee.

"Hello, Kelly," Sharpe said, noting the girl's nametag. "My name is Emily. I'm guessing you've had just about as much coffee as you can stand, huh?"

The girl blinked. "Yeah. Making me jumpy. Rather have something a little stronger, know what I mean?"

Emily smiled. "Yeah. You like beer or wine?"

Kelly squinted. "I wouldn't say no to a PBR tall boy."

Emily turned to one of the cops. "Deputy, would you please fetch me a couple from the cooler? You and your partner can have one, too. For after work."

When the tall guy gawked at her, she gave him a wink and a smile. "It's okay. Uncle Sam is buying." She fished her money clip out and put a twenty on the counter.

Kelly looked at her, put the coffee away, wiped fresh tears from her eyes, and sniffed. "I just don't understand..."

Sharpe took the two beers, popped one, and handed it to the girl.

"Shh, now. Have a sip or two. Calm down. Then we'll talk." When Kelly turned the Pabst Blue Ribbon up and chugged, Sharpe opened the other and took a long drink of her own. She wanted to drain it in a gulp but reminded herself of her audience. And her responsibilities.

"They looked so... normal..." Kelly wiped her lips and suppressed a burp. "It was all just so damned *normal...*"

Sharpe waited, watched the girl's old eyes drift into memory and her mouth twitch, trying to form the words. She took another sip, noted the two cops staring. She gave them a nod, directing them to give some space. Thankfully, they complied. A little.

"What happened?"

Kelly licked her lips, took another swig of beer, and said, "Helen was in the back, cleaning the bathrooms, finishing her shift... I was going over the till and all the other start-of-shift BS we have to do. In comes these two. They looked like a couple of drowned rats, like they'd walked here in the rain all the way from Karns or Oak Ridge or something, but they were driving this dinged-up old 4Runner..."

Sharpe listened to the tale, making mental notes, not interrupting. She knew the surveillance tapes would fill in any blanks. She just wanted to know what the girl knew, what she suspected. She was the first confirmed civilian to have contact with the subject and survive. Sharpe could not afford for this girl's story to wind up in the tabloids, or, heaven forbid, the legitimate news cycle.

This male accomplice... is he an unwitting civilian? Or could he be a contact? Another of her kind... a fifth columnist? Are there more of them? How long have they been here? How deep does this thing go...?

"... and that's how I found her..." Kelly broke into fresh sobs, snapping Sharpe out of her thoughts. "She was a grandma... Who would do that to a grandma cleaning shitters for a living? Who could? It just doesn't make any damned sense..."

Sharpe patted the girl on the back, handed her the rest of her beer. "I know," she said. "People do strange things sometimes."

Kelly looked up at her, hatred and fear in her wild eyes. "That woman was not *people.* She was a monster. And you've got to stop her."

"That's the plan, Kelly. Now, let these officers take you home so you can try to get some rest, okay? And do me a favor. Don't talk to the press or anybody else about this for the next seventy-two hours, huh?"

With a little luck, the President will say something stupid and piss everybody off, or a celebrity will accuse another of misogyny or racism, or some left-wing hacker group will shut down a pipeline or something. Anything to take the spotlight of short attention spans off this little Tennessee shithole.

As the deputies escorted the poor girl out, Sharpe joined Helbourne and Honcho in the restroom. It was cramped, and the combined girth of the doctor's waistline and the Ranger's shoulders made it even more so. Thankfully the CSI people had cleared out.

Helbourne and Honcho stood on either side of the opened handicap stall, staring at the dead woman sitting on the toilet inside.

Sharpe caught her breath. The woman looked to be about her own age, with a short, greying afro and relatively pale skin. Her dark eyes stared into infinity and her mouth hung open in an almost comical expression of shock and surprise. An arterial splash of bright crimson arced at a forty-five-degree angle nearly a foot up the stall divider from her opened throat. Her calloused hands rested gently on her lap as if positioned.

Kelly said this woman was a grandmother. She couldn't have been more than forty-five... "What have we got, Doctor?"

Helbourne glanced at her. "Well, the wounds are much less savage than those inflicted upon the soldiers. I suppose that is only to be expected considering the combat scenario in which those occurred. It appears that the subject somehow duped this poor woman into a passive condition, and then... I don't know, convinced her to sit still and allow herself to be murdered."

Sharpe tilted her head back and exhaled. "Are you insinuating *mind control*, Doctor?"

Helbourne did not look at her, seemed to find something interesting on the top of his wet wingtips. "Well, I believe the subject may have some form of telepathic abilities—"

"Fuck me running." Sharpe breathed. "How long were you going to sit on this little tidbit, Helbourne? How many more fucking body bags do you need to see before you realize the next one might be *yours?*"

She didn't add that she might be the one to put the motherfucker in it.

"Well..." He cleared his throat, flushing pink around his flabby jowls. "Well, I wasn't exactly sure." She could tell he was lying. "But on the plane, just before she broke free, I thought she was... I don't know, somehow in my head."

"Great," Sharpe snapped. She turned to Honcho. "What about you? Your guys got anything that can fight a psychic alien vampire warrior bitch?"

The soldier smiled. "We got guts, brains, brawn, an unlimited supply of ammo, and several million dollars' worth of taxpayer-funded elite spec-ops training. We're Alpha for a reason, Colonel. Me and my guys? We get shit done. No matter what."

She glared at Helbourne. "Okay, Doctor. Here's what's about to happen. The three of us are going back to McGhee Tyson, and once we get there, we are going into a small, soundproof room. And I am going to ask you questions about the subject. And if I don't think you are being one-hundred percent honest in your answers with me, Honcho here is going to hurt you. Do you understand?"

Helbourne blinked, looking somewhere between indignant and terrified. He started to say something but glanced at the big man standing behind her. He dropped his eyes and nodded.

"Good." Sharpe turned back to Honcho. "While we're doing that, I'll have the body and the CCTV tapes brought to us. You've got a tech guy on your team, right?"

"Petty Officer Michael Tan, Navy SEAL. We call him Hack-Job—"

"Whatever. While you and I are playing Twenty Questions with the good doctor here, have him go over the footage with a fine-toothed comb and get the guys in the C&C looking for that vehicle and the two people who were in it."

Turning back to the corpse in the stall, she said, "After that, Doctor, you can examine poor Helen here. That is, if you can still stand."

Sharpe was gratified to see Helbourne's Adam's apple bob through his neck fat. "All right. Let's go."

***

"I know it's a nice ride," Jon French said. "But don't get used to it. It's new, and that means it's probably LoJacked. But I know a guy in LaFollette—well, he's actually in Jacksboro, but anyway…"

Idegen tuned him out as he rattled on about something called a muscle car and a place called Kentucky. He was talking fast, his voice tight and high. As it had been ever since they stole the vehicle and medical supplies from Doctor Kirby's house.

He was afraid. She had sensed a residue of fear in his mind when she had nearly fed on him at the river, but now it roiled off him in waves.

Just like the frail woman she had killed at the fueling station. When she had fed on her, Idegen had felt her fear. Not of her death or even of her killer. It was a constant fear of virtually everything in her life: fear of poverty, violence, failure, loneliness… the list went on and on. The fear was as much a part of her as the blood Idegen had taken from her veins, making what little life force she had taste weak and bitter.

Though the feeding had barely staved off her hunger and had done little to help her heal from her injuries, Idegen counted the kill a

87

mercy. That was why she had not fed upon Dr. Kirby. He deserved to wallow in his tremendous fear for the contemptible and vile thoughts he had entertained about her, as much as for his duplicitous intentions concerning Jon French.

That pathetic creature deserved no such mercy as death.

They're all afraid, all the time, Idegen thought as she turned her attention to the beautiful scenery whisking past the speeding vehicle. Even in the rain, this land of rolling green hills and rushing rivers was a visual wonder. The misty clouds settled like grey memories into the ageless emerald and jade valleys as if hiding from a sky of tarnished silver. *So different from Logonijy and the worlds of the Black Star... How can a people on a world as lovely as this be so constantly afraid?*

She accessed the data her neural web had collected during her stasis—the decades of broadcasts from this planet that had filtered out into the cosmic ether. *No wonder*, she thought as she absorbed and processed the world's memories of the last century. *It has been a generation or more since they've had a leader who* didn't *tell them they should be afraid. Afraid of words, thoughts, ideas... afraid of each other, anyone who didn't look like them, talk like them, worship like them, think like them, or even love like them... afraid of disease and disaster, afraid of the world itself. Afraid the planet is marshaling its strength to wipe them out in its own death throes. The people of this world thrive on fear and its twin sister, hatred.*

Idegen shook her head, thankful that she feared nothing and thus hated nothing. But then she paused in her smug satisfaction. *That is not entirely true. In that swamp, I did discover my fear. Even worse than the degradation of my captivity was the isolation. The loneliness and the utter separation from my own kind, the members of my sister cell. Never knowing if I will see Vodie again... Yes, I was afraid. And I still am.*

A gaudy green monster loomed out of the mist on a hill to the right of the road. Idegen blinked, trying to make sense of the thing. It was some sort of primitive idol, a bipedal saurian reptile that stood several times her own height. She almost asked Jon French if it was an effigy of his god before remembering her ruse. The fact that he paid the artificial beast little, if any, heed as he guided the vehicle onto the access ramp indicated that it was nothing special. Indeed, she could find no exact match or reference on the neural web, and so disregarded it as a trivial thing.

Fear and trivialities. That is how they cope, I suppose. The trivialities lull their fears to sleep so they can go about their meager lives. All the while, they do not realize that their chemicals and entertainment only feed the evil beasts in their bellies, making them stronger, rather than killing them. When the Fleet arrives, it will truly be like... She searched the neural web for a proper analogy, an Earth analogy. *Yes, it will be like wolves among the sheep.*

"You happy about something?" Jon asked. "Or are the meds kicking in? You're smiling."

Idegen looked at him. "Was I? I suppose I just thought of something funny. You wouldn't understand."

***

"Boss?"

Craig rose from the couch with a start. He touched his chest, his heart pounding. "What? What the hell?"

"He still ain't talkin'," one of the big gomers said. "Sneed wants to know if he can break out the toys."

Craig swung his feet around to rest on the carpet and rubbed the sleep from his face with both hands. "No," he said through his fingers. "No, he's told us all he's going to. Let him down and take him home." He coughed to clear his lungs as the bulky kid stomped out of the sports bar-themed man cave and back into the torture chamber.

Craig had known he wouldn't get anything out of Frank Gill, but he'd needed to hurt someone at that moment, and the gun broker just happened to be handy. So Craig had gone to work on old Frank as soon as they got him trussed up in the basement, venting all his pent-up anger at his disparaged lot in the organization, at his frustration at his failing health and lost youth, at his hatred for his own body and its betrayal. And even at his disappointment at how quickly he tired after only a dozen or so punches.

He'd forced himself to keep hitting Frank until he drew blood, and then, sweating and out of breath, he had turned the exercise over to Jesse. After only a few minutes of watching, he had gone into the adjacent room and stretched out on the old plaid couch. It wasn't long before the sounds of fists on flesh, grunts, and groans lulled him to sleep.

"You okay, Craig?" Jesse Sneed asked from the door, wiping blood from his scraped knuckles on a pink shop rag. "You don't look so good."

Craig gave him an eat-shit-and-die look. "Of course I'm not okay! I've got the Feds building a case against me. My best man is in the pokey. My mid-state lieutenant is AWOL. My best chance at getting a handle on this is in the wind. And I've got you, Florida's golden boy, looking over my shoulder and watching my every fucking step. Would you be okay?"

"Sorry." Jesse grinned, holding his bloody hands up in surrender. "Just asking. And, for the record, I'm not here to watch your every step, Craig. I may be Florida's golden boy, but I know that territory's a dead-end for my ambitions. I'm here to help you make the mid-South a powerhouse again. I'm on your side, Craig. Believe it or not."

Craig didn't believe it. Not for one damn minute. But before he could say so, his phone rang. He pulled it out and looked at the name on the ID, doubting what he saw.

"Who is it?" Sneed asked.

"The last person I thought would ever call me. Not unless he's got a gun to his head." He answered Doctor Kirby's call and heard this:

"Change your mind? I'm old and lonely. It won't take long, and she'll be right as rain by morning."

A loud crashing noise. "You piece of shit!"

... The sound was muffled but still audible.

"Please...! I-I wasn't—"

"You knew I was on the outs with the operation, didn't you?"

"Y-yes! Everybody knows! Word's out, Jon! They're coming for you, and there's nowhere you can run. Please don't take me down with you."

"Let me get this straight, Doc. You were going to shake us down for everything you could get out of us, and then rat me out to Byce anyway! You knew the whole time—?"

Craig jumped to his feet, fought the light-headedness that came with the sudden movement. "Hot damn, we've got the son of a bitch! Get the car!"

Twenty minutes later, he and Jesse Sneed stood in Dr. Kirby's empty and trashed garage/ER. The fat doctor sat on a rolling chair, holding an ice pack to his head. A bandage stretched across his black and swollen nose. If ever there were a more pathetic sack of shit in this world, Craig had never seen one. "So, Jon French did this?"

Kirby gave him a sullen look. "Yeah. He brought some broad up here for me to patch up, but when I told him what it'd cost, he got chippy."

Craig and Jesse exchanged looks, wondering if this could be a point of leverage. "Broad? What'd she look like? What was wrong with her?"

Kirby looked at the bloodstained ice pack before reapplying it. "She was hot. Like a Dallas Cowboy Cheerleader or something. Definitely not from around here... she didn't look like a pot whore, a meth head, or a coke skank. Except for the two in-and-out bullet holes in her side, she appeared to be perfectly healthy."

"Bullet holes?"

"Yeah, you know, the holes left by bullets."

Craig didn't have to ask. Jesse reached out and thumped Kirby on his sore head all on his own. "Don't get smart, shit heel."

Kirby winced and gave Sneed a dirty look. "Sorry." He waved his hand at the shattered, empty medicine cabinets and the sample boxes scattered across the garage floor. "But as you can see, I've had an unusually long fucking morning."

Craig scanned the clutter. "They take anything they can sell?"

"You mean aside from my new truck? Yeah, they got close to six grand in pain killers, tranquilizers, and nerve pills. Not to mention the antibiotics and bandages. Hell, they could set up shop in a Podunk like Rocky Top or Jellico with what they took off me."

Sneed looked at the empty garage. "You said it was a new truck? You have it LoJacked?"

Kirby kept his eyes on his feet. "Yeah."

Craig noted the CCTV camera in the corner. "Okay, Doc, first we're gonna check on where they've taken your ride. Then I want a look at your security footage before we erase it."

Kirby looked up in a panic. "Erase it? I need it to make my insurance claim and file the police report. It's bad enough I didn't have the damned alarm turned back on when that son of a bitch kicked the door in on me."

Craig sighed, feeling tired and bloated. "Can't be helped. No insurance and no cops. We'll get your truck back, but I don't want any video evidence linking me to this French kid and his new honey. Not with what I've got planned for them. I don't intend to leave much behind or in any place they can be found, but you can never be too careful about this sort of thing."

12
BLOOD ON MY NAME

Jon parked the stolen Range Rover at the edge of the crumbling, pot-holed lot. They sat almost a hundred yards from the row of warehouses and shops just off Highway 63, which constituted the main drag of Jacksboro/LaFollette. He took a deep breath and looked at Idegen as rain continued to fall. "I've got something to tell you, and I guess now is as good a time as any to do it."

She narrowed her pale eyes, gave him the knowing hint of a smile. "You are afraid for your life, and you do not wish to risk mine. Is that what you would say, Jon?"

Jon blinked, broke into a wide grin. "Probably not as succinctly. But yeah, that's what it comes down to. Look, the guys in that garage aren't *technically* on the DM's payroll—the Dixie Mafia, the outfit that wants my hide. But they do run grass and pills out of their shop in Knoxville's backyard, which means they probably pay tribute money to Craig Byce—"

"Which means they are as likely to... 'rat you out' as the unpleasant Doctor Kirby," Idegen finished for him. "So you do not want me to go in with you. Is that correct, Jon?"

Jon fished another straw out of the RaceTrac bag, folded it in thirds, and popped it into his mouth. "That about sums it up. I know you've got your own problems, but you've not really bettered your situation by hitching your wagon to my horse. You really ought to think about bailing on me."

She frowned. "I do not understand..."

He thought it odd how it seemed like she could read his mind one minute and then be completely dumbfounded the next. "Look, here's my plan. The guy who runs this shop and I go way back. I'm hoping to trade him this new ride and the loot in the trunk for an older model, fast and reliable car. Then, I'm gonna cut over to Harrogate and the

Cumberland Gap, and make for the Tri-Cities and I-81. If I can get far enough north, I might be able to get away from these guys. So, unless you want to come along for that kind of ride, now's your chance to cut your losses and run."

"I am not going anywhere." She raised her chin defiantly. "You saved my life this morning, Jon French. I must repay that debt."

He decided not to tell her that she'd already done that, even if it was only for a little while. "Just stay here, keep the motor running, and if I don't come out in ten minutes, or if somebody else comes for the car, then you get the hell out of here as fast as you can."

"The problem with this plan, Jon, is that I cannot operate this vehicle."

The straw almost fell out of his mouth. "You don't know how to drive?"

Idegen shook her head. "No, but I do know how to fight, Jon. So it would be best to take me with you."

He shook his head. "No, you're still too weak."

"I am fine, Jon. Let us just go and get this over with, shall we?" She stared at him without blinking.

Jon shrugged. Clearly, Idegen was the latest in the long line of women he could not beat in a debate. "Fine. It's your funeral. I just thought I might make my morning swim worth the effort, y'know?"

She chuckled at that as they stepped into the rain and hurried to Augie's Garage. He gave her another glance. She did seem better off than when they'd left Clinton. He just hoped her recovery wouldn't be stymied by whatever happened next.

"Julio!" Jon beamed as they stepped into the small front room of the garage. "My man! How you doing?"

The heavyset man with slicked-back black hair and full sleeve tattoos on his beefy arms looked up from a *Hot Rod* magazine. It was dark in the lobby/waiting room, the grey light from outside the closed blinds barely amplified by the chrome wheels on display. The man stood up straight behind the counter and sighed theatrically. "Jon French, as I live and breathe. I should call the cops."

Jon beamed and extended his hand. "And I should call Immigration."

Julio, whose real name was August Winchester, grabbed the offered hand, pulling Jon into a bear hug. The countertop between them was the only thing saving him from cracked ribs.

"You rat bastard!" Julio slapped Jon on the back. "What brings you to this neck of the woods? Haven't seen you in a coon's age." His eyes alighted on Idegen. "And who's your friend? Please tell me she's your sister or your cousin. Not that it makes much difference with you hillbillies, but at least it would give me a shot."

Jon relaxed a little, feeling like old times with Julio. They used to burn the midnight oil in Knoxville, shutting down the bars and haunting the private card games peopled by the upper crust's wannabe Doc Holidays. Julio had sold him the Toyota master key, among other vehicle-related essentials like bogus insurance accounts and license plates.

Jon smiled, noticing the dingy old Mr. Coffee in the corner. "This is Idegen. She's a friend of mine, but she's had a rough time lately, so go easy, huh?"

Julio stepped around the counter and gave Idegen a playboy smile. "If you've had to keep company with this loser, no wonder it's been rough going, my dear. Hi, I'm Augie."

"But you can call him Julio," Jon laughed, helping himself to a Styrofoam cup of mud.

"Only if she's a racist redneck like the rest of you Peckerwoods. My dad's from Rocky Top."

Jon winced at the cold, bitter coffee, not commenting on the fact that the elder Winchester had married a senorita from Juarez.

"Hello, Augie," Idegen said before punching him in the face.

August "Julio" Winchester dropped to the dirty cement floor like a sack of wet flour. All two-hundred sixty pounds of him out like a light.

Jon sprayed cold coffee across the room. "What the—?"

"They are here, Jon," Idegen said a moment before the door to the workshop opened and three big men with guns rushed in.

"Don't move." The lead grunt leveled a Ruger Blackhawk at Jon's face. He was tall and thick, wearing an oil-stained Carhartt all-weather coat and a wet ballcap. He wasn't as big as the other two, but by the sharper look of his eyes he was the brains of this particular outfit.

Jon glanced at Idegen, saw her tensing for an attack.

"Easy." Jon held his hands up in surrender. He slowly sat the Styrofoam cup on the table and knelt down to check on Julio. "Easy, everybody. This is all one big misunderstanding. No sense in anybody else getting hurt, much less killed, over a little bit of confusion."

"That's right," Blackhawk said as the two guys with the Glocks flanked them. "I want you to be in pristine condition when Craig gets here. He likes to take before and after pictures of his special projects. So's he can circulate 'em among the boys as an object lesson from time to time."

Jon felt his bladder shrink and his guts twist at the mention of Byce and his torturous proclivities. He motioned Idegen to help him get

Julio off the floor. "Good." He forced himself into full-blown bluff mode. "I'm looking forward to clearing the air so we can all get on with our lives."

As the goons herded them into the back of the garage, Jon told himself he still had a chip and a chair, and all was not yet lost. But deep down inside, there was a little voice fervently praying for a stray asteroid the size of the Sunsphere to find its way to Jacksboro, Tennessee, in the next few minutes.

***

Helbourne sat in the uncomfortable aluminum chair with the flimsy, vinyl-covered cushion, his arms folded and his chin tucked. He sat alone in the small debriefing room, screwing up his courage to face the fascist intimidation he was about to endure. He was scared, sure, but more than that, he was angry. In truth, he was angrier at himself than at Sharpe or her jackbooted thugs. He knew that he was the real reason he was sitting in this room, waiting to star in his own personal rendition of *Marathon Man*.

I underestimated the subject, and I underestimated Sharpe's recklessness. Just like I underestimated the jealousy and ire of those at SETI and NASA. If only I knew how to read people the way I can read equations and star charts! If only I could get out of my own damned way, I could be running this country's—hell, maybe this planet's—space program, guiding our species on its next evolutionary steps to the stars!

When the door opened, he surprised himself by saying, "Well, it's about damn time. Are we ready to get this farce over with?"

Sharpe walked in, Honcho behind her. The big Ranger was now dressed in black BDUs and a fully loaded combat rig. The Colonel looked tired and old, and he could tell by the stiffness of her stride that the weather was playing hell with whatever injury she'd been trying to conceal. She sat on a desk against the right wall and motioned Honcho to stand at the closed door.

"Doctor Helbourne..." Sharpe rubbed her temples. "I don't want to waste any more time on this than we already have. So I'm hoping this will be a short and forthright conversation."

Helbourne raised his chin. "Then let's get to it, Colonel."

"Tell me, in as clear a language as you can, everything you know about the subject. Especially everything you've held back until now."

Helbourne licked his lips, deciding what advantage was to be gained by keeping secrets at this point. "Okay. I'll give you everything in

THE WICKED TWISTED ROAD

exchange for your word that when that ship is found, I'm placed exclusively in charge of analyzing it."

Honcho cracked his knuckles and rolled his impressive shoulders.

Sharpe glowered at Helbourne. "Are you fucking kidding me? You really think this is a negotiation?"

"Every human conversation is a negotiation, Colonel. And unless you want to waste even more time having your pet gorilla pound on the only real intellect you've got on this project, I suggest you agree to my terms." He cut his eyes at Honcho to see how he had taken the slight. Helbourne could have called him the sexiest man alive or the son of a disease-ridden whore for all the emotional reaction evident on the Ranger's square face.

Sharpe stood up and sighed. "Fine. Just spill it, Helbourne. We're on the clock."

He exhaled in relief. "First, her name is Idegen Videshee, and I think she comes from a world called Logonijy. From what I gathered from those DNA results, it must lie in a completely different galaxy, which leads me to believe that her people have traveled here via a wormhole or some other form of interspace gateway. Though, given her surprisingly advanced age, it is possible, if highly unlikely, that they do possess some form of travel that's faster than light."

Sharpe pulled another chair from behind the desk, turned it backwards, and faced him, her arms resting across the chair's back. "Go on."

"Obviously she's a soldier or warrior of some kind, which leads me to believe that her society is almost certainly a militaristic one." He glanced at the armed Honcho with a sneer. "Much like our own."

"So far, this is nothing new or Earth-shattering, Doctor," Sharpe said, her face taut with frustration.

"Fine, how about this, then? I believe that her people's technology is a blend of advanced cybernetics and preternatural psychic ability. Our initial X-rays showed a large concentration of metallic implants in her skull, specifically around the right posterior cortical and hippocampal regions. A recent, if inconclusive, study showed this as a possible center of psychic abilities in humans."

"And?"

Helbourne sighed in exasperation. He'd forgotten how hard it was to speak to mouth breathers for any given amount of time. "It means, Colonel, that she is not only physically superior to us, but also *psychically* superior, and that her race has found a way to use technology to enhance these superiorities. It means, Colonel Sharpe, that if there is an alien army up there and heading this way, there is very little chance we can stop them if they set foot on terra firma.

"It means, dear *friend*, that unless we find her and get her on our side, and somehow convince her to be an emissary to her people on our behalf, then those people up there will either enslave or annihilate us."

"Or," Sharpe said, slowly rising from the chair, "it means we find her, capture her, and systematically take her apart to find the weaknesses of these psycho super soldiers from outer space, Doctor. That's what we do here. We assess threats, and then we deal with them."

"The military solution," Helbourne said with disgust.

"The human solution, Doctor. You of all people should realize that there aren't any descendants of the Neanderthals running around on Planet Earth anymore because our ancestors saw them as a threat. It is simple human survival instinct."

Helbourne jumped to his feet. "But what if there's a better way?"

Sharpe stayed Honcho with a raised hand. "So far, Doctor, your *better way* has racked up one hell of a body count. Speaking of which, I think you need to get to work examining our first, and hopefully last, civilian casualty. While you're up to your elbows in a defenseless grandmother's ribcage, I want you to think about this... Idegen Videshee... and how she could possibly be on our side.

"In the meantime, I've got some intel on her male accomplice to go over."

When Helbourne started to follow Sharpe out of the room, Honcho dropped him to his knees with a quick shot to the solar plexus. As Helbourne knelt on the concrete floor, sucking air, his diaphragm spasming, the big soldier leaned down and whispered in his ear, "That's for the gorilla remark, Doc. Let's try to keep it civil from here on out, huh?"

***

Sharpe had Archer and Ramrod, the two Marines from Honcho's team, escort Helbourne to the medical building to perform the autopsy on Helen Woodbury, mother of four, grandmother of seven. She and Honcho headed over to the command center where Hack-Job, the tech specialist, and Tunes, the team's communications specialist, collected and collated the data gathered by the C&C squadron.

"I get that you don't like him," Sharpe said to the big Ranger. She didn't look at him or raise her voice as they strode down the empty hallway. "I don't like him, and from what I've gathered from his file, nobody does. But, for the time being, Doctor Helbourne is an asset just like one of your weapons and should be treated as such. Savvy?"

"Yes, ma'am," Honcho said in the same reserved, professional tone. "Just sometimes a weapon jams in the field and needs to be reminded of its purpose with a good blow to the action."

Sharpe couldn't argue the point, almost smiled at the analogy. Probably would have if the pain in her lower back wasn't trying to invite a migraine to the party. When they stepped into the control room—which was completely dark save for the multitudinous glow of computer monitors and a bank of HDTVs displaying rotating feeds from CCTV cameras in the area—the headache may as well have jumped out and shouted "Surprise!" over the din of murmuring techs and beeping computer commands.

Sharpe exhaled, gritted her teeth, and stepped over to the light table where the two black-clad members of Alpha Team were looking over data. "All right," she said to Petty Officer Michael Tan—Hack-Job. "What have you got for me?"

The short, wiry SEAL swung a laptop around for her to see the picture and data on the screen. "His name is Jon Rodney French. Born in Dayton, Tennessee, on April 1, 1989, to Rodney Howell French and Lois Marie French, né Montgomery. He was the second of two boys. His older brother, Kevin Mark, committed suicide in October of 2000."

Sharpe rubbed her forehead, studying the picture of the ruggedly handsome young man. "What else? Are we sure this is real? He's not a plant?"

SFC Dunte Lunis, the stocky Army Ranger they called Tunes, turned another laptop in her direction. "We've got his school, medical, and criminal records. He's a hundred percent legit."

"Criminal...?" Sharpe murmured as she scanned the data. She saw the dirty secrets of a man's life painted in broad strokes on the computer screen.

Good student at first, then a bad one—coinciding with the death of his sibling—until high school, where he became a star multi-sport athlete... Two ER visits in early childhood: a broken left wrist at age six and a false case of appendicitis at age nine... DCS alerted on first occasion, but no follow-up... attending physician on second instance attributed false alarm to nervous stomach brought on by emotional trauma... Full athletic scholarship to Middle Tennessee State University... arrested for illegal gambling... time in county...

"And then he goes off the grid? No residential address, no credit cards, no voting registration, not even a phone bill?"

"Not completely." Hack-Job brought up DMV records. "He's kept a valid Tennessee driver's license, using various fake mailing addresses or the addresses of friends and associates. He's been picked up a couple times for vagrancy, public drunkenness, and even one count of assault in Pikeville, Tennessee, a few years ago, but nothing serious has ever stuck. Usually time served, community service, and counseling. All small-time stuff."

"Until yesterday." Tunes displayed another page of data. "Looks like he got himself tied up in a big multi-departmental sting going after the Dixie Mafia."

Sharpe scanned the data. "And they just let him go? Show me everything you've got on this lawyer, this Angela Lawman. Maybe she's got some insight into where he might go to ground."

A few minutes later, she saw the connection: high-school sweethearts featured in the yearbook as Mr. and Ms. Rhea County, and an announcement the following year in the *Dayton Herald* of their pending nuptials. But now the lawyer was married to someone else, an airline pilot, and had a kid of her own. Sharpe studied the happy teenager in the yearbook photos, the smiling girl in the black-and-white engagement photo, and the hard-faced woman in the online law firm ad.

"Nope," she said. "That's a dead end. I'm betting she cut Jon French loose a long time ago and just got him out of the can because of some misguided sense of nostalgia or guilt. Have one of the local boys pay her a visit and see what she knows, but we need to keep our eyes out for something else."

"Like what, Colonel?" Tunes asked.

Sharpe frowned. "I wish I knew, Sergeant. If I did, I probably wouldn't need you guys, now, would I?"

"No, ma'am."

"Right. Just let me know if anything else comes in."

"Yes, ma'am."

Sharpe turned to Honcho on her way out of the C&C. "Get some of your guys out in the field. I want boots on the ground as soon as something comes in. In the meantime, I've got some thinking to do."

And some self-medicating.

***

Idegen allowed herself to be led into the small room behind the shop's front chamber. Though it had a high ceiling, the white-walled office was a narrow rectangle. The scarred and dirty walls were adorned by ragged images of nude and partially nude females. The room's corners were cluttered and it smelled of sweat, petroleum, chemicals, and artificial flora.

She sensed Jon's frustration at her striking this Julio person as much as his overwhelming fear of their current situation. His mind swirled with gruesome images of death and torture. Clearly, he was out of sorts and was not going to be of much use in extricating them from the scenario.

She studied their captors and was unimpressed. True, they were large specimens of the human male, and all were armed with the chemical projectile sidearms, but they did not seem to show any semblance of military discipline or even combat alertness. In fact, they appeared to be under the influence of some form of relaxing herb or medication. She smelled a strange smoke clinging to their clothes as well as the scent of foodstuffs.

She and Jon settled the unconscious Julio onto a low couch in front of a cluttered desk.

"All right," the apparent leader of the trio said. "Time for a frisking."

Jon turned and raised his hands. "I got a pistol in my belt," he conceded as one of the other two men patted him down and removed his weapon. "She's not armed."

"I'll be the judge of that." The other stepped close to Idegen with the same lascivious smile she had seen on Doctor Kirby's face. Jon tensed and started to step between them, but the man who had disarmed him struck him in the midsection, dropping him gasping for air onto the sofa next to Julio.

Idegen smiled at the man about to search her and raised her arms invitingly.

Licking his lips, he said, "I'd better use both hands and take my time, darlin.' You look like you could have all *kinds* of weapons on you."

He set his pistol on the desk beside her and cupped her breasts.

She reached into his mind, past the vulgar thoughts swimming at the fore until she found his memories about his weapon. In the moment it took him to start lifting her shirt, she understood how the pistol worked and knew that it was loaded.

She picked up the weapon, placed it against his head, squeezed the trigger.

The gunshot was deafening in the small chamber. The other two men stared at her through the pale haze of smoke and aerated blood, dumbfounded. Just long enough for her to fire twice more.

In as many seconds, three dead humans lay bleeding out on the filthy floor tiles.

"Holy shit... You killed them!" Jon gaped wide-eyed at her from the couch. "Holy shit, you *are* Jason Bourne. Holy shit!"

Idegen scanned his thoughts for the reference. When she understood, she smiled and winked. "Jason Bourne wishes he was me."

"What... the... shit," Julio groaned, regaining consciousness and rubbing his jaw. "What happened?" He blinked, looking around at the carnage in the smoky room. He stared at Idegen, the smoking weapon still in her hand, and shook his head. "Never mind. I'm guessing *you* happened."

Jon turned to Julio. "Man, I am so sorry to drag you into this shit..."

As the two began discussing the unusual situation—the fact that Julio had not been given a choice or a chance to warn them, and Jon's plans for escape—Idegen knelt and started looting the dead men for more weapons, ammunition, and other resources. Sensing a surprising kinship between Jon and Julio—almost as if they had fought on a campaign together as members of a brother cell—she felt some small regret for having struck Julio.

She shook the useless thought away, made certain that they were ignoring her, and slid her hand under the garments of the man who had touched her. *How do you like it?*

Her talons extended, burying themselves in his abdomen. While Jon and Julio continued to speak, she drew the last remnants of the man's fading life force up through the biomechanical blades and into herself. There was not much, and what little she was able to extract took enough time that she knew the other two would be useless as sustenance.

But at least I won't starve today.

"That was three gunshots," Jon said. "Somebody's gonna call the cops."

"Doubtful." Julio staggered from the couch. "This place makes so much racket that the neighbors are probably all desensitized to it. I'm more surprised nobody called the cops when we *stopped* making noise this morning."

Jon looked at him. "How's that?"

"They took my scattergun and sent my crew home." Julio flopped down behind the desk and began rifling through the drawers. "Jimmy Ray there—" he nodded in the direction of the erstwhile leader of the gunmen— "remembered us running around from the old days and decided to sit on me just in case you showed up. Bastards been smoking my grass and eating my mama's tamales all morning."

He found what he was looking for and lit it, filling the room with that same smell Idegen had sensed on the dead men. He inhaled the herb, coughed, and offered it to Jon, who declined, as did she when he held the... "joint" toward her.

THE WICKED TWISTED ROAD

Jon's face was pale as he stared at the dead men on the floor. Idegen sensed surprise and mild disdain at her actions, but not shock and revulsion. This was not his first encounter with sudden, violent death. He was unsettled by it but not crippled. *That is good. He may continue to be of use in the future...*

"I can't believe this," Jon muttered in a tight voice. "Just yesterday, I was a short drive from Tunica and living my dream. Now I'm running for my life and surrounded by corpses."

"So, what's the play?" Julio asked, his nerves apparently calmed by his aroma therapy. He, too, was no stranger to violence, it would seem. "I mean, you've got a kick-ass bodyguard here." He smiled at Idegen. "She hits harder than an MMA fighter I once tussled with. So, you gonna turn and face Byce when he gets here? If so, I'll back you, but even if we win, we're all dead once the cops show up and we go inside."

Idegen was genuinely surprised at Julio's forthrightness. He was scared, but he was also willing to stand beside his... *friend. Yes, they are cell companions, like Vodie and myself. Only not the same...*

Jon rubbed his face. "Believe me, I know... Julio, the reason I came was I've got a hot Range Rover Sport with a trunk full of meds and drugs. I was hoping you would trade me something fast, old, and reliable to get me out of the South. I reckon if I can make it past the Mason-Dixon Line, I'll double my odds of survival."

"I've got what you need, Jon-boy, but you can't run forever."

Idegen scanned Julio's thoughts closely but could detect no deception or duplicity.

"I know, man. What other choice I got? You already said we either go down in a blaze of glory or get shanked in gen-pop."

"Do you remember Wayland Moore?"

Jon frowned. "Moore? No, I don't think so."

"Me neither. But he was Byce's predecessor back in the day. Stepped down in the eighties, but he's still around. Maybe he's got enough juice to call for a face-to-face—a safe meeting between you and Byce under the bosses' supervision. Maybe give you the chance to talk your way out of this."

Jon ran a hand through his hair and stared at the bodies at Idegen's feet. She sensed his hopelessness, his desperation, his desire for his predicament to simply be over. His weakness. "Okay. I guess it's worth a shot. One in a million, but it's probably the only one I got at this point... Where's he at?"

"Middlesboro," Julio said. "If he won't help, it's basically on your way to the Tri-Cities and 81, anyway, right?"

"Yeah." Jon turned and smiled. "Thanks, Julio. I owe you one."

"Add it to the list. Now, y'all need to get some gone while the gettin' is good. Byce could already be on his way."

Jon tucked the Taurus Judge back into his jeans. "You going to be okay when he shows up?"

Julio winked at Idegen as she slid the other three handguns into the pockets of Jon's Doctor coat. "Sure. I'll tell him how your one-woman army here took us all apart. I'm sure my security camera got a good shot of her dropping me like a bad habit out front."

Idegen smiled. "For what it is worth, August, I am sorry that I struck you. I assumed you had betrayed Jon."

"I would have done the same thing, sweetheart. No hard feelings." He tossed Jon a set of keys. "Now get."

***

"Nice bird," Craig said as the blacked-out, fully restored 1968 Plymouth Road Runner pulled past them at the light and headed northeast on Highway 25. He smiled, hearing the engine purr. "I had a blue one back in the day, but mine didn't have the Hemi."

Jesse Sneed grunted beside him. "Not bad for an oldie, I reckon." The light changed, and he guided the white Maserati into the industrial park. The rain had slacked off a bit, so Doc Kirby's stolen Range Rover was clearly visible in the semi-crowded parking lot.

Craig was about to launch on the virtues of old-school auto mechanics when his burner chirped in his pocket. He saw the number that coincided with the jacked-up, mud-crusted Ford Bronco parked in front of Augie's Garage. He answered, "Jimmy Ray?"

"Hello? Is this Craig? Craig Byce?"

"Who the hell is this?"

"August Winchester." The voice was shaky. "I need to tell you something."

"Tell it to my face," Craig said. "We're here."

He snapped the phone off and stuffed it back into his pocket. "Something's wrong. You packing?"

Sneed smiled as he parked the car beside the Bronco. "Always."

"Good."

They hurried into the front room of the garage to find August Winchester putting the phone down on the counter and holding an ice pack to his face. Craig recognized him now: the beaner half-breed dealer who always paid his protection money on time and never rocked the boat. The guy even sent him a bottle of Patrón every Christmas to keep on his good side.

"What the hell's going on here, Julio?"

"I'd better show you," he said, opening the door to the back.

"Shit on a stick," Jesse said with a low whistle. "Looks like you got some 'splaining to do, Ricky."

Winchester gave Jesse a dirty look. "Look, Homes, I'm just as unhappy as you about this shit. And I'm damn lucky I got off with a slight concussion instead of a hole in the head. And just who the hell are you, anyway?"

"He's with me, that's who," Craig said, surveying the tiny office that smelled of death and pot. "And he's right. What happened here?"

Winchester stepped over the dead men to get to his desk. Turning the computer monitor where they could see it, he pulled up footage from his front room security camera. "*They* happened here."

Craig watched as Jimmy Ray and his boys showed up and intimidated Julio into clearing his garage and turning over his personal defense items. A bit of fast-forwarding showed Jon French and the woman walk in the front door. After some silent movie banter, the woman dropped the muscular greaser to the floor with a single punch just before Jimmy Ray and his boys rushed the room, guns drawn.

Craig scanned the office. "No cameras in here?"

Winchester pulled the ice pack from his swollen face. "Never needed one before today. So how we going to handle this? I mean, *shit*, man..."

Craig scowled. "Did *you* see what happened in here?"

"No. I came to just as the shooting ended. Jimmy Ray and the others were already worm food by the time I knew what was going on."

"Then what?" Jesse asked, pulling his Beretta from under his shirt. Craig was satisfied to see Julio's eyes widen. "How come they didn't just waste you, too?"

"The b-bitch w-wanted to, man," Julio stammered. "But Jon stopped her. I reckon he's the sentimental type. Remembers the good times we had back in the day."

Craig took a deep breath, feeling the bloated pain in his guts. "So they just walked out of here?" He looked around. "This couldn't have happened more than half an hour ago, and the car they came in is still out front. They get wheels off you? They say where they were going?"

"They took my El Camino and all the cash I had in the drawer, which thankfully wasn't much, just a couple hundred. But no, they didn't say where they were going."

"Description of the El Camino," Sneed said.

"Gold with black and red pin-striping. Lift kit with chrome spinners. Personalized plate that reads C-N-Q-S-T-D-R."

Jesse looked at Craig. "Want me to get that description out to the boys?"

"Nope," Craig said. "He's lying. He had me going right up until that fancy spic-mobile. No way this chick—who seems like a pro—would take something that conspicuous from a scene where she'd just dropped three bodies."

Craig watched the color drain from Julio Winchester's face. "No, he's holding something back. Fortunately, I know just the place and the methods to figure out what that is. Get him up; he's coming with us."

"L-look..." Winchester licked his lips, his eyes bugging out. "M-maybe I do know something, but..."

He reached for something under the desk.

Jesse shot him.

Julio spun around in the office chair before toppling to the floor. A huge red splatter painted the dirty wall behind him.

"Dammit, Jesse!" Craig shouted over the ringing in his ears. "Now how we going to get anything out of him?"

Jesse laughed as he safetied his weapon and returned it to the small of his back. "Easy, Craig. That was a flesh wound. He may never be able to throw a fastball again, but so long as we get him patched up before he bleeds out, he'll be healthy enough for a visit to your rumpus room."

Julio lay on the floor, groaning in pain and shock.

Craig ran a hand through his thin, wet hair and sighed. "Well, good... Okay, let's get him in Jimmy Ray's Bronco and get him back to the house. I'll drive the mudder; you pick up Doc Kirby on the way."

13
WAGON WHEEL

Helbourne examined the sample through the microscope and grunted.

"What's up, Doc?" SFC Adam "Patches" McKinney asked from the other side of the examination room, where he stitched up the earthly remains of the late Helen Woodbury. Patches was one of the Alpha Team grunts, an Air Force Pararescue medic. But he was the least grunt-like of the bunch to Helbourne's way of thinking. The lanky, sandy-haired man put him in mind of Jimmy Stewart's George Bailey at the beginning of the Christmas classic: good-natured with a quick wit.

"The tissue from around the wounds..." Helbourne pushed himself away from the microscope and rubbed his eyes. "It is not nearly as desiccated as that of the soldiers I studied in Florida. This in spite of the subject having more time and ease in which to... feed."

"Uh-huh." Patches carefully continued his work. "And what does that mean?"

"I believe it means that this victim had less... essence, or energy, to convey than did the younger, more virile men killed in action."

Patches looked up at him. "Like in that old space-vampire movie, *Lifeforce?*"

Helbourne smiled. The medic apparently shared his taste in pop culture schlock. "Indeed. I'm surprised the analogy didn't occur to me sooner, considering the similar comely appearances of the subject and the female 'vampire' of that film."

Patches went back to work. "Mathilda May sure kept my teenaged motor running. I wore my dad's VHS tape out before I was fifteen..."

"Yes, I'm sure you did." Helbourne turned back to the labs. "Now, could you hurry that business up over there and help me load the centrifuges? I have another suspicion about the blood samples."

Patches sighed but did not move. "You know, Doc, this is a human being I'm sewing up over here. She was a hard-working mother and grandmother, loved by people who are going to miss her terribly. You could show a little—"

"Respect?" Helbourne scoffed. "That is dead, inanimate tissue, Sergeant. Whatever it was that made Helen Woods a person is long since gone. I'm trying to save living people with what I'm doing here."

"Compassion." Patches looked up with cold blue eyes. Now he was Jimmy Stewart in *The Man from Laramie*. "I was going to say 'compassion.' And her name was Helen Woodbury. And thanks to... whoever screwed up on that plane, she won't be going home to her family tonight, but right now, she is doing her best to help us catch this monster."

Helbourne raised his chin, accepting the rebuke. "Of course, you are right, Sergeant. My apologies... However, I think her blood can help us in that task *if* we can examine it quickly."

"Almost finished here," the medic said, returning to his work. Helbourne watched him cut the suture and carefully cover the body with the medical blanket. The tall man's actions were almost reverent, loving.

"I think you might have a career in the mortuary arts after you're done with the service, Sergeant."

Tossing his latex gloves in the bin, Patches retrieved a fresh pair before walking over to the counter. He took the prepared blood samples from Helbourne and began loading the centrifuge. "I've seen a lot of dead bodies in this line of work, Doc. Some of 'em were dead when I got to 'em. Some of 'em weren't. I reckon I got a clearer picture than most of what's waiting at the end of the line for all of us. That's all... Death ain't got no dignity on its own, so it don't hurt us to try and give it some."

"Hm, perhaps a poet, then."

"So, what's your theory on the blood, Doc?"

"First, I don't think our 'vampire' woman actually feeds on the blood itself. I think it is merely the vehicle by which she absorbs the *life force*, as you put it. Just as the water, barley, and hops of beer are merely the vehicles by which the human body ingests alcohol."

"And second?" Patches asked as the centrifuge whirred to a stop.

Helbourne clicked on a result on the computer screen. Then two more. "Aha. As I thought, Helen Woodbury's blood shows a high concentration of dopamine, serotonin, and endorphins. High, but not unnaturally so."

"Meaning?"

Helbourne smiled indulgently at his mundane lab assistant. "Meaning that the subject was able to affect Mrs. Woodbury's emotions, but not her cognitive reasoning. If she were capable of true 'mind control,' as the Colonel called it, the blood samples would be absolutely flooded with these 'happiness hormones.'"

"So, she can't make us turn on each other or ourselves?"

"No, nothing like that. But given the right set of variables or situations, she could get you to lower your guard enough that you would give yourself to her willingly. Our subject seems to have the seductive abilities of a very powerful Mata Hari—a super sex symbol version of Raquel Welch or Bo Derek... Though I suppose Scarlett Johansson or Jennifer Lawrence would be the proper analog for your generation, Sergeant."

Patches laughed. "You mean she's 'Love Potion Number 9' in person."

"No. I mean she is the Kiss of Death personified. And you, my virile young friend, appear to be just her type."

***

"So," Jon said as he guided the black Road Runner out of LaFollette and headed northeast onto the long, straight, open country road that was either Tennessee Scenic Route 63 or General Carl W. Stiner Highway, depending on which sign you believed. "Are we going to talk about the fact that you just murdered three men?"

Idegen looked at him with a crinkled brow. "Murdered? I killed three enemies who would have been more than happy to kill us, Jon, and happier still to beat and molest us first."

Jon cocked his head, conceding the point. He moved the straw around in his jaw, noting that the rain was easing up. Even if the world might be a slightly better place without Jimmy Ray and his goons in it, he realized that Idegen now made him nervous. And he was trapped in a car with her on a lonely stretch of road. "I know you're probably right... It just seems like, I don't know, that it doesn't even bother you... like you're a machine or something..."

"Were you trained by some special military unit to be a killer, or did they recruit you because you already were one?" *Funny: In real life, maybe Jason Bourne would be a psychopath...*

She chewed her lower lip, staring out the windshield. "I... I never really thought about it in those terms. I was raised to be a... soldier. I excelled at my training, which I suppose is what drew the attention of the... special unit..."

"Wait." Jon stared at her and put his foot down on the accelerator. "You were *raised* to be a soldier? Surely not by this country! Please tell me we don't have child soldiers in America!"

Idegen inhaled sharply as if realizing she'd accidentally divulged a secret. "No. Not in this country. I cannot speak on the subject any further."

Jon chuckled, half nervously and half bitterly. "'If I told you, I'd have to kill you.' That old schtick, huh?"

She smiled at him. "I won't kill you, Jon. I owe you my life. But yes, I have secrets that I should not share with you, just as I am certain that you have secrets of your own."

Jon shook his head and flipped the straw to the other side of his mouth. "None that would require me to kill anybody."

"And yet it is *your* situation that resulted in the three dead men at your friend's place of business. Not mine."

Jon cut her a dirty look. "That's not my fault. I'm just trying to stay alive. Just trying to mind my own business. They're the ones that won't let me."

"And what is your business, Jon French?"

Jon sighed, looked at the speedometer. He backed off the pedal when he saw the needle approaching ninety. *Never seen a cop out here, but the way my day's going...* "My business is... well, my business."

"Fair enough."

An uncomfortable silence settled over them. The only noise was that of the 426 Hemi's throaty growl reverberating through the bench seat and the floorboards. The grey-green scenery slid past in a muted blur. For some reason, as many times as he had driven this road, it always seemed like the least traveled highway in the entire state of Tennessee. Nothing to see for miles at a stretch, save for rolling fields of stunted cotton or corn, little old cemeteries on cow pasture hilltops, stands of twisted trees, muddy or rocky creeks, fenced-off farmsteads, the occasional out-of-the-way gas station with the old school pumps out front and a graveyard of old cars out back, and the dead-and-gone skeletons of mom-and-pop businesses—roadside groceries, small engine repair shops, fruit stands, beauty parlors, and the like. And of course, the low, hunched mountains rolling behind it all.

In a word, it was boring. In another, it was depressing.

"All right." Jon took the mangled straw from his mouth and tossed it to the floor. "I don't really have a business. I... well, I had plans. Big plans. But then life happened."

Idegen studied him. "Explain, please."

Jon frowned, not really wanting to get into this Dr. Phil sort of shit.

"Well, I used to play football. And I was good at it, too." He smiled, remembering the pep rallies and the touchdowns in high school, the after-game dances, and the awards banquets.

"I even got a scholarship to play in college. Not a big college, but I was good enough there, too, that I could have probably made it to the NFL Combine..." The smile widened as he recalled the cheers and his name echoing over the PA system. "The student section used to bring this breakfast cereal to the home games, Cinnamon Toast Crunch. And when I'd lay a big hit on a receiver or sack the quarterback, they'd toss it in the air and chant, *French Toast!*"

He glanced at her, noting her confusion. "Well, if you're not from the U.S., I guess you don't understand American football—"

"No." Her eyes narrowed as if slowly reading something in a foreign language. "I understand... football... I do not understand the wanton waste of foodstuffs."

Jon laughed. "I think it started from a line in an old movie. About a cop who fights terrorists during a Christmas party in a skyscraper. There's this scene where one of the bad guys is narrating the action, and when they blow up a police tank, he shouts, 'And the Quarterback is toast!' My last name being French, it was a short leap of coed imagination to 'French Toast.'"

He focused back on the road. "I guess you just had to be there."

After a moment, she smiled. "*Die Hard.* Now I get it... Still seems a terrible waste of resources to me."

Jon did not comment on the fact that she seemed more bent out of shape over the waste of Cinnamon Toast Crunch than the cold-blooded execution of three men.

Creepy.

"And what, exactly, about life happened to upend these *big* plans, Jon?"

He scowled at her. "Would you quit saying my name every time you ask me a question or tell me something? You sound like a teacher I had when I was a kid."

She arched an eyebrow and waited.

Jon chewed on his cheek and winced, wishing he hadn't tossed the straw. "I got arrested for playing poker, okay? It was an illegal game and a dumb mistake, and I went to jail for almost a year. When I got out, nobody would touch me with a ten-foot pole. I was damaged goods, poisoned fruit, whatever... Nobody but the damned Dixie Mafia, that is.

"I've spent the past decade crisscrossing the Southeast at their beck and call. 'Pick up this car in Memphis, take it to Chattanooga. When you get there, they'll have another job for you.' Usually to take another car with another load of contraband someplace like Rome, Georgia, or Florence, South Carolina, which usually led to another haul to Asheville, or Bristol, or Knoxville, or Mobile, or wherever...

"But I guess it wasn't all bad. Every now and then, I could have a good time between jobs. Find a card game or two, hook up with an old girlfriend or a drinking buddy, maybe make some new ones, but for the most part, I've lived the past ten years at seventy miles an hour... So yeah, life happened."

Idegen turned and stared out the passenger window for a while. "It sounds to me like you made a bad decision and suffered the consequences. And then followed that up by continuing to make worse decisions.

"Yes," she said, turning back to face him. "'Life happened.' But it happens that way for everyone, J—it happens that way for everyone. You are not special, nor are you immune. We all make choices, some good and some bad. These decisions and what we learn from them is what defines us."

"Thanks for the life lesson," he grunted. "You should really have your own TED Talk. Make sure you mention that you're a cold-blooded killer when you introduce yourself."

He immediately regretted the words. *Shit, she could kill me.*

Idegen gave him a smile that made his hair stand on end. "Yes. But you should be thankful that I am on your side, *Jon...* for the time being."

He laughed, trying to settle his nerves. "You're right. I guess I had that one coming... Sorry about the cold-blooded killer thing."

She shrugged. "No need. I am what I am, just as you are what you are, Jon. I am a killer, and you are a runner. I eliminate my problems; you flee from yours."

Jon stomped the brakes and spun the screaming car into a gravel clearing in front of an abandoned restaurant, spraying the broken windows and decaying walls with rocks and debris.

"Just who in the hell do you think you are?" he shouted. "You don't know the first thing about me!"

Idegen looked at him and her evil smile widened. "Good. You've got some fight in you, after all. I can use that... and so can you."

Jon shook, his heart pounding in his temples. His mouth went dry, and he sucked air like a blast furnace. He clutched the steering wheel until his fingers turned white and numb.

Just to keep them from finding their way to her throat.

I'll show you fight, you bitch! But it was his father's voice he heard in his head. His father's and his own, and it terrified him.

"Get out," he said through gnashed teeth. "I don't need this sort of shit from nobody, least of all some crazy bitch I just met."

Idegen didn't move. "Oh, but you do, Jon. You need someone to tell you like it is. Someone to call you on your... bullshit. You need a *friend* now more than you ever have before. And besides, I owe you. You saved my life, remember?"

"And you saved mine at Julio's. We're square; now get out."

"No, Jon. I'm not running out on you. And you're not running out on me. We are a team now. Our lives are bound together. Our fates are intertwined."

"Who the hell are you? Who even talks like that?"

"I am Idegen Videshee. I am a soldier and a killer. And right now, I am your friend, Jon French. Perhaps the only one you have."

Jon tried to make sense of what was going on, what she was saying, but all he wanted to do was punch her in the face. Repeatedly.

"Julio is my friend. I've got others." Though he knew that was not entirely true. He had acquaintances and contacts—*drinking buddies and ex-girlfriends*. He hadn't had a real, honest-to-God *friend* for a long time, not since he and Julio had rolled up the Knoxville streets back in the good old days.

She kept that sphinxlike smile in place. "For all you know, Julio could be dead by now. We did leave him to take responsibility for our escape, after all."

Jon flung the car door open and stepped out into the cool drizzle. A logging truck roared by, spraying him with diesel-scented mist. He ran his hands through his hair and tried to calm down. He shut his eyes tight and thought about what she had just said.

"No," he said aloud. "No. Julio's a smart cat. He wouldn't have taken this on if there had been any danger. *I* sure wouldn't have. We're both survivors, right?"

He stopped and looked up into the glowering sky. *That just proves what she said. I am a runner. I am a coward. Cowards tend to survive while the brave ones die...*

"You are not a coward, Jon French." Idegen stood on the roadside in front of him. He stared at her, wondering why he had said that out loud, wondering if he actually had.

She stared into his eyes. "That is not what I said, and that is certainly not what I meant. You simply have not yet found a worthy cause for which to fight. A cause for which to live."

"You don't understand..." His sudden rage washed away in the rain. He thought about the revolver in his hand, pressed to his temple just a few hours ago. He thought about the ridiculous amount of alcohol he'd had to consume to work up his courage for even *that* cowardly act. How those three men would still be alive if he'd just had the guts to pull that trigger. How Julio would be going about his life right now, never knowing any troubles because of him. "You just don't understand, Idegen..."

"Perhaps not. But get back into the vehicle, and you can explain it to me as we resume our trek... That is, if you desire to do so."

Jon looked down the highway in the direction of Jacksboro and La Follette. "Maybe we should go back and check on Julio."

Idegen stepped beside him and took his hand in hers. "If that is what you desire. Of course, by doing so, you could undo whatever effort—or sacrifice—your friend is making. Like you said, he knew the risks and made his choice. Perhaps you should have the courage to honor it."

"Damn." He looked into her grey-green eyes. "I think maybe... you're right... I'm sorry. Let's go."

Suddenly calmed, Jon wondered how she could have incited such a rage in him so fast, and then dismissed it just as quickly. But as they got back on the road, headed toward Harrogate, home of Lincoln Memorial University, his mind turned to another woman who had always been able to put him into a tailspin: Angela.

She was wearing an LMU sweatshirt... And why did she even have to be there this morning? Why her, of all people? I've put her out of my thoughts and out of my heart for years (that's not entirely true, you know)...

His mind wandered over all the good times they'd had. And there were a lot of them. He and Angie had shared the first two-thirds of their lives together, after all. Growing up in the trailer park, walking home from elementary school, saving milk money to buy dinky little toys, boxes of crayons, and bubble gum for each other at the local five-and-dime. Trading comic books and marbles at the Pines during recess and riding their secondhand bicycles around Graysville all summer long. Her helping him with his homework every night, and him teaching her how to throw a football, a baseball, to dribble a basketball.

The first time they held hands and understood that they were more than friends. Sitting out under the stars on a clear autumn night, telling each other all their inner hopes, dreams, fears, and pains. Adults would call it baring their souls, but they were young, and it was more intimate and more real than that phrase could ever describe—more perfect and powerful.

Their first kiss.

Their first date.

The first time they held each other close and danced.

The first time they...

And now, on the absolute worst day of my life, I've got her ghost haunting my skull. Karma, kismet, fate, or just good old-fashioned shitty luck, it all comes down to the same thing. Jon French, you live a charmed life, my boy.

In a way, he reluctantly had to admit, maybe he did live a charmed life. After all, his mom had been there to keep the worst beatings from doing any real permanent damage (though his wrist still hurt on cold days, and he knew he'd have arthritis when he got old—*if* he got old). Coach Jackson had pulled him out of the downward spiral after Kevin's death, had gotten him into sports and back on track for college. And Angie had always been there, no matter what. Especially to help deal with all the heavy stuff after his mom took off, somehow even showing up out of the blue to spring him this morning.

And now there was Idegen. She had appeared in that river at just the right moment to keep him from putting the gun back to his head. And then she had taken out Jimmy Ray and his crew, saving him from Craig Byce's basement dungeon...

He looked at her as she seemed to doze. *Who knows, maybe Somebody Up There likes me. Maybe she's my own personal guardian angel.*

He chuckled to himself and put his foot down, giving the Road Runner its head. "And maybe I'll win the damn Mega Millions while I'm at it."

***

Sharpe sat with the lights off in her appropriated office, riding the soothing wave of half a Vicodin. The constant pain in her back was bearable, but the migraine still had its claws dug into her brain. The text message from Mr. White staring up from the phone on the desk in glowing letters didn't help: *SITREP.*

She rubbed her temples, willing the pain to go away. Taking a deep breath, she snatched up the phone and hammered out her reply: *Subject still active. One civilian casualty. One civilian compromised. Blackout in effect. All assets deployed. Will keep you informed.*

She hit send without second-guessing herself. *He's going to burn me over this, no matter what I say. The only way to make this good is to capture or kill the subject. And I'm doing everything in my power to make that happen.*

Which was true. Honcho, his two marines, and one of his SEALs were all riding shotgun with the Kiowas, searching the entire region for any sign of the gold 4Runner or the subject and her male accomplice. Hack-Job and Tunes were still in the C&C, feeding data to the searchers as fast as it came in. Patches, Alpha's medic, was keeping Helbourne on task in the medical building.

And while she sat here in the dark, nursing a headache like some pathetic gold brick, Alpha Team's assistant squad leader was overseeing things on her behalf. The handsome Air Force master sergeant went by the odd nickname "Frankenstein" for some reason. Sharpe assumed it was because his last name was Steiner, but she had to admit he did seem to have a rather wooden personality. *Enlisted men and their knack for nonsense and nicknames... I wonder what nom de guerre they'd come up with for me. Probably best to never know. I'm sure it wouldn't be very flattering...*

For some reason, the image of a green dragon flashed in her mind. A gaudy bipedal statue like something at a roadside attraction from the '50s or '60s.

"You're getting goofy, girl," she told herself in the empty room. "Chasing stray thoughts down rabbit holes. Time to get back to the war."

Sharpe forced herself out of the office chair, forced herself to ignore the dull ache that shot from her buttocks up to her shoulders and back down again, and forced herself not to puke at the sudden queasiness in her guts brought on by the railroad spike to her forehead. She white-knuckled the edge of the desk for a moment, took a deep breath, and then made for the door.

And almost ran face-first into Frankenstein on the other side.

"Colonel," he said, snapping to attention. "Apologies. I was coming to let you know that Dr. Helbourne has finished his examinations and is prepared to report his findings."

Sharpe scowled at the man, mostly because of the jump scare he had given her. It was very difficult to look at his high cheekbones, full lips, and dark-chocolate eyes and be angry. Even if he did have the personal charisma of a cardboard box, he was still very pretty. "I assume he wants to hold court in the medical lab, so he'll have home field advantage. That's why he sent you instead of coming to me himself, isn't it?"

Frankenstein's pretty face rippled slightly. "I am merely conveying his wishes, Colonel."

Sharpe stepped past, motioning him to follow. "Doesn't matter. If he needs it, I'll give him another ass-chewing wherever we're at. What about the Kiowas? Any news yet?"

"They've located the Toyota, abandoned behind a gas station in Clinton. Honcho and Shaq are focusing their searches in that vicinity. Archer and Ramrod are sweeping the area south from Oak Ridge to Harriman. The weather is hampering progress, of course."

Sharpe tried to picture the map of the region she'd stared at all morning, but it was just a big fuzzy green blur covered in red and black scribbles that should have been roads. *Damn pills. Damn pain. Damn old woman...*

"And what about this Lawman? Anything on her?"

Frankenstein nodded, eyes front as they strode out of the building and onto the covered walkway. "As you suspected, local law enforcement says she was a dead end. But it seems that this Jon French does have several connections throughout the state's criminal network, the so-called Dixie Mafia. We're trying to get access to the DOJ files as well as the current departmental investigations."

"What about his family?" The rain beating on the aluminum awning overhead sounded like machine gun fire inside her skull.

"His father is still alive, still living in Rhea County. Best we can tell, he hasn't had any contact with the man in several years. Nothing on his mother at present."

Sharpe rubbed the back of her neck as they stepped into the air-conditioned cold of the medical building. "Well, it's not much of a lead... But, when the chips are down, sometimes there's no place like home... Reach out to the local law enforcement in Rhea County, have them keep an eye out for French."

Her phone rang.

It was Hack-Job, the Navy SEAL in the C&C. "Colonel? We've just intercepted a 911 call about a triple homicide at an automotive repair shop in Jacksboro. You said—"

"Jacksboro." She suddenly saw the map clearly in her head. "That's just up I-75 from Clinton. Get Honcho over there ASAP. Have him shut down the scene and get those bodies back here. And any witnesses, including whoever made the 911 call."

"Yes, ma'am."

She looked at Frankenstein. "Bad news: three more bodies. Good news: as long as she keeps dropping them like breadcrumbs, it makes it easier to track her."

***

Idegen watched the lovely, rain-swept scenery pass by and listened to the soothing growl of the primitive engine. Jon had slid back into his own thoughts of a remembered, cherished, and complicated relationship, and she was reluctant to pry. Primarily because it made her think of Vodie and her own regrets, complicated feelings, and, of course, her terrible isolation.

What if I am permanently stranded on this world? What if my brothers and sisters never received my transmissions? What if Fleet Command has decided this system is unworthy of exploration, or even conquest? What if they've already departed this galaxy?

What if I never see Vodie again?

Idegen pushed that painful possibility deep down into her subconscious and buried it beneath her current priorities. She was still wounded and had not yet secured a viable source of nourishment. And she was still being hunted by this world's military. Not to mention the criminal organization that was pursuing her traveling companion.

But I am armed, and, at least for the moment, I am not starving. My wounds will heal, and I will feed again. And soon...

She looked at Jon. Brow furrowed, his jaw worked as if chewing. His characteristic mannerism.

Not on him, not unless I absolutely must. He saved me from the river and he put himself at risk to acquire medical treatment for me. He has provided me with opportunities for nourishment and something perhaps even more important. If I am to remain on this planet for any length of time, I will go insane if I continue to fret over my isolation and possible abandonment. Until I am rescued, I need to occupy myself with constant activity. Protecting Jon French from his Dixie Mafia seems an ideal distraction.

Besides, I have known him only a few hours, as they gauge time here, and I have already killed four humans and fed on two. If I stay with him long enough, there may be no limit to the amount of combat and nourishment to be had.

"Well," Jon said, guiding the vehicle to the left at an intersection, "we're in Harrogate. Just over this hill and past the college campus is our Robert Frost moment. So, what'll it be? Do we go through the tunnels and head into Kentucky to find Wayland Moore? Or do we take Highway 58 and make for the Tri-Cities and try to escape the big, bad Dixie Mafia?"

Idegen looked at him. She cocked her head and waited, honestly wanting to see what he would decide on his own.

Jon smiled. "Okay. Like Julio said, I can't run forever. Might as well take a shot right now and see if I can find a way to face this shitstorm head-on."

She returned the smile as they drove over the hill toward the twin tunnels piercing the mist-shrouded mountain. "Good choice."

***

Craig shifted on the folding chair, trying to find a spot that didn't make his ass want to turn inside out.

"You okay, Craig?" Jesse asked, a smile on his blood-streaked face while Doc Kirby tended to August Winchester, who was strapped to a chair in the center of the basement floor. "You look like you need to go to the shitter. I can wait 'til you get back if you want." He tossed the bloody needle-nose pliers onto the tray and reached for the box cutter.

If only. How long has it been since I've had a nice long, comfortable shit? Craig shook his head and stood up to pace around the basement. "I'm fine. Just wondering how far away Jon French has gotten while we've been down here fucking around with this beaner."

Jesse smiled, wiped some blood and sweat from his face. "He's a tough one. I'll give him that."

Craig looked at the Florida Golden Boy's thorough, grisly handiwork. *And you're having the time of your life, you sadistic son of a bitch.* "He is that. I reckon this whole world is just getting meaner all the time. Time was, you could get just about anything out of anybody just by showing 'em a baseball bat, a tire iron, or a switchblade. Nowadays, everybody's gotta show you just how tough they are. They gotta pretend to be Rambo or something."

"Which suits me just fine." Jesse clicked the cutter's razor blade in and out like a snake's tongue tasting the air. "You about done there, Doc?"

Kirby grunted, checking the dressing on Winchester's gunshot wound. "He's lost a lot of blood, and the smelling salts are having less effect. You should really let him rest while I give him a transfusion."

Craig leaned against the cinder block wall and folded his arms. "No time. Every minute he holds out, Jon French and his killer bitch get another mile away."

Kirby looked up at him, a rare fire in his eyes. "And if he dies, then what? Look, Byce, I didn't say much when you wouldn't let me fetch my car from a crime scene. And I didn't put up much of a fuss when you told me I had to help you torture this man," which wasn't true at all; he'd said plenty on both topics. "But I will not be a party to murder."

Craig glared at him. "And how much you owe us, Kirby?"

The fat veterinarian looked at the concrete floor.

"That's what I thought. Besides, this ain't murder. From where I'm standing, it looks like suicide."

Winchester's bloody head rolled back on his brawny shoulders. He fixed Craig with the better of his two eyes, the one that wasn't swollen shut. "Fuck... you..." punctuated with a dribble of blood from split lips that must have been intended to be a dramatic spit of defiance.

Craig inhaled sharply and stood up straight. "Stand back, Doc. I'm tired of playing with this asshole. Jesse, get his pants off." The terror that filled Winchester's one eight-ball hemorrhage of an eye was gratifying, just as the absolute childlike glee he saw on Sneed's face was revolting. "And hand me the vice grips."

"*Wait!*" Winchester shrieked as soon as Jesse grabbed his bloody jeans and started tugging. "Wait! For the love of God, I'll tell you, I'll tell you!"

Craig waved Jesse away, ignoring his obvious disappointment. He stepped over, grabbed Winchester's greasy hair, and stared hard into his face. "Talk to me, or I'll turn your junk into guacamole."

Winchester started sobbing, but he also started talking. "... Sixty-eight Road Runner... Black... Headed to... Middlesboro... Wayland Moore... Ask for a sit down... I'm sorry... I'm sorry..."

Craig let go and stood up. "Son of a bitch."

"Wayland Moore?" Jesse asked. "Wasn't he the head of the region back in the old days?"

Craig picked up a shop rag to wipe his hands. "Yeah. The old days... But he's still got enough juice with Angola that if he goes for what this French kid is selling, he might get them to go for it, too."

His phone rang.

It was a Nashville number, not one he recognized. "Hello?"

Craig listened to the short, nervous report, then hung up without another word.

"You look like you just saw a ghost," Jesse said.

Craig threw the phone against the cinderblock wall, smashing it into a dozen pieces.

Kirby let out a little girl squeak.

"Motherfucker." Craig knotted his fists so tight his arthritis screamed. His gut filled with boiling water that threatened to force its way up his throat. "*Motherfucker!*"

"What is it?" Jesse's voice was barely above a whisper.

Craig turned, looked at the other three men in the room. Stepping to the tool cart, he picked up a ball-peen hammer, turned on Winchester, and vented his rage until it was all gone.

"Oh my God..." Kirby whispered from where he was huddled in a corner, his eyes stretched wide, staring at the bloody pulp that had been a human being's head just a few moments before.

Sneed held a fresh shop towel out to Craig, ropes of blood splashed across his fancy shirt, khakis, and dripping down his face.

Craig dropped the hammer. Its clanging rattle echoed for what seemed like forever in the silent basement, drowning out his own heavy breathing.

"That..." He wiped the blood from his hands and face. "That was a contact in Nashville. That... son of a bitch, Joey Green, has turned state's evidence. He's the one who set me up with that shipment. The feds and the TBI are building their case, and they'll probably be issuing a warrant for my arrest in the next twenty-four to forty-eight hours."

"Then we've got just that much time to catch this Jon French and find out what he knows about Green's evidence..." Jesse looked at August Winchester's shattered remains. "What we gonna do with this?"

Craig turned to the cowering veterinarian. "You've got hungry dogs at your office, right? How are you at using power tools?"

Jon blinked, letting his eyes adjust to the unexpected sunshine on the Kentucky side of what the old-timers used to call "Massacre Mountain." The Cumberland Gap Tunnels, which had replaced a bloody stretch of dangerous switchbacks on 25E a couple decades before, were a marvel of transportation engineering, running nearly a mile beneath the National Historical Park on the Tennessee-Kentucky line. But to Jon, they felt like a portal into another world, one of freedom and hope.

Where ever-present rainclouds had glowered over his head and shadowed his thoughts all day long in Tennessee, late afternoon sunshine fell across the small town of Middlesboro, Kentucky. He breathed a sigh of relief. "We just might make it."

A mountain and a miles-wide storm standing between him and Craig Byce gave him a little bit of hope. He looked at Idegen, who studied the blue-green hills and flowing traffic like a painter preparing a composition. *She's given me hope, too... helping me to make a decision instead of just turning tail... Hope and confidence.*

"We need to get you some new clothes," he said.

She looked at herself. "What is wrong with these?"

Jon chuckled. "Well, they're mine for starters, and they need a good wash for another. Besides, you might be more comfortable in stuff that, I don't know, was actually designed for somebody with curves...?"

She looked at him with an inscrutable glare, then broke into a warm smile. "I see. And where do I get these clothes for some-*body* with curves, Jon?"

Jon flushed at the way she said the word "body." It made him feel like she'd seen the fleeting stream of thoughts he'd had a moment before: *I wonder what she'd look like in a short t-shirt and shorter shorts... I wonder what she'd look like in a swimsuit... I wonder what she'd look like in her underwear... I wonder what she'd look like out of it...*

Clearing his throat and focusing on the traffic, he guided the Road Runner through the first intersection in the small town, past the KFC on the left and the Food City on the right. "Just up here, the Middlesboro Mall should have everything you need. While you're getting gussied up, I'll see if I can track down this Wayland Moore character."

Parking on the back side of the mall, Jon checked his funds before they went in. Thanks to Julio's donation, they had about six hundred bucks to work with. He tried to calculate the cost of gas, food, and maybe a motel room for the night, but the numbers were fuzzy. *Damn, I'm tired... how long's it been since I got a good night's sleep...? Maybe I should find a Goodwill to get her some clothes...*

He shook his head, deciding the odds were still against them living to the end of the week. If everything went south in the end, Idegen deserved to die in new clothes. "Come on."

An hour later, Jon sat on a bench, charging his phone in the center of the mall, waiting for Idegen to finish her purchases at J.C. Penny. They'd bought a few things at Rose's first: new underclothes, socks, toothbrushes, soap, shampoo, toothpaste. He knew they probably looked like a couple of hobos or meth heads to the store clerks and the mall cops that shadowed their steps, but since they paid with cash and didn't slip into any of the changing rooms, they were eventually left alone.

When his phone had enough power, Jon began searching the local directory for a Wayland Moore. He made several cold and unsuccessful calls before Idegen came out of the store carrying two big bags stuffed with shoe boxes and clothes. He grimaced, instantly regretting giving her a full three hundred bucks. "Please tell me you've got something left over."

She beamed at him. The euphoric smile which seemed so out of place on the face of a woman who had just killed three men was worth every cent of whatever she'd spent, and then some. "Sales, Jon. Everything was *on sale.*" She fished into the pocket of his *Kriegsmarine* and handed him a wad of bills. "I got everything for just over one hundred of your dollars."

Jon glanced around to see if anyone noticed the hand-off. Or the glint of gunmetal in her coat pocket. He forced a smile. "Great. Have a seat... I've still not found our guy, and I'm starting to feel the noose tighten. We may be in Kentucky, but we're still technically in Craig Byce's backyard. If he hasn't already, he could make one phone call and have an army of Bluegrass Gangsters hunting for us any minute."

She chewed her lip, studying his words before nodding solemnly. "You need rest, Jon. I can see it on your face. In your body language. We should find some place to hide until you have recovered your focus."

Jon rubbed his face. *You're the one who's been shot...* "I'd come to the same conclusion. But we're low on funds and... well, I didn't know how to approach this..."

She raised her chin. "We'll need to share quarters. Of course. What is the problem?"

Jon blinked. "Well, we just met, and... we're under a lot of stress. Emotions are high. We're both young, reasonably attractive, and alone... Like you said, *our fates are intertwined*, or whatever... These sorts of things have a way of getting... personal. Intimate..."

Idegen's eyes widened. She threw her head back and laughed, the Predators cap falling to the floor. It was a loud and raucous cackle. Jon scowled, looked around at the mall-goers staring at them. "Okay, okay! Shush! I don't know what's so damn funny about it, but I get it. Nothing personal, nothing intimate."

Idegen wiped at the corners of her sparkling, luminous eyes, continuing to chuckle. "Thank you, Jon. It has been so very long since I had a good laugh... So long, I cannot even remember it. But please forgive me; I did not mean to offend you."

He stood, giving the onlookers a polite *Go to hell* smile. "That's okay. No big deal, but we should get going. There's a Days Inn nearby that's got cheap rooms. I can continue the search for our man there. And we can get some rest."

***

Helbourne leaned comfortably against the metal counter, feeling like Quincy at the beginning of every episode. Sharpe and her Alpha Squad stood on the other side of the row of gurneys containing the four corpses. Though not quite at attention, the nine soldiers all stared impatiently at him. He knew he had the room.

"So," Sharpe said, her tawny arms folded across her chest. He could tell she was in pain but had to admire the way she mastered it. "Do these three GSW stiffs tell us anything? Are they related to the woman at the convenience store somehow?"

Helbourne moved to stand near one of the three dead men. "As a matter of fact, Colonel, yes they do, and they are. Though at first, it appears that they were all victims of a single, fatal gunshot wound to the head, this gentleman here tells a slightly different story."

He pulled the plastic sheet back to expose the naked corpse and the five puncture wounds just below the gaunt ribcage. "Unlike her previous victims, it would seem the subject did not use her teeth but instead was able to feed, for lack of a better term, through her talons. We saw firsthand how effective they can be as weapons on the plane. But now it appears that they can also be used to siphon off the life force of her victims as well."

"Let's not get tunnel vision here, Doctor." Sharpe rubbed her forehead and continued to frown. "So what does this really tell us? How does it help us catch her or deal with her when we do?"

Helbourne stepped over to the counter and held up a microscope slide for dramatic effect. "Well, for one thing, we know that the claws are not completely organic. They seem to be a part of her cybernetic system judging by the trace elements left in the wounds. And for another thing, based on the limited amount of cellular degradation around these wounds, I'm guessing that the claws are not the preferred method of feeding. Either that or, since the victim was already dead, there was not enough essence remaining in the body."

Sharpe stepped over to the corpse. "His shirt wasn't pierced, was it?"

Helbourne frowned. "No, I don't think so. Why does that matter?"

She looked at him with a pained smile. "I think it means she did this on the down-low. If so, it means Jon French doesn't know what she is."

Patches said, "It also means she's still hungry. If the life force she got from Helen Woodbury was not sufficient, and she was only able to get residue off this guy, then it means there should be another body or two turning up very soon."

Helbourne was not happy that they had stepped in to steal his thunder. "Yes. That would appear to be the case. And I may actually have a way to predict where that might take place, hopefully before it happens."

Sharpe narrowed her eyes. "You could have led with that, Doctor. What have you got?"

"The metal." Helbourne smiled and waggled the slide. "I noticed that her biological tissue showed traces of radiation not known in our part of the galaxy, but this metal shows a much higher concentration. It holds it longer. Once I analyze these elements, I should be able to determine how they react to different forms of radiation, including those occurring naturally here on Earth."

Sharpe smiled for the first time since he'd met her. A real smile, at any rate. "Once you know what her cybernetics are made of, you can build us a detection device. A Geiger counter keyed on her signature?"

"Better. If you can get us access to one of NASA's satellites, I can program it with an algorithm that will home in on the particular radiation signature."

Sharpe's phone rang. She stepped away to take the call. "Excellent. Get it up and get it to the Oak Ridge National Lab ASAP." The smile widened as she hung up. Turning back to Helbourne, she said, "Good news, Doctor. The Navy just found your rocket ship."

***

Idegen stood beneath the jet of hot water, letting it wash some of the tension from her exhausted muscles and the stink of river water from her hair and skin. She examined the throbbing wounds on her side. They were better than they had been at the beginning of the day. Still, she needed a more substantial meal if she was to fully recover her health and her strength. Despite what little energy she had taken from the armed man earlier, she could feel the hunger sawing at her insides like a dull blade.

Jon had insisted she take the first shower after the simple meal of bread-enfolded roasted meat, fat-fried curled tubers, and carbonated sugar water. The roast beef sandwich hardly sustained her, but it did provide calories and some nutrients that her body needed, and at least it kept her belly from joining in the demanding chorus for *real* food.

Taking the scented lathering agents and putting them to use, she wondered if she should probe Jon's mind. She was curious to see if he was still stressing over the sexual feelings he had for her. In truth, when she had first sensed them in him, they had surprised her just as they had surprised him, which is why she had laughed. And in her mind, he was still only one step above a possible meal.

Besides, up until that point, she had thought his physical affections were completely tied up in his memories of this woman he called Angie or Angela.

Though in retrospect, she should not have been surprised at all. She had sensed the same emotions and urges from every human male she had encountered on this planet and even a slight variation on them from the dark-skinned warrior woman. She understood it to be a useful weapon against them. But for some reason, probably his preoccupation with his own fear, Jon French had not reacted in the same fashion until they had emerged from the tunnels.

But even then, he had instantly felt guilty over the thoughts.

Guilt... An odd sensation, and quite unpleasant. The only time I have ever felt a... similar experience, was when I accepted the invitation to the Order of the Black Star, when I left Vodie... If I had known that was to be the last time we were to be together, would I have made the same decision? Am I feeling guilt for it still?

Emerging from the shower, Idegen shook the painful thought away and tried to touch Jon's mind. But he was asleep. *Just as well... This way, I will not have to persuade him to let me go outside alone.*

After toweling off, she donned the new clothing she had purchased: denim pants that, as Jon had said, were designed for her curves, an uncomfortable yet practical garment that restricted and supported her breasts, a hooded, long-sleeved black tunic, a pair of short cotton stockings, and ankle-high rugged leather boots. In the darkened bedroom, where Jon snored peacefully on one of the two beds, she pulled on his Doctor's coat and Predators cap, pocketing the three dead men's pistols before slipping out into the night.

The sun had set, but the darkening sky was filled by an orange glow from the city's streetlights and the humid air was heavy with the scents of fried food from nearby restaurants and the natural, earthy aromas of the woods that edged the back of the motel's property. Beyond the thick stand of trees, Idegen could hear and smell the signs of a residential area: sweaty children laughing and shouting, domestic animals moving about on fresh-mown grass, and the ever-present stench of petroleum from the primitive vehicles that constituted this planet's Prime Mover.

Unlike the towering black structures of Logonijy, these human buildings were only one, two, or sometimes three levels in height and spread out along neatly arranged streets, lanes, and roads. An unsuccessful attempt had been made at incorporating the natural environment into the settlement, leaving isolated trees or thickets as decorative measures among the blocks of squat buildings lit with electric light. Still, the overall impression was one of unwanted refugees or outmatched interlopers huddling around a campfire, dreading the wild mountains that surrounded them in the dark.

Idegen closed her eyes and took a deep breath. *Now, to feed... I must find someone who will not be missed, someone young and healthy. The old woman this morning was an impulsive mistake and hardly worth the risk. From what I have seen of this society today, I am certain that her corpse has already been found by my hunters... And possibly the man I fed on at August's business. I must be more careful. They may be only a few steps behind at this very moment...*

Sending out telepathic filaments, she stood in the parking lot of the Days Inn, hoping to brush against the mind of a suitable victim. It only took a few minutes.

Idegen pulled the hood over her hat and walked into the woods.

Toward the sound of laughing children.

***

Jon woke from the familiar nightmare in a cold sweat, his heart thundering in his chest and vomit rising in his throat. "Damn," he whispered into the darkness. "Damn." *How many times have I torn out my father's throat with my own teeth?*

Coming to his senses, he turned on the nightstand lamp. "Idegen?"

His heart still raced from the bad dream when real panic hit him. Lurching to his feet before his equilibrium had returned, he staggered and bumped into the small table in the corner. "Where the hell...?"

He scanned the room. The bathroom door was open, shopping bags scattered on the floor, the other bed undisturbed, but his ball cap and coat were gone. And so were the three pistols she'd taken from the men she'd killed. "Shit!"

He grabbed his wallet off the dresser and counted the money. It was all there. He sighed in guilty relief. *At least she didn't rip me off... Glad that was my first worry... selfish son of a bitch...*

He dropped back onto the bed and clutched at his sweat-soaked head, trying to make sense of things. "Okay," he told himself. "No sense in running off half-cocked. She didn't take any cash, so she means to come back. Right? Maybe. Hell, I don't know."

What do you really know about her, Jonny-boy? You fished her out of the Tennessee River this morning, where she'd been dumped after taking a double-tap to the side. Who put her there? She sure didn't volunteer that information. In fact, she hasn't told you shit. Other than she's a soldier trained by some elite military unit. From another country... And aside from being a cold-blooded killing machine, she's, well, just plain weird...

He stepped over to the tiny coffee pot and grabbed one of the plastic sleeves containing the sweetener and creamer. Ripping it open, he snatched out the black plastic stirrer and jammed it into his mouth. "Damn. Just damn."

Feeling a bit calmer and more in control, Jon took a deep breath and talked it through. "Okay. Either she comes back, or she doesn't. No sense in me going out looking for her. If she's done with me, I'll never find her, and even if I did, things could get messy." He took another deep breath. "So in reality, I'm no better or worse off than I was this morning. My problems are still the same, and I still have the same options."

He looked at the Taurus Judge sitting on the nightstand.

"No... I've been down that road, and that's not who I am. Not anymore. I can either get back on the highway, heading for I-81 and parts north, or I can keep trying to find Wayland Moore and see if there's another way out of this..."

But first, I smell like a dumpster behind a Chinese restaurant. I need a shower...

He heard a knock at the door just before he turned the water off. Still chewing the plastic straw, he cursed for not bringing the pistol or his clothes into the bathroom. "Shit."

The knocking became more insistent.

Jon hurried out of the shower, wrapped a towel around his waist, and ducked into the larger room. Snagging up the revolver, he stepped to the door and looked through the peephole. He was surprised and relieved to see that it was Idegen.

Dripping wet, he opened the door. "Where the hell have you been?"

She smiled, looked him up and down, and stepped into the room. "I went out for a walk. I thought you could use the privacy."

Closing the door, he felt like an idiot, standing there wet and all but naked with a gun behind his back. "You could have woke me up to tell me."

"You needed your rest." She tossed the Predators cap onto the bed and flopped down beside it. She looked even more stunning than she had earlier, more vibrant, more alive. "What's that?" she asked, pointing at the tattoo on his left deltoid.

He glanced at the royal flush design, the spades replaced with fleur-de-lis. "My tattoo? Just a good luck charm. Y'know, the fleur-de-lis is the symbol of France, and my last name is French, and I like to play poker..." He lost the thread of his own story. Even fully clothed, the sight of her stirred his desire and made him painfully aware that only a thin layer of old cotton covered his body.

He could feel a raw energy rolling off her, causing his blood to rise. Clearing his throat, Jon hurried to the bathroom to finish drying off. He grabbed his backpack on the way. *I should have taken a cold shower...*

When he came back out, wearing clean(ish) jeans and his Oddball: "Why Don't You Knock It Off With Them Negative Waves?" t-shirt, Idegen was stretched out on the bed, sleeping contentedly. In her bra and panties. Her hands folded over her breasts and her hair splayed out around the pillows in a black halo, she looked like something out of a sexy Hammer horror vampire movie.

Jon rolled his eyes and swapped out the tattered stir straw for a fresh one before donning his socks and boots. *I don't need this kind of distraction right now...*

Sitting at the little desk with his back to the beds, Jon took up his phone and the dog-eared directory from the nightstand and resumed his search for Wayland Moore. As the night dragged on and his efforts flagged, it got harder and harder not to turn and peek at the sleeping beauty on the other side of the room. But every time he did, he heard that hysterical, demeaning laughter in his head.

"She's just not into you," he'd whisper. "Which is good, because if you fool around and get your head snapped off by another girl, you are a dead man, Jon French."

These little pep talks helped, and sometime around midnight, he finally found Wayland Moore.

***

WayMo Feed & Seed and Farm Supply was a sprawling old one-story clapboard covered in flaking white paint beside Sam's Mountain Road, just outside of Middlesboro, where Pineville Road turned into Wilderness Road. A row of muddy, beat-up farm trucks and a Bell County Sheriff's patrol car were parked out front. An old-school phone booth sat beneath a dingy porcelain sign hanging from a cockeyed pole at the edge of the highway and the gravel parking lot. A tall chain-link fence topped with razor wire surrounded a few rows of rental tractors, backhoes, and bobcats in the overgrown back lot.

Jon pulled the Road Runner in at the opposite end of the row of parked vehicles from the patrol car. It was early on a Friday morning, the sky still an iron grey as the sun tried to find its way into the Kentucky hills. Jon figured the place was filled with the old boys' club, chewing the fat and drinking the first complimentary cup of coffee while they pretended to make business plans and purchases. Small town farmers were the same no matter where you went.

"What are you waiting for, Jon?" Idegen asked.

"For that cop to leave." He chewed the end of the straw he had gotten with his Hardee's breakfast. "This Wayland Moore doesn't know me from Adam, and I'm pretty sure it's going to be a tough sell to get him to dip his toe back into Dixie Mafia business. It'll be damn near impossible if I traipse my shit into his store and wave it around in front of one of the local county mounties."

She nodded, her eyes narrowing. He watched her for a moment, never certain what was going on behind those beautiful eyes when she did that. It was like she was changing channels on the world, leaving this situation to check for something better someplace else. He shook his head and looked back at the store as he finished his sausage, egg, and cheese biscuit.

A few minutes later, the front door opened, and an old, bow-legged man in a sweat-stained Co-Op ballcap and bib overalls waddled out, a fifty-pound bag of feed on one shoulder. Behind him came a younger, straighter man with two on his. They exchanged some rough laughter, tossed their bags into the back of a green, turn-of-the-century F150, and headed out to start the day.

"You not gonna eat that?" Jon asked, motioning at the Hardee's bag on the floorboard. Idegen hadn't touched her biscuit. He wasn't really hungry; he just wanted something to occupy his time while he tried to think of the best way to approach Wayland Moore, the former capo of the Southeast.

Idegen shook her head, handed him the bag.

As he dug his way through the greasy paper avalanche, she tensed. "I think the officer is leaving."

Jon looked up as a hulking deputy stepped out the front door. His face was a red storm cloud, and his crooked-toothed mouth worked in mumbled profanities. An old man stepped onto the porch behind him. He was tall, thin, with snow-white hair and patrician features. To Jon, he looked like he should be wearing a white Colonel Sanders suit, standing on the front porch of an antebellum plantation house, a cigar in one hand and a mint julip in the other—not wearing flannel and jeans, standing on the front porch of a rundown farm supply store.

"Don't go off in a huff, Bubba," the old man said, his voice muffled inside the car. "You know I can't do nothing about what them sons o' bitches do up in that holler. Not now, anyhow."

The deputy, Bubba, turned at the front of his car. "I come to you on account o' you supposed to be able to do stuff around here, Wayland. Stuff we can't. Stuff nobody else can. I thought you was supposed to be somebody. I guess I was wrong. I guess I gotta call somebody down in Knoxville."

The old man scowled. "You don't want their shit up here, Bubba. You call them, there's no tellin' what you'll stir up. You want niggers and spics running roughshod in this town? You want the Jews to get their hands on Bell County like they have in Knoxville?"

Jon blinked, looked around to see if anybody else was watching or hearing this. *Racist much?*

"All I know is I got a problem. A real problem, not just—" the cop caught himself and looked around, finally noticing Jon and Idegen. Stiffening and taking a deep breath, he opened the patrol car's door. "Either you handle it, Wayland, or I'll find somebody who will."

Dropping his girth into the car, he started it up and tore out of the gravel lot.

"Great." Jon wiped his hands and opened the door. "Now the old man is pissed. Perfect timing."

Idegen smiled at him. "Maybe it is. Maybe we're just what he needs right now."

Jon raised an eyebrow, then got out of the car. "Mr. Moore?" he called before the old man could step back into the store. "I was wondering if I could speak to you for a moment."

Wayland Moore stopped, glowered at them. He blinked when Idegen stepped closer. "Damn," he muttered. "You look familiar, girl. We met before?"

Jon took a deep breath. *Great, a dirty old man with the oldest pick-up line in the book.*

"No, sir. I believe we have not," Idegen said. Jon cast a sly look her way. He hadn't noticed until now, but her accent had faded tremendously since he'd first met her less than twenty-four hours ago. Now, however, it was even more pronounced.

The old man blinked, smiled. "I know... You look just like one o' them European actresses from the old movies..."

Jon cleared his throat. "I'm sorry, Mr. Moore, but what I've got to say is very important... a matter of life or death, if I'm totally honest."

Wayland Moore blinked at Idegen again, dragged his eyes back to Jon with an effort. He sized him up for a second, then with a shrug, said, "All right, come on in for a spell. I've got a few minutes to kill this morning, anyhow."

Jon gave Idegen a curious look. She smiled and winked at him as they followed the old man into the business. The sweet and earthy scents of livestock feed blended with the machine oil and plastic smell of a hardware store, the aroma of cheap coffee suffusing the whole. A handful of farmer-types hunkered around a pretty young blonde girl at the counter, sipping coffee and trying to make her laugh while pretending they weren't married.

They all looked up as the trio walked through the store, but a shake of the old man's head quickly put them back to their own business. Moore led them past the counter, down a short hall and into what must have been his office, though it looked more like a sports fan's man cave and smelled of fine cigars and bourbon whiskey. The wood-paneled walls were covered in framed University of Kentucky Wildcats posters and photos. There was no desk, just a brown leather three-piece living room sofa radiating out from a sixty-inch plasma TV surrounded by an impressive Bose speaker system.

"Have a seat," Moore said, closing the door behind them.

Jon and Idegen took the sofa, leaving the big chair for the older man. As soon as they were situated, Jon said, "Mr. Moore, my name is Jon French—"

"No shit," Moore said with a grin. He chuckled and slapped his leg. "If that don't beat all."

Jon's brow knotted. "You know who I am?"

"And probably why you're here. Let me guess; you think I can pull some strings and get Byce to call off the dogs, right?"

Jon took a deep breath. "Can you?"

Moore shook his head and stood up. "I don't know who you've been talking to, boy, but I haven't kept in touch with that crowd in a long time. We came to an agreement back in the good old days of Ronnie Reagan. I let Byce take over without bloodshed, and they let me walk away."

Jon's heart sank. He stared at the mud on his boots. *This was it. My last chance.*

"Not even if we did you a favor?" Idegen asked. She sat ramrod straight on the end of the sofa, her eyes hooded and leveled at the old man. "Perhaps an exchange of services?"

Jon blinked, aghast. But before he could protest, Moore smiled and put his hands on his narrow hips. "What you got in mind, girlie? At my age, I don't reckon even a looker like you can make it worth my while."

"I am a trained soldier," she said. "Perhaps you have a problem that requires a specific level of action. One that outmatches your current resources, perhaps?"

Moore tilted his head. "You hear my little chat with Bubba, did you? You know about the Tackett boys, huh?"

Jon shook his head. "Not exactly." He glanced at Idegen, trying to take back control of this negotiation. "Not all of the conversation, and no, we don't know about the Tackett boys."

Moore rubbed his smooth chin. "I did hear 'bout what you done to them fellers in Jacksboro. I also heard that the bodies didn't make it to the morgue and the story didn't make it to the news. Almost like somebody important didn't want nobody to know about it."

Jon inhaled sharply. Even if the old man wasn't in touch with the Knoxville crowd, he was still well informed on the goings-on in his old fiefdom. Jon had been so absorbed in his own run from Craig Byce that he had completely forgotten that whoever had put Idegen in the river might still be on the hunt.

"Then you know I am not without skills," Idegen said.

"And that you might be bringing too much attention my way,

darling," the old man said. He continued to smile, but Jon thought there was a menace in his voice.

Jon took another deep breath, wishing he'd brought his straw from the car. "Okay, how about this? You tell us what you need done with the Tackett boys, we do it, and we get the hell out of town. In return, you make a couple calls to Louisiana and Cincinnati. That's all I'm asking."

Moore tilted his head to the other side, stared at them for a long while. "Well, I reckon it couldn't hurt... You succeed, and I get my cred back with the local sheriff. You fail, and the Tacketts will bury you in a hole in them hills so deep the Almighty'll have to send out a search party on Judgment Day. I can't promise the bosses will put much stock in what I've got to say, but if you can take care of the Tacketts, I'll make the calls."

Jon sat up and exhaled in relief. "Okay. Good. Thank you. Now, who are the Tackett boys, and what do you want done with them?"

Moore chuckled like a man about to tell a ghost story over a campfire on Halloween night. "The Tackett boys are three of the meanest things to ever crawl out of the hollers of Harlan County, and I want them dead."

15
DEADMAN'S CURVE

Craig sat on the crapper and stared at the clean tile floor. He hadn't slept worth a damn all night, pissed off and worried, his guts in a knot. He hadn't eaten much yesterday, which only made the bloated pain in his belly lonely and loud. There really wasn't much in his system to pass, but you'd never know it to listen to his angry colon. Sometimes the bastard just decided to act like it was shitting of its own accord. He'd be sitting on a barstool or on his sofa, and for all the world, it would suddenly feel like he was dumping on himself. He'd jump up, run to the john only to find... nothing.

"Dammit," he whispered into the empty bathroom.

He checked his phone, saw that it was just after seven in the a.m. on a Friday morning in September. He heard Jesse downstairs in the kitchen frying bacon and eggs and making toast. That made him both hungry and nauseated. He closed his eyes. *Maybe I could just punch my own ticket and be done with all this horse shit. I got all the options in the house: pistols, blades, pills, booze. Hell, I even got a pretty good toaster and a comfy bathtub.*

"Chickenshit," he growled, finishing his disappointing business and flushing. He didn't bother checking for blood anymore. It didn't matter now.

The phone rang while he washed his hands. It was a Middlesboro, Kentucky number.

"Byce," he said, answering with wet hands.

"As I live and breathe," the old man's voice said on the other end. "How's things going in K-town, boy?"

"Wayland," Craig said. "Good to hear from you. You still got all your teeth? If so, I reckon that would make you mayor up there, right? How's your wife-slash-sister?"

"Now I remember why I was so glad to get out of Knoxville. But I didn't call to exchange pleasantries, Craig."

"I reckon not."

"I heard about your little French problem. In fact, I've heard about everything, including your big Green problem."

Craig rubbed his forehead, squinting his eyes hard. "And?"

"And I might be able to help you out."

Craig exhaled, closed the toilet lid, and sat down. "Why? How?"

"That boy's traveling with a looker of a gal. She says she's a soldier, but she ain't one of ours. Might be a kike outta Israel or something. Anyhow, she's on the lam, and I don't want her folks chasing her in my hills and hollers. That's the why.

"As for the how, well, what if I told this Jon French feller that I'd made the calls and got a sit-down organized in Atlanta? And what if you and your hosses showed up to meet him?"

"Atlanta, huh?"

"A good sight away from my neck o' the woods, and maybe if you put in an appearance down there, you *might* be able to help Crabtree take his city back from all the niggers. I say might, because if you were worth a damn, you'd never have let him lose it in the first place."

"Not that you did such a bang-up job in your day, Wayland. Folk Nation had a grip on that town a good while before you stepped down, as I recall."

There was a sniff at the other end of the line. "Do you want my help or not?"

"Fine. Yes, okay."

"Good. I've sent them off on a suicide mission up in Harlan, but if they manage to come back out, I'll send them that-a-way. If not, then problem solved, right?"

Craig inhaled sharply. "Not exactly! I need to know what this French kid told the TBI and the Feds before they issue a warrant, Wayland."

The old man chuckled. "Well, can't fix all your problems, sweetheart. Who knows, maybe that bitch is a badass after all. I'll let you know."

Craig sighed as the line went dead.

Jesse yelled from downstairs. "Craig! Breakfast is ready!"

Craig took a deep breath and hollered back through the door, "Make it to go! We're going shopping!"

***

Idegen watched the high, blue-green hills roll past the windows as the black hood ate up the road. Jon's hands clenched in white fists on the steering wheel, and his jaw worked on the plastic in his mouth like a machine. His mind writhed with a multitude of thoughts and emotions. The ever-present human fear was there, but she was pleased to sense rage, anger, and an unusual hatred as well.

"I have a plan," she said.

Jon glanced at her. "Good. You're the soldier. If you leave it up to me, the best I can come up with is challenging them to a game of Russian roulette, saying my prayers, and crossing my fingers."

Idegen took a moment to collate the idioms. Her feeding the night before had restored her systems to optimal capacity.

The man had sat alone in his darkened car, watching children play in a field across the street while he pleasured himself. She had read in his thoughts that he lived alone and worked from home. After the feeding—and learning how to drive via her refreshed neural web—she had put him in the backseat and taken his car deep into the woods. It would be some time before he was missed. With a little luck, even longer before he was found.

"Based on what Wayland Moore told us about the three brothers, I think we can lower their guard with a ruse of a sexual nature," she said. *It seems to be the common denominator of this species, or at least the male.*

Jon's anger flashed bright red in her mind, and his hands twisted on the leather of the wheel. He lowered his chin and glared out the windshield but said nothing.

"We should approach them claiming to be a gift or bribe sent by a rival organization. You pretend to be the mouthpiece or representative, and I will be the offering."

Jon gave a short, bitter laugh. "You want me to be your pimp? Say that I'm from a Peckerwood gang, hoping to recruit them away from the DM?"

Again, she had to scan for references; this time took a bit longer. "Racism... yes. Odd that the two organizations seem to have this in common and yet remain rivals."

Jon laughed. "I reckon the big difference is that the Peckerwoods openly embrace that shit, wearing their rebel flags and swastikas like badges of honor while the old-school Dixie Mafia guys like Wayland Moore keep theirs hidden under nicely pressed white sheets and hoods."

Idegen sensed a wave of guilt rising in Jon. "You are also a racist?"

He looked at her, a mixture of surprise and disbelief. "What? Me? No. Well... at least not anymore. I don't think so, anyway."

"Very confusing answer, Jon."

He scowled. "It's complicated, okay? You grow up in a trailer park where your old man spends days he should be out working and earning a paycheck griping about how the blacks and the Mexicans are taking over all the good jobs, and how the Confederacy should have won and saved the country from the liberals and the Jews, and it... well, it messes with your head. You don't know any better when you're a kid..."

Idegen's neural web fed her the appropriate information. "But you don't think like that anymore?"

"Of course not. I went to college, met new people, got exposed to new ideas. I learned some things, like how to think for myself. I learned that assholes come in every spectrum of the rainbow and every political stripe, and no matter what color we are, we're all just trying to deal with our own shit. It's the universal Human Condition."

"Good for you, Jon French."

"Well, I'm glad I meet with your enlightened and cosmopolitan sense of approval, Idegen Videshee. Now, about this plan...?"

She gave him as much detail as she could while they made their way toward Possum Hollow Road, just off US-119 on the way into Harlan. Until they had the exact layout of the property, there were no details to share. The gist was, Jon was to talk their way into the three brothers' compound—a small, isolated farmstead according to Wayland Moore—where she would do the rest.

Idegen licked her lips in anticipation of the coming feast.

***

Jon pulled the Road Runner onto the gravel patch just off Possum Hollow Road. A cattle gate secured by a logging chain crossed the driveway, and a stand of tall cedar trees screened the property from the road. Half a dozen of the trees to either side of the gate bore faded and torn NO TRESSPASSING signs. One on the gate declared, TRESSPASSERS WILL BE VIOLATED.

Jon took a deep breath and popped a fresh straw into his mouth. "You really want to do this?" he asked Idegen. "I don't like you going in there unarmed."

"Do you not think an armed prostitute might be suspicious?" She took the Predators cap off and shook out her long black hair. "Relax. Just get us in, and I'll do the rest."

Jon looked at her. Without makeup and revealing clothes, she didn't really look like a prostitute, but she was still gorgeous. She tilted her head, then slipped out of her pullover hoodie. "What the hell are you doing?"

She laughed. "I need to look the part." She reached in the back to grab his Doctor's coat. In a moment, she'd slid it on over her lacy black bra. "Now, how do I look?"

Jon nearly swallowed the straw and turned away. "Like the best honey trap in Kentucky."

"I shall take that as a compliment, Jon. Now see if anybody is home."

He shook his head and stepped out of the car, hating that her guns were in the trunk. There was an old-school callbox wired to one of the cedars beside the gate. Jon pushed the button and said, "Hello?" into the squawking feedback. "I'm looking for the Tackett brothers. Is anyone there?"

Releasing the button, he waited. Just past the trees, the rutted gravel drive bent to the left and climbed a hill. Off to the right, he could see what looked like part of an ancient cemetery. Over a dozen stones jutted up at odd angles around a timeworn granite obelisk.

Crows cawed and cicadas sang in the trees.

"Who are ye?" a gruff, nasally voice blasted from the speaker. Jon jumped straight up.

Clearing his throat, he pushed the button. "My name's Jon English. The boys in Frankfurt sent me over to see if y'all want to come work for their team. They sent a... a present."

There was another long pause, and Jon continued to sweat beneath the late morning sun. He swatted at a mosquito that was trying to feed on his eardrum.

"Wait there. I'll be down in a minute."

Jon sighed and looked back at the car. A moment later, he heard a small engine fire up somewhere in the distance behind the cedars. The rumbling noise grew louder and closer until Jon saw a big man in a dingy John Deere ball cap, baggy jeans, and old work boots come around the curve on a battered and muddy red Honda four-wheeler. The man wore no shirt, so the jailhouse tattoos covering his sweaty, sunburnt muscles were on display. A thick patch of scraggly red beard covered most of his face. He looked like a cross between a mountain man and a serial killer. The big, ivory-handled Bowie knife strapped to his side suited both roles.

Jon chewed the straw like his life depended on it.

The man cut the engine and dismounted the vehicle. He was even bigger standing up. "What you say yer name was?" he grunted, stepping to the fence.

Jon thought about the Taurus Judge he had tucked into the back of his pants. *I could pull it and drop him; then we could climb the fence and hunt down the other two. Only, I've never shot another human being. Hell, I've never shot any living being...*

"Jon." He slid into bluff mode. "Jon English. The boys in Frankfurt sent me." He waved at the car, and Idegen got out. "With a gift."

The big man grunted, eyed her up and down without showing any interest. "Which boys in Frankfurt?"

Jon smiled. "The New Reich." He hoped he'd picked the right name out of the Big Hat o' Neo-Nazi Assholes. "They've heard good things about what y'all have done down here for the Dixie Mafia, and they think you would be a good addition to the team."

The Tackett grunted and stepped over to the callbox. "Dan, Ben," he said into the machine's static. "Pretty boy down here says they's with the New Reich. Got a good-lookin' whore says is a gift. Got a fancy ride, too. What y'all think?"

"Shit, Jim," a voice crackled back. "Bring 'em up."

Jim Tackett grunted, gave Jon a narrow-eyed look, then produced a big keychain and proceeded to undo the lock on the gate. Jon smiled and returned to the Road Runner.

"I've got a bad feeling about this," he grunted as he started the car. "I hope you know what you're doing, 'cause I sure as hell don't."

Idegen stared at the big man waving them through the opened gate and licked her lips. Jon wasn't sure if she was turned on by the monstrous, tattooed hillbilly or if she was wondering what he'd taste like after a few hours in a smoker. "Trust me," she said.

They waited for Jim Tackett to resecure the gate, mount his Honda, and then followed him back up the winding gravel drive. The left side of the hill was covered in more cedar and pine trees, thick with an undergrowth of ferns, kudzu, and creeper vines. To the right was the ancient cemetery, which was at least three times the size of what Jon had first thought. He guessed every ancestor of the Tackett family since the Revolutionary War was buried there.

The house was a weathered, ramshackle, three-story monstrosity that was probably almost as old as the cemetery and the tree. The lower part looked like it had started life as a log cabin, with add-ons and additional stories that shared traits with Victorian and Edwardian architecture but showed no real sign of a plan or blueprint. Orange and yellow extension cords ran from the opened windows out to several other buildings, strung between stunted trees, clotheslines, and old fence posts like tentacles impersonating Christmas tinsel.

Chickens and hogs wandered through the whole compound without supervision. A pole in front of the house displayed a faded Klan flag and that of the Commonwealth fluttering in the warm breeze.

"Looks like the House of Redneck Usher," Jon muttered. After a moment, he was surprised to hear Idegen laugh.

He almost joined her, but then the other two Tackett brothers emerged from the old house. Though not as big as Jim, Ben and Dan looked older and meaner. Their reddish beards were slashed with silver and grey, and no ballcap concealed the hill-bred cruelty in their blue eyes. One brother wore all camo and tan combat boots, the other had a blue and white bandana around his unruly hair, a sweat-stained Mountain Dew t-shirt, and old jeans tucked into scuffed-up motorcycle boots. Both wore pistols on their belts, and the camo guy had an AR-15 in his hands.

"Outta the car," the Tackett with the rifle said. "Hands where we can see 'em."

Jon forced a pleasant smile as he complied. "Hey, we're here to play nice, friend. No need for that."

"Shut up." Camo man kept the AR leveled at his chest while Mountain Dew frisked him and came away with the Taurus.

"Man's gotta protect himself these days." Jon shrugged, still smiling.

Nobody was really listening to him, though. All three brothers were looking at Idegen.

"We gonna do this or not?" she asked, and Jon almost lost his straw at the perfection of her poor white trash accent. "One at a time or all together?" She smiled at the big Tackett and winked. "I ain't never done three brothers at once before."

Jon was surprised to see the big guy flush and look away.

"What's a matter, Jim?" Mountain Dew said with mocking laughter. "Cat got yer tongue? She too much fer ye?"

"Let 'im be, Dan," Ben—the one in camo—said, shouldering his rifle. "If he don't want to play, that's more for the two of us."

"Damn right!" Dan slid Jon's revolver into the waistband of his jeans. "Come on girl, we'll break you in. Meantime," he looked at Jon and winked, "you, pretty boy, can keep Little Jimmy company while he works up his courage."

Jon tried to keep his face neutral as he glanced at Idegen. *What now? They weren't supposed to split up!*

She didn't seem to notice as she stepped between the two older brothers, letting them put their arms around her to guide her into the house. A moment later, Jon stood in the dooryard with the silent hillbilly giant. Jim Tackett gave him a glare, then turned and walked across the driveway to the pig pen, cursing under his breath.

Jon stood there, not sure what to do. He had to trust that Idegen could handle herself with the two horny, distracted bastards. He also had to make sure that the big guy didn't come in and catch her by surprise. He stared at the skull and crossed sabers tattooed over Jim

Tackett's broad back beneath the words HATE IS HERITAGE. Surprisingly spelled correctly, the inked motto reminded him why they were here.

"Bubba's daughter, Becky Lynn," Wayland Moore had said. "She was running around with the sheriff's son for a while. Going steady, you know? Well, over the past few months, Ronnie—the sheriff's boy—got it in his head that he was untouchable on account of who his daddy is. He was becoming a real hellion, right up until the time he decided he'd go pay the Tacketts a visit.

"Now, I don't know where he got the notion that he could waltz right up to their house and demand their pot at his prices, but that's what I reckon happened. Unfortunately, Bubba's girl was with him at the time.

"They taught Ronnie a lesson he'll never forget. Not only did they give him the beatings his daddy should have, all in one go, they made him watch while they showed him how they treat a woman up in the hollers. If you ask me, Ronnie got off easy, but poor Becky Lynn was the one to pay the real price. They had to send her off to one of them state hospitals for crazy folks in Louisville..."

Remembering the tale, Jon bit down on the straw, felt it almost separate in his teeth. He curled his hands into fists and walked across the driveway to join Jim Tackett, where the big man tossed scraps over the fence into a trough.

"So, Jim..." Jon knew how to get under another player's skin, how to make him lose his cool and make a stupid mistake, to bet or fold the way Jon wanted him to. "Why you out here with the pigs while your brothers are in there with the chick? You like sloppy seconds, or you just not like girls?"

Tackett turned on him, his yellow teeth a jagged line beneath his thick beard. "Watch it, pretty boy." His hand lowered to the handle of the big Bowie at his side. "You might not be so pretty when you come out of this holler."

Jon forced a smile, knotted his fists tighter. *I just hope I'm not the one losing my cool. Not the one making a stupid mistake.* "Let me guess. She's too old for you, right? You like 'em on the young side. The *small* side. Makes your little pecker seem bigger, right?"

Jim Tackett dropped the bucket of scraps. Jon noticed human fingers, toes, and other bits when it spilled on the ground.

A strangled cry came from the house. It was one of the brothers.

Jim Tackett's eyes flicked that way. The Bowie knife came out of its sheath.

Jon punched the big man in his bearded jaw with all he had in him.

Tackett staggered back against the fence, but Jon was damn sure he'd just broken a bone in his hand. Pain rocketed up his wrist and into his shoulder, and the appendage went numb. *Oh shit... Didn't plan this out all that well, did you, Jonny-Boy?*

He leapt back as the big blade scythed past his belly.

Jon grabbed for the big man's wrist with his good hand, but Tackett shook him off, mainly because of the ferocious, if off balance, left cross. It still knocked the straw from Jon's mouth like a KO'd boxer's mouthpiece.

Jon took the blow on the right cheekbone, felt fire explode under his eye. He turned, rolling with the impact, and ran for the parked Road Runner. And the three guns in the trunk.

I just hope Idegen's having better luck than I am. I just hope she's still alive.

He tried to fish the keys out of his jeans pocket, but the bolt of fire-and-ice pain that shot through his right hand caused him to lose his breath. Black suns pinwheeled across his blurring vision. He tripped on a cackling chicken and went sprawling headfirst into the gravel driveway.

The rocks dug into his palms and knees like dull knife blades. The pain in his right hand exploded again. He heard big Jim Tackett bearing down on him, breathing hard and cursing. Jon grabbed a handful of gravel, spun, and hurled it as hard as he could. Tackett yelled as the rocks peppered his face.

Jon scrambled back to his feet, changed direction, and bolted for the horse barn.

"I'm gonna cut your dick off and feed it to the hogs!" Tackett roared. "Then I'm gonna use a rake handle on your asshole!"

Jon's mind reeled at the variety of awful things Jim Tackett listed as he came after him. He was genuinely surprised at just how creative and depraved the man was. Which made him wonder, exactly, what the three brothers had done to Bubba's poor daughter.

What are the other two doing to Idegen right now?

Bolting into the darkness of the barn, Jon's senses were assaulted with a panoply of unexpected smells. Rather than the scents of horseflesh, feed, hay, and the like, the barn reeked of alcohol, chemicals, and smoke. His strained vision fell on the source in one of the stalls: a sizeable moonshine still, bubbling away.

As Jim Tackett's huge frame filled the barn door behind him, Jon pulled his Zippo from his left pocket, flicked it, and tossed it into the stall with the contraption. "Looks like Andy and Barney missed this one, you son of a bitch!"

Tackett rushed into the stall as something on the floor caught fire. An orange glow filled that part of the barn, accompanied by a soft whumping noise. It didn't last long as the cursing man kicked and stomped it out. Just long enough for Jon to find something he desperately needed.

"Now, you little shit," Jim Tackett growled, turning around, stepping out of the stall, and right onto the rusty tines of a hayfork in Jon's clenched and bleeding fists.

Jon glared up at the surprised Tackett as blood boiled out from the four puncture wounds in his belly, then started to dribble from his beard.

"This is for Becky Lynn," Jon said through clenched jaws, pushing down on the handle so that the tines dug higher into the big man's innards. Jerking it up, then to the left and right, he tried to pull the fork free, but there was too much suction.

"You... shit..." Tackett gasped in agony. He grabbed the fork with his left hand, swung the Bowie at Jon's face with his right.

Jon let go of the hayfork and stepped back. The tip of the blade carved through the bridge of his nose. Blood exploded across his face, tinted his vision. The pain came next, sharp and fast.

Jim Tackett tugged the bloody hayfork from his body. His legs moving awkwardly, he lunged after Jon, impossibly picking up speed. Blood ran out of his belly and his mouth in crimson fountains.

"Why won't you die, you hillbilly monster bastard?" Jon shouted as he turned to run from the barn. He wiped blood from his face with his throbbing hand.

The Bowie sliced into his right ear before cartwheeling past to bury two inches of blade in the barn door. Jon stumbled into the doorframe, the side of his head on fire. He could hear Jim Tackett gasping and shuffling after him. He turned, saw the huge, wounded man using the hayfork as a crutch, murder in his bloodshot eyes.

Lunging through the door, Jon bolted straight for the old house, praying that Idegen was okay and that the other two brothers were already dead. If he found himself alone and unarmed on this hill with the pissed off Tackett clan, there was no telling what he'd suffer before being fed to their pigs. *No, that's not entirely true. From the things Jim said, I've got a pretty good idea of what will happen to me...*

His eyes stinging and swelling shut, his hand in dull agony and blood pouring down his face, Jon stumbled up the front porch and into the log cabin's darkened lower floor.

Even though he had resigned himself to the fact that he was now smack dab in the middle of the Bluegrass State's version of *The Texas*

Chainsaw Massacre, Jon French was wholly unprepared for what he saw in the filth-cluttered living room of the Tackett house, illuminated only by the broad blade of sunlight falling over his shoulders.

A slack-jawed, shriveled corpse in bloodstained camouflage lay sprawled over a threadbare antique sofa. Jon knew that those were the clothes Ben Tackett had been wearing a few minutes ago, but he could not understand how this desiccated corpse, like something from an Indiana Jones movie, had gotten into them.

As troubling as that was, the sight of a topless Idegen Videshee straddling a quickly shriveling Dan Tackett on the stained and torn loveseat, her face buried in his throat, bothered Jon even more.

He froze in the doorway and swatted at the crimson haze of his vision. "Idegen?" he whispered before clearing his throat.

She turned and stared at him with glowing white eyes, blood smeared over her face and dripping from her extended fangs.

That's it... I can't believe I'm about to—

Jon fainted.

***

Sharpe hurried into the C&C despite the throbbing spasms in her lower back. The bunks at McGhee Tyson were better than those at Canaveral, but not by much. And she was struggling to make do on half a Vicodin a day. "What have we got?" she snapped at Hack-Job and Tunes.

"We got a hit from a CCTV camera at the Cumberland Gap Tunnels. A 1968 Plymouth Road Runner registered to one August Winchester passed through yesterday around 1630. Winchester's garage was the site of the shooting where we found the three bodies."

"Tunnels?" Sharpe inhaled, feeling that sense of déjà vu again, and clutched the back of Hack-Job's chair. "Yesterday? Around 1630? Why the hell am I just now hearing about this?"

Tunes shrugged, his mahogany skin shaded blue in monitor light. "We're not exactly working with Delta Force here, Colonel. These folks are weekend warriors. The feed must have come in on someone's break or between shifts, and I guess it just fell through the cracks 'til Hack and I could go over the footage."

"Excuses," she growled. "Do we have a positive ID?"

Hack-Job shook his head. "No. The resolution on the cameras isn't that great, even with all the scrubbing and enhancements I can do. But we know there's two Caucasians in the car, one male and one female."

Sharpe stood straight and rubbed the bridge of her nose. "It'll have to do. Get Honcho and the two Marines up there ASAP. The rest of us will continue expanding our search outward."

"Yes, ma'am," the two tech specialists said.

Sharpe turned to go. "And find out what's taking Helbourne so long with that damn NASA algorithm. I want a SITREP within the hour." She stalked out of the C&C without waiting for their affirmation. The pain was getting worse, and she needed to be alone.

Her phone rang.

She slipped it from her pocket, knowing who it was before she even saw the number. Mr. White had a knack for reaching out at the absolute worst times. "Hello," she said, keeping her voice as neutral as possible.

"SITREP, Colonel."

"Status hasn't changed, but we have made progress. Helbourne believes he can reprogram a satellite that will allow us to track her—"

"*Her*, Colonel? Don't you mean *it?*"

Sharpe leaned against the cool cinderblock wall in the corridor. "Yes, sir. It, the subject. He should have the device operational within the next few hours. In the meantime, we've picked up a visual lead which indicates the subject and its accomplice are now in the Kentucky border region. I'm sending a heavy weapons detachment that way, ASAP."

"Detachment? Do you think that will be sufficient, Colonel?"

Sharpe bit her lip. *Do you want me to call out the entire National Guard in two states, asshole?* "Yes, sir. Sergeant Conrad and his men are the absolute best. I'd lay odds on any one of them against any platoon our enemies can field."

There was a sigh or a grunt on the other end of the line.

"Is there anything else, sir?"

"Just let me know as soon as you think you're in over your head, Colonel. This one could be for all the marbles. We just don't know right now."

"Yes, sir. Wilco." She hung up and shook, resisting the urge to smash the phone against the floor. *Of course you just don't know right now! You're not the one with boots on the ground. You're not the one counting corpses and waiting to see where the next one turns up. You just sit in your boys' club, smoking your Cubans and drinking your single malt, waiting for the poor little colored girl to call for help so you can swoop in and save the day...*

Sharpe chuckled as she regained her composure. "If I get in over my head, *sir*, you'll be at the bottom of the pool with me. Right alongside the whole rest of the fucking planet."

***

Jon smelled mold, mildew, and gun oil. And blood.

He opened his eyes, feeling like he'd slept for a week and needed another. It took a moment to realize where he was, to remember what had happened. But then the pain coursing through his body reminded him. "It wasn't a nightmare..."

Blinking the crust from his eyes, he saw Idegen standing over a card table in the middle of the dingy room. Ammo boxes, weapons, and magazines crowded the table's surface. She wore his *Kriegsmarine* over her hoodie while cleaning an assault rifle beneath the naked glow of a dangling hundred-watt lightbulb.

There were traces of dried blood on her chin.

Jon jolted to a seated position, adrenaline dulling the pain. He realized he was on the threadbare couch in the Tackett house's front room. He noticed the dried-out husks of the two dead brothers lying among the tottering stacks of hunting, car, and porno magazines on the dirty hardwood floor.

His mouth worked; his lungs tried to push a scream up through his constricted throat.

Idegen smiled. "Good, you are awake, Jon. We've got some work to do before we get back on the road. Do you think you can start loading these magazines for me?"

That smile and matter-of-fact way in which she spoke froze the scream on the back of his tongue. "Wh—who are you? *What* are you?"

She frowned without slowing in her task. Her pale fingers fluttered over the brass cartridges she pressed into the plastic AR magazines. "What a silly—and rude, if I am to be honest—question, Jon. I am exactly who and what I said I am. I am Idegen Videshee, and I am a soldier and a killer. Nothing has changed."

Jon stared at the two dead men on the floor and shuddered. "The hell it hasn't," he whispered, trying to work saliva into his mouth.

Idegen's glance followed his line of sight. "They are no more or less dead than the three men I killed at August's garage, Jon. Yet it seems that the manner of the killing is what bothers you. Please explain." She continued to load rifle and pistol magazines.

Jon swallowed, unable to look away from the mummified hillbillies. "Are... are you a v-vampire?" *Or am I losing my mind?*

Idegen chuckled. "That word. I find it interesting. The reference to a parasitic reanimated corpse from your mythology. When what you actually mean is, do I feed off of living things? The answer is yes, just as almost all life in the universe does. Just as you do. Or do you think the meat you ate for breakfast this morning sprang into existence upon a whim?"

Jon rubbed his face, winced at the sharp pain in his hands, his cheek, his ear, and across his nose. He looked at the ragged holes the gravel had made in his palms when he fell in the driveway. He put a tentative finger to the gummy scab forming across his nose, then felt another on the upper edge of his right ear. *I must look like De Niro in* Raging Bull... *or in the Branagh version of* Frankenstein...

"Yes," Idegen said. "You are not seriously injured, but there is a chance your limited physiology may become infected from your wounds. It is a shame we no longer have those medical supplies we took from Doctor Kirby... I have searched this structure but have been unable to locate anything that might be of use. Other than the munitions, that is."

Jon blinked, barely hearing her words as he remembered the moonshine still in the barn and the monstrous Jim Tackett hot on his heels. "The other one," he gasped, feeling a tightening in his chest. "The big one..."

Idegen smiled again. "Oh, you killed him, Jon. So you see, we are not all that different. We both kill to ensure our own survival."

Jon lumbered to his feet, carefully sidestepped the corpses and the trash, and looked through the opened door. On the front lawn, the massive body of Jim Tackett lay face down in the grass beneath a swarm of shiny green flies. A large spotted sow was nuzzling at his neck, giving the body a taste test before settling in for the meal.

Jon tried to say something, but no words seemed right for the occasion. *If I had a beard, I'd stuff a bone in it and promptly go mad...*

He turned back to the room and stared at Idegen. "Okay." He forced himself to stay in the hand, hoping for a favorable flop. "Okay. Let's have it. I want all of it. The whole truth, every bit of it. Who and what you are. And why haven't you...?"

"Killed and fed upon you, Jon?" Idegen did not look up but was plainly amused by his discomfort.

"Yes. All of it."

She stopped assembling her arsenal and turned to look him full in the face. "I am Cell-commander Idegen Videshee of the Logonijy Empire's Deep Space Exploration Fleet; Balor Task Force, Seventh Group, Reconnaissance Battalion. And I am currently trapped on your primitive world.

"I was deployed as a scout, but was shot down by your military and subsequently captured, tortured, and studied before making my escape. You found and rescued me, Jon French, and for that I owe you a debt of honor: my life for yours. That is why I have not killed or fed upon you." She turned back to her weapons. "That, and I have grown... fond of you."

Jon blinked, and his jaw worked on a straw that wasn't there. *Deep Space... Exploration Fleet... Empire... primitive world...? She's from outer space? She's a vampire warrior woman from outer space? How the hell do I even begin to process that?*

Something about the way she said the word "fond" made him think of Golden Retrievers and German Shepherds. This, at least, got a neuron or two firing. "Wait. I'm your *pet?*"

She laughed. Almost as hard and raucously as she had at the mall. "We do not keep pets, Jon, but that is an interesting analogy... No, if I were to use one of your words, I would say *friend.*"

Jon collapsed back onto the sofa and put his battered head in his aching hands. "This is all way too much..."

Two days ago, I was about to join the World Series of Poker. Yesterday, I held a loaded gun to my own skull. Today, I've killed a man, and am sitting in a room with an alien vampire, a pair of mummified bodies, and an arsenal... and I still have one of the nation's biggest criminal organizations out for my blood. Where and how did my life go completely off the rails and into the Twilight Zone?

"Come now, Jon. You could do a lot worse than having a professional soldier from a superior spacefaring race as your friend. Especially right now. Or have you forgotten your feud with Craig Byce and his Dixie Mafia?"

There is truth to that. "But... you *eat* people!"

Idegen sighed and went back to work, loading the weapons and ammunition into a dirty old Gladiator gym bag. "And how is that any different from what you eat, Jon?"

"Cows and pigs and chickens are not people!"

"Perhaps not to you, but to their own kind, I suppose they might be."

"But you, you look human. That's... *cannibalism!* You look just like one of us, maybe better, but you've got... all the same parts we do."

"And then some." Idegen zipped up the bag. "It is entirely possible that there was a common ancestor of our two races at the beginning of time, but mine has evolved to the point that there is a very, very wide gap now between our species." She hoisted the bulging bag onto her shoulder as if it were no more than a purse. "Now, shall we go?"

"Why do you think I would go anywhere with you?"

Idegen cocked her head. She looked annoyed, yet Jon was surprisingly unafraid of her. She set the bag on the floor beside the dead brothers. "You are right, of course. I should not assume anything or take your continued friendship for granted. What do you want to do, Jon? How can I assure you of my intent?"

He looked at her, seeing the myriad versions of her flash before his eyes. The pale, wounded, and drowning woman he had saved from the rain-swollen Tennessee; the weak and shivering woman he had patched up with stolen medical supplies in a stolen car; the strong, calculating woman who had coldcocked his street fighting friend before killing three armed thugs in the blink of an eye; the incredibly vibrant and sexy woman he had gone shopping with; the terrifying vampire woman he had seen just a little while ago. And finally, the powerful, confident alien warrior woman standing before him now, offering him her friendship and protection in exchange for his continued trust and cooperation.

"Okay." Jon extended his hand. "But there's got to be some rules. You may not be human, but you're going to start acting like it if you want me to hang around. No hunting and killing people just for the sake of a snack and the like."

Idegen smiled and accepted the handshake. "It is, as they say here, a deal, Jon French. I will restrict my diet to our enemies. Fortunately, it seems we have an abundance of those."

He could not resist a chuckle at the truth of those words, despite the horror story situation. "Apparently. And by the way, like I said before, quit saying my name every time you speak to me. We humans don't do that unless we're sleazy motivational speakers or used car salesmen."

She winked at him as she picked up the bag of weapons. "Very well. Now can we go? I suspect that my hunters have not been idle, even if yours have."

***

Sharpe watched the live feed from Honcho's helmet cam. The big Ranger hopped from the skid of the Kiowa into the hillbilly compound, the barrel of his carbine flicking into and out of frame as he swept the insertion zone. Glimpses of the two Marines, Archer and Ramrod, came into view as they joined the hunt.

"Alpha One is in," Honcho said. "No sign of hostiles yet."

Sharpe gripped the back of Hack-Job's and Tunes's chairs as she watched the three overhead monitors in the C&C. The two techs had located the classic Road Runner less than an hour before with the DOD satellites and had directed Honcho's detachment to the site as quickly as possible.

The three men swept the farmstead while the hovering Kiowas

covered them with their light machine guns and rockets. Sharpe's eyes flicked from feed to feed as they moved from hovel to hovel. She held her breath, remembering those fierce, dead-white eyes, bloody talons, and extended fangs, the carnage from the C-130. She expected to see the subject flash from the shadows at any moment, the feed going dead or breaking into static at the sound of wild gunfire and a man screaming.

"Clear," the three troops declared as they moved from structure to structure.

Please let this be the end of the hunt. Please let them find her. Please let them bring her down and put an end to all this bullshit...

"Got one KIA," Honcho said, his feed displaying a large, tattooed corpse sprawled on the lawn. Flies and crows scattered at Honcho's approach. The body's face and entrails had been devoured. "Looks like the pigs got to him first. I'd say this happened a few hours ago."

"Car's empty," Archer announced, revealing how he got his nickname. The Marine sounded like the cartoon secret agent on television. His feed showed the abandoned Road Runner.

"Two more KIA," Ramrod said, his monitor revealing his M60E6 sweeping the front room of the main structure. "Definitely the subject's handiwork, based on what the doc said. Looks like she took her time with these."

Sharpe pursed her lips at the sight of the two shriveled things on the monitor. "If she had that much time, then they're already gone. They've switched vehicles again."

She turned to Hack-Job. "Find out who owns that property and see if all the vehicles are registered to the same name." To Tunes, she said, "Tell Honcho to catalog all the vehicles still there. We need to find out what they're driving now."

Sharpe stood straight and rubbed the small of her back with both hands. *So this wasn't the end of the hunt. Still, we are closing in... But if she's fed that much off two victims, how much stronger will she be? Will that much energy give her additional abilities that we don't know about...? And why them? That address is almost the definition of Bum-Fuck Egypt. There has to be some connection between these victims and this Jon French and his criminal ties. That is a lead that should be revisited... But first...*

"I need to talk to Dr. Helbourne."

16
TAKE ME HOME, COUNTRY ROAD

"What do you mean it's not working?"

Helbourne took a deep breath at Sharpe's visceral tone. He could see the veins in her throat, and her eyes were wide and bloodshot. He could tell she was in pain, which meant he'd already won this particular altercation. If he wasn't so frustrated by his own failed endeavor, he might have even taken some small pleasure in her discomfort.

"I mean, Colonel, it simply isn't working." He pushed himself away from the computer. "This satellite was built to examine phenomena light years away, not miles. It's like trying to study microbes with a telescope."

"You mean you've wasted hours on this faulty algorithm, after I put my ass in a sling to get you access to a multi-billion-dollar satellite?"

Helbourne threw his hands in the air. "It is a matter of hardware, Colonel, not software. My algorithm is not faulty. If I had the right kind of satellite, it would work."

Sharpe folded her arms and stalked stiffly around the lab. "What kind of satellite do you need?"

Helbourne rubbed his chin. "One that can detect multiple spectrums of light, a wide range of differing types of radiations, subsonic to supersonic frequencies. Do you happen to have one like that lying around somewhere?"

She sighed and rubbed her bloodshot eyes. "Maybe. The DOD has a few satellites they use to look for nuclear activity in restricted regions. Why didn't you say that in the first place?"

Helbourne shook his head. "I asked for a NASA satellite because that's what I'm familiar with. You're supposed to be the soldier-slash-spy. You could have told me you had something like that."

She gave him an eat-shit-and-die look. "I am *so* sorry, Doctor, if I haven't kept you up to speed on things in the real world. Just in case you haven't noticed, I'm up to my armpits in casualties since your precious subject showed up, and it's all I can do to try and keep the body count from rising.

"But, by all means, play with your computers and your slides, and keep your little secrets if it makes you feel better. Meanwhile, the grownups are going to try to keep this monster from killing again."

Helbourne felt his face and neck flush. He was on his feet, and his words came out in a harsh flurry. "You don't understand! You and your gang of super soldiers strut around here like you're all Real American Heroes: God's gift to the Red, White, and Blue. You think you're the only ones trying to save people."

He stepped closer to her, rage coursing through his body like he hadn't felt in years. He jammed a finger hard into his own flabby chest. "Well, *I'm* trying to save the entire planet!"

Sharpe's brow furrowed. "What the hell are you even talking about?"

"You don't see the big picture, Colonel. You're trying to save what, a dozen, a score, a hundred lives? Don't you see—they won't matter at all in the end if we don't learn to understand her, to communicate with her."

When Sharpe looked at him like a cat contemplating a canary, he said, "Let me ask you this, Colonel: What would you do if one of your pilots got shot down by some third-world banana republic? Then, before you could enact a rescue, said pilot was captured, tortured, then hunted down and exterminated like an animal?"

Sharpe still didn't say anything.

Helbourne took a deep breath and exhaled. "Idegen Videshee has killed, what? Around twenty or so people since she's been on Earth. And that was while unarmed, weak, and wounded. Now, imagine a hundred or a thousand of her kind at full strength, all armed with technology that makes your state-of-the-art weapons look like flint-tipped spears. And they've never heard of the Geneva Convention and have absolutely no ties to the United Nations."

"Okay, you've made your point," Sharpe said grudgingly. "Since you brought it up, tell me this. Do you know what her—*its*—physical and psychic capabilities are at full strength?" She rubbed her temples and took a deep breath. "How powerful can the subject become if fully 'charged' on this life force or essence deal?"

Helbourne blinked. "She's killed again? And fed?"

Sharpe stared at him in confirmation.

He ran a sweaty hand through his thinning hair. "Who knows? Based on what our initial cellular studies showed... Somewhere between Steve Austin and Superman? Between Kreskin and Professor X?"

Sharpe rolled her eyes in exasperation. "Pretend I didn't grow up living and breathing pop culture references, Doctor. Be as specific as you can. We are trying to apprehend or kill a monster from outer space here."

Helbourne flopped back into his rolling chair, hating her dogged devotion to the idea of terminating the subject. "Okay, maybe she can bench press a Volkswagen Bug, maybe a cruise ship. Maybe she can tell you what you had for dinner last night and how you feel this morning, maybe she can tell you how your great-great-grandparents died and how the world is going to end... That's all I can give you without more data, Colonel. I'm sorry."

"All the more reason to work faster, Doctor," Sharpe said. "Faster, harder, and smarter. We've got to bring her down before her people get here."

Helbourne gave her a bitter chuckle and looked at the overhead lights. "That's my point, Colonel. They're *already* here. Hers could not have been a long-range ship capable of intergalactic travel. Somewhere up there, possibly even within the confines of our own solar system, her people are already on their way."

***

Jon slumped against the door, strapped into the passenger seat of the brand new Ford Raptor that had been lovingly covered beneath a tarp in the back of the Tackett barn. He was surprised that the hillbilly psychopaths had owned such a pristine ride, though he would have preferred something a little less flashy than the University of Kentucky-blue paint job. But it was either this or an old yellow 1966 Mustang convertible the brothers had been restoring in one of the outbuildings. The Tacketts had also used one of the outbuildings as a garage for their three Harleys (another being the home of their hydroponic pot operation), but Jon had absolutely no desire to ride a motorcycle across Kentucky, through Tennessee, and half of Georgia.

"I knew they were getting close," Idegen said. Jon blinked, hearing the helicopters as she guided the truck onto 25E on the outskirts of Pineville. "I hope the route you have chosen is a good one."

"It is," he said with more confidence than he felt. Hearing the helicopters made the threat of the military suddenly real. He tried not to think about all the movies he'd seen of swarms of soldiers and scientists in hazmat suits hunting down aliens. Gangsters were one thing, but the U.S. Government's war machine was something else entirely. "We'll make a left onto 92 up here on the other side of town and just stay on it 'til we hit Highway 27, then take it back into Tennessee and all the way to Georgia."

"And you think this Wayland Moore is to be trusted? You think he will arrange an armistice with your Dixie Mafia?"

Jon had called Moore as soon as they had picked up cell coverage on their way back from the Tackett farm. The old man had promised to make the calls as soon as he'd verified their claim. He told them to make for Atlanta in any case. Jon hated not knowing for sure, but what choice did he really have? Driving south put them in no more danger than heading into the DM-held Virginias would.

"I honestly have no idea. All I can do is hope now."

When Idegen didn't say anything, he tried to relax and take in the scenery. The highway curved around the hill-nestled town of Pineville off to the left, separating it from the Cumberland River like a retaining wall. There was a pair of giant concrete and steel gates flanking the roadside on either end of the Southeastern Kentucky Medical Center, and Jon could never pass through them without thinking they had been built to save the hospital from the outbreak of a zombie apocalypse—or to seal such an event inside.

It was unusual for him to be riding instead of driving, and he couldn't quite get the hang of it. He had been behind the wheel since before he'd had a driver's license and had probably logged several million miles across the mid-South and Appalachia in the past sixteen years. Unable to rest, he looked at Idegen. "So, how do you know how to drive an Earth car all of a sudden?"

"I have an integrated neural web that accesses your Ethernet and radio broadcast."

Jon blinked, then laughed. "So, you're a Wi-Fi hotspot?"

She smiled. "Yes. Something like that. But I also gain much of my understanding of your speech and mannerisms by studying your thoughts and memories."

Jon sat upright, awakening all the pain in his body. He winced. "What? You... you can read minds?"

She glanced at him, furrowing her brow. "To a certain extent. This bothers you?"

"Hell, yes, it does. That's an invasion of privacy. I don't want you poking around in my head. Not ever again, you got it?"

She pursed her lips and turned back to the road. "As you wish. Though, I must confess I do not understand your objections, Jon. It was by looking at your thoughts that allowed me to judge you as a worthy companion. You are not driven by the wickedness I have found in the minds of other humans."

"Oh, really? You had to read my mind to figure that out? The fact that I risked my life to save you from drowning didn't give you a clue?"

Idegen's head rocked back slightly, acknowledging his point. "Yes. You are correct. I am sorry. It will not happen again."

"Good." Jon curled up and felt like every dirty little thought since childhood had been on public display for the past twenty-four hours. "In our society, we tend to judge people by their actions and their words, not by what might or might not be going on inside their heads." Though, deep down, he knew that wasn't entirely true.

"So I have gathered. But tell me, do you object to me reading the thoughts of our enemies? If so, it will drastically increase the chances that we are both captured or killed."

Jon frowned. The obvious answer made him feel like a hypocrite. He took a deep breath and rubbed his eyes, painfully remembering the slice across his nose. "Fine. But just the bad guys, okay? No digging in the heads of everyone else."

"And how do I know who is and who is not a 'bad guy?'"

Jon rolled his eyes. "If they're shooting at us, or look like they're about to, then they are probably the bad guys. Until then, no mind-reading."

"As you wish, but you do love a challenge, Jon French."

Jon started to say something about the name thing but let it drop. He was tired and hurting, and things just kept getting weirder and weirder. He had absolutely no idea if Wayland Moore would even make the calls or whether they would make a difference if he did. He had no way of knowing if Craig Byce would honor the sit-down or just use it as the opportunity for an ambush. Jon admitted he had done a pretty good job of pissing in Byce's cornflakes on the way out of Knoxville, thanks to Idegen.

And now there was the military to worry about. He had to assume that they would use every possible asset on the table to track down Idegen. Way more than they'd ever consider to bring him, Byce, or even the entire Dixie Mafia down. In truth, he was surprised they had made it this far without seeing any soldiers.

Who knows? Maybe whatever military agency responsible for hunting down alien life forms is just as inept and inefficient as every other government operation. Maybe if we just keep overestimating them, we can keep one step ahead.

But for how long? Jon glanced at Idegen. There was no Wayland Moore, no sit-down, for her. As long as she was here on Earth, she would always be hunted. And as long as he was with her, probably even after, they would hunt him, too.

"So, what's your endgame?" he blurted.

"Endgame?"

"How do you see this ending for you? Even if you manage to elude the military for as long as you can. What's next?"

"Before I was captured, I sent a distress signal. I'm hoping that someone from the fleet will come and rescue me."

Jon swallowed, finally acknowledging what that meant. "So... you are a warrior... and your fleet is up there, nearby. Were you planning on invading us? Is that why you're here?"

Idegen looked at him, then made the turn onto the winding country highway that would take them through miles of farmland, forested hills, and not much else. "I had no specific orders to that effect. My mission was to observe and report only. A mission at which I failed, obviously. There was an accident as I entered the planet's atmosphere that kept me from making a stealthy insertion. This resulted in my confrontation with your Air Force."

"Accident?"

"When we came to this galaxy, your world had not yet put anything manmade into orbit, so my preliminary approach vectors had not been programmed with sufficient data. When my ship approached Earth, a bit of space flotsam managed to breach the shields at sufficient velocity to cause several systems to malfunction."

Jon blinked, wishing he had a straw to chew. "Wait... we've had satellites up since *Sputnik*; that was in the fifties, if I remember right. How long has your fleet been in our galaxy?"

Idegen kept her eyes on the road, and Jon got the sense that she was doing some form of algebra in her head. "According to timing and naming conventions, our fleet reached the outer edge of the Orion Spur on January 17, 1901."

"Holy shit," Jon said. "What have they been doing in all that time?"

Idegen sighed. "I only wish I knew."

***

Craig stretched out on the leather sofa of the Thor Outlaw 37BG as it shushed down rain-soaked I-75. Jesse sat at the little dinette on the other side of the big RV. Two of Craig's best bruiser boys sat at the wheel and in the passenger seat. Four cars and SUVs containing sixteen more of his crew ranged out in front of and behind them, keeping the speed limit and looking as innocent and as much unlike a convoy as possible.

"Lucky the manager owed you a favor," Jesse said, admiring the posh new vehicle.

"Hell with luck. That bastard's on the hook. Every year, he gets his college buddies and best clients together for a big Smoky Mountain getaway, and I supply the blow, the weed, and the girls. He owes me plenty of favors, sure, but luck had nothing to do with it."

Craig could tell Jesse wanted to say something more, and his anxious silence was as annoying as the bacon and eggs twisting in his guts. "What's really eating at you?"

Jesse sighed and ran a hand through his short hair. There was a slight tremor in that hand. "I don't like this, Craig. I don't like reacting instead of taking the initiative. I hate trusting that Moore's telling you the truth. That French is going to just walk into the trap. I think we should be out there beating the brush until we've got him strung up by his thumbs, and we can go to work."

Craig grunted. *So that's it. Jesse just needs to hurt someone.* The ex-soldier hadn't had any fun since they had killed Winchester in the basement, though Jesse had laughed quite a lot watching the squeamish Dr. Kirby take the Husqvarna to the corpse before feeding the bits to hungry German Shepherds and Rottweilers in his office. "Well, I'm glad to know what you don't like, what you hate, and what you think, Jesse. But seeing as how I'm still running things, we're gonna play this my way.

"Besides, we know the Feds were gonna issue a warrant for me today, so I needed to get out of town under a plausible excuse. An impromptu road trip to Atlanta's Cheetah Club with my boys does the trick nicely, and I just happened to forget my phone on the kitchen counter before leaving... So, shut up."

Jesse grinned, and there was murder in it. "Sure, Craig. I'll shut up."

Craig settled back into the sofa cushions and pulled his cap over his eyes. The rain was gone, and the sun was coming out. "Try to relax or something, will ya? When we get to Chattanooga, we'll stop for lunch and then make a little social call."

"Social call?" Craig didn't have to look to know that Jesse had sat up like a terrier hearing a UPS truck.

"Yeah. Been meaning to flex my muscles on some of the Folk down there for a while; just been too busy 'til now. So, I figured we'd kill two birds with one stone."

"Two birds? Or a few blackbirds? Sweet."

Craig closed his eyes and tried to go to sleep. He didn't have the heart to tell Jesse that he didn't want to kill anybody if he didn't have to. Besides, he'd let Jesse do the wet work when they caught their pigeons... *Blackbirds... I kind of like that...*

Several hours later, after a hearty lunch at Hamilton Place's Sticky Fingers Ribhouse, Craig sat on the sofa of the RV, watching the news. He had sent Jesse and two cars to the notorious Park City neighborhood near downtown to snag a couple gangbangers for an object lesson. He knew that Folk Nation had a sizeable presence in the city, but that neighborhood was where they were strongest, and the local cops tended to leave them alone so long as they stayed there.

Craig hoped that level of concentration and autonomy would not only make Jesse's mission easier but also make him more cautious. He had brought his biggest and best guns from Knoxville, but they were still heavily outnumbered unless he called in his reserves off the mountains and out of the suburbs, which would take time. Besides, Craig just wanted to make a demonstration, not start a full-scale gang war. Not yet, at any rate. He had other fish to fry.

"Your slick just called, boss," the driver said. "He said the Feds have issued the warrant, and a group of cops are on their way to serve it at your house right now."

Craig frowned at the expected news. He had hoped for a few more hours, enough time to get deeper into Georgia. But now the race was officially on. He had only so much time before they tracked him down, and he needed to make sure he had every bit of info he could squeeze from Jon French before they got him in cuffs. He also needed to make sure that French could not be called upon to testify against him. Time was now of the essence.

"Dammit. Where the hell is Jesse?"

The squeal and bark of tires answered.

"Shit," the driver said, looking through the huge windscreen. "That don't look good."

Craig started to jump to his feet, but the door flew open before he could. Jesse stood on the step, a broad smile on his blood-spattered face. He smelled of gunpowder. "Message delivered, boss!"

"What the fuck did you do?"

"The coons were having a barbeque down at the park," Jesse said, taking the hand towel from the kitchenette and wiping his hands and face. "A whole mess of 'em. I fanned us out in perfect military order, and we hit 'em from three sides. They never even saw it coming. Maximum casualties, minimum effort."

Craig looked over Jesse's shoulder at the overgrown parking lot behind the abandoned hosiery mill. The white X-terra they had taken was raked with bullet holes, the back windows were shot out, and a finger of smoke rose from the grill. "You maniac. How many did you lose?"

"None." Jesse picked broken glass from his hair. "Just some damage to the one vehicle and a few cuts. We were in and out before they knew a thing. We didn't even hear sirens until we were nearly back here, and they were all going the other way."

Craig grabbed him and yanked him into the RV. He shouted to the men standing around the wounded X-terra, "Burn that shit and get in the other rides. We've got to get the hell out of here, right now!"

He slammed the door and turned on Jesse, who still looked as proud as a peacock. "I told you I just wanted a prisoner or two. Not a fucking ambush!"

Jesse flopped onto the sofa as the big rig got moving. "You said you wanted to send a message, Craig. So that's what I delivered: the Dixie Mafia will not suffer nigger gangs in Chattanooga. I'm guessing when the dust settles, Folk Nation will have lost anywhere from six to a dozen of their best shooters, plus whatever collateral damage."

"Collateral damage?"

"I told you it was a barbeque. Girlfriends, baby mamas, kids, the whole works."

Craig felt so very old. He slid into the kitchenette chair and put his head in his hand. "You idiot," he said, but there was no force in his voice. "Don't you see what you've done? You just declared war, and now we're heading straight into their stronghold."

Jesse smiled. "Bring it. We'll call every gun-toting, sheet-wearing Son of Dixie in the Tri-State region and have 'em meet us there. We'll take Atlanta back in one, maybe two, nights, and the streets will run red with black blood."

He's a madman... How long has he been planning this? Has he been planning it? Did he just decide he was tired of playing my lapdog, and now he's got the war he was born and bred for? Or was this Orlando's plan all along? Get me embroiled in a struggle for Atlanta until I'm forced to beg them for help? Damn, damn, damn...

***

It was dark by the time they got into Rhea County. They had stopped for fuel, snacks, and some light first aid supplies in the wide-spot-in-the-road town of Helenwood and then again in the larger town of Harriman. Jon had Doritos breath and a sour stomach full of microwave burritos and Snickers bars, chewing on the straw from a forty-four-ounce Orange Crush fountain drink. He now had a pink

Dora the Explorer Band-Aid across the bridge of his nose, one wadded around the top of his right ear, and several more on the palms of his hands. Rinsing the wounds out with peroxide hadn't been much fun.

He also had a slight fever and was shivering despite wearing his Doctor's coat and having the heater vents aimed at his face. "There's no telling what that hillbilly son of a bitch used that knife for. I've probably got hoof-and-mouth disease, herpes, leprosy, and West Nile," he said through chattering teeth.

"You need antibiotics." Idegen guided the Raptor through near-empty Spring City. "From what I can tell, this medication is difficult to acquire without a medical professional's written consent. Is that correct?"

Jon grunted. "Yep. Best way to control folks is to hold their healthcare hostage. But if we go to a hospital, the cops are likely to get involved, or even worse, Big Brother's goons who are after you."

Idegen nodded. "I could break into one of your... pharmacies."

Jon shook his head. "Too much risk. Maybe my body can fight this off, whatever it is. Just need some vitamins and orange juice. Maybe some chicken soup."

"I do not think that is sufficient, Jon." He knew she was right by the way he already felt. Like a corpse that had forgotten it was dead.

"Well..." He regretted thinking this, much less saying it. "I might know someone who has antibiotics on hand. It's even odds if he'll give them to me or not, though."

"Who?"

"My father."

Blue lights flashed behind them, and a siren warbled once.

"Damn," Jon said. "How fast were you going?"

Idegen frowned. "I was following the posted speed limit, Jon."

He sighed. "Just some bored local Barney who happened to notice the out-of-state tags. Pull us over and pray he'll be content with a look at your cleavage."

"Oh, I can do better than that, Jon."

Before he could ask for elaboration, a stocky, flat-topped Rhea County Sheriff's deputy was standing at Idegen's window, waving a flashlight into the cab. "License and registration, miss."

Jon couldn't see Idegen's face, only the back of her head as she spoke. "I'm sorry, officer, but that won't be possible."

Jon cleared his throat to try and start some kind of fast talk, but nothing came to mind.

"And just why not, miss?" The cop leaned down on the door. Jon could see his face clearly, and he didn't need to be a mind reader to know what he was thinking.

Jon thought about the Taurus Judge tucked into the back of his jeans. He thought about the two or three pistols Idegen had on her person. He thought of the various rifles, shotguns, handguns, and ammunition in the Gladiator bag in the backseat.

There are only two ways this ends: either we kill this cop and keep going, or we give up and go to jail, which means both of us are dead within the next few days... But killing a cop is an entirely different thing from killing a psycho rapist redneck who's trying to gut you and feed you to his pigs...

Idegen's chuckle brought Jon out of his thoughts. The cop was smiling. He touched the arm she had put up on the door. "All right, Ms. Dawn," he said with a wink. "I'll let you go with a warning this time. But I'm gonna stop by Kelly's Motel and check on y'all first thing in the morning, just to make sure you got there safe, okay?"

"Thank you, Deputy Norris. I'd like that. Perhaps we could get some coffee and breakfast? My brother likes to sleep late."

"Sounds good. And call me Steve."

"Okay, Steve. I'll see you at breakfast."

He patted the doorframe and stepped back. "Be safe."

Idegen started the truck and slowly pulled back onto the highway. She glanced into the rearview mirror as the blue lights vanished. "Human males are so easily manipulated by their sex drives."

Jon sighed, pushed himself back into the seat, and closed his eyes. "More like we're easily manipulated by a pretty face and a soft touch. Both of which you have, by the way. You could have been Helen of Troy, the Face that Launched a Thousand Ships."

"You flatter me, but that may be the fever talking."

"It's true, though. You're gorgeous..." He thought about how she had laughed at him in the Middlesboro Mall and how she had bedded down in her skivvies without a thought of him. "But I guess I'm just not your type, huh?"

"You are not even my species, Jon. But no, I suppose you are not 'my type.'"

"You have a special someone up there?" He waved at the stars beyond the windshield. "Some Han Solo or Captain Kirk type?"

She furrowed her brow, probably searching her neural web for the references. "No... More like a Leia... or a Ripley..."

Jon blinked. "You mean Princess Leia from *Star Wars*? Ripley from *Alien*? Carrie Fisher and Sigourney Weaver?"

Idegen smiled. "Something like that, though perhaps Aeryn Sun from *Farscape* might be more accurate. Her name is Vodie

Shalamazar, and we were inseparable and unconquerable. She is strong and beautiful. She is... perfect."

Jon exhaled. "Wow, that's a... a bombshell from a bombshell. Now I don't feel so bad."

"And why would you feel bad? I do not understand."

Jon opened his mouth to explain, then realized he couldn't. "Nothing. Doesn't matter."

Idegen studied him from the corner of her eye, and he was afraid she might be looking at his thoughts, so he imagined Barney the Dinosaur at a strip club doing body shots off the naked *Golden Girls*. He shook the thought from his head, hoping it was as distasteful to her as it was to him.

"And you, Jon," she prompted. "What of this one you love, this Angie? Did you and she not grow up together in this area?"

Jon frowned. "Yes, but you said you weren't going to snoop around in my head anymore. That's private."

"I am sorry. That was information I gathered yesterday on our way into Kentucky. So, please, tell me about her. I told you of Vodie."

Jon rubbed his face, grimaced at the pain in his nose and hands. "Nothing to tell, really. Boy meets girl, boy falls in love with girl, boy and girl get engaged, boy boinks another girl, girl hates boy and never wants to see him again. You know, that old chestnut."

"You do have a habit of making poor decisions, Jon."

"Thanks for the news flash. Let's just hope going to visit my dear old dad isn't one of them."

But his irritable gut told him it would be.

17

17

Mdegen watched the prosaic scenery slip past them in the dark. The wide, four-lane highway seemed superfluous as it passed through the rural, lightly populated landscape. There were other vehicles on the road, but not many. She thought Jon might sleep until they reached his father's home, but every minute or so, he would say something about another obscure landmark.

"There's where I went to high school," he indicated a sprawling complex flanked by athletic fields and parking lots in a depression at the foot of a forested hill to the right of the highway. Nodding to a building across the road that looked like a chimera of market, gas station, and apartment building, he added, "And that's where I bought my first beer on a fake ID."

Miles and minutes later, he shook his head. "Place has changed a lot since the last time I was here. Not for the better, as far as I can tell... That used to be the drive-in movie theater," his voice sounded sad as he indicated a used car lot beneath a massive political billboard. "I saw my first movie there right before they shut it down. Damn. Never thought I'd spend another Friday night in this town."

Just over the hill from this memorable milestone was the medical center where he had been born. Right across from the place was where he had rented his first dirty movie, which was now, ironically enough, a Baptist revival hall. Fast food joints, barbeque stands, antiquated strip malls, car washes, oil change facilities, and a surprising number of Mexican restaurants edged the shoulders of Highway 27 as it passed through Dayton, Tennessee: the historic site of the infamous Scopes "Monkey Trial."

After passing the brick monstrosity where Jon had gone to middle school (and where he had kissed Angie for the first time), he waved at a large, impressively columned building on the left beside yet another car wash. "That's where we had my brother's funeral." He was quiet for a long time after that.

Idegen did not need to read his thoughts to know that he was wrestling with vivid memories and emotions conjured by this town.

"I assume we are getting close to your father's house?" She hoped to drag him away from the internal discomfort she could see hardening his injured face. His dark hair was damp at his temples and brow. The fever had not yet broken.

Jon rubbed his nose and winced at the sudden pain. "Yeah, at the other end of the county, just a few miles south of town. He got a big settlement after falling off a roof a couple years ago, and finally moved out of the trailer park. It's an old farmhouse up on a hill just off from the highway. Pretty secluded, which is good for us."

After passing new strip malls, the Walmart Supercenter, Rhea Memorial Gardens, the 84 Lumber, and leaving the Dayton city limits, Jon said, "So tell me about your home. Your world. What's it like up there?" He waved a shaky hand at the roof.

Idegen smiled at her memories. "It is …amazing, Jon. There are hundreds of thousands of worlds inhabited by sentient beings. Many so different that you can scarcely imagine them, and many more who look much like you and me. So many of them subject to the Empire—"

"So, you are a race of conquerors?" She heard the fearful accusation in his voice.

"And you are not? I have looked at the historical record of this world, Jon. Shall I elaborate for you?" When he shrugged in capitulation, she continued. "My home world is not very unlike this one. Larger, and with less ecological diversity, perhaps, but still a world of vast cities and sprawling agricultural reserves. Lit by a singular star by day and a singular moon by night. In truth, our civilizations are not all that dissimilar."

"Aside from the spaceships and the blood drinking, you mean."

Idegen winced. "The… blood drinking, as you call it, is not a natural trait of my species, Jon. It is a result of my indoctrination into the Order of the Black Star Worlds, the elite military unit I mentioned earlier. It is a means of perfecting our physical powers so that we might better serve the Empire in all facets of war."

"And your… Vodie? Is she also a member of this Black Star organization?"

Idegen frowned and shook her head. "No, Jon. As I said, she is perfect." She looked at him, reached over and pulled the collar of his coat tighter around his pale chin. "Maybe you should get some rest before we get to your father's. I am sure that he will be glad to see you."

"Yeah," Jon said, breathing hard. "And I am sure Craig Byce wants to shake my hand... His place is just over that hill on the left."

Idegen was about to comment when Jon's eyes rolled back in his head, and he passed out.

***

So it's come to this.

Craig sat on the tiny crapper in the moving RV, his head in his hands, his pants around his ankles, and his "empire" slipping through his fingers while broken glass and barbed wire moved slowly through his colon. "Damn," he whispered, wiping sweat or maybe tears from his eyes. "Damn."

He could hear Jesse laughing as he made his phone calls, just as he was sure Jesse and the two bruisers could hear his grunts and farts. *The old man's shitting himself to death while our new king is making plans for war.*

And he was, too. Jesse had already called Dillon Crabtree in Atlanta, letting him know they were on their way to help take back his city from Folk Nation. Then he had called somebody named Hammer, who apparently was a big cog in the machine of White Atlanta Reich, a Peckerwood gang trying to earn its way into the Dixie Mafia. He was spreading the word: "Sharpen your knives. Load your guns. Call your friends. Change is coming. Atlanta will be pure again."

This started out as a hunt for a snitch, and now he's turned it into a damned crusade...

And then, as Craig had expected, Jesse called Orlando. His tone changed significantly. Much of his swagger and bravado was replaced by matter-of-fact soldierly discipline. He was Florida's man and would probably continue to be once he sat on Craig's "throne." At least for the first few years. Then, Craig could see the ambitious little shit growing ballsy and turning on the hand that feeds. He could see a Dixie Mafia civil war coming down the pike in the next ten years or so, with Jesse Sneed at its center. And then Folk Nation and the Peckerwoods would sit back and watch, wait for the dust to settle. Then, they'd fight for the leftovers.

At least I won't be around to see that happen.

Craig gnashed his teeth and rocked as the pain writhed through his innards, forcing the air from his lungs and the tears from his eyes. And then it passed. For the moment, at least. But he could already feel the next wave coiling, ready to strike. "Damn," he whispered. "Maybe this situation is a blessing in disguise. Maybe I'll go out in a blaze of glory instead of rotting away from the inside out. Maybe this is what I've always really wanted."

He nodded in acceptance, swallowing down the fear. *The fear of death, the fear of the pain growing worse and more frequent as time goes on. The fear of all that happening as I waste my final days behind bars. Hell of a choice, but I gotta think the bullet is the better of the two.*

Concluding his business, Craig flushed and washed his hands, hit the air with some Glade Tropic Mist. Squeezing out of the tiny lavatory, he stepped into the bedroom at the back of the RV and opened his suitcase. Buried at the bottom was his gun, an old school, Vietnam-era Colt 1911A1. A commander's gun. He pulled it from its case, checked the loaded magazine, and slid it into the concealment holster before tucking it into his jeans.

"So, the old man finally goes to war."

***

Jon woke to the overwhelming smell of cigarettes. Marlboro reds.

He sat up, his head feeling too big for his battered body and his mouth tasting like the floor of a public toilet. He had no idea where he was, and almost every inch of his body ached. The room was dark, faint grey light filtering in through yellow-tinted curtains. Then he saw the bright orange pinpoint in the corner.

"Still alive, boy? Well, I reckon we got that much in common."

"Dad." Jon swung his feet off the old sofa, awakening a new level of pain. "How are you?" It seemed the appropriate thing to say and the only thing that came to mind.

"Fair," the old man said before breaking into a hacking cough. Jon heard him spit something wet into a mason jar; then he took another pull from his cigarette. "I'm fair. Maybe even better than you, from the looks of it."

Jon's eyes adjusted enough to see his father, or what was left of him, cradled in the old La-Z-Boy. The mason jar sat on a small table next to his recliner. His slippered feet were up on the elevated footrest, an oversized and stained Alabama Crimson Tide hoodie enveloping his emaciated frame. A slender green oxygen tank stood just to the side of the chair, its clear plastic tubes running up the arm to his father's nose. Just an inch above the lit Marlboro. A much bigger chrome tank stood behind the chair.

"Shit, Dad, it's a wonder you haven't blown yourself up yet."

The old man chuckled, coughed. "You'd like that, wouldn't you? Show up for the funeral and the insurance payout, and then be back on the road to your next card game or whoring one-night stand before the grave dirt even settled."

Jon sighed and rubbed his face, winced at the throb in his cheekbone and nose. "We haven't seen each other in a long time. Do you really want to start criticizing each other's lifestyles right off the bat? Or do I need to go see how much booze you've got stashed in the kitchen?"

"Show's what you know. I haven't had a drink since I fell off that roof. I'm clean two years, seven months, and sixteen days. Got the chips to prove it."

"Well bully for you." Jon got up and tried to stretch. "Why is it so dark in here? And warm? Don't you have power?"

"Sure. Just don't want to pay for it if I don't have to. Not much to see around here. And I stay cold nowadays, so don't need no air conditioner."

"Well, I'd like to see where I'm going. Care if I turn on a light or two?"

"Sure, if you're willing to pay the bill."

Jon grunted. "I'll leave a few bucks on the table."

He flicked on a lamp and wished he hadn't.

The room's hardwood floor was bare and dirty, littered with old newspapers, magazines, and fast-food wrappers. A pair of overstuffed garbage bags sat in the corner beside the recliner. *At least the cigarettes are covering the smell of those.* The wallpaper was peeling and stained almost brown by nicotine, and the plastered ceiling was yellowed and chipping. The sofa, the recliner, and the curtains all looked like they had been brand new in 1976 but had seen a hell of a lot of mileage in the ensuing decades.

But the crowning horror was the mummy enthroned on the threadbare goldenrod La-Z-Boy. Jon's father had never been a big, powerful man, but now he looked like a shriveled bag of sticks that was too fragile to lift his cigar store Indian of a head. The old man's hair, once black and lustrous, was now iron grey and white, cut to a short bristle that exposed his liver-spotted scalp. His cheeks had hollowed to such an extent that his blue eyes bulged like robins' eggs on jutting cheekbones flanking a razorblade of a hooked nose. Only the lips working around the lit Marlboro even remotely reminded Jon of the man who had terrorized him as a small child.

"Damn, Dad. You look like hell."

"Seen a mirror lately, bucko? You ain't exactly Mr. Rhea County no more."

Jon subconsciously increased the distance between himself and the lit cigarette and oxygen tank combo. He looked around but saw no sign of Idegen. *Surely she didn't dump me and tear out on her own. Of course, if she shared more than two words with him, I couldn't blame her if she did.* "Where's Idegen, the girl who brought me here?"

"The Polack? Or is she a Jew? Whatever she is, she ain't American. What the hell you doing bringing somebody like that into my house? She's easy on the eye, but she might as well be a colored girl."

"Well, I see your newfound sobriety hasn't changed your redneck prejudices." Jon ran a hand through his greasy hair. "So, where is she?"

The old man took another slow drag on the cigarette. "She'll be back. Why you care? You in *love* with that Polack? You makin' Jew babies?"

Jon closed his eyes and tried to stay calm. "Look, I need some antibiotics. If you'll give me a couple, we'll be on our way."

"Already did," the old man growled, stumping out the butt in an overflowing ashtray and reaching for the pack. "That gal forced one down your throat before she stretched you out on the couch, and she pocketed a couple more for later."

Jon raised an eyebrow, wondering exactly how that conversation had gone down. *Did Idegen threaten him or use her psychic mumbo jumbo?* "And how did she convince you to agree to that?"

His father looked away as he lit the next cigarette. Jon winced at the Bic's flame so close to the oxygen line. "I don't rightly know. Musta caught me in a moment of sentimentality. I just saw you was in a bad way, and, well... hell, Jon, I'm still your daddy."

Jon inhaled sharply. *Yeah, and I can never change that.* "Well... thanks. Do you need anything before we go? I've got a little cash..." He looked around. "Maybe I could clean up around here a bit. Maybe go get you some dinner."

"Your gal's already gone up to the KFC. Should be back in a bit. But don't do me any favors."

Jon shook his head, wondering why things had never been easy between the two of them, never been good. Once, when he was very young, he had heard his mother and aunts talking about something of that nature, but he did not remember it. Not really, and so he always wondered if it had really happened at all or if his childish mind had just created the confusing images to go with the angry tale.

"Did you really try to drown me when I was a baby?" The blurted question surprised him as much as it did his father.

"No," the old man spat. He looked at the floor. "Not really... It was a long time ago..."

Jon sat on the arm of the rickety sofa. His heart pounded. "What are you saying?"

His father's eyes flicked at him, then returned to the filthy floor. "I was giving you a bath while your mama was at work. I'd already given Kevin his... he was squalling on the bedroom floor, raising all kinds of racket, getting on my last nerve—"

"You had a hangover," Jon whispered with certainty.

"Maybe," his father grunted. "Who the hell knows? Anyways, you shit in the tub... And my first reaction was to—" he swallowed and lowered his voice— "to rub your nose in it."

Jon looked at the cracked ceiling and gave a bitter chuckle. "You almost killed me as a baby, and then you killed Kevin years later."

"You shut your filthy mouth!" the old man snapped. He sat up, trying to look formidable and failing miserably. "I loved Kevin. He was a good boy, a strong boy. Not a shit heel, crybaby mama's boy like you!"

Jon stood over the old man and licked his lips, cherishing the coup de grâce that he'd wanted to deliver most of his life. "Dad, Kevin was gay."

"Bullshit!" But Jon could tell by the hollow look in his father's eyes that he had always known, that the shot had struck the mark. "When that Polack Jew bitch gets back here, you and her get the hell off my property, and don't you ever come back!"

"Kevin was gay, Dad. And your bigotry killed him. He knew he could never live up to what you expected. He knew he could never be the son you wanted him to be, and so he couldn't live with that failure. He was the one who hanged himself, but you're the one who put his head in that noose."

The room was quiet. Jon heard the blood rushing in his ears and the air wheezing through his father's lungs.

Tears welled up in the old man's eyes, and his narrow chest heaved. "I know," he whispered, his lip trembling. "Just like I know I'm the one that drove your mama off. It's always been me, my fault." He swatted at his eyes and looked up at Jon, trying to firm up his quivering jaw. "I reckon I drove you off, too."

"Yeah, you did. The night I brought Angie over to tell you we were getting married, and you ran her off, saying she was a whore who was just trying to ruin my future. That pretty much did it. In fact, I thought about killing you that night."

The old man smiled a nasty-toothed grin. "Oh yeah? And what changed your mind, bucko?"

"The coach at MTSU called that night, offering me the scholarship. That's probably the only thing that saved your miserable life."

The old man wheezed a bitter chuckle and waved at the squalor surrounding him. "Like I said, don't do me any favors, Jonny-boy."

Jon wanted to say either something even more hurtful or something that would start to heal the breach, but he couldn't decide which. Headlights raked the window. The rumble of the Raptor's engine outside saved him from making the decision. "Sounds like your dinner's here."

Jon opened the front door and stepped onto the wraparound concrete porch, gulping in the fresh night air. Idegen slammed on the brakes beneath a pole-mounted security light at the end of the driveway, jumped from the Raptor without turning off the engine.

"They're coming, Jon! We have to go!"

***

Sharpe stood in the C&C, watching the overhead monitors. They displayed the green-tinted night-vision feeds from Honcho's, Archer's, and Ramrod's helmet cams and similar feeds from the hovering Kiowas. The three Alphas made another textbook insertion into another hillbilly homestead, this one less cluttered and unpopulated by livestock. Almost abandoned. Again, she clutched the back of Hack-Job's and Tunes's chairs, silently praying this was the end of the line for the alien invader and her miscreant sidekick.

Come on, come on, get her, get her...

"Vehicle's secured," Archer announced, his feed displaying the empty Ford Raptor parked in the driveway. The vehicle the targets had taken from the Tacketts in Kentucky had subsequently turned up on a routine traffic stop just an hour or so before. "Hood's still warm."

"Outbuildings secured," Ramrod declared after clearing the empty barn, tool shed, and detached garage.

Honcho gave hand signals. His men fanned out, approached the dilapidated old two-story farmhouse from three sides. Honcho climbed the steps to the front door, paused, then whispered into his mike. "It's dark, but somebody's in there. Knock or breach, Colonel? Your call."

Sharpe resisted the urge to rub her forehead in hesitation. *Making war on our own people...* "Do it," she said. "Full breach."

Honcho kicked in the front door. A quick glance at the other monitors showed Archer and Ramrod forcing entrances into the house.

"Well, come the hell on in," a spindly old man in a recliner said, his scratchy voice filled with bitterness. "Not like this is private property or nothing."

Honcho kept the old man at gunpoint while the other two cleared the house. There was no sign of either the subject or the human accomplice.

"Ask him where they went. How long they've been gone," Sharpe said through gritted teeth. *Not again, not again...*

Honcho relayed the questions. The old man coughed, slid a cigarette out of a crumpled pack on the side table. "I got rights, y'know. A whole Bill o' Rights, as a matter of fact, and you sonsabitches are trampling all over 'em. I also got me a pretty good hotshot lawyer up in Dayton who has a taste for fancy cars and pretty young ladies. I bet he'd love to sink his teeth into your ass right about now."

"Mr. French," Honcho said, his voice cold and hard. "We represent the United States Government in the lawful pursuit of an enemy of the state. You will cooperate with our efforts, or you will face severe consequences. Now, where is your son? Where is the woman who was with him? How long have they been gone? What did they do or say while they were here?"

"My son..." The old man rolled the cigarette around in his fingers as if studying it, admiring and savoring it. "My son is a damn fine man, in spite of all the shit I put him through." He looked up at Honcho. "He's all I got left in this world, mister. So, if you think I'm gonna help you lot run him down, you got a thing or two coming. Now get out of my house."

Sharpe could see in the man's hateful eyes that he wasn't going to talk. She was about to tell Honcho to bring him in when she noticed the thin tube running across the old man's upper lip. The oxygen tanks beside the recliner. She saw the Bic lighter in his hand.

"Honcho!"

All three feeds went white and staticky. Hack-Job and Tunes jerked back, yanking their headsets away as the explosion fed directly into their ears. The feeds from the choppers showed flames blowing out the windows of the lower level.

Sharpe bit her lip, felt the pain swell in her hips then stampede up her spine like an elephant in high heels. "SITREP!"

The feeds came back online. She heard the men coughing, could see bright white glares from fire scattered around the hazy room. Two of the feeds showed movement, the third did not. "Man down," Archer coughed. "Man down! Honcho's down!"

"How bad?" Sharpe snapped.

"Burns," Archer replied, still coughing. "Some slight shrapnel. Probably a concussion. The civilian is toast, though."

"Get out of there," Sharpe said. "Get Honcho back ASAP. And let that place burn to the ground." Turning to Tunes, she said, "Notify Park West Hospital, have a trauma team standing by. Route Honcho's chopper there and have the other two report to me the moment they touch down here."

She stormed from the C&C. The phone in her pocket vibrated. It was a text from Mr. White: *SITREP.* Sharpe rolled her eyes and went straight to her appropriated office, slammed the door before flopping down behind the desk.

She stared at the phone for as long as she dared before typing in her response: *Subject still MIA. Alpha one man down. Helbourne almost finished with tracker. Ship located. Scheduled for transfer to ORNL.*

A spectral knife of burning ice entered her left hip, severed her tailbone, and lacerated her right ass cheek when she hit SEND. The pain was so sharp and sudden she almost cried out and doubled over in the chair. Her hands shook and tears filled her eyes. She gulped air and rubbed the muscles of her hips, trying desperately to make the pain go away.

The phone rang.

Sharpe closed her eyes and swallowed, bracing herself. She answered, "Colonel Sharpe."

"This FUBAR situation has gone on long enough, Colonel," the man said. "I've one more thing to take care of here, and then I'll be on my way to Knoxville. You've got about twenty-four hours to get your house in order, or I'm bringing a big-ass broom, and I'll be the one cleaning up. Copy that?"

"Yes, sir. Will comply."

The line went dead. She felt cold all over, and the numbness that spread through her body was not as much a relief as she had hoped. It was exhaustion, not relaxation. She still hurt, but her body simply couldn't deal with the pain anymore. She put her face in her hands and wanted to cry, which only made her angry. *I'm just so tired. When was the last time I slept a full night? When was the last time I didn't hurt? When was the last time I took a break and thought about anything but all this? How long have I been burning the candle at both ends?*

The door flew open, and Dr. Helbourne stormed in. "This is entirely unacceptable, Colonel!" he snapped, waving a printout like a torch or a pitchfork.

Sharpe pulled herself together in a flash. She sat up straight behind the desk and glared at the little man. "Dr. Helbourne, I've just had a man severely injured in an attempt to recapture the subject and have been informed that my superior will soon be relieving me of my command. So, for your sake, I sincerely hope that this unprofessional demonstration is merited by the severity of your complaint."

Helbourne's face drained in the blast of her icy tone. His lips moved and his jowls quivered, his wide eyes blinking. "I... I'm sorry, Colonel," he said, licking his lips and dropping his gaze to the floor. "I... I didn't realize..."

"What is so unacceptable, Doctor?"

Helbourne cleared his throat. "The Navy just reported that a storm in the Gulf is hampering their efforts to retrieve the craft. They've pulled their ships back to base to wait it out."

Sharpe closed her eyes and rubbed her temple. "A purely sensible precaution, Doctor. How many U.S. servicemen have already perished because of the subject's intrusion? No need to add an entire ship's crew to that total, I should think."

Helbourne's shoulders sagged, and he looked at the printout as if there were more guidance to be had. "I'm... I'm sorry," he said. "I just keep thinking that the sooner we understand them and their technology, the better our chances of survival when they arrive in force. To my way of thinking, there is no price too high to make sure of that."

"Duly noted, Doctor. And what about your tracking algorithm?"

"Some finetuning left to do, but almost finished. Should be ready by morning."

Sharpe raised her chin, saying nothing else.

Helbourne turned to go, then stopped in the door. "Who was hit? How bad?"

Sharpe studied him for a moment, wondering about his sincerity. "It was Honcho. A civilian accomplice detonated an IED in his proximity. He was badly burned, but I think he should pull through."

Helbourne gave a curt nod. "I hope so." He closed the door behind him.

Sharpe sat back in the uncomfortable chair and exhaled. She fished into the breast pocket of her BDUs and pulled out the Vicodin bottle. She did not think twice before swallowing a whole pill this time. And for some damn reason, despite everything else, she found herself craving the Colonel's Original Recipe.

18
REMEMBER TO BREATHE

It was all Jon could do to keep the 1973 Plymouth Barracuda from demolishing the posted speed limit as he headed back into Dayton. Though it was primed gray and unpainted, his father had poured a good portion of his dwindling finances into restoring the classic muscle car, including dropping a 426 Hemi big block under the hood. Where and how the old man had gotten his hands on that, Jon would never know.

"I hope this works." Jon wiped the sweat from his aching face. His fever was all but gone, but the multitude of hurts he had taken at the hands of big Jim Tackett were still raging in full force.

"We have been moving south," Idegen said. "They will not expect us to reverse our course. Not anytime soon, at any rate."

Jon planned to take 60 over to Highway 58 in Georgetown and follow it all the way into Chattanooga before jumping on I-75 and making for Atlanta. He hoped that was the best route to stay off the military's radar. Trying to relax, his thoughts drifted back to the moments just before they'd left his father's house.

"I figured you was on the run," the old man had snapped as Jon and Idegen had hurried back into the living room. "What is it this time? You owe money to the wrong folks? She somebody else's wife?"

Jon had frowned, trying to ignore his father. "How do you know?" he asked Idegen as she handed the old man the red and white box of the Colonel's Original Recipe.

She had glanced at his father and said, "I just *know*. They are close, and they do not plan on capturing me this time."

Jon had felt all the wind go out of his sails. "Sorry to rush off, Dad, but we've got to go."

His father had surprised him. "Take my car. It's faster than anything you've got, and whoever they are, they're not looking for it yet." He fished into his sweatpants and pulled out a small keyring with old Chrysler keys on it.

Jon had reached for the keys. "Thanks..."

The old man had grabbed his hand like a vice grip, fixing him with his watery blue eyes. "I know I never did right by you... or Kevin or your mother, for that matter. But I've always loved you, boy. I'm sorry I just never knew how to show it."

Jon's Adam's apple had felt like a bowling ball. He took the keys with a curt nod and hurried from the house. "Leave him the keys to the truck," he told Idegen, his voice barely a whisper. "I'll fetch the guns..."

Idegen was watching him from the passenger seat. He could see her face glowing in the light of passing headlights, her eyes fierce and green. "Penny for your thoughts," she said. "I believe that is the expression."

"That man back there..." Jon swallowed hard and wished he had a straw. "He wasn't the man who raised me. More like his shadow. Or his ghost."

She turned back to face the windshield. "I never knew my parents."

"Really? How's that work? Were you an orphan or something?"

"No. I was bred for the military and raised in a sister cell with eleven other female warriors. We lived and trained as a single unit. That is where I met Vodie."

He started to comment on how weird it was that Vodie had started as her sister before becoming her special someone. But then it occurred to him, *Isn't that exactly how my relationship with Angie progressed?* He thought about that old Brooke Shields movie, *The Blue Lagoon.*

"So..." He cleared his throat. "Your race, your people—they don't have courtships, date, marry, have kids, get divorced, like we do?"

Idegen shook her head. "Not really. There are some old, powerful families who still have ceremonial and arranged unions. But our entire culture is centered on perfection, Jon. Couples are selected and matched by the Empire for their genetic makeup and the offspring their union is projected to produce. In many cases, such as in specialized roles like mine, the parents never even meet. Their genetic material is harvested, combined, and matured in a fertilization facility."

"You're a test-tube baby?"

Idegen laughed. "I suppose that is an accurate, if incomplete, analogy. Yes."

Jon inhaled. "What you're talking about is eugenics. The creation of a 'master race.' You know they've tried that here on Earth a couple times... So, what you're telling me, in essence, is that your people are space Nazis?"

Idegen rolled her eyes and sighed. "You humans and your labels. In *essence*, Jon, I am Idegen Videshee: Warrior of the Order of the Black Star, and Cell-commander, Scout-section of the Deep Space Exploration Fleet of the Logonijy Empire. And, as I have said before, and I hope that I have proven, I am your friend."

Jon cracked a smile. "How messed up is it that you're probably one of the best I've ever had?"

She laughed. His phone rang.

"It's Moore," he said, answering. He listened to the information the old Kentuckian rattled off before hanging up. He turned to Idegen. "Our meeting is set for a chop shop in Kirkwood, midnight tomorrow. He said I was promised 'safe passage,' like we're in the Middle Ages or something."

"You think it is a trap?"

"Oh, I *know* it's a trap." Jon chewed on the inside of his swollen jaw. "But I've got a hotrod muscle car, a trunk load of guns, and a sexy vampire-cyborg-Nazi-warrior woman from outer space. What could possibly go wrong?"

***

"There," Helbourne said before breaking into a gargantuan yawn. He hit the ENTER key and watched the data transfer begin. As the percentile bar slowly filled, he rubbed tired eyes and stretched, glancing at his watch. "No wonder... Nearly five in the morning. I wonder if I should even bother going to bed..."

He looked around the dark, empty lab. "Humph. Talking to myself. Not a good sign, Marty, old boy. Pushing yourself too hard these past few days." Thankfully, another yawn cut off the stream of babble. When the upload was complete, he ejected the flash drive, grabbed his suit jacket, and headed for the C&C. "I wonder which of Sharpe's cyber-warriors will be on duty."

As it turned out, none of Alpha's personnel were there. Just a handful of exhausted and bored Air Guard NCOs. Most of these didn't give him a second glance as he entered the darkened room that reminded him of a video arcade from the eighties. Suppressing another yawn, he stepped up to a middle-aged Hispanic woman wearing her salt and pepper hair pulled back in a tight bun. He noted the star and four rockers on her camouflaged sleeve.

"Where are the Alpha specialists, Sergeant?"

The woman looked up with an expressionless gaze. "Gone to see their squad leader in the hospital—Doctor."

Helbourne frowned. "Here's the tracking algorithm." He held out the flash drive. "Get it loaded into the DOD satellite, and I'll start the fine-tuning myself."

The staff sergeant looked at the drive for a moment, then looked back at him with those dispassionate brown eyes. She did not move to accept the device. "I'm sorry, Doctor. I have no orders permitting me to install new software on any of our systems."

Helbourne was exhausted, hungry, and extremely irritable. And he had lost his last confrontation with Sharpe, slinking away like a whipped dog. "Now see here, Sergeant..." he glanced at the nametag sewn above her breast pocket. "Vasquez. I am Doctor Martin Helbourne, and I have been working side by side with Colonel Sharpe on this case from the beginning. *Before*, actually. And I have just spent the better part of the past twelve hours writing this rather extensive program. I would try to explain it to you, but I doubt you could comprehend even the most rudimentary points of my equations or, I very much doubt, the advanced mathematics systems used in constructing those equations. So, I want this installed on that satellite right now."

Staff Sergeant Vasquez folded her arms and sat back in the chair, cocking her head. "And I want a full body massage with a happy ending from Idris Elba." She pursed her lips. "But, as you may or may not understand, Doctor, we very seldom get what we want in this life. Now, unless you've got written orders from Colonel Sharpe or can get her to come over here and issue them in person, you might as well take your little equations and insert them into a slot where the sun don't shine."

Helbourne's nostrils flared, and the hair stood up on the back of his neck. He gnashed his teeth and squeezed his fists. "How... dare... you..."

The woman stood and, in her military boots, was a few inches taller than he. "I may not be able to do your fancy math, but I do know how to follow orders and protocol. And right now, I'm responsible for these machines, including that taxpayer-owned DOD satellite you're so interested in.

"Now, I could explain the chain of command and custody to you, *Doctor*, but I doubt you would care about even the most rudimentary procedures or, I very much doubt, the ethical purposes thereof."

Helbourne raised his finger but couldn't think of anything to say. Or rather, he thought of a hundred things to say, and they were all very nasty. Instead, he turned on his heel and stalked from the room, making a beeline for Sharpe's office.

"I'm sorry, Doctor," the red-eyed orderly said over a Styrofoam cup of coffee. "The colonel left strict orders that she is not to be disturbed before 0700 hours."

"You mean to tell me there's absolutely no way I can get my tracking algorithm loaded onto that satellite before then?"

"I'm afraid not. I'll be happy to give Colonel Sharpe a message when she comes in."

Helbourne rubbed his eyes. "No. That won't be necessary. If I'm not here waiting for her, she'll come find me. Thank you."

Taking a deep breath, he reluctantly decided it was probably all for the best. *I could use a couple hours' sleep myself.*

Only it wasn't a couple of hours. Sharpe didn't wake him until almost eleven o'clock. She, too, had overslept. And she was not happy about it. "Why the hell isn't that tracking algorithm uploaded?" she barked through his room's door while pounding on the other side.

Helbourne sat up, angry before he was even awake. "Ask Staff Sergeant Vasquez!" he shot back. "Give me a damn minute!" He cursed under his breath as he pulled on his wrinkled pants and shirt and looked for his socks and shoes. *Hell of a way to start a Saturday...* Finding them, he unlocked the door and sat back on the bed to don the sweat-damp footwear.

Sharpe entered the room like a storm cloud about to spit lightning and tornadoes. "What are you talking about? Did you finish the program or not?"

Helbourne indicated the flash drive on the dresser. "Of course I finished it! But you'd left no orders with the people in the C&C to upload it, so I got snagged in red tape. I went to your office looking for you, but you'd left word not to be disturbed." He looked at his watch and rolled his eyes. "I thought it was only a two-hour difference. I figured you'd wake me at seven like the orderly said."

Sharpe stood straight, closed her eyes, and rubbed her temples. Taking a few long breaths, she finally said, "Okay. We've still got time." She snagged the flash drive and turned to leave. "I'll get this in the works. Go ahead and take a shower and shave, Doctor. That's an order."

Helbourne glared as the door slammed behind her. "Bitch," he said before sniffing his armpit. He decided to obey the order.

Thirty minutes later, freshly scrubbed and in clean clothes, he walked into the fully staffed C&C to find Sharpe conferring with Tunes and Hack-Job. She turned to give him a quick appraisal without comment. "The programs are uploaded, and the system is rebooting. It should be back online in a few minutes. The problem is, right now, the satellite is over the South China Sea. It'll be a few hours before we can focus it on the continental United States."

Helbourne frowned. "Still wouldn't hurt to run those tests. We don't know for certain that she's the only visitor we have."

Sharpe pursed her lips. "I'd already thought of that. And I seriously hope that is not the case. As much trouble as this one has caused, I'd hate to think we have an unknown infestation."

Helbourne folded his arms. "Infestation or invasion, Colonel, the end result will likely be the same. I still strongly suggest that when we do find her, we bring her back alive and try to establish peaceful communication. It may be our only chance at survival when her people arrive."

She turned back to the monitors. "I am well aware of your position and your opinions, Doctor. Feel free to discuss them at length with my superior when he arrives later today."

Something about the way she said that made him raise an eyebrow. "You don't plan on being here?"

She shook her head. "With Honcho down, I intend to lead Alpha personally and in force when we go after her this time. I'm throwing everything we've got at her."

Helbourne gave her a wry smile. "Your Hail Mary play, Colonel? Or your swan song?"

She frowned. "We'll just have to see, won't we?"

Her phone buzzed. She took the call, gave a few curt responses, and hung up. "Well, Doctor, it seems somebody upstairs likes you. That storm changed course, crossed the Florida Peninsula, and is now tracking up the East Coast. The Navy operation to recover the ship is back on schedule."

Helbourne smiled. "Well then, it seems that not every force in the cosmos is aligned against us today, eh?"

***

The legal operation of Bash & Body Works was humming with activity: men in sweaty coveralls using power tools to remove damaged parts from or attach new(-ish) ones to wounded cars, trucks, and SUVs. The racket of compressors, grinders, and air hammers was deafening, and the smell of machine oil, aerated automotive paint, and singed metal all but choking.

Craig and Jesse followed Dillon Crabtree and his swaying old-man ponytail past the legal operations, through a labyrinth of offices and breakrooms, and into a much bigger space filled with top-end vehicles, awaiting their turn on the lifts where they would be broken down for parts to be shipped all over the region for a hefty profit. A pair of musclebound and tattooed skinheads in wife-beaters and black BDUs tucked into spit-shined tactical boots stood waiting for them. Otherwise, the chop shop garage was empty.

"Craig, Jesse," Crabtree said, his false teeth square and white beneath his neatly-trimmed grey goatee. "This is Hans Hammer and Jefferson Himmler, the leaders of White Atlanta Reich. I've been working with them for the past several months, and we've managed to take back a couple of operations from Folk Nation. I think if we expand our partnership, we can drive them out altogether."

Jesse shook hands with the two men. Craig gave them curt nods. "So why you boys want to hitch your wagon to the DM? I thought all you Peckerwoods believed our days were done."

Hammer smiled, revealing blue-etched canines. "We did. But like the Little Engine Who Could, you just keep chugging along. So, why fight each other when we've got the same goals? A White America free from the corruption of the Jews and the jigaboos."

Craig pointed at the swastika tattooed on Hammer's throat, "Because of that—" and at the SS lightning bolts tattooed on Himmler's deltoids— "and those. We fly the Stars and Stripes as well as the Stars and Bars. We're patriots, not Nazi scum."

Himmler bridled, but Hammer held up a hand, his smile widening. "And that's worked out great so far, right? A losing Civil War, Civil Rights, welfare broodmares living off hard-working white folks, filthy illegals from Mexico and Guatemala raping and murdering white girls and selling children on the Internet, Jews and niggers in the government, and even a half-breed Muslim President... Only Hitler had the balls to do what was best for his country. To make Germany great again, he knew he had to exterminate or drive out the lesser races, build up a strong military, and instill national pride in the purified people. That's why *we* honor him and the Reich."

"Look," Jesse said, stepping in as the mediator. "You're right, Hammer, we do want the same thing; we're just going about it in different ways." He looked at Craig. "You have to admit; it's always better to have an ally than an enemy. What's the old saying? 'The enemy of my enemy is my friend.' No sense in fighting a two-front war."

Craig frowned. "I'd like to remind you that I didn't want to fight *any* war. I just wanted to catch a snitch and find out what he told the cops before they clamped irons on me. You're the one who's turned this thing into a flaming shitstorm of epic proportions."

"And that's why you're losing, old man," Himmler growled. "The war's here, and the kikes and niggers are winning it because you refuse to fight."

Craig raised an eyebrow at the blue-eyed Aryan piece of shit. "So, your bitch can talk, Hammer. That's impressive. Keep her quiet, and maybe I'll toss her a bone when we're done."

Himmler's hand went for the small of his back.

Everyone tensed, but Hammer grabbed his man around the shoulders. "That's enough. I know you old guard types don't like us, but we don't have to like each other to work together. So, tell me, Byce, what's it going to be? You want me and my crew to help secure this place while you grab your snitch? Or do you want to be looking over your shoulder all night, waiting for a boatload of ghetto sleds crammed full of gangbangers to roll up your backside?"

Craig smiled at the fascist asshole, wanting to beat Jesse Sneed to death with a ball-peen hammer just like he did that beaner in his basement. *This is your fault, and Orlando's... And mine, for letting it get this far...*

"You know this is for the best, Craig," Crabtree said, licking his lips, his eyes darting between the two leaders. "If we don't unite, the Nation will own Atlanta and most of Georgia by the end of the year. I've been fighting a losing action for over a decade. Without WAR, we're done here."

Craig swallowed what was left of his pride and held out his hand. "All right, Hammer, you've got a deal. You and your boys do good tonight, and we'll see about officially getting you all into the Dixie Mafia."

He hated himself for making the deal, but he knew it would never stick with the bigwigs in Ohio and Louisiana, probably not even with Jesse's people in Florida. Craig's only consolation was that he didn't plan on being around when it all went to shit.

***

Having driven through half the night, Idegen felt refreshed as she stepped out of the shower. But before she had finished toweling off, she sensed a heaviness in the other room. Hurrying into one of Jon's oversized shirts—emblazoned with a THE PORKCHOP EXPRESS logo—she resisted the urge to reach out and read his mind before stepping into the motel room.

Jon sat on the edge of one of the two beds. Awaiting his turn in the shower, he was barefoot and stripped to the waist. His head in his hands, his shoulders shook with restrained sobs. The television was on a news channel. The digital plaque beneath a pretty woman speaking into a microphone read: UNEXPLAINED HOUSE FIRE KILLS TENNESSEE MAN.

"Jon, what's wrong?"

"He's dead," Jon said through his hands, his voice low and thick. "They killed him. The sonsabitches hunting you killed my father..." There was no rage in his voice, no blame. Only pain and regret. She sensed that he did not yet know the full extent of what he was feeling or how to begin processing it.

She sat on the bed beside him, the t-shirt clinging to her damp body, and placed her hand on his back. He tensed, then relaxed. "I am so very sorry for your loss, Jon," she said in a tone of voice she could not recall using before. She found herself hoping it was soothing.

He gave a bitter chuckle and sniffed. Wiping his hands on his jeans, he stared at the wall. "I can't remember ever liking the old man." His voice was raw, like he was regurgitating his words. "But I reckon at some point, when I was a kid, I must have loved him. And then, the last thing he said to me..." His bruised and cut face contorted, and fresh sobs escaped before he could hide them.

Idegen tried to understand the... *grief...* she sensed in him. *I never had parents. I've lost members of my sister cell in combat and testing, but I do not recall any of us ever having such a reaction... Of course, we were born and bred to accept death in battle, in service to the Empire. Apparently most humans, for all their fragility and short lifespans, never come to understand and fully accept the finite nature of existence...*

"You know..." He regained control for the moment. "When I was in high school, a few years after my brother Kevin... died... my mom ran off with a black man. He was a football coach in Chattanooga. They got married and moved to Tuscaloosa. I hated her so much for that. Hated the man more. Not so much for running off but for leaving me alone with my dad.

"But they'd send me a check for my birthday and Christmas every year." He wiped at his face with his bruised and scabby hands. "I tore the first one up and threw it away. When my dad saw it in the trash, he beat me. Said money was money, no matter where it came from. Told me if I didn't want it, to give it to him and he'd drink it. So that's what I did for three years.

"And you know what? It really was a present, in a way. Every time I'd get one of those checks, I knew the old man would be getting ripped for a day or two, and I'd be free to see Angie or hang out with my friends without worrying about him screwing it up."

"I... am sorry, Jon," she whispered, gently rubbing his back. His skin reacted to her touch, and she sensed confusion in him, a mixture of powerful emotions. "Is there... anything I can do to make you feel better?" She understood what she was asking, how he would interpret it. And, as... unusual as it might be, she was willing to do it for the sake of her friend, Jon French.

They sat on the bed in silence. Close and breathing. Her hand on his naked back.

He stood and crossed the room to the sink. "No," he murmured. He turned on the water and splashed his face, leaned on the counter with shaking hands. "I'm okay... Besides, I... I don't want to screw things up between us by making a mistake like that. Right now, you're the only friend I've got. I've tried to have it both ways in the past, and it just don't work. Believe me. I know."

Idegen smiled. He had surprised her. "I understand... Just know that I am here for you no matter what you need, Jon."

He turned, the white towel coming away from his face with traces of blood. He returned the smile. "Thanks. But I think I've outgrown the willingness to accept a pity screw." He laughed and looked at the ceiling with red-rimmed eyes. "I don't know. I guess I just need someone to talk to."

Idegen stood, went to the mini fridge, pulled one of the plastic-wrapped packs from the coffee tray, and handed it to him. "And a plastic straw to chew on, I suppose."

He accepted the token with another, more genuine laugh. "Thanks. And it wouldn't hurt if you put some pants on while you're at it."

"So, what happened with your mother and this black man?" She carried a pair of jeans and underwear into the bathroom and partially closed the door to dress. "Did you ever go and live with them?"

"No." She heard Jon pop the straw into his mouth. "But when I went to college, they started coming up on the weekends to see my home games, or if we were playing somebody in Alabama, they'd meet me after the game. That's when I began to understand that my mom hadn't wanted to abandon me, but she had no other choice if she was going to find some happiness in her own life. Lord knows there was no chance of finding it with my father."

Dressed, Idegen opened the bathroom door.

"And I realized that Coach Lee, her new husband, actually loved my mother and wanted to make her happy in a way that my father never had... or never could." Jon wiped at his eyes again and looked at the stained carpet. "He was the one who called and told me about Mom's death. She had cancer but had kept it a secret, even from him. He got up to go to the bathroom one night and just found her lying on the bedroom floor. Just like that."

Idegen leaned against the doorframe and looked at him. He seemed so soft—so full of weakness and useless emotion and sentimentality. And yet, she now saw the inner strength that kept him going, the iron rod of character that had been forged in the crucible of his life. "You have lost everyone."

"Lost them or run them off, just like dear old dad. I guess the apple doesn't fall far from the tree, huh?"

"You have not run me off, Jon. And I promise you never will."

He looked up at her and smiled. "I'll hold you to it, though I don't know how I'd punish you if you did."

Idegen smiled back. "You could try a hammer and wooden stake, I suppose."

Jon rolled his eyes. "I'm going to take a shower and try to get some sleep before we have our Showdown at the O.K. Corral."

Idegen scanned the neural web for the reference. "And I shall make sure our 'shooting irons' are in working order, Doc."

19
GUNSLINGER'S GLORY

"Got them," Hack-Job said. "A motel in Marietta, just north of Atlanta."

"Atlanta," Sharpe muttered. She and Frankenstein stood behind the two techs in the C&C. "They've covered a lot of ground in a short time." She turned to Tunes. "Alert the Blackhawk crews to be ready to move out." To Steiner, she said, "Get the team together. We're deploying in one hour." She took her phone from her pocket. "I'll call the commander at Fort Benning and have backup from the 75th Rangers ready to converge on the target."

After making the call, Sharpe felt like a crushing weight had been lifted from her shoulders. At least part of that could be attributed to the fact that Helbourne had relocated to ORNL in anticipation of the recovery of the alien craft, and she finally had a reprieve from his bitching.

No more waiting around, playing cat and mouse and always coming up empty-handed. This time, I'm going in personally, and, win or lose, I'm the one playing the game instead of watching it on TV.

This time, it's all or nothing. Do or die time.

***

Atlanta traffic was as heavy and nerve-jangling as ever, even as a Saturday night fell on the city. Funny enough, Jon didn't mind for a change. *I guess it's hard to get stressed out about the possibility of a fifteen-car pileup when you're on your way to a showdown with heavily armed gangsters...*

He chewed on a straw and thought about Jim Tackett, the first and only man he had ever killed. Deep down, he knew the man and his brothers had deserved what they got, but then he wondered how he had any right to be the one to decide that. *After all, I'm not exactly in the running for sainthood. It may have started out as an attempt at justice or vengeance, but it ended up being a matter of pure survival. It was him or me, just like tonight's going to be. I got lucky...*

He looked at Idegen, cool as Frosty the Snowman's underwear, almost smiling. Gorgeous. *Speaking of lucky, I wonder if I shouldn't have taken her up on her offer back at the motel. After all, I might be dead—or worse—in an hour's time. I'm not sure if there's a heaven, but having sex with her might have come in a close second...*

He shook his head and focused on the road, fearing she might be reading his mind despite her promise. *Probably best not to think about that stuff, anyhow. Time to get my game face on. This is for real.*

Jon kept the 'Cuda on the congested interstate system, moving from I-75 to I-85 and then onto I-20, knowing that it was still the best way to make time in the metropolis. Besides, there were so many traffic and security cameras throughout the city that the government would have the same chance of spotting them on the surface roads, if not a better one. "Glad we left early," he muttered. "Looks like we'll be pushing it for time."

"Good," Idegen said. "Never do what your enemy expects, especially *when* he expects you to do it."

"Thanks, Sun Tsu... So, you're good with the plan?"

Idegen nodded, touching the bulges in the *Kriegsmarine* where the automatic pistols were concealed. "We park the car a block away; I take the guns to the roof across the street and set up a shooting position."

"And," Jon prompted.

"And... I commune with your mind to establish targets and give you situational awareness."

Jon was unsure how he felt about giving her an all-access pass to his melon. But it was the one advantage they had over the Dixie Mafia. In fact, he had no idea how many guns Craig Byce would bring to the party or even if the old man would actually be there. "The .30-06 should have enough punch to shoot through anything but layered brick or steel. Glass and sheet metal should be no problem."

"I understand the capabilities and limitations of your primitive weapons, Jon. Trust me."

He glanced at her. "I am. With my life."

Bash & Body Works was in an industrial park just off Memorial Drive, in the tastefully wooded hinterlands between Edgewood and Kirkwood. Jon guided the prime gray 'Cuda into a small church parking lot across the street from the park's entrance. Cutting the engine, he handed Idegen the keys. "Remember, if it all goes south, don't try to save me. Just get back here and get out of town."

"Do not worry. I will be watching." She smiled at him in the dark without taking the keys, and he dared to hope this might just work. Before he could change his mind, Jon got out of the car and jogged across the deserted street and into the industrial park.

He walked beneath the bright white streetlights, past a book warehouse, a heat and air supply store, a beauty supply wholesaler, and an importer of foreign motorcycle parts. All sheet metal and glass constructions. The high-end body shop was easily the largest complex in the park. Its sheet metal exterior had also been upgraded since the photos they'd seen on the website. It had been covered over with a concrete mixture that approximated old stone.

No way the rifle punches through all that.

Five pickups and SUVs were parked in front of the multi-bayed building. Jon could see baldheaded men in some of the parked cars and another four smoking cigarettes in front of the three big bay doors on the nearest wing.

His optimism vanished. He almost swallowed the straw. *Skinheads. Byce must be desperate if he's cutting the Peckerwoods in on this. I'm as good as dead...*

—Do not worry, Jon. I am here. Idegen's voice in his head was both alarming and reassuring.

He took a deep breath, felt for the Taurus Judge at the small of his back—though he knew he'd have it taken away long before he ever saw Craig Byce—and thought, *Well, at least I'm wearing my lucky t-shirt.*

—I do not get it.

Jon glanced down his chest, saw the mighty Cthulhu raising a frosty pint to him above the motto I LOVECRAFT BEER. *If I live through this, I'll explain it to you.*

Jon staggered for a moment as the world turned into a kaleidoscope of images, words, and sounds. His insides heaved up toward his mouth. And then the sensation was gone. *What... the* hell *was that?*

—Oh. I am sorry, Jon. I scanned the neural web to understand your shirt. I did not think to sever our connection first. I hope it did not unsettle you, but I do now understand the joke. Clever.

"Yes," Jon said, taking a deep breath and gnawing on the straw to regain his composure. "Clever. And now I know the complete works of H.P. Lovecraft by heart..." *The man must have lived a sheltered life to create such a vast array of otherworldly terrors. There's plenty of horrifying things to be found in the real world, and you don't even have to look very hard to find them.*

He walked to the body shop.

The smoking men were the first to notice his approach, and he could see them breaking up their little ring and stepping to the edge of the parking lot. The tall one in the center, the one with the SS lightning bolts tattooed on his shoulders, raised his voice and called, "Can we help you?"

Jon smiled, going all in. "I'm here to see Craig Byce. Name's Jon French."

Another man laughed. He wasn't a skinhead but looked somehow familiar. Like a male model out of a Ralph Lauren catalog. Only the pistol on his belt and the tribal tats peeking out from under his expensive polo marked him as anything more than a pretty boy. "The snitch showed, boys." To Jon, he said, "Don't you know snitches get stitches? In the joint, they usually get 'em in the asshole first."

Jon halted six feet from the four men. The guy was the Man with No Eyes he'd seen driving the Maserati outside of Hopper's, Craig Byce's man.

Jon's smile widened—a bluff. "You look like the type to miss those Halcion days of sodomy and pruno. What's the matter? Can't find a date on the outside?"

The three skinheads chuckled with gusto, reinforcing the fact that the blond guy was an outsider. Surprisingly, he only smiled back. Like a psychopath. The tall Peckerwood with the SS ink said, "You've got safe passage by the DM. But we ain't officially their boys just yet, French. So I'd watch my mouth if I was you."

Jon noted the array of Nazi and White Power tattoos adorning the rest of the thugs, the pseudo-military fatigues and boots. The half-concealed guns. "Fine by me. I'm here to talk to Craig Byce, anyhow, not swap breath with you guys."

The SS guy gave him a smirk. "All right, inside." Jon followed them in through the front door. They grabbed him just inside the fully lit, white-walled reception/waiting area/showroom.

"Easy, Jonny-Boy," the male model said with that psycho smile as Jon struggled against the three skinheads. "Easy, we just gotta frisk you. Trust me, I ain't the type to enjoy petting another man's junk, so stay still, and this'll be over in a second."

—I am here, Jon. Do not worry.

Jon bit down on the straw and forced himself to relax. He was promptly divested of the Judge before they released him. "Happy?"

"Ecstatic. Now follow me."

He was led down a short corridor, through a metal door, and into the vacant garage. The smell of automotive supplies was stifling. A silver Mercedes S-Class was up on a lift to his right, and a vintage-green

Jaguar XK-8 sat parked across the way, beside a dinged-up black Escalade awaiting cosmetic surgery.

They went through a man door beside another closed bay at the back of the huge space, through a small office and lounge area, and into a tiny, concrete vestibule containing a heavy steel door secured by three different types of locks. The pretty boy pushed an intercom button. "This is Jesse. Open up. We've got him."

After a moment, there was a buzz and click, and the big metal door opened. Jon was ushered into the secret workings of the chop shop. *Idegen? You still there? How's things going outside?*

—I am here, Jon. In position... There are fourteen armed men in the front of the building... another twenty-two inside, including your escort...

"Great."

The skinheads led him to the center of the big back room, which was lined with four rows of parked high-end automobiles, gleaming beneath the overhead lights: BMWs, Cadillacs, Mercedes, Jaguars, Porsches, Ferraris, Lamborghinis, a Bentley, and something that may have been a McLaren or the Batmobile. And standing in the center of this petrol-head paradise like an Anglo-Saxon king in his great hall was white-haired Craig Byce in a khaki outdoorsman's shirt, jeans, work boots, and a .45 on his hip. The half-dozen men flanking him were armed with ARs and submachine guns. Jon recognized one of these as Dillon Crabtree, the ponytailed and embattled head of the Atlanta chapter. There was also another skinhead, an older man with White Atlanta Reich tattooed around his neck. Jon figured him to be the Peckerwoods' leader. The rest were just muscle, as far as he could tell.

Jesse, the male model, handed Byce the Taurus Judge. "Had this on him. Numbers are filed. Must be the piece he got off Frank."

"Well..." Byce tucked the revolver into his own waistband. "We meet at last, Mr. French. Where's your girlfriend? The one who shot my boys at Winchester's place."

"We parted ways in Chattanooga. She's not the go steady type." Jon forced a calm smile. "And actually, you and I met a few years ago, Mr. Byce. I delivered a package from Joey Green to your favorite watering hole in Knoxville."

"Joey Green. Funny you should mention him, Jon, seeing as he's the reason we're all here right now."

Jon glanced around at the small army, noticing other armed men lining the walls beyond the automobiles. "Really? I thought we were here because of what happened at Hopper's the other night... I just need you to know—"

"That you're a stooge for the Feds?" Jesse said. Someone had handed him an AR, and he held the thing like he'd been born with it. "That you're in on the setup with Green?"

Jon blinked.

Byce's eyes narrowed as he raised a hand to quiet his subordinate. "Easy, Jesse. Let's hear him out. Then, if we don't like what we hear, we can always string him up. It ain't my basement back home, but I'm sure they got plenty of toys we can use around here. I promise, we'll take more time with him than we did the beaner."

Jon felt his stomach fill with cold water. A fierce stab of guilt. *Julio... Because of me... Julio and my dad... both...* He nearly bit the straw in two.

—Concentrate, Jon! Focus on the task at hand!

Jon blinked, licked his lips. "I was promised safe passage."

"Which you got. Now start talking, Jon-Boy. What do you know about Green's deal with the DEA and the ATF? Who else is he in bed with? What did you tell them?"

This was not going according to plan. Not at all. He'd thought that he would walk into the trap, maybe get roughed up a little, and then Idegen would come to the rescue, taking down Craig and his posse once and for all. Then, just maybe, the big dogs of the Dixie Mafia would forget about him or at least give him the time to escape the country. Instead, he was in the heart of a veritable fortress, surrounded by close to fifty shooters, all itching for his blood.

Jon knew he had to look like a fish, his mouth puckering with no noise coming out. Finally, he managed, "What? I didn't know—"

—Trouble, Jon.

You think?

That's when he heard the first gunshots outside.

Craig gripped the Colt on his hip. "That your girlfriend, Jon-Boy? She trying to shoot her way in to save your sorry ass? Well, I don't care if you've got all of Charlie's Angels out there; you'll be dead before anyone gets to you. Or you'll wish you were."

Crabtree's phone rang. He answered, and his eyes went wide. He turned to Byce. "Folk Nation is here. At least fifty bucks."

—Jon, I hear helicopters.

***

—Go! Jon said in her head. *Save yourself. This is my mess, not yours.*

Hold on, Jon. I am coming for you.

From the rooftop across the street, Idegen watched a dozen big-wheeled cars and SUVs tear into the industrial park, skid to a halt in front of the body shop, or careen into its parking lot. The dark-skinned men in the cars opened fire with automatic weapons, raking the building and the vehicles parked out front. Windshields and the building's glass exploded and shattered. Tires went flat with angry, hissing pops. Vehicle body panels erupted in tattered holes, and the building's metal roll-up doors rattled beneath the hail of bullets. The barrage was wild and apparently devastating but in reality, caused very few casualties.

The pale-skinned men abandoned their damaged vehicles and returned fire. More took up positions inside the building, firing from the broken windows. In a matter of moments, the front of the body shop was a war zone.

The helicopters drew closer.

Idegen raised the hunting rifle to her shoulder, sighted through the scope, and added to the confusion and carnage below. Even if she had not owed Jon French her life, she knew that her only hope of escape was to draw her own hunters into the violent maelstrom now unfolding. She hoped to use the chaos as a distraction, allowing her to rescue Jon and make good on yet another escape.

When the rifle was empty, she tossed it aside, snagged the Gladiator bag, and leapt from the rooftop to the roadway thirty feet below. The cybernetic enhancements that had enabled her to survive the fall from the aircraft two days before now allowed her to land on the run with ease.

Shouldering the automatic carbine, she opened fire on the embattled men, dark- and light-skinned alike. From what she could gather from their jumbled, violent, and hate-filled thoughts, they were all suitable enemies. And they stood between her and Jon. Her only regret was that she did not have time to feed on any of them.

She was terribly hungry.

The first helicopters arrived as she made her way into the building. A moment later, the lights went out.

***

"What a cluster," Sharpe said into her headset's microphone. The Blackhawk circled the industrial park to which the DOD satellite had tracked the subject. She had not expected to find her in the middle of a full-fledged gang war. "Looks like downtown Fallujah!"

Turning to Tunes, she said, "Get ahold of somebody at Atlanta PD, preferably in the gang task force. Tell them that we are conducting a

Homeland Security operation and would appreciate their full cooperation. Tell them we need a mile-wide perimeter around this location. Then get us backup from GHP and the Fulton County Sheriff's Department. I don't want anybody getting out this time.

"Hack-Job, tap into Georgia Power and get this block cut off. Maybe these gangbanging assholes will be less likely to shoot what they can't see."

Pointing at Frankenstein, she said, "We're going night-vision. Relay that to the Rangers. Have them set up a tight perimeter around the property. They are not to engage the civilians unless it is in self-defense. And make damn sure they do not use explosives—no grenades or rockets. Small arms only—unless they have a positive ID on the subject."

Taking a deep breath, she turned to the Blackhawk's crew chief. "After you drop us in, maintain elevation and cover us with your fifties. No rockets; keep collateral damage to an absolute minimum."

As soon as the orders were carried out and the block fell into complete darkness, Sharpe pulled on her night-vision goggles, flipped on the power, and checked her M4. "Here we go."

There was a grinding pain in her hips, but she hardly felt it. Adrenaline raged through her body like a flood-swollen river, and it was now, at long last, officially go time.

***

Craig stared the kid down. He was scared, but Craig was probably the only one in the room to know it. Jon French had a good poker face. Of course, his face looking like a so-so prize fighter at the end of the twelfth round made it a bit easier to look tough. His right eye sported a fading greenish-purple shiner, the bridge of his inflamed nose was crossed by a fresh Band-Aid, and another crimped the top of his right ear. And what the hell was with that red piece of plastic moving around in his teeth?

"Jesse," Craig said, not taking his eyes off French. "Take half the men through these back rollups, circle the building, and hit the bastards from both sides.

"What are you going to do with him?" Jesse asked, motioning the gunmen toward the rear of the building. "You know he's probably responsible for this shit."

No, asshole, you *are responsible for this particular batch of shit. But we'll talk about that later...*

Craig pulled his .45, appreciated the widening of the kid's eyes, and then smashed the butt across Jon's already injured nose. French staggered with a surprised grunt, then toppled to the ground, clutching his face, his eyes filling with tears. "Don't worry about him. Just take care of the Nation. This is the fight you wanted, so go enjoy it."

"My boys can handle this," Hammer said. Craig ignored him.

The rollup bay doors were halfway up when the power died, and everything went black. The gunfire outside tapered off for a second, and Craig heard the unmistakable thudding of approaching helicopters.

Crabtree activated the flashlight app on his phone. A few others followed suit with lights on their weapons.

"Who the hell is that?" Craig demanded, kicking Jon French's leg. "You bring the Feds with you? This a sting?" He worked the slide on the pistol, chambering a round.

"No!" French said, raising his hands and staring at the floor. "No. That's the U.S. military. They're after the girl. Let me go, and I'll get her as far from here as possible, and they'll follow. I promise, you'll never see me again."

Craig sighted down the barrel of the gun, squinting to focus on the dark shape at his feet. Cellphone flashlights and gun lights swept the big room. "I ought to blow your brains out, right now... Tell me what you know about Joey Green."

The gunfire was louder, some shots coming from inside the building. Followed by screams.

"I know he's an asshole," Jon French said, meeting Craig's stare. Blood streamed from the reopened cut on his nose. "I know he set me up. I reckon his plan was to set you up, too."

"How come the cops cut you loose?"

French swallowed. "I cut a deal with TBI. They bagged me in Crossville. Wanted to be cut in on the federal investigation. I was their ticket. All I had to do was show up, turn over the car, and they were in, and I was out."

Craig squeezed the handle of the pistol, his finger tight on the trigger. "You've got balls, kid. You should be shitting yourself right about now."

The son of a bitch actually smiled. "One of us should be, for sure."

The cinderblocks near the inner iron door exploded into the garage. Craig looked up in time to see... *Someone crashing through the fucking wall?*

The kid came off the ground like a pit bull, hit him in the chest with his shoulder. The blow knocked the air from his lungs, the pistol from his hand, and him to the cement floor.

Deafening gunfire erupted in the darkened room. Blinding strobes from muzzle flashes. Whining ricochets. Shattering glass. Men screaming. The smell of burnt powder and fresh blood.

Craig drove his fist up into the kid's face, knocked him off his chest. Ignoring the pain in his gut, he scrambled onto his hands and knees, looking for the pistol.

He saw movement beneath the half-raised doors. Men coming across the darkened back parking lot. Men moving in slow, professional order. Men with long weapons. Soldiers.

"Shit." He grabbed the .45 and dragged himself to his feet. *Where the hell is that damn kid? I'll kill him if it's the last fucking thing I do...*

By the strobing light of gunfire, he saw her. The black-haired beauty standing on the hood of a Jaguar, an AR in one hand and a Glock in the other. Bullets zipped around her unnoticed. The bitch was actually smiling as she dropped men left and right. Hammer was sprawled on the concrete floor, half his head a bloody pulp. Crabtree lay curled and whimpering in front of a gore-splattered yellow Ferrari, a huge pool of blood fanning out from his midsection. Half a dozen other bodies lay motionless or writhing and screaming around the room. Men were firing blind on their way to the escape promised by the half-raised back doors.

Craig raised his pistol, put her forehead in the sights, and—

Pain exploded in his belly. Sharp, piercing pain like he had never known, surprisingly. He took a step back, hearing the gunshot a moment later. He didn't feel the impact of the second round. His knees buckled. He blinked, straining to see through the haze of gun smoke in the dark room. Straining to catch his breath.

That little bastard, Jon French, had shot him with the very gun he'd bought from Frank Gill to off himself. The kid lay on his back, aiming the Taurus Judge at him from between his knees.

Craig realized that he was on the floor, too. He tried to raise his own weapon to return fire. But nothing wanted to work. Even his lungs. It was getting dark. Darker. The pain rose, spread out, ebbing and flowing, throughout his body. And then it faded away.

He blinked. The only thing he saw was a Band-Aid over a bloody nose.

He tried to take one last breath. And then the light was gone...

***

"Are you well, Jon?" Idegen asked, leaping from the hood of the car.

The room had gone quiet as the last of the enemy had fled out the back. She could still hear a few sporadic shots from outside. Her nocturnal lenses were in place, so the details of the dark garage were completely visible. She pulled a fresh magazine from her jacket and reloaded the carbine.

"I'll live." Jon stared at one of the corpses, his smoking revolver in hand. "More than I can say for Craig Byce."

Idegen sensed relief, guilt, and emptiness swirling among his thoughts. Images of Julio, his father, Jim Tackett, and this Craig Byce. A wave of uncertainty and doubt rising from somewhere inside his psyche, threatening to overwhelm him.

"Well, one problem is solved, but we have more than enough to take its place. We are surrounded, and the confusion of the gang fight is dying down. We must hurry, Jon."

He shook himself, knelt, and took the pistol from the dead man's hand. "Okay, which way?"

Idegen crouched, trying to ignore her ravenous hunger brought on by the bloodbath. She reached out to focus on the minds of the military hunters closing in. "There are thirty men that way." She used the rifle barrel to indicate the rear. "They are forming a perimeter. Seven coming in the front."

"Seems like an easy decision." Jon checked the magazine on the new pistol.

Idegen shook her head. "We will need to draw them in here, then try to break past them. If we are caught in the open, they will cut us down. They have a helicopter with machine guns covering the front."

Jon looked around the garage. "If you can keep them busy for a few minutes, I might have an idea."

She saw it in his mind and smiled. "I like it, Jon."

He frowned. "I think it's safe for you to get out of my head now."

"Sorry."

***

At least one of the idiots on the ground decided to take a pot-shot at their Blackhawk. The crew chief looked at Sharpe. She pointed at one of the abandoned vehicles in the parking lot.

"Rock and roll," the chief said, grabbing the handles of the door-mounted fifty-cal. A big, roaring burst of ol' Ma Deuce and the black SUV flew apart in a cloud of debris and began to burn. The ground fire came to a sudden stop, and empty hands, both white and black, went into the air.

"You still have a lock on the target?" Sharpe asked Hack-Job.

"She's in the building's wing to our right."

"Then let's go."

She led Alpha Team in a fast-rope insertion from the hovering helicopter. Above, the pilot used the chopper's loudspeakers to order the gangbangers to get on their knees with their hands on their heads. Some complied more quickly than others, but as soon as they saw the heavily armed team of commandos hit the pavement, the rest quickly followed suit. Sharpe took some pride and satisfaction in that.

At least we look like hell on wheels. I wonder if the subject will give us the same kind of respect...

An engine roared, drowning out the noise of the helicopter and the crackling fire of the burning SUV. Sharpe turned in time to see one of the bay doors on the building's opposite wing blow out of its housing, smashed to the front of a huge motor home. The lumbering vehicle made a hard turn, coming up on its right wheels before settling back and thundering straight at them.

Alpha Team scattered, but one of the kneeling gang members was not fast enough and was ground into pulp beneath the heavy vehicle's wheels. The RV knocked two more parked cars out of its path on the way out of the industrial park.

"Should we take it down?" the crew chief asked over the coms.

She looked at Hack-Job. He shook his head. "Target is still inside."

"Negative. Let the cops handle it. You guys keep these gangstas from following us in or wandering off."

"Yes, ma'am."

She turned to Frankenstein. "Have the Rangers secured the perimeter?"

"Affirmative. They've got the entire back side locked down and have taken a dozen prisoners."

"Good. Move out." Sharpe took up the rear position in the stack. She hadn't trained or operated with the team before, so she wasn't about to horn in on their routine while initiating a hostile breach. Frankenstein was in tactical command, so he was the number-three man, with Ramrod and Archer in the lead. Hack-job, Tunes, and Patches filled the gap.

But turning over operational lead allowed her mind to wander back to the horrifying experience on the C-130, when the subject was a foot away from tearing her to pieces. *And she was weak and wounded, and unarmed then... Now, she's strong, healthy, and probably armed to her pointy teeth... Get a grip, girl! She's a Tango, that's all. And in just a few minutes, she'll be Tango Down...*

The mental pep talk did nothing for her sudden craving for a beer or a Vicodin. Or... something else. *Blood?*

They entered through the shot-out entrance, and by the green light of her night-vision goggles, Sharpe saw the carnage left in the target's wake. There were nearly a dozen dead men scattered across the front room, stretched on the floor, the wraparound sofa, and the reception desk. All covered in blood. She paused to examine one, a single shot to the throat—all but instantly fatal. *Too precise to be a gangbanger unless it was the luckiest shot in the world...* She looked at the wall the man had been using for cover and shook her head.

They followed the trail of gore down a narrow hallway, through a steel fire door, and into a sizeable garage. Several dead neo-Nazis and hillbilly gangsters lay sprawled on the concrete floor among dropped weapons, spent brass, and the paraphernalia of auto body repair and damaged vehicles. An opened door in the rear wall led into another darkened chamber.

They passed through a small, bullet-riddled office and into a lounge, where a bald and tattooed brute lay in the midst of a broken folding table, his throat torn out. An arterial spray arced up the wall and across the mounted flatscreen TV.

"Shit," Archer muttered.

Sharpe turned from the grisly wall art to see the roughly man-sized hole in the plaster and cinder block on the opposite side of the room. She could make out the shapes of parked cars in the large space beyond.

"This security door," Hack-Job said from a vestibule just past the sundered wall, "it's a mother. I can get us in, but it'll take some time. Like half an hour."

Steiner looked to her for orders.

"Looks like we go down this rabbit hole."

"Flash-bangs," Frankenstein said in response. "Full breach."

They flanked the hole in the wall, half the team on either side. Archer and Ramrod tossed in the flash-bang grenades. A boom and splash of light. The team moved in.

Automatic weapon fire met them. Both Marines went down in the first barrage; Frankenstein returned fire with his M4, raking the front of a parked Bentley. This gave them just enough time to get the rest of the team through the breach.

Sharpe again felt that unsettling sensation of déjà vu or vertigo, only stronger. For a brief moment, it was like she was looking through someone else's eyes, watching herself follow the team through the wall. And that someone else was spraying them with gunfire. It took a moment to pull herself out of the disorientation and the anger.

"Flash-bangs were for shit," Tunes shouted, pulling the groaning Archer behind a Ferrari. Bullets hammered the other side. "Next bright idea?"

Sharpe knelt beside him and returned fire over the hood, then ducked back.

"Ramrod's dead," Hack-Job said. "Took one in the face."

"Shit," Frankenstein said from behind a Maserati across the way. He and Patches were taking turns pouring it on, sweeping the garage with bullets. "Your orders, Colonel?"

"Patches, you stay with Archer and Ramrod. Steiner, you take Hack-Job and flank right. Me and Tunes'll go left. Bound, fire, and maneuver. We go first. On three."

Bullets rattled against the cars they were using for cover.

"One... Two... Th—"

Almost every car in the garage started its engine with a roar. Headlights erupted in high beams. The green and white images on their night-vision goggles went bright white.

They were blind.

A throaty engine drowned out the others, revving to life on the other side of the garage. Another sound, like rattling chains and clanking machinery.

Sharpe flipped her goggles up from her face and stood. Blinking, she could just make out two figures diving into a dark vehicle on the far side of the big room. She didn't have time to aim. She swung her rifle from the hip and squeezed the trigger. One of the figures went down under the hail of bullets.

"No!" a male voice shouted above the echoing gunshots.

Something hit her in the right shoulder. She dropped her rifle and tried to reach for her pistol, but her arm wouldn't work. Another gunshot, glass shattering in her face. Sharp pain. Someone grabbed her and pulled her to the ground.

She felt dizzy, weak. "Get them..." Her mouth was dry, her throat tight. "Get them," she said again, but she couldn't hear herself over the thunder of gunfire and the roar of a big engine. Tires squealing. Another distant crash.

"It's not too bad," she heard Patches say. "But we've got to get her CASEVAC right now if we want to save the arm."

"Get them," she said again, but nobody seemed to hear. The world was melting into a kaleidoscope of colors and shapes. "I hit her, dammit... She's wounded..."

"Someone is escaping in a black sports car," a voice said over her radio. "Please advise."

She's hurt. I know it. Hurt bad. Now's the best chance to get them. To get her...

"Disengage," Frankenstein said. "We've got wounded to evac."

No, you asshole! Light them up! Do it now!

And then she slipped into a profound darkness...

***

Jon crashed the McLaren through the front bay door, swerved to miss a couple kneeling gangsters, jumped the curb, and cut hard left onto the road, weaving between parked ghetto sleds. He saw the big helicopter hovering only a dozen or so feet above the ground but tried to ignore it. *If they decide to shoot, nothing I can do about it... And I thought I was being so clever using the keys and remote starters to blind those assholes inside...*

He looked at Idegen in the passenger seat. She was pale, her face rigid, breasts rising and falling with each labored breath. He could see the *Kriegsmarine* stuck to her body, her hands soaked in blood. "You're okay," he said. "I'll get you out of here. I'll get you fixed up."

"I am fine, Jon," she whispered, forcing a blood-streaked smile. "You should leave me and save yourself. I can manage." She coughed, and blood flecked the cracked windshield.

"Hell with that." He glanced at the supercar's dashboard, lit up like the Starship Enterprise's alert system after taking a direct hit from a photon torpedo. What the hail of bullets in the garage hadn't damaged, the crash through the bay door had. The front tires were flat, the front suspension was shot, and the fuel gauge was dropping like the President's approval rating.

Changing gear, he aimed the dying penis envy on wheels for the tiny church across the street. "The old 'Cuda is almost as fast and a hell of a lot less noticeable, anyhow," he muttered.

He heard sirens as he crossed Memorial. Blue lights coming from both directions. "We'll need to make this fast."

And they did.

By the time the GHP cruiser and the Atlanta PD patroller arrived at the entrance of the industrial park, Jon and Idegen were already in the restored Plymouth and backing out of the parking space. He thought about playing it casual and just creeping out and slipping past the cops, but when the State Trooper flashed them with his lights and honked his siren, Jon put the pedal down.

The Hemi roared, the tires barked and squealed, leaving a cloud of smoke as the 'Cuda tore out of the parking lot and shot past the two police cars like a loosed arrow.

"Hang in there, Idegen." Jon licked his lips and chewed the pulped straw. "Now you're about to see the skills that got me into this mess in the first place."

This time of night, the surface road was abandoned, allowing him to reach the ramp to I-20 at a full hundred miles per hour. Of course, the souped-up Georgia Highway Patrol Dodge Charger was in hot pursuit and probably radioing his buddies to set up a roadblock.

If one hadn't been set up already.

The interstate was busy, even after midnight. But Jon used the traffic as an obstacle course to shake loose the trooper. Shifting gears and keeping his foot on the accelerator, he pushed the 'Cuda over 115 miles per hour. The big engine growled like a wild beast as tractor-trailers, box trucks, SUVs, compacts, and pickups all turned into multicolored blurs, flashing in the muscle car's headlights for a second, then vanishing to one side or the other.

The blue lights continued to strobe in the rearview mirror, getting closer. The siren couldn't be heard over the Hemi's roar.

This guy is good. Well-trained and experienced. But has he been on duty all night? Has he got the adrenaline rush I do? The motivation to do the crazy shit I'm willing to do to keep her safe? We'll see...

When the trooper's headlights got close, Jon cut left just a few feet ahead of a horn-honking tanker truck, then hauled the wheel back to the right, the car screeching across three lanes of sparse traffic and hitting an offramp at somewhere north of eighty miles per hour. The blue lights missed the ramp and kept going.

Jon almost laughed, thinking of Roscoe P. Coltrane cussing the Duke Boys. But he was too busy slamming on the brakes, grabbing the emergency brake, and cutting the wheel to the left at the bottom of the ramp to fishtail through an intersection, forcing three Atlanta night owls to put their cars in the median or on the sidewalk.

At the next intersection, he turned right onto Flat Shoals Road and made for Panthersville. "From here, I can take the backroads all the way into South Carolina. I'm sure they've got an APB out for us, but on those dark country roads, this thing will be camouflaged until daylight. I think I can make the state line well before then."

"Jon," Idegen said. "We have to get back to Knoxville."

He blinked. "What? Are you crazy? We'll never be able to do that after the manhunt we've instigated tonight."

"We must try. I saw the warrior woman's thoughts. They have recovered my ship and are taking it to their laboratory there in Oak

Ridge. If they somehow manage to activate the deep space engines, they will ignite your planet's atmosphere."

Jon licked his lips, kept his eyes peeled for blue lights, glanced at the speedometer showing seventy-five as they rocketed through a thirty-five zone. "Ignite the planet's atmosphere?"

"Your world will be incinerated in a matter of hours."

20
THE DEVIL WEARS A SUIT AND TIE

Helbourne hadn't slept in twenty-four hours. Not since he'd heard the news about the ship's retrieval and before his subsequent relocation to the Oak Ridge National Laboratory. He had immediately gotten to work, setting up his labs, ordering equipment, and requesting personnel and their ensuing security clearances. But he wasn't tired. He felt like a kid waiting for his promised BB gun or bicycle on Christmas Eve. In just a few hours, he would be examining an extraterrestrial spacecraft. The prospect excited him even more than his study of the subject, Idegen Videshee, as alluring as she was.

With a machine, I won't have to hold back any tests. I can tear it apart, piece by piece, until I've unlocked all the technological secrets of this advanced civilization.

The security door of the massive, hangar-like laboratory buzzed, clicked, and opened. Helbourne looked up from his laptop, where he reviewed the list of assistants. No one was scheduled to enter for hours.

A tall, handsome man in his early fifties walked in, accompanied by a pair of black-clad troops in full combat gear. The man, in contrast, wore a pretentiously expensive grey Italian suit and black wingtips. His salt and pepper hair was just long enough not to be military, but still all business. He smiled with impossibly white teeth, his pale blue eyes sparkling as he extended his hand. "Doctor Helbourne. A pleasure. You can call me Mr. White."

Helbourne frowned as he stood, shaking hands out of reflex. "And you would be?"

Mr. White looked around the expansive room, admiring the technological gear already assembled for use on the pending arrival. "I would be one of three top dogs in the United States intelligence community, Dr. Helbourne. Colonel Sharpe is my latest charge, and I have had to step away from very important activities to come down here and clean up after her."

"I see."

"I very much doubt that." Mr. White flashed another smile. "But let's try to understand each other. I don't know if you've heard, but Colonel Sharpe got herself shot up while allowing the subject to escape yet again. What is this, the third time? She also lost another two members of Alpha Team. One fatally."

Helbourne blinked, licked his lips. "No. I... I hadn't heard. Is she all right? Who... which team member was killed?" He surprised himself by caring, hoping it was not Patches, the idealistic medic who had helped him with the autopsies.

"She'll live. She's in surgery, I believe. They're trying to save the use of her right arm. But between me, you, and the fence post, she might be better off if she loses it. That way, we can push her out with a purple heart, a combat commendation, and an honorable discharge. If she comes back on active duty, on the other hand..." White shrugged.

"As for the KIA, both Marine LRRPs got hit. I don't know which one didn't make it."

Helbourne sat back on his stool and swallowed, relieved and saddened at the same time.

"But I didn't come to give you box scores, Doctor." Mr. White strolled around the workbench, picking up a microscope and examining its weight. "I'm not entirely sure how forthcoming Sharpe was with her reports. Especially where your findings are concerned. So, I need you to fill me in on everything you know about the situation." He set the device down. "Especially your opinions."

Helbourne frowned at this revelation. "You mean she didn't tell you that I've been arguing for capture rather than termination from the beginning? That I believe that the subject is a member of an advanced spacefaring civilization that, if it were so inclined, could destroy or conquer us on a whim? That our only hope of avoiding such a possibility is by making amends for our initial treatment of the subject and establishing peaceable communications with her?"

White smiled. "Oh, she told me you were waving the white flag on this, but she didn't go into detail about how passionate you were on the subject. But believe me, Doctor, there are people in the Pentagon discussing those very things right now. What you and I need to focus on, however, is how best to recapture the subject, what to do with her once we've got her back, and how to get every last tidbit of information we can out of her. And her vehicle."

Helbourne rubbed his face. "You know, if I had only been permitted to speak with her when she was first captured, I believe that all of this bloodshed could have been avoided."

White's smile vanished. "Water under the bridge, Doctor. Unless you've got a time machine somewhere around here, that statement is useless. Besides, she's the one who drew first blood, so we proceeded on the assumption that she is an enemy hostile. From what I've gathered thus far, there is no evidence to contradict that estimate."

"What about this Jon French? He's a human being, and she hasn't harmed him. In fact, we think they may be working together for mutual benefit and protection."

Mr. White scoffed. "So she's got a human pet. Big deal. It's not like we humans have never employed natives to do our dirty work when we go in to conquer a new region."

Helbourne acknowledged the undeniable truth of that argument. "Very well, Mr. White. What is it, exactly, that you want from me? Aside from what I'm already doing, that is."

White's smile returned as he stepped to the door. "I just want you to do your level best, Doctor. And, if it occurs to you in your spare time, I'd also like you to prepare a report on how *you* think Colonel Sharpe mishandled this situation. Be as thorough and precise as possible... And the sooner you can get that to me, the better. The... *gratitude* of your government is riding on it. It was nice to meet you, Doctor Helbourne. I look forward to working with you over the next few days."

Helbourne watched the man and his armed escort depart. He suddenly hated White, himself, and the whole twisted mess. *I was never overly fond of Sharpe, but I did respect her. And now, that... that monster wants me to throw her under the bus while she's fighting for her life in a hospital bed. And that little threat, assuring me that my career is at stake, pending what I say in that report. Damn Mr. White. Damn this government. Damn the entire human race and all its misguided wickedness...*

***

They sat in the car, hidden beneath a thicket of stunted palmettos and crape myrtles, surrounded by pines. The sun came up like a gunshot wound in the eastern sky, a bloody rift between the horizon and the black clouds of the coming storm. The radio had said it was going to be another tropical one, this one named Stanley.

Jon sipped a cup of cold convenience store coffee, listened to the ticking of the 'Cuda's cooling engine and the drone of insects outside the opened window. He looked at Idegen, barely awake in the passenger seat. Slow, shallow breaths. They had managed to bandage and wrap her torso to stem the bleeding. Thankfully the three bullets had gone straight through without hitting bone and ricocheting or tumbling through her body. But she was still a mess. *I wonder what kind of song Kristofferson would have written if he'd had this Sunday morning coming down.*

"I know of a guy," he said, clearing his throat. "A guy in Charleston, about two or three hours from here. From what I hear, he's a bad guy. We can bag him, and you can..."

Idegen gave a weak smile, her grey-green eyes like glass marbles. "Feed on him, Jon? Yes, that would be nice..."

Jon frowned. "I don't think you can make it that long, though. What if I gave you some... blood?"

Idegen shook her head. "No. I... need more than blood. I need... *essence*. I cannot take that from you, Jon. You saved my life."

"And you've saved mine a couple times, now. Besides, it's not taking if I give it." He pulled his shirt over his head. "Come here. How does this work?"

"No, Jon..."

He grasped her hand. It was ice-cold and heavy. "Shit. You feel dead already. Quit screwing around and take a bite out of me before it's too late."

Idegen's eyes did that scary thing where they turned a glowing bone white. He heard a wet click, and when she spoke, he saw her fangs had extended. "I... I am sorry to do this, Jon. I will... try not to kill you... and I will make it as painless as possible."

She moved more quickly than he had expected, with more strength. The seat slid backward to its limit. She was on top of him, straddling him. Her breath was hot and moist on his naked shoulder. He could still smell the sweet scent of herbal shampoo in her hair, mingled with the smells of burnt gunpowder, blood, and gasoline.

Then all was pain. Sharp, digging, piercing pain.

He gasped, swallowed down a scream.

The pain was gone. He relaxed, felt sleepy. And why not? He had been running on adrenaline and caffeine for the better part of a week. Why not take a little nap and let Idegen have her snack?

Her body was warm, both soft and hard in all the right places. She enfolded him, and he returned the embrace, becoming aroused. "Oh man..." he murmured, running his fingers through her silky black hair, down her muscular back, grasping her powerful buttocks. He pressed himself against her, felt like he might burst through his jeans.

The physical sensations faded, replaced by something deeper, more important. He was inside her, and she was inside him. Their minds, their consciousness, their souls were one. In a moment, he saw her life as it had unfolded—centuries like days, months, and years. Vast, towering alien metropolises on distant worlds lit by Technicolor suns. Interstellar ships the size of small cities in immense armadas hurtling through space. Strange and wonderful beings that Hollywood could never imagine. Tall, beautiful people with stern, unforgiving faces, and a rigid formality.

He saw Vodie. A woman much like Idegen, though with hair the color of sunlight on snow and eyes like burning sapphires. He watched the two of them grow from small children to full womanhood in the blink of an eye: playing, fighting, learning, training, and eventually loving, and sadly parting.

All too quickly, the joyful memory was gone, replaced by pain. A pain so profound and extended, he could not fully comprehend it. It was the pain of the Black Star, whereby she was unmade and then remade to the rule of perfection. Her body was ripped to pieces, shredded, flayed, and dismembered. Each piece alive and in agony as it was reconstructed and improved with implants and injections. The reassembly hurt just as bad, if not worse.

Jon blinked, breathing hard. He was crying, tears hot and wet on his face. His groin and belly ached like he had been kicked hard in the nuts. He shook all over, but he was himself again, sitting in the old Barracuda in the early morning, just off a rural South Carolina road. On Earth. He reached up and touched his neck. The wound was sore and fresh but bled very little.

Idegen sat curled against the passenger door. She looked only marginally better, but her eyes were alert, watching him. After they stared at each other for a while, she raised a shaking hand and wiped his blood from her lips. "Thank you, Jon. I am... sorry I hurt you."

Jon wiped his face and slid back into his t-shirt. "I'm fine," he lied, fighting a sudden swoon. He was lightheaded as hell. "I've had hangovers that were worse." Which was probably true, though he couldn't remember one now. "How are you feeling?"

She forced a smile. "I will live. But I am very tired. I need to rest until we find this bad man... Are you able to drive?"

Jon licked his lips. "You kidding? That's the one thing I can do in my sleep. And have on occasion." He slid the seat back into position, turned the key in the ignition. "Go ahead. Get some shuteye. I'll wake you when we get there."

She grasped his hand. "Thank you, Jon." She turned against the door and was quickly asleep.

An hour later, after snagging a sausage biscuit and OJ at a roadside mom and pop, he turned onto Highway 78 and aimed the 'Cuda's gray hood at Charleston and the big black cloud coming in from the Atlantic. The air was already cooler, and he could see the flicker of distant lightning along the horizon. "Come on, Tropical Storm Stanley," he whispered. "Keep those helicopters out of the sky until we can find another ride."

He winced at the words as soon as he said them. The car was the last connection he had to his late father. The one and only nice thing the old man had ever done for him. He hated to part with it but knew if he didn't, they would be caught for sure.

Jon didn't know if it was the sudden sentimentality or the near erotic encounter he had shared with Idegen that made him suddenly think of Angie. He guessed it was probably both, as they equally incited a certain amount of guilt within him, and that was the one emotion he had come to associate with his true love for almost a decade. He felt for the phone in his pocket. Looked at the time display. "I wonder..."

Before he could think better of it, Jon dialed information and was connected to Angie's office in Knoxville. *I'll just leave a message on her voicemail...*

"Hello, Angela Lawman."

Jon spit out his straw.

"Hello?"

"Angie," he said. "Sorry, I thought I'd get your voicemail..."

She inhaled sharply. "Jon. I'm kind of busy getting ready for a big case. I thought this might be one of my assistants with some information I need."

"Right. Sorry. Look, since I've got you here, I just want to say thank you. Not just for getting me out of jail. I want to thank you for everything. All of it. My whole life. You were always there for me—when Kevin died, when my dad broke my arm, when Mom left. Every nasty bit of it. And I never appreciated you the way I should have. In fact, I treated you like shit. I'm sorry..."

There was silence on the other end of the line.

"Angie?"

There was an audible sigh. "Yes. I've always been there for you. And I guess a part of me always will be, which is why I came down the night they bagged you outside Hoppers. Now, what's this about, Jon?"

He pursed his lips, wiped at the corner of his eye. "Closure, I guess. That's the word you used. I just want you to know that whatever good I've ever done, and I know it's not much, it's because of you. You made me a better person. I should have been better to you. For you."

"Jon, are you all right? What's going on? Are they... are they going

THE WICKED TWISTED ROAD

to kill you?"

Jon laughed so he wouldn't cry. "No. I think that problem's solved. Nothing's wrong. I'm sorry to bother you. Just wanted to get all that off my chest and wish you the best life this world can give you. You deserve it, and then some."

"Jon—"

He ended the call and turned off the phone. "I love you, Angie. Always did and always will."

He looked at Idegen. *I love her, too. I've got to help her get back to Vodie, so she doesn't make the same mistake I did. No one should ever give up on love, no matter what planet they're from...*

Wiping the last tears from his eyes, he put his foot down on the accelerator and reveled in the throaty roar of the Hemi as the Barracuda ate up the shitty South Carolina road.

***

Idegen stared through the windshield as Jon pulled the car up to the gate. Beyond the wrought iron bars, she could see a driveway winding through a manicured lawn lined with swaying palmetto trees, terminating in a wide ring in front of a colonnaded three-story manor house. She also noted the security camera staring at them from inside the ten-foot brick wall.

She touched Jon's arm.

"I see it," he said, chewing on a new straw. "But I doubt very seriously if Andrew Summers has a public company handling his security. Too much of a chance for his secrets to get out to the world. I'm betting it's on a private system, with a monitoring station somewhere in the house."

He looked at her, concern etched on his pale, battered face. "How are you doing? You up to this?"

In truth, she was hurt and did not have very much strength. The effort of refraining from killing Jon had all but exhausted her. "I suppose I have no choice. Either I feed on this Andrew Summers or I die."

A ripple of guilt worked across his face. "I know. Well, just stay inside my head and follow my lead. If we work together, we might be able to pull this off. Hopefully better than we did in that showdown in Atlanta."

"In your head, Jon? I thought—"

He put the car back in gear and eased up to the call box. "After what we... shared, I reckon secrets don't matter anymore." He smiled. "It's okay. Trust me."

"I am, Jon. With my life."

"Can we help you?" an unhelpful voice demanded from the box.

"I need to speak to Mr. Summers. Dillon Crabtree sent me from Atlanta. It's urgent."

"Just a moment."

—*I hope this works*, his mind said to hers.

Either it will, or it will not. Worrying changes nothing.

—*Thank you, Yoda.*

She scanned her neural web for the reference and chuckled just before the gates opened. Jon drove up to the house. "Yes," she said, reading his thoughts. "It does seem that Mr. Andrews fancies himself a plantation owner, a member of the genteel Southern aristocracy before your American Civil War."

Jon scoffed. "These old school Dixie Mafia bastards and their racist paradise. At least the Peckerwoods don't wrap their bullshit up in pretty paper."

Two muscular white men in red polos and black slacks met them at the house. Both wore sunglasses and earpieces, Sig Sauers on their hips. "Mr. Summers will see you, but you must be searched before entering the house."

They had expected as much, so Jon surrendered the pistol he had taken from Craig Byce, as well as his revolver. Idegen was unarmed. They followed the two men into the spacious—if apparently empty—house and through a shrine to antebellum grandeur and glory. It was like walking through the set for Tara before the Yankees came—at least according to Jon's thoughts.

On the screened-in back porch, they found Andrew Summers, his lanky, middle-aged frame housed in a lovely seersucker suit. He smoked a cigar and enjoyed a pitcher of dark beer at a white wicker dinette. His backyard was separated from a golf course by a line of trees and a small creek. He watched as Charleston's doctors, lawyers, and executives finished their ninth hole under a glowering sky on a Sunday afternoon. The dark screen, combined with the landscape and distance, meant he could watch the course at his leisure without their seeing him.

Thunder rumbled and crackled in the distance.

"Well?" Summers said without looking up from his distraction. Idegen touched his mind and sensed irritation bordering on anger. She conveyed a warning to Jon.

"Mr. Summers, I'm Jesse Walker. One of Dillon Crabtree's lieutenants. This woman is an FBI agent—"

Summers cut them with his dark eyes, pursed his wrinkled lips. "So? Get to the point, Mr. Walker. I want to know why you have brought a *wounded* federal officer to my home. I am—as I am sure Mr. Crabtree has told you on many occasions—a law-abiding citizen and an upstanding pillar of this fine community."

Idegen dug deeper into the man's mind. She saw images of him in a red room, using a whip on dark-skinned people. Mostly women, but a few men. She sensed not only a physical pleasure in this form of degradation but also a personal, emotional one. She saw an exchange of money for these acts but still sensed the revulsion and self-loathing of the people he used. More, she sensed a deep, burning desire within the man to increase the sadism of these actions. These consuming fantasies were not limited to consenting adults...

"...It was an ambush," Jon was saying. "During the shootout, Crabtree told me to get to you. He said Atlanta couldn't fall and that you were the only person he trusted to take over after he and Byce were gone. He was already hit pretty bad... and Byce was dead."

Summers stared at the golf course, took another long sip of beer. "Atlanta has been a mess for years, and now you tell me it's even worse. Why on God's green Earth would I want to step into that Vietnam?" He looked at Jon and waved at the extravagant surroundings. "I'm done with the DM, boy. I got out, and I'm staying out. I do legitimate business now." He laughed. "Or what passes for legitimate business in the Old South."

Idegen saw more money and favors changing hands. This time with elected and appointed officials, men and women in power. Contracts signed, regulations ignored, statutes pushed aside, and zoning boundaries changed. She saw car washes and tree-trimming companies, beer and liquor distributors, and bars and restaurants. She saw a web of corruption stretching across the entire state of South Carolina, with Andrew Summers at its center like a bloated spider in a seersucker suit.

This isn't going to work, Jon.

—I'm open to suggestions.

"Andrew Summers," she said, raising her chin in judgment. She downloaded the data as she spoke. "We've got a file on you at the Bureau. Racketeering mainly, but I think they're looking for a few more charges to make sure you go away for good this time. Shouldn't take too much longer. I hear they got somebody in Columbia to roll."

Summers went rigid, bit down on his cigar. "What the hell are you talking about, bitch?"

She smiled, leaned on the back of a wicker chair. "I'm just a grunt, assigned to the Interstate Gang Taskforce, but I hear things from other departments. And I've heard your name once or twice. Not surprising, since we've still got a few things tucked away from your turn with the DM during the Reagan administration."

Jon blinked. "Guess I got lucky when I bagged this one on the way out, huh?"

"What do you want, girl?" Summers was leaning forward now. Angry but interested.

"A deal. I've been doing the good girl routine for eight years, and all it's gotten me is shot and kidnapped. You give me, say, thirty grand in cash, cut me loose, and I'll give you the name of the stooge they've got in Columbia."

Summers grinned as he stood. "You've got balls, girl. But no brains. Ain't nobody but the three of us even knows you're here." The door opened, and the two clean-cut bruisers stepped onto the porch. "And in a couple hours, it'll just be me and the gators down in the swamps feeding on your two sorry carcasses. But by then, I'll know what you know." Smug hatred rippled across his twisted face.

Now, Jon.

She summoned the last of her reserves and lashed out. She sensed Jon's attack at the same moment, felt his satisfaction as he broke Summers's nose and sent the man crashing to the concrete.

Idegen extended the claws of her right hand and spun, tearing the throat from one of the guards. As blood splashed the startled face of the other, she drove her knee into his groin and delivered a hammer blow with her left fist to the base of his bent neck. He dropped to the ground, cracking his skull.

She half-turned as she knelt over the big man bleeding out at her feet. "Hold him, Jon, while I deal with this one."

"Who—*what* the hell are you?" Summers shrieked as she sank her fangs into the shredded meat of the dying guard's throat.

"Karma," Jon said just before the ecstasy of the life force hit her.

The sudden glut of nourishment and energy overwhelmed Idegen. The man was still strong and virile, healthier than most of her recent meals, with a purity of blood that astonished her—devoid of pollutants and chemicals. She was locked in the eternal dance between life and death, host to it and part of it all at once. Infinity flowed from the dying man and into her, and she could feel the cells of her damaged body being reborn newer and stronger than before. Her death staved off by his life.

And then it was done. She let go of the shriveled corpse and stood, turning her eyes on the cowering man at Jon's feet. "Your turn, Mr. Summers."

He screamed, but only she and Jon French heard. He had built his secluded plantation too well.

Idegen and Jon spent the rest of the afternoon recovering from their recent ordeals while taking advantage of Andrew Summers's "hospitality." Hot showers were followed by long naps on expensive sheets in four-poster beds, and then Jon feasted on the stores found in the gourmet-style kitchen. Meanwhile, Idegen located and destroyed the estate's security system's hub and hard drive before looting Summers's personal safe. She came away with six thousand dollars in cash and the key to his gun safe, which offered up an arsenal that surpassed even what she had used in the battle at the Atlanta chop shop.

She found Jon in the detached six-car garage, four plastic bags of purloined provisions at his feet, his hands on his hips. He stood in total admiration. "Say what you will about that old douchebag, but Summers had good taste in cars."

"Which one shall we take?" Idegen hefted two bags filled with weapons and ammunition.

Jon rubbed his chin and slowly walked past the new silver Aston Martin Vantage. "Too flashy." He stopped in front of a fully restored, racing-green Jaguar E-Type. "Pretty to look at, but probably not the most reliable." He strode past the black Mercedes E 450 and the red Ferrari 458 Spider.

"What do you think?" He raised his hands over two cars, one orange, the other black. "The '68 Camaro Z/28 or the '63 Corvette Stingray?" He smiled, tilting his head repeatedly at the black and chrome Corvette.

She laughed. "I do not know, Jon. What do you think?"

"I think I've always wanted one of these," he said, opening the Stingray's driver's side door and whistling. "Go ahead and load up the trunk. We'll take her!"

They left Charleston just as Tropical Storm Stanley arrived.

21
RENEGADE

"Are you sure about this, Colonel?" Frankenstein's handsome face showed unusual emotion as he handed her the clipboard, genuine concern. "I mean, the docs are all against it. You could still lose that arm."

Sharpe struggled to write with her left hand. The pain in her reconstructed shoulder rivaled that which she had grown accustomed to in her back, but both were being held at bay by a wall of prescription painkillers. Barely.

"How's Archer?" She turned the clipboard over to the nurse at the station. She had just officially signed herself out of the hospital against recommendations. And against orders from Mr. White.

Frankenstein sighed and took the handles of her wheelchair. "Better than you, if I'm honest. His vest took most of the rounds. One clipped his left bicep, and another took a chunk out of his right deltoid. He'll be in rehab for a while, but if all goes well, he'll be a field operator again."

"That's good," she said. "I am... sorry about Ramrod."

There was a pause as he wheeled her down the hall crowded with doctors, nurses, and visitors—smells of antiseptics, urine, and flowers. "It's part of the job. I reckon we're lucky, considering what she's capable of."

Sharpe grunted agreement, shifted uncomfortably in the chair, and tried to readjust the heavy brace on her right arm. "Lucky." She thought about Brock and Race, about the squad of Air Force security troops on the C-130, about Honcho, Archer, and Ramrod. She tried to swallow down the guilt. "I've racked up quite the body count on this one."

"Like I said, Colonel. It's the job."

"Well, it may be my job, Sergeant, but it doesn't have to be yours anymore. I've officially been relieved of command for this operation, so you and the rest of Alpha are free to return to base and await new orders."

They boarded the elevator, and Sharpe was surprised to see Patches, Hack-Job, and Tunes waiting in fresh BDUs. They gave her grim smiles of encouragement. From behind her, Frankenstein said, "With all due respect, ma'am, to hell with that. We've got one motto at Alpha: Charlie Mike. Continue the Mission."

Sharpe forced herself to return the smile until she could get her emotions under control. *It's the damn medication and the fatigue. I can't get all dewy-eyed in front of the men...* Taking a deep breath, she cleared her throat. "Charlie Mike. Now, let's get to ORNL and set a trap for that alien bitch. Something tells me she'll be coming back for her ship."

She did not tell them that all the growing waves of déjà vu had come together and finally made sense. The "something" was, in fact, a psychic bond she had somehow forged with the subject, this Idegen Videshee of the Logonijy Empire. Something even she didn't fully comprehend until that moment in the garage when she'd seen through Idegen's eyes during the firefight.

Ironically, she realized that only Helbourne would be able to understand that connection, and she would have to now rely on *his* good will in order to stay on the case. *The good doctor, expert in all this shit that he is, may just be the only one able to convince Mr. White that I still have a job to do.*

***

Idegen watched the wiper blades battle the sheets of rain as Jon kept the Corvette moving northeast through the storm-racked countryside of South Carolina. But Idegen's thoughts were not on the weather, the road, or the classic rock on the car's radio. Her mind was far away, touching that of the dark-skinned warrior woman who had almost killed her in the firefight at the chop shop. Try as she might, she could not break the connection. This woman, this Sharpe, was now aware of the bond and was clinging to it, holding it open with her formidable will. Idegen had to admit she was impressed.

She is also returning to Oak Ridge. She plans to use the ship to lure me into a trap. She knows I am coming. How can we hope to outwit an enemy who can see into my mind, even if only instinctively? Though I can see her plans as well, she still holds all the advantages: larger, more heavily armed forces, a strongly defended installation, and she will soon possess the ship. As Jon would say, she is holding all the cards.

"Penny for your thoughts," Jon said with a smile. "Since we've been doing the Psychic Friends' Network thing, it's kind of lonely whenever you drift off like that."

Idegen rubbed her face with both hands. "Sharpe, the leader of the soldiers hunting me. She knows we are coming. And her superior has arrived, which means he will be able to bring even greater forces to bear against us."

"Well, it's not like giving up is an option. I mean, so long as they've got your ship, they're holding one hell of a big gun to the planet's head. If we don't stop them, we'll die anyway, along with several billion of my closest friends."

"I know," she said with a weak smile. "We do not have a choice. I am just unaccustomed to facing a hopeless battle."

Jon laughed. "Well, if that's all that's bothering you, don't fret." He gave her a playful wink. "Hopeless battles are my specialty. I've made a life of perfecting the underdog role. But I guess you've figured that out by now."

Idegen returned the laugh, let it lighten her spirit.

"Besides," Jon said, smoothly changing lanes to pass a slow-moving semi and guiding the car through a tidal wave of spray. "We need to get to that ship so you can get back to the love of your life. Somewhere up there, I'm sure Vodie is still waiting for you."

Idegen winced at the unexpected pain in her chest. "That is not a realistic option, Jon. Even if the ship were not all but destroyed in the crash, I might never see Vodie again."

"What do you mean?"

She wiped at the moisture of one eye. "When I was selected for the Order of the Black Star Worlds, Vodie and I had an altercation. She did not wish me to accept the honor, and I believed it was because she was jealous—that at long last, I had outdone her.

"When I informed her of my decision, she left me. We did not communicate during the entire period of my indoctrination and training. When I returned to the home world, I learned that she had joined the Conquest Fleet and had departed for the Savage Frontier.

"If she still lives, she has been at war for centuries. I fear that neither of us is the same person who once loved the other."

"But you don't know that, Idegen. You have to take the chance."

She shook her head. "I am sorry, Jon. And I thank you. But trying to save my relationship with Vodie will not heal the wound you feel for your Angie."

His jaw clenched. "I know that. I just thought it might be nice for *somebody* to have a happy ending, for love to actually win one for a change. And if I could be a part of that, then so much the better."

Idegen placed her hand on his wrist. "Jon, you have already helped love to 'win one.' When I came to your world, I was an invading soldier who regarded your species as no more than one of your big-game hunters might regard a particularly savage wild animal. But you have shown me the human race is just as sentient, complicated, and at times, noble as my own kind. It is because of you, Jon French, that I hope that the communications are still operational on my ship. I must try to contact the fleet and urge them not to attack the Earth."

Jon grinned. "Well, at least I've got that going for me: 'Jon French, Goodwill Ambassador to the Stars'... So, about this Sharpe, and how she knows we're coming... do you have any suggestions for how we handle that?"

"A few. Of course, all of them involve me feeding until I am all but glutted with essence and power. That means a lot more killing, Jon."

He sighed, and she sensed his internal conflict. "Well, as luck would have it, I know a few more guys in Asheville who might just have it coming to them."

***

"I am sorry, Colonel." The guard at the gate leaned down to talk across Frankenstein in the driver's seat. "But your clearance has been revoked."

Sharpe glared at the young DOE security officer. She fumbled her phone out of her pocket and struggled to text with her left hand. "Just a moment," she said as she sent the message to Mr. White: *I'm @ gate. Have plan to trap subject.*

Thank goodness for autocorrect.

A moment later, the phone in the guard shack rang. The young man stepped back into the booth, answered, gave a quick "Yessir," and hung up the receiver. "I'm sorry, ma'am. You're good to go; please proceed to Building Five." He pushed a button, and the crossbar raised.

"Not exactly a welcome with open arms," Tunes said from the backseat of the Humvee they had taken from McGhee Tyson. "You'd think *we* were the bad guys."

"They'd better be thankful we did come back," Hack-Job said as Frankenstein drove through the ORNL complex. "All these high-dollar security guards with their high-dollar toys... I doubt half of them have seen any real combat. Probably cousins, nephews, and brothers-in-law of folks with connections. They'll be kissing our boots when that space bitch shows up."

Sharpe tried to ignore the grumbling. She knew the real reason White had permitted them to enter. He wanted to humiliate her face to face, preferably in front of the men. She swallowed down the impotent rage that realization inspired. It didn't matter how much shit they heaped on her. The only thing that mattered was stopping Idegen and keeping more of her kind from coming to Earth. Even if it cost her a dishonorable discharge or time in Leavenworth, it would be worth it if she could make sure the United States was safe.

Right. And maybe someday, I'll even believe that. But right now, I still want my fucking star, and that sanctimonious son of a bitch White is not going to stand in my way. This is still my mission, and I aim to see it through to the end.

Parking in front of Building Five, they heard the air brakes of a huge flatbed. She turned to see the semi and its tarp-covered payload easing around to the rear of the building. "Looks like we're not the only ones arriving just now," she said as Frankenstein helped her out of the vehicle.

He followed her gaze. "So that's the honest-to-gosh spaceship... Sort of makes it all real now, even though we saw the alien face to face... sort of."

They were waved into the building by more DOE security, these armed with submachine guns and sidearms. Inside, they were met by another armed man who directed them to follow him through a short maze of corridors and security locks before guiding them into an expansive, whitewashed laboratory the size of a football field. At the far end of the lab, the semi was backing in, and a small crane waited to remove the cargo.

Doctor Helbourne and Mr. White stood in front of a pair of black-clad operators with M4s and full tactical gear. White was absorbed with making a text report on his phone, but Helbourne turned as they entered the room. Sharpe was surprised at the look of happiness that crossed the irascible doctor's face. He hurried to greet them.

"Colonel!" he said, taking her good hand in his sweaty grip. "I am so glad to see you up and about." His eyes swept the remnants of Alpha. "And you, I am sorry about the loss of your teammate, but I am glad to have you all back. And just in time to see the most significant moment in the twenty-first century! Perhaps in recorded history!"

"Must not have had anybody to talk to lately, huh, Doc?" Patches smiled, slapping Helbourne on his hunched shoulders. "It's only been a couple days."

Sharpe left the men with their reunion and walked over to face Mr. White. "Sir," she said, "I would like to offer my continued service to this project in whatever capacity you see fit."

White continued to scroll on his phone. "Well, you could fetch me a cup of coffee, Colonel." He glanced up, a grin creasing the side of his face. "But I see you can hardly manage even that at the moment."

She inhaled slowly, trying to restrain the rage. "I admit that my performance in this matter has been less than satisfactory. However, I must point out that we hardly have a set of guidelines concerning this scenario. I did the best I could with what I had."

White put the phone away and looked past her to watch the unloading process. "Not exactly the inspiring words of a historic leader, Colonel. 'I did my best,' doesn't quite have the gravitas of George C. Scott at the beginning of *Patton*, now does it?"

Sharpe smiled to keep from punching him with her good hand. The painkillers were wearing off, and her entire body was haunted by the ghosts of former agonies. "Perhaps not, sir. But I am not quitting. In fact, I have another plan. And I have new information."

White raised an eyebrow. "Really?"

Helbourne and Alpha joined them. "Has Dr. Helbourne informed you of the subject's psychic capabilities?"

"I am up to speed on all the pertinent data," White said.

"Then you will understand when I tell you that I have somehow formed a telepathic bond with her and can sense her desire to return to this ship."

White smiled like a wolf. "One hardly needs ESP to come to that conclusion, Colonel Sharpe. If there is anything still working on that craft, my guess is that it's a signal or homing beacon that your subject's cybernetic system has already picked up. She knows that it's her only way of escaping this planet, short of hijacking one of our rockets."

Helbourne cleared his throat. "Mr. White, if I may? Since that tropical storm is playing havoc with our satellite coverage right now, I do believe that Colonel Sharpe's link to the subject, if it is *legitimate*—" he glanced at her— "may constitute our best chance of tracking and catching the subject... for the time being."

"Fine, Doctor. Do whatever tests you feel are necessary to ensure that Colonel Sharpe's claims are founded and not just an attempt to salvage her career. Now, if you'll excuse me, I need to take some photos of our newest acquisition."

Sharpe watched White and his guards walk to the ship as the tarps were removed. It was rather small, about the size of an F-16 fighter jet, only more disc- or oval-shaped, and covered with a matte-black finish as she'd seen on the old SR-71 Blackbirds. The canopy was gone, and much of the rear section and one of the wings was heavily damaged.

"Legitimate, Doctor?" Sharpe asked as they both stared at the alien craft.

"I needed an excuse to speak with you in private, Colonel." Helbourne's voice was low. "I think you and I may now have a mutual enemy that requires our formal alliance. And I am not talking about Idegen Videshee."

Sharpe glanced at the little scientist and smiled for the first time in what seemed like forever. "I think you might be right, Doctor."

***

Jon pulled the Corvette to the curb in front of the big taproom and restaurant on the corner of Biltmore Avenue and Market Street. The painted windows on the block-long building read BREWER'S FINE FOODS & BEVERAGES. It was after midnight. The rain-washed windshield glowed with the twisted colors of neon lights. Thankfully, the weather kept the late-night crowd off the streets.

"Ready?" he asked, popping a fresh straw into his mouth.

"Ready." Idegen adjusted her push-up bra. Not that she needed one, but impressive cleavage was still the best distraction known to man.

They had stopped at a Target and used a few hundred bucks of Summers's money to spruce up their appearance and sell the notion that they were high rollers looking for a big-money game. Idegen wore a low cut red top under a new jacket, extra-tight jeans, and knee-high black leather boots. Her newly dyed red hair trailed loose and free over her shoulders, and she'd done an amazing job on her makeup and nails in the store's ladies' room.

In a word, she was a knockout.

Jon glanced at himself in the rearview mirror, not liking the Billy Idol bleach job he'd done on his own hair or the hipster-framed cheaters he wore to disguise the damage to his nose. He also wore jeans and a grey sports jacket. A wild-eyed monochrome Gene Wilder declared IT'S FRONKENSTEEEN! on the t-shirt beneath. Replacing his Bates tacticals were a pair of brand new Nikes that hurt his feet.

"I look like I should be working for Google or something," he grumbled as he put on the little black fedora.

Idegen chuckled. "Well, after this is all over, you will be looking for a new line of work."

Jon shook his head. They were leaving all the guns in the car. "Or an undertaker. Come on, let's go."

"Jon," Idegen said as they hurried across the sidewalk in the rain.

"I see it." He glanced at the silvery North Carolina Highway Patrol cruiser parked two cars ahead of them. "I half expected him to be here, anyway."

Brewer's was all but empty on this particular Sunday night. The tastefully dim dining room to the right of the entrance was peopled by a handful of late-night diners in corner booths, two servers, and a busboy. The extensive bar on the left side of the big room was more populated, with nearly thirty drinkers, bartenders, and cocktail waitresses.

The pretty brunette hostess smiled tiredly. "Two for dinner?"

Jon returned the smile, watched her appraise Idegen with jealousy. "We're here to see Tommy. He in tonight?"

The girl frowned. "Who's asking?"

Jon patted his breast pocket. "Tell him Mr. Green and a few of his *presidential* pals are looking for a game."

The girl raised her chin. "Just a moment."

—There are a lot of people here, Jon. Most of them innocents by your standards.

I know. But Tommy Brewer's got a basement room where he has his poker games. It's secluded and insulated. We could set off a bomb down there, and it wouldn't even cause somebody up here to spill a drink.

—And you are sure he will not recognize you?

Who knows? But I doubt it. The few times I brought him deliveries, he had his face buried in either his ledgers or a hand of cards. I was a peon, a nobody. Tommy Brewer is the DM's big man in the Carolinas, even bigger than Summers. Why would he ever pay me any mind?

"Follow me," the girl said, returning from a room behind the bar.

Showtime.

They followed her through the bar area. Jon noted the way all heads turned in their direction. He saw Rick Brewer, Tommy's state trooper son, sitting at the end of the bar. He got up to follow just as they entered the backroom.

—Do not worry, Jon. He is coming as a security precaution, and I am certain I can take him if it comes to that.

The hostess opened another door at the end of the storeroom stocked with cases of liquor and glassware. A stone stair led down. "Go ahead."

Jon smiled and pressed on. *Can you tell how many more are down there?*

—Six. I sense this Brewer and five subordinates. All armed.

Great. Why do I keep hearing Brad Pitt yelling something about starting a gunfight in a basement?

Reaching the foot of the stair, they found themselves in a low-ceilinged yet luxurious room that was half man cave and half gentleman's club. The far wall was covered by a projection screen in front of two rows of leather recliners. To the right stood an old-school bar complete with brass footrails and an antique odalisque painting above the row of top-shelf booze and tap handles. The left side of the room was dominated by mirrors along the walls and a low, under-lit stage sporting three floor-to-ceiling brass poles.

A trio of green felt-covered gaming tables occupied the center of the red-carpeted chamber: poker, roulette, and craps. The poker table was surrounded by five big, cigar-smoking men. The sixth man stood behind the bar, idly watching ESPN on the flatscreen mounted in the corner. Johnny Cash's "Folsom Prison Blues" played over the surround sound system.

"Who the hell are you?" Tommy Brewer asked from the wet end of his cigar. The fat, bald man in suspenders didn't look up from his cards until he sensed a wave of awe slide across his companions. Then his bright blue eyes widened as they took in Idegen.

Jon stepped into the room but was dragged to a halt by a hard hand on his shoulder from behind. "Easy, slim," Rick Brewer, the state trooper, said, his breath heavy with Jack Daniels. "Let's see what you're carrying first."

Jon submitted to the pat-down. He accepted the leisurely tour the crooked cop took over Idegen's body with less grace. "Find anything you like there, Barney?"

The big cop stood and smiled, his hand resting on the stun gun on his belt. "Sure. You want to make something of it?"

"No, he doesn't," Idegen said. "Please forgive my brother. He's just a little overprotective." She gave Jon a mock glare. "I can take care of myself, and I actually *liked* it." She turned a glamorous smile on Rick Brewer.

"As much as I enjoy a good soap opera," Tommy Brewer said from the card table, "you still haven't told me who the hell you are and what you want."

"Sorry, sir." Jon stepped closer to the table. "Name's Jon Reagan, out of Charleston. Andrew Summers said you had the best game in town. My sister and I are on our way to Atlantic City to see if I can score a seat at the World Series of Poker. Thought I might stop a few times along the way to keep my skills frosty and maybe add a few bucks."

One of the bruisers, the flat-topped guy to Tommy's left, sat back and shook his head. "He sounds like a sharp, Uncle Tom. I say we send him and his sister packing."

Jon glanced at Idegen, who had joined Rick Brewer at the bar for a glass of whiskey.

"Let 'em stay awhile," the trooper said, smiling at Idegen like a kid with a new toy.

"How much green you pushing, kid?" Tommy asked, pulling on his cigar until the tip glowed bright orange.

"I've got five K." Jon pulled the envelope from his pocket and set it on the table. "Is that enough for a buy-in?" He glanced at the flat top. "Or are you tough guys scared to play with some new blood?"

"Sit down." Tommy reached his bulk across the table to scoop up the envelope. "Bradley, deal him in."

Flat top grunted but did as his uncle instructed. Jon smiled, chewed on his straw, and sat down at the table. He was surrounded by big, armed gangsters, and his back was to the door.

I wish I hadn't gotten blood all over my lucky shirt. I can't think of a worse way to start a game of poker.

"We're gonna watch a movie, Dad." Rick Brewer took Idegen by the hand and made for the back of the room. Idegen carried a bottle of Jack and a pair of glasses. She winked at Jon as she passed the table.

"Whatever," the fat man said. "Just keep it down back there."

The end of the room went dark and a moment later the grindhouse opening credits of *Death Proof* appeared on the screen.

Stage one complete, Jon thought. The plan was to divide and conquer. Jon would keep them occupied on the card game while Idegen lured them away to feed, one by one.

He folded the first two hands. They were dealing him shit cards on purpose. He'd seen the scam before: make the new fish desperate as he watches his stack dwindle for the first hour, then give him the promise of a good hand, only to lose to a bad beat or two. Then, he'd get reckless, be forced to go all-in, get beaten for good, and sent on his merry way.

He tried to slow play, but in truth, he was only half paying attention to his cards or the game. He was still connected to Idegen, and the euphoria as she quietly murdered and fed on Rick Brewer washed over him in waves.

"You sure do smile a lot for somebody losing his shirt," one of the bruisers said.

"Looks like we might be saving you a trip, son," Tommy grunted, laying down a king-high flush, trumping Jon's queen-high straight. "If you can't do no better than this, you don't need to go to no World Series of Poker."

"Like I said," Jon whispered, trying to shake off the lingering high.

"I'm a little rusty. But I've still got a few chips."

Flat top gave him a lewd grin, tilted his head toward the movie screen. "Once you're out of dough, I guess you could wager a go-round with your sister. So long as Rick don't mind."

—Jon, someone else is coming down. More armed men.

Jon turned just as the door opened. In stepped the blond pretty boy with the tattoos and fancy clothes, the man Byce had called "Jesse." Two more bruisers were behind him on the stair.

"Brewer!" Jesse boomed as soon as he was in the room. "We got lots of problems. Byce and Crabtree are dead, and we've lost two dozen shooters from Atlanta to Knoxville. I just barely—"

Jon's and Jesse's eyes met. Recognition flashed across the man's handsome face. "Why, you little son of a bitch! It's *you!*"

Jon came out of his chair, grabbed it, and hurled it into the three men clustered in the doorway.

"What the hell?" Tommy Brewer shouted.

The men at the table clawed at their concealed pistols, trying to get to their feet.

The bartender reached beneath the bar.

The first gunshot splattered his head across the framed reclining nude. Idegen had taken the dead Rick Brewer's sidearm.

Jon dived across the bar. Bullets, shattered glass, and splashing liquor followed him.

Jon found the scattergun the bartender had been reaching for. He sensed Idegen had already dropped four of the men at the table.

The air in the room was thick with the smell of burnt powder, alcohol, and blood.

An arm reached over the bar above him, a pistol in its hand, muzzle pointed down.

Jon squeezed the shotgun's trigger, the barrel still beneath the bar. His ears rang and his eyes stung from the explosive blast. The man on the other side screamed, and the arm disappeared.

Rolling out from behind the bar, he swept the room with the shotgun, working the pump. Tommy Brewer had flipped the card table on its side. He and one other man were using it as cover, firing at Idegen behind the leather chairs. Kurt Russell ate nachos on the bullet-riddled movie screen.

Wounded men cried out and writhed on the carpet.

Two shots tore into the bar just inches above Jon's head, spraying him with splinters and dust. Jesse knelt behind the heavy door, pointing a smoking pistol in his direction.

Jon squeezed off a shot, then ducked back behind the bar to clear the debris from his face.

—*He's coming over the bar, Jon!*

Jon worked the pump and swung the gun around. He saw Jesse slide across the bar's surface, leading with his pistol.

Jon pulled the trigger.

The report was louder than before. Something hot and sharp punched him in the left shoulder, knocking the wind out of him.

A wet, warm, and heavy mass fell across his legs. Jon blinked, realizing it was the mangled, faceless corpse of his attacker.

Jon's mind reeled. He felt weak and cold, the gun slipping from his hands. The warmth he felt on his legs seemed to be spreading across his chest and back. He slid down the wall until he was prone. He closed his eyes, saw through Idegen's as she moved across the room at superhuman speed, her teeth and claws sinking into throats in a red haze.

Just like my nightmare as a kid...

22
AIN'T NO GRAVE

"Fascinating," Helbourne murmured. He made another notation on his tablet and traced the circuitry through the ship's canopy until it abruptly ended. "Everything was relayed into a command module, which is now sadly missing."

He thought of the pile of slag the Army had recovered from the Everglades about the same time they had captured Idegen. *All the secrets in the universe could have been in that melted metal...*

His requested personnel had not yet arrived. A technologist from DAARPA, a Nobel-nominated engineer from MIT, a computer scientist from Cal Tech, and a cyberneticist from Texas A&M would eventually make this task so much simpler. Or so he hoped. But for some inexplicable reason, Mr. White was dragging his feet on the security clearances, so Helbourne was making do with the dunces he had to work with at ORNL.

All they seemed interested in was determining if the ship's power was fission- or fusion-based atomic energy. He had already had a few headbutting sessions with the facility's top dog, informing the man in no uncertain terms that the engines and their power source were the last part of the ship to be examined. Helbourne reasoned that anything capable of interstellar flight might possibly be something above the ken of mortal man, and he was determined to understand everything he could about the alien technology before he decided to poke that particular bear.

And then there was the constant maneuvering between Sharpe and Mr. White. White had all the power, or so he thought, but Sharpe was slowly putting together a mutiny that could dethrone the would-be king of ORNL. At times, Helbourne felt that he was the swing vote and was being pulled apart by two powerful forces.

But despite all this, he was happy. He was sitting in the canopy of an actual extraterrestrial spacecraft, and he was sussing out the thing's inner workings. At long last, he was at the pinnacle of Maslow's pyramid: the much sought after and rarely attained self-actualization.

"We've finished cataloging the ship's circuitry, Dr. Helbourne," one of the assistants said. "What's next?"

He looked up at the pretty young woman and scowled. "Have you uploaded the data into the system?"

"Not yet."

"Then do it. When that's done, get some tools and start disassembling the exterior. *Carefully.*"

"Yes, sir."

Helbourne watched her stalk off, admiring the slight movement of her hips for a moment before turning back to his tablet. "Yes, just a few more notes, and I think I might be able to put together an interface... then we'll see what secrets you hold for me and the human race, my beauty."

***

It was almost one a.m. on Monday morning. Sharpe sat in the corner booth of the Waffle House on Illinois Avenue in Oak Ridge. Her back ached and her shoulder hurt, and she wanted a Vicodin like nobody's business. She settled for a cup of sugar-loaded coffee. Not because she liked overly sweet coffee, but because she had tipped too much in with her left hand. Clumsily stirring the drink only reminded her just how useless she now felt.

Can't even put sugar in my coffee. How the hell am I supposed to pull this off? Usurp the authority of a CIA and DOD top brass player, take over ORNL, and capture an alien warrior who has kicked my ass every time I've gone up against her? Maybe I'm stupid. Maybe I should have taken White's deal—accepted the Purple Heart, the commendation, and the honorable discharge. Retired someplace nice, maybe take over a college ROTC program, and shape the country's warriors and leaders of the future...

"Hell with that," she muttered into her syrupy coffee. She'd never quit anything in her life, and she wasn't about to start now. It just wasn't part of her genetic makeup.

She checked her watch. He was late.

The door opened, and Helbourne stepped into the near-empty restaurant. He wore an old-school fedora and a raincoat, like a dime-store Bogart. She resisted the urge to roll her eyes when he spotted her and came to the table.

"I've finished the interface," he whispered as he sat down. "I'm running a full diagnostic as we speak. It's possible that tomorrow morning, I might be able to access the navigation computer and the engines. Do you know what that—?"

"Have you thought about it?"

The waitress was there asking for his drink order before he could answer. Sending her away with a request for coffee and ice water, he nodded. "Yes, I have. But I want to know your full intentions before I say one way or the other. Your plans."

Sharpe sipped her coffee and waited for Helbourne to accept his drinks. She sent the waitress away without ordering anything else. "We're waiting on a third party."

Helbourne glared at her. "Who?"

Sharpe chuckled and inclined her head at her arm brace. "Who do you think, Doctor? I've got a busted wing, and you're not exactly a crack shot unless you've been holding out on me. We're going to need muscle if we're to pull this off."

Helbourne leaned over the table and whispered, "Alpha? You can't be serious!"

"We're about to find out." She raised her chin to Frankenstein as he walked through the door, dressed in jeans and a faded Georgia Bulldogs sweatshirt. Sharpe felt her cheeks flush at the sight of him out of context. Just a damn good-looking man about to have coffee with her.

After they all had drinks and Helbourne and Frankenstein had ordered pecan waffles and steak and eggs respectively, she got down to business. "I think you are right, Doctor. I think I've been going about this the wrong way all along."

"How's that?"

Sharpe closed her eyes and took a deep breath. She blocked out the pain in her body (and the pleasure of Frankenstein's proximity) and reached out with her mind to the alien yet familiar mind somewhere in the distance. She concentrated and felt... *concern... love... fear*, but not for herself...

"I don't think she's the bloodthirsty monster I had assumed."

"Begging your pardon, Colonel," Frankenstein said, "but you couldn't prove that by me. We've got two men in the hospital and one under a flag because of her. And that's not counting all the other G.I.s and civilians she's put in the ground."

"I know," Sharpe said. "And that's why I wanted to talk to you about this. In an unofficial capacity. I don't want to order you or anybody else in Alpha to go against your conscience. As I've said, I don't have any official authority over you anymore. I'm not here as a Colonel but as a human being who wants the best for Earth."

Helbourne smiled. "You finally want to *talk* to her? You've sensed something through your... connection, haven't you?"

"I think we can lure her back to her ship without any more killing."

"It could be a trick." Frankenstein pushed his half-empty plate away. "If she's aware of your bond, she could be trying to lull you into lowering your guard. Hell, she could know you're planning to trap her. Maybe this 'bond', or whatever you call it, is just one more weapon in her arsenal. Or a means to get ahold of one she's got hidden in that ship. And from what I've seen, she doesn't need any more weapons."

Sharpe pursed her lips. "You're right. And it's because of that ferocity and killing efficiency that I think we need a change in strategy. You realize that all Mr. White intends to do is increase the manpower and firepower, which is likely to increase the body count."

Frankenstein sat back and sipped his coffee.

"But... I don't know..." She rubbed her temple. "I just remember when she escaped from that C-130... when we locked eyes, and we both wanted to kill each other..." She shook her head. "Now, it's like she's a completely different... person."

"Or you are," Helbourne offered.

Sharpe frowned. "Meaning?"

"Well, I don't know, maybe we're all different people now. I know when I took this job, my primary goal was to become a Nobel winner and the Grand Poobah of human-alien relations. Now..." He rubbed his wrinkled face. "Now, I just want to make sure that her people don't come down here and lay waste to our entire planet and the human race."

Sharpe looked at Frankenstein. The handsome soldier raised an eyebrow. "Don't put this on me. I'm an Air Force grunt. I go where I'm told, do what the mission calls for. I'm not even the leader of Alpha."

"You are so long as Honcho's in a burn unit," Sharpe said. "And you're not just 'a grunt.' You're Pararescue and one of the best. That means you're in the business of saving lives, right?"

"Yes, and I reckon saving the planet falls into that category... even if it does include Commies and terrorists. So, you two think this is the best plan?"

Sharpe laughed. "Hell no. It's not even a plan. It's just an idea, but right now, it's all we've got."

Frankenstein smiled. "I'll have to sell it to the team, but who am I to argue with a full-bird colonel and a Ph.D.? What's a little treason in the face of a global invasion, right?"

So, they hashed out the bare bones of a plan. And after Helbourne returned to his lab, Sharpe popped a Vicodin and checked into a motel with Frankenstein. After all, no matter what happened next, it might be the last chance to get her rocks off for a long, long time.

***

—*I am coming for you, Jon... Do not worry...*

Jon woke to a dull white glow, the sound of low beeping, something over his face, the smell of sterile plastic, and pain, dull and enveloping. He tried to move but felt sluggish and fuzzy. His right wrist caught on something cold and hard.

Cuffed. It took a few seconds before full consciousness dawned, and he understood. *I'm handcuffed to a hospital bed.*

—*Do not worry, Jon*, the voice in his head said again. *I am coming for you...*

Idegen? He remembered the alien woman he had saved from the Tennessee River and who had saved him from the Dixie Mafia. She was in his head, only very far away.

"Idegen," he slurred into the oxygen mask covering his face.

"Good," a gruff voice said from somewhere to his right. "You're awake. About time, too." A shadow loomed into his field of vision and slowly took form. A large man with short reddish hair and a deeply lined face, eyes the color of night. Instinctively, Jon knew he was a cop.

"I'll start easy," the man said, pulling the mask from Jon's face. "I'm Detective Anderson, Asheville PD. I reckon I'm first in line, but there's a guy from the state police and another from the FBI out there waiting to have a crack at you, Mr. John Doe. So, let's start there. What's your name, son?"

Jon giggled. "Puddin' Tame."

Anderson was not amused. "Fine, tough guy. I'll have them cut your pain meds down to shit, and then we'll see how fast you want to talk." The man tapped the bullet wound in Jon's shoulder for emphasis. It felt like he was being shot all over again.

"Son of a bitch," Jon grunted. "I got rights..."

"To hell with your rights," Anderson said. "You were the only survivor of a shootout in a downtown business involving known members of the Dixie Mafia, a North Carolina State Trooper, and an upstanding member of this community."

Jon glared at the cop. "That upstanding member of the community would be Tommy Brewer, right? Well, news flash, detective. That asshole was a DM big cheese. But if you didn't already know that, I'm guessing someone in your department, probably higher up than you, was on his payroll." He took a deep breath and closed his eyes. "Now, that's the only freebie you're getting from me until I see a lawyer. Now get out."

Anderson raised his angular jaw. "I'll be back, you little shit heel. Me or one of the others, and I've got a feeling they won't be as nice."

"Bring flowers or chocolates next time, asshole."

When Anderson left, Idegen told him, *I am coming, Jon. I am close. No... too many cops. I'm caught. Save yourself...*

Jon dozed off again...

He woke to panic. Something was wrong. Someone was in his room. It was dark, but he saw someone, someone big. Dim light from the window reflected on metal. Buckles, buttons, a badge. "Who—?"

A powerful hand pushed him back into the bed; another covered his face. "Hush up now, Jon-Boy," a gravelly voice said.

His mind reeling, Jon thought it was the ghost of Rick Brewer.

"Settle down, and this'll be painless and quick. Make trouble, and I'll have to make it look like an attempted escape."

Jon tried to relax.

"That's better," the state trooper said. He kept his hand over Jon's mouth. "You call out or scream, and I just shoot you in the balls and then in the face. Get it?"

Jon nodded. When the cop let go, he licked his lips. "Who are you? What's this all about?"

"It's about the Dixie Mafia tying up loose ends, Jon-Boy." The trooper pulled a capped syringe out of his breast pocket. "And let me tell you, brother, you are one hell of a loose end."

Jon stared at the syringe, outlined against the pale light from the room's window, the needle glinting as the trooper removed the orange plastic cap.

"I don't know what you're talking about." Jon tried to buy as much time as possible. Just a few more seconds of life.

The cop laughed. "Right. You don't know anything about that multi-departmental sting that sent Knoxville into a tailspin, which somehow led Byce and Crabtree to a terminal case of lead poisoning in Atlanta." His voice went hard when he added, "And I'm sure you don't know jack shit about what happened to Jesse Sneed and my pal and his daddy down in that basement last night."

Jon licked his lips and chewed on the inside of his cheek. "Okay, maybe I do. But don't you want to know? The truth, I mean."

The cop paused, the needle inches away from the IV. "What?"

"Didn't you see the crime scene? Didn't you see the condition of Rick

Brewer's body? Were there any more like that?"

The trooper stood straight, the needle easing to his side. "No... I was on a... What the hell are you talking about? Like what?"

"Go to the morgue and take a gander at your pal's corpse. I'll bet it looks like a piece of beef jerky. Then come back, and I'll explain it to you."

"Ha!" The man bent back to the IV. "Nice try. Now it's time for you to say goodnight, Jon-boy."

The window slid open behind the cop. He turned.

Jon didn't see what happened in the gloom, just a dark blur. But he heard a wet crunching sound and the soft clatter of the syringe falling to the linoleum.

—Rest, Jon. I am here. You are safe.

'Bout time... He surrendered to his exhaustion and vanished into oblivion.

When he woke next, he was in the leather passenger seat of the Corvette Stingray. The classic car's engine purred like a contented panther, and the fog-shrouded trees of the Smoky Mountains slid past the windshield in a silvery green blur. He looked over and saw Idegen at the wheel, her red-dyed hair shining in the dull morning sun, pale skin aglow, and grey-green eyes sparkling. She was dressed in a zipped-up black hoodie and yoga pants instead of the flashy outfit she'd worn during the gunfight.

"What the hell happened?" he croaked. He sounded like Gollum from *The Lord of the Rings* flicks.

She smiled. "You were wounded. I knew the best thing I could do was to let the authorities take you to a hospital where you could get proper medical attention. So, I refueled the car and got supplies while I waited until you were well enough to travel, and then I came and got you. After placing the dead policeman in your bed, I carried you out through the window. It was just after dawn, so no one saw us get away, and I had parked the car two streets over."

He was more than thankful he'd passed out before she removed his catheter. Now, his mouth was dry as the Sahara, and his shoulder hurt like hell. "You cut it pretty close. There had to be security cameras..."

"Yes," she admitted. "Easily disabled with thrown rocks."

Jon chuckled, which turned into a cough. "I guess, if you have an onboard targeting system like a Terminator and the arm strength of a superhero."

"There is water and aspirin, as well as some nourishment in that bag at your feet... I am sorry for my delay in extracting you, but I had to make certain that we would be able to escape Asheville without further pursuit. We are far too close to ORNL to try another roundabout getaway."

Jon winced as he reached down and pulled the bag into his lap. "How'd you get out of that basement without being seen after that shitshow?"

Idegen winked at him. "I removed my bloody clothes and ran out naked, screaming. There weren't that many people still in the restaurant by that time. The few remaining witnesses were completely caught off guard. I was in the car and a mile away before I heard the first sirens."

Jon remembered the stripper stage in Tommy Brewer's man cave and shook his head. "The cops'll be hounding Asheville's exotic dancer community for months looking for you." As his head cleared, he realized they weren't on I-40. "You're taking the Parkway? They watch for speeders like hawks on this thing."

"Do not worry, Jon. I am monitoring our velocity. Besides, you need your rest, and we need darkness before we arrive at the facility."

"And once we get there, then what?"

"I do not know. The only thing of which I am certain is that Colonel Sharpe knows I am coming and that she has made her plans accordingly."

"So, it's a trap. We're just walking right into their trap after all this shit." He bit his lip, thinking about the last time he had seen his father. The last time he would *ever* see his father because Sharpe and her troops had killed him.

"Do you have a better idea, Jon? If they test those engines—"

"Yeah, I know. Your Space Modulator will detonate the planet." He washed down the aspirin and was about to get angry until he saw a bundle of plastic straws in the bag. He sighed and rubbed his face. "You're right. What choice do we have? I guess we go in the front door, guns blazing. At least we've still got Summers's hardware collection."

"Indeed, we do."

He looked at his bare legs and the wrinkled hospital gown exposing his backside to the leather seat. "Well, before we go out like Butch and Sundance, I need to put on some damn pants."

23
STONE

The ORNL campus was a sprawling complex of regimented brick buildings and smokestacks nestled in the forested hills just outside the town of Oak Ridge, Tennessee. On the surface, it appeared to be a quaint relic of a bygone era, the idealized golden age of post-war science and American ingenuity. In truth, it housed some of the most advanced technologies and facilities on the face of the Earth.

Idegen knew all this not only from her neural web but also from the impressions she had received from Helbourne and Sharpe during her captivity, as well as the current bond she shared with the colonel. She also knew it was heavily guarded by its own private security force. A *well-armed* security force.

"They have automatic weapons, Jon." They sat in the darkened Stingray at the edge of the road that branched off from the highway and led to the main gate. "And armored support vehicles. I'm sensing at least sixty armed men on duty, with possibly more in reserve somewhere within the complex."

Jon chewed on a straw behind the wheel. Beneath the blue nylon arm sling they had picked up at Walmart, he wore a black t-shirt with a small red-and-white patch printed on the right pectoral, which read, HELLO! MY NAME IS: INIGO MONTOYA. YOU KILLED MY FATHER. PREPARE TO DIE.

When she had pointed out that it looked like a tempting target, he had said, "Still. I think it's appropriate."

When she found the reference with her neural web, she could not argue.

"And you say Sharpe knows we're coming?" Jon said. "So much for the element of surprise."

Idegen reached for the door handle. "You should go, Jon. I will see if

I can sneak in and destroy the ship on my own."

Jon started the car. "Hell with that. We've come too far not to see this thing to the end." He glanced at her in the dim light of the dashboard. "Together."

She smiled as he put the car in gear and got back on the road. She also cocked the four pistols she had on her person. The carbines, the shotgun, and the submachine gun on the floor were already chambered with safeties on.

Jon pulled the car up to the security gate and rolled down the window. She could feel his tension but also his practiced poise. He planned to fast-talk their way in first, as futile as the attempt seemed. "Evening," he said to the handsome soldier who stepped out of the glass booth.

Soldier? Idegen frowned when she saw the camouflage BDUs instead of the blue uniform she had seen in her psychic scans. She focused on this man and realized he was one of the warriors Sharpe had used to hunt her. One of the men she had seen in Atlanta.

She gripped one of the pistols.

"We've been expecting you, Mr. French," the man said as the gate opened. "You and... uh, Miss Videshee. If you'll follow us, we'll take you to Colonel Sharpe and Dr. Helbourne."

Jon turned back with wide eyes. They both shrugged, and Jon pulled in behind the Humvee the soldier had boarded. "Well," he said, "this is a new one. Can you tell what they're planning?"

"No. It is... confusing. The men in that vehicle are the ones we fought in Atlanta... They want to kill me, but... for some reason, they are not. I cannot tell if they are merely waiting to spring a trap or whether they have new orders that countermand their personal intentions. I do know that Dr. Helbourne—despite being my chief torturer—has always been a proponent of peaceful communication, if only for the sake of his own professional vanity. But if he is here, that may be a good sign."

They drove deep into the benighted complex, near the back where the buildings hunched against the ring of mountains.

"Even if they do draw down on us," Jon said, "and even if it looks like we're not going to make it out alive, we need to make sure they know about the dangers of that ship. We've got to try and make them understand, no matter what."

"I know, Jon. I agree. I have tried to convey this information to Sharpe via our connection, but she does not seem to grasp it. Perhaps she is not yet skilled enough in her psychic abilities, or she is too focused on me and the threat I pose as an individual."

They pulled in beside the Humvee in front of a long, five-story brick building that had very few windows. The number 5 was painted in a big, two-story white numeral on its upper corner. "My ship is here, Jon," Idegen said as she got out of the car. "I can sense it."

"Have they monkeyed with the engines yet?"

"If they had, we would not be standing here, Jon."

"Fair enough."

Two soldiers, both armed with carbines and sidearms, exited the Humvee and motioned them toward the entrance. "If you'll be so kind," said the handsome one.

They entered the building. Idegen's eyes adjusted quickly to the sudden stark brightness of the interior lighting. A squad of security guards stood on either side of a metal detector, all holding submachine guns at the ready. She felt Jon tense but put her hand on his shoulder. "Easy, Jon. We might as well surrender our weapons; they would not save us at this point, in any case."

"They might give us a chance at a stalemate," he mumbled around his straw. "Time to think of a way out."

She shook her head and drew her pistols, ejecting the magazines and the chambered rounds before placing them in the heavy plastic bins provided. "There is no way out, Jon. This is the endgame. We either continue to run, or we try to save your world. We cannot do both." She looked at the soldiers and the security men. "Your metal detector will pick up my cybernetic enhancements, but I assure you, I have no more weapons on my person."

The handsome soldier grunted as Jon dropped his revolver and speed loaders in the bin. "That's fine; just don't make any sudden moves. We know about your... 'natural' weapons." He glanced at Jon and his left arm in the sling. "And the fact that he is quite a bit more vulnerable to small arms fire than yourself."

Idegen narrowed her eyes at the obvious threat. "I am ready to meet with Colonel Sharpe and Dr. Helbourne."

The two soldiers led them through the maze of corridors, eight security officers walking behind. At a set of heavy double doors, the handsome soldier used a magnetic key card to access a series of security locks, and they stepped into an immense hangar of a laboratory. The civilian guards remained outside.

"Looks like something out of *2001: A Space Odyssey*." Jon's eyes darted around the huge white room, taking in the banks of computers and scientific equipment before settling on the large black shape in the middle of the room. "And that looks like something from *Independence Day*."

Sharpe and Helbourne were flanked by two more armed soldiers in camo, standing near the spacecraft. Sharpe turned as they entered, and Idegen saw a strange smile cross her face.

"Ah, Frankenstein, you've got 'em." Sharpe stepped forward, her right arm in a heavy brace strapped to her torso. She was also armed.

***

Sharpe met Idegen's eyes and smiled for some reason, as if she'd just recognized a long-absent friend. "I'm glad you came, Ms. Videshee," she said. And then she spoke to the alien with her mind, but it was a conversation that went far beyond the scope of mere words or even of conscious thought.

In a few moments of silence, they passed into each other's lives, wandered the halls of memory, saw every triumph and tragedy in vivid display—every pain and pleasure. Sharpe saw the vast personal history of Idegen Videshee, and she knew Idegen saw every minute detail of her own life journey as if they had lived each other's lives. They felt the camaraderie of their gender, their shared profession, and their similarly strong wills, just as they shared shock and disdain at some finer points of each other's personalities and experiences.

When the connection ended as suddenly as it had begun, Sharpe blinked and took a deep breath to maintain her balance. She felt, in a strange way, closer to this warrior from another world than she did to her own sister. That moment of fear and hatred she had felt on the C-130, the frustration of the hunt, and the pain of the firefight in Atlanta was all but washed away by this connection. In a moment, she had truly experienced what it means to "put yourself in someone else's shoes." She could even understand Idegen's reasons for the lives she had taken since coming to this planet. She could not fully justify them, but she could empathize. They were both soldiers, after all.

Helbourne cleared his throat and launched into his rehearsed speech. Sharpe knew he was looking to add the Peace Prize to his list of future Nobels. If he could keep Idegen's people from squashing Planet Earth, she figured he deserved it. "Ms. Videshee, on behalf of the people of Earth, I would like to formally apologize for your treatment upon your arrival—"

"Unnecessary." Idegen's eyes scanned the ship. "I am as much to blame as you. Or rather, my superiors are as much to blame as yours. We both followed orders. Orders that barred us from attempting peaceful contact. Human contact."

"That doesn't change the fact that you fascist sonsabitches killed my father," Jon French said through gnashed teeth. Sharpe could see the sudden rage boiling off the young man, his hazel eyes darting from her to the members of Alpha.

"I am sorry," Sharpe said. "There have been unfortunate casualties on both sides."

"She killed a hell of a lot of us," Frankenstein said, pointing at Idegen. "Including one of our team. Two others are in the hospital."

Sharpe raised her good hand, smiled, and tried to diffuse the rising tension. Another firefight would not do anyone any good, much less the Human Race. She'd seen Idegen's intentions in that moment of shared consciousness; she understood the gravity of the immediate situation.

At that moment, however, she saw something in Dale Steiner's hard eyes that let her know things were about to go spectacularly south. "What have you done?"

He and the rest of Alpha drew their weapons as the doors to the lab opened, and a sizeable force of black-clad operators in full tactical gear and brandishing submachine guns swarmed the room. Mr. White strolled in behind them.

"Well done, Sergeant," White said to Frankenstein. He pulled a clunky, plastic-cased device from his pocket. It looked like it might have been hi-tech in the 1960s, a refugee prop from the original *Star Trek* series.

"Thank you, sir." Steiner did not look at Sharpe.

Turning to Helbourne, White said, "And you were quite right, Doctor. This new psychic 'bond' between Colonel Sharpe and the subject was indeed the key to capturing her. As soon as I realized that the poor colonel had been compromised by this connection, it was very easy to convince Master Sergeant Steiner of this fact, though I'm sure he and his fellow Alpha members were also motivated by the personal losses they have suffered at this monster's hands."

"I am here to warn you," Idegen said. "You cannot—"

Mr. White pushed a button on the device.

Idegen's eyes rolled back in her head, and she gave a fang-baring scream that doubled her over backward and left her convulsing on the floor in agony.

"Took me a while to get my hands on this," White said, raising his voice above Idegen's animalistic howls. "It was developed by the MK Ultra program to combat Commie psychics back in the day, but I figured it would work just as well on an alien one. And what do you know? I was right."

Sharpe took a step toward Idegen, as did Jon French, but they were both checked by the automatic weapons thrust in their faces. She glared at Frankenstein. "You son of a bitch," she whispered as all her familiar pains cranked up to eleven.

***

Helbourne licked his lips, his mouth completely dry while every square inch of the rest of him was suddenly covered in perspiration. His heart rocketed in his chest, and he felt like his bladder had shrunk three sizes.

He stared from the writhing, screaming form of Idegen Videshee on the floor to the grinning, cruel face of Mr. White while he brandished his techno terror like a Golden Ticket. Sharpe and the French kid stared at the soldiers with undisguised hatred, both itching to do something but frozen by the numerous guns in the room.

"Now see here, White!" Helbourne stepped forward. "This is a place of science! Of human endeavor and learning, not some arena for your primitive sadism. I don't care what authority you have; I'm in charge of this laboratory!"

"Oh, really?" White said. He twisted a knob on the device and Idegen's agony intensified. Her long red hair lashed back and forth, and her claws shredded the floor tiles.

"Don't you see what you're doing?" Helbourne shouted, trying to be heard over Idegen's horrific wails. "You may be able to bully her, but you are condemning this planet to the vengeance of her people when they arrive! You dumb son of a bitch, you're not killing her; you're killing *us*!"

He reached to take the device from Mr. White.

That's when someone shot him.

He felt the pain before he heard the report or even smelled the gun smoke. It was sharp—piercing and blunt at the same time, and it knocked the wind out of him. His knees, already shaky with fear- and rage-fueled adrenaline, went completely limp, and he sat down on the floor. Hard. He looked down, saw the bright red stain on his lab coat growing wider and wider. A trickle of blood pumped in shallow spurts from his chest.

Numbly, he thought it an altogether fascinating experience: being shot and seeing the anatomical results... *I must be going into shock...*

He heard voices muffled behind what sounded like a thick wall. He looked up and saw a familiar face, Patches, the bright young medic who had helped with the postmortems. He was arguing with Mr. White.

Helbourne struggled to understand the words as darkness edged his vision.

"He'll bleed out, sir," Patches shouted over the high-pitched keening that echoed around the room.

"Let him," White snarled. "He's been compromised just like Sharpe. He's an enemy of the state. You take another step to give him aid, Sergeant, and I'll declare you the same. And my men will shoot you down where you stand."

"It's okay," Helbourne whispered, though he didn't think anyone could hear him. He tried to catch his breath to raise his voice but couldn't. He lifted a weak hand to wave the medic off. *No reason for both of us to die...*

Clearly no one was paying him any mind, because Patches clenched his jaw, glared at Mr. White like *The Man from Laredo*, and took another step.

Gunshots followed.

***

Jon had been biding his time, waiting for his chance. All those years wasted sitting at poker tables had given him the insight to read what men were going to do seconds before they did it.

When one of the men in black shot the doctor and the Air Force medic in camo made his play, Jon knew his chance had come. All the men in camouflage turned on the men in black as if they were a single person, and the big white room turned into an arena for a live-action game of *Call of Duty*.

All those years spent on practice fields, in the weight room, and on football fields had given him the speed, the strength, and the agility to use his body like a battering ram. Jon launched himself at the asshole in the Italian suit holding the device hurting Idegen, the one they called Mr. White.

Bullets zipped through air thick with gun smoke, reverberating thunder. Jon hit White square in the chest with his good shoulder, felt the man come off his feet, and the air rush from his lungs. They toppled to the slick linoleum floor in a heap and went sliding on White's back. Jon heard the device clatter to the ground and crack.

He looked up to see Idegen come off the ground as if she'd been shot out of a cannon. She was a wild-eyed blur and was soon surrounded by a crimson cloud as she moved through the black-clad men like a tornado of razor blades.

"Get the fuck off me!" The asshole in the suit snarled, tried to catch his breath.

Before Jon could retort, Mr. White smashed a fist into the side of his face. Jon saw stars and rolled to the floor, dazed.

Shaking his head to regain his senses, Jon clambered to his knees. The well-tailored man was nowhere in sight, and the opposing forces had spread out behind cover, still spraying the huge lab with lead. The floor was littered with dead and dying men, spent brass, and dropped weapons in pools of blood. In the middle of the chaos, Jon saw the medic crouching over the wounded doctor, firing a pistol.

"Shit." Jon chomped down on his straw and low-sprinted to the man's side. "Here, let's get him to cover." He grabbed one of the doctor's limp arms. The medic nodded, and they pulled the wounded man behind the alien spaceship.

"Thanks." The medic dug in a pouch on his web belt.

"No problem." The day-old bullet wound in his left shoulder screamed bloody murder as he shucked the sling. Jon glanced back at the battle and caught sight of Mr. White rising behind a bullet-riddled array of sparking machinery with a submachine gun. Jon followed his line of sight and saw Idegen thrashing a trio of black-clad troops, her back to White.

"No!" Jon took off at full speed straight at the man, waving his right hand over his head and wishing he'd grabbed one of the dropped guns. "Over here, asshole!"

Mr. White swung on instinct, and Jon found himself staring down the muzzle of the weapon, murder in the blue eyes glaring through the loophole sight.

The room was full of gunshots, but Jon imagined he actually heard the one that would kill him. He froze where he was, standing in the open and staring at the suited man with the gun.

Jon bit down on the straw in his mouth, felt it snap in two. But he did not feel anything else, not the now-familiar sensation of a bullet tearing into his body. He blinked and touched his chest with his good hand, felt no blood, no wound.

Mr. White stared at him for a moment, then slumped to the ground.

Jon swallowed as the gun smoke thinned. Colonel Sharpe, the woman he had shot in Atlanta, now stood in his line of sight, behind where the well-dressed asshole had been, a smoking pistol in her left hand.

24
THE ROAD GOES ON FOREVER

Idegen rose from the shriveled corpse she had just drained. The shooting was over, and a heavy quiet had settled over the cavernous lab. The muffled groans of a few wounded men were the only noises to be heard after the last echo of falling brass had faded.

Her clothes were riddled with bullet holes and soaked in blood, but her body had already healed from its many wounds. She could not say the same for the other survivors in the room. Jon and Sharpe were the only others standing, each with a useless arm. The colonel held a smoking pistol in her hand, its muzzle pointed in Jon's direction.

She lowered the weapon and slumped into a nearby chair.

"Are you all right, Jon?" Idegen stepped to him and scanned his body for fresh wounds. "Are you hurt?"

He shook his head, glanced around at the carnage, and smiled. "I'm fine. What about you? I thought he was going to scramble your brains for good with that thing."

Idegen rubbed her temple. There was still a slight buzzing behind her eyes, but it was fading. "He very well may have if you had not saved me."

"We're really starting to make a habit of that, aren't we?"

She returned his smile and walked over to where two of the soldiers crouched over Dr. Helbourne. "How is he?"

"Not good," the medic said. "I've done what I can to stabilize him, but he needs to get to a hospital ASAP."

The other soldier, the dark-haired man with narrow eyes, clenched his jaw. "He's better off than Tunes and Frankenstein, no thanks to you, lady. At least he's got a chance to make it."

Idegen accepted the accusation without comment. She turned and climbed into the cockpit of the Outrider.

"Hey!" the dark-haired soldier shouted. "What do you think you're doing up there?"

Jon stepped to intercept the man. "She's trying to save the world. That's the only reason we came back. If those engines are fired inside the atmosphere, this planet becomes a charcoal briquette."

"A likely story," the soldier said, sliding a fresh magazine into his pistol.

"He's right," Sharpe said, stepping into the confrontation. "If we don't let her do whatever she needs to do, all of this... will have been for nothing."

Idegen ignored the drama. She removed the primitive device wired into the cockpit by the human scientists and inserted her claws into the auxiliary interface system, hardwiring her neural web directly into the ship's computer.

***

Sharpe stared at French and the alien woman in the spacecraft and waved Hack-Job back. "There's been enough killing."

She turned and surveyed the carnage. Mr. White lay face down on the floor in a slowly expanding pool of blood, surrounded by upwards of thirty of his men. Tunes sprawled across a bank of smoking computer terminals, half his head gone. Frankenstein stretched out at her feet as if asleep. He was one of the first ones to die when the shooting started. She wanted to ask him why he had turned on her, but she already knew.

Why wouldn't he? If it were me hearing a crazy story of psychic bonds with alien warriors, I would have gone to another superior and asked for clarification, too.

"Thank you, Colonel," Jon French said. His face was hard, his voice strained. It was not easy for him to say. "You saved my life."

Sharpe looked at White's body and shrugged. "I never liked that asshole, anyway."

French's face softened. He gave her a sheepish grin and pointed at her shoulder. "I'm... sorry about that. I guess I'm the one that shot you."

She pointed at his limp left arm with the muzzle of her pistol. "Looks like we're even. But you should know, we didn't kill your father, Mr. French. He did that himself, putting one of our men in the hospital in the process. I believe he did it to help secure your escape."

Jon French lowered his head and took a deep breath. "Yeah... I guess I suspected as much... I just wanted to blame somebody, you know?"

"Yeah. I know." She meant what she said, too.

Idegen hopped down from the canopy, a sour look on her face. "Colonel," she said. "I have a proposition for you."

Sharpe almost laughed. "Sure, why not? Not that I'm in any position to cut any deals after this fiasco, mind you. I did just kill my supervisor, a high-ranking government official. If I escape a firing squad, I'll be buried under Leavenworth for the rest of my days."

The alien woman waved that off as inconsequential. Blinking, Sharpe realized that their psychic connection was gone, somehow severed by whatever White's device had done. This Idegen Videshee, with whom she had been so intimately familiar just moments ago, was now just another person.

"I have a possible solution for your situation, as well," Idegen said. "But right now, I want to make a deal with you. Woman to woman, warrior to warrior." She held out her bloodstained hand.

Sharpe eyed it for a moment, realizing she still held her weapon. Holstering it, she shook hands. "Okay, what have you got?"

Idegen Videshee rubbed her temples, smearing blood around her grey-green eyes. "There was a communication from my fleet stored on the ship's log. It came in right before I reached Earth's orbit, but because of the system malfunctions on my ship, I was unable to access it until now."

"Yes?"

"The fleet has returned to our galaxy. Apparently, the Logonijy Empire is now in the midst of a civil war. As far as I can tell, I am the only member of my race still in this part of your galaxy, Colonel. I am alone."

Sharpe pursed her lips. "Well, from my point of view, Idegen, that is fan-fucking-tastic news. So, what is it, exactly, that you are proposing?"

Idegen looked at the ship. "I am proposing, Colonel, that I help your scientists and engineers advance your technology while they help me repair my craft so that I can one day return to my own people. A mutually beneficial arrangement, I should think."

"A good start to interplanetary relations, I guess. That would certainly make Helbourne happy... But we need to discuss your diet."

Idegen flushed. "I am certain that we can find mutually agreeable prey in due time."

Sharpe rubbed her face, too tired to be shocked at discussing putting other human beings on an alien's menu. "I guess the Earth has no shortage of assholes who have it coming. Okay, sounds all right to me, but again, I'm not the last word on the matter. Now, how do we clean up this mess?" She waved at the battlefield.

Idegen turned and pointed at White's body. "I am guessing you did not know that he was, in fact, an agent for the Russian government."

"Bullshit."

Idegen smiled. "It is true. I saw it in his thoughts as soon as he entered the room. He was placed in your organization quite some time ago and actually participated in affecting some of your latest elections. I am certain that if you relay this information to your superiors, they will find evidence to verify what I have said."

"And if they don't," Hack-Job said, "you're starting a damn witch hunt!"

Sharpe shook her head. "Either way, it takes the heat off us for a little while. At least until they sort it out. I know White's plan was to dump this in my lap and let me be the scapegoat from the beginning. Well, now they'll have no choice. They'll have to listen to *my* story."

"Colonel," Patches said. "I don't care what you and Vampirella plan for Earth's future right now. I need to get Dr. Helbourne to a hospital, like, yesterday."

Sharpe cleared her throat. "Hack-Job, make the call to security. Get a trauma team in here and arrange for a helicopter medivac. I'll handle the details for the rest of it."

"One other thing, Colonel," Idegen said. "I want you to help Jon French disappear from the public record. He should not have to spend the rest of his life looking over his shoulder for your people or the Dixie Mafia."

Sharpe raised an eyebrow at that, glancing at French. "I guess he did have a... *humanizing* influence on you, after all."

"And lucky for all of you that he did," Idegen Videshee said.

She did not smile when she said it.

***

Jon sat on the hood of the 1963 Corvette Stingray, drinking lukewarm coffee from a Styrofoam cup, and watching the spectacle of blue and orange lights flashing in the pre-dawn darkness. The helicopter had left ORNL with Helbourne and another severely wounded combatant just a few moments before, and he could still hear the dull thump of its rotors above the din of radios squawking and EMTs jabbering reports and orders. FBI, DOD, and DOE agents strutted around, trying to find someone to throw their clout against.

The doors to Building Five opened, and Idegen walked out, a pair of armed security guards behind her. She smiled and sat down beside him. Jon looked at the federal rent-a-cops and gave them a *Go to hell* look. When Idegen did the same, they took a long, respectful step back to the sidewalk.

"So," Jon said. "You decided to save the ship, after all. I'm glad. Maybe you can get back to see Vodie one day."

Idegen tilted her head back and stared into the starry sky. "No, Jon. The engines were already beyond repair, and the ship's power source had drained away. There was no need to destroy the ship any more than it already is. And it will take at least a century for your people to gain the advancements, even with my help, to rebuild it."

"The power source drained away? How dangerous to the environment is that?" He ate a lot of fish tacos, and most of that fish came from the Gulf.

"Not very. We have a clean energy system that does not rely on chemicals or radiation, Jon. The only side effect was the tropical storm caused by the sudden, radical imbalance in electromagnetic energies in the region."

Jon tossed this nugget of info aside and returned to a more pressing concern. "So, you're trapped."

She folded her arms and glanced sideways at him. "Trapped is a harsh word, Jon. I am actually beginning to like it here."

He looked at the two guards standing six feet away. "But will you like being on a government leash?"

"No, but I suppose it is better than running from them for the rest of my life. At least now I will be afforded some modicum of respect." She bared her fangs at the two men, causing them to take another step back. "After all, they know what I can do, and they will live in constant dread of what my people will do if they ever return, and I am not here to greet them."

Jon shook his head. "You ought to use your neural web to check out the Trail of Tears and Wounded Knee, the Japanese Internment Camps during World War II, the Patriot Act, and the holding pens on the border. This government does not have the best track record when it comes to keeping promises or dealing with strangers, no matter what Lady Liberty says."

"I will be fine, Jon."

He dumped out the cold coffee. He reopened their psychic connection. *That true about the guy in there? Was he really a Russian spy?*

Idegen gave him a playful wink.

—I do not know, but it is possible based on what I have seen in your news lately. Even if he wasn't, he was still a very bad man, and, as Colonel Sharpe would say, he had it coming. I think those in charge will be willing to sacrifice him in exchange for what I can provide them

in new technologies. I know I can work with Sharpe, so her superiors will want to keep her as my... liaison. And Dr. Helbourne, provided he recovers from his wounds.

"And upset the balance of power," Jon muttered. "You could start a whole new arms race, a new Cold War that might actually get hot."

"As I understand it, my presence is not required for that possibility." Idegen frowned. "Besides, it is the only play, Jon. I cannot trust enough to make a deal with anyone but Sharpe and Helbourne, and if we do not pursue this course, they will be removed. And then you and I will have to go on the run again."

Jon sat back and sighed. "We split the pot."

"Exactly. Now, what do you propose to do, Jon?"

"I honestly have no clue. I've got two legally marketable skills. I know football, and I know poker. My reputation and my age bar me from football, and if I go back into the poker scene, I'm bound to run up against the DM again. Craig Byce is dead, and the rest of the mid-South gangs might be in shambles, but the higherups in Ohio, Louisiana, and Florida still know who I am and could put a hit on me like that." He snapped his fingers. "So, no televised World Series of Poker events for me." He looked at her and sighed. "I've got nobody and no place to go."

She put her arm around his shoulders and leaned her head against his. "You have got me, Jon French, and you always will."

He smiled, felt a lump in his throat. "I know. And you've got me, too, Idegen Videshee."

AUTHOR'S NOTE
A NOVEL SOUNDTRACK

You may have noticed that I chose this story's title and chapter headings from song titles. Below is the "playlist" garnered from countless hours of driving across Tennessee, Kentucky, the Carolinas, and Georgia with the windows down and the stereo turned way, way up. Some songs are already timeless classics, while others eventually will be. I hope you'll search them out, give them a listen, and decide for yourself whether or not they make for a good soundtrack for Jon and Idegen's adventures.

— D.S.H., 2021

Title: Reckless Kelly, "Wicked Twisted Road," *Wicked Twisted Road*, Sugar Hill, 2005.

Chapter 1: "The Wayfaring Stranger," Traditional Folk Song, originally published in 1858.
Author's note: You can't go wrong with Johnny Cash's version, but I really like the acoustic take by Rhiannon Giddens for BBC Northern Ireland in 2017, available online on YouTube.

Chapter 2: Wall, Colter, "Sleeping on the Blacktop," *Imaginary Appalachia*, Young Mary's Record Co., 2015.

Chapter 3: Reckless Kelly, "American Blood," *Bulletproof*, Yep Roc Records, 2008.

Chapter 4: The Dead South, "In Hell I'll be in Good Company," *Good Company*, Devil Duck Records 2014.

Chapter 5: Rateliff, Nathaniel and the Night Sweats, "I Need Never Get Old," *Nathaniel Rateliff and the Night Sweats*, Stacks/Concord, 2015.

Chapter 6: "The Gallows Pole," Traditional Folk Song.
Author's note: Most people are familiar with the Led Zeppelin 1970 version, but I recommend tracking down Lead Belly's 1939 recording.

Chapter 7: Simpson, Sturgill, "A Good Look," *Sound & Fury*, Elektra, 2019.

Chapter 8: The Builders and the Butchers, "Bringin' Home the Rain," *The Builders and the Butchers*, Bladen County Records, 2007.

Chapter 9: Alabama Shakes, "Hold On," *Boys and Girls*, ATO 2012.

Chapter 10: Rateliff, Nathaniel and the Night Sweats, "S.O.B.," *Nathaniel Rateliff and the Night Sweats*, Stacks/Concord, 2015.

Chapter 11: Uncle Lucius, "Keep the Wolves Away," *And You are Me*, Entertainment One, 2012.

Chapter 12: The Brothers Bright, "Blood on my Name," *A Song Treasury*, Whitestone Nocturne, 2012.

Chapter 13: Old Crow Medicine Show, "Wagon Wheel," *Old Crow Medicine Show*, Nettwerk, 2004.

Chapter 14: Scott, Darrell, "You'll Never Leave Harlan Alive," Aloha from Nashville, Sugar Hill Records, 1997.
Author's note: This song was made famous by Patty Loveless. There are several versions of this one, but they're all good in their own way.

Chapter 15: Childers, Tyler, "Deadman's Curve," *Live on Red Barn Radio I & II*, Hickman Holler Records, 2018.

Chapter 16: Denver, John, "Take me Home, Country Roads," *Poems, Prayers, and Promises*, RCA, 1971.

Chapter 17: Cross Canadian Ragweed, "17," *Cross Canadian Ragweed*, Universal South, 2002.

Chapter 18: Simpson, Sturgill, "Remember to Breathe," *Sound & Fury*, Elektra, 2019.

Chapter 19: The Dead South, "Gunslinger's Glory," *Illusion and Doubt*, Curve Music, 2016.

Chapter 20: Wall, Colter, "The Devil Wears a Suit and Tie," *Imaginary Appalachia*, Young Mary's Record Co., 2015.

Chapter 21: Styx, "Renegade," *Pieces of Eight*, A&M, 1978.

Chapter 22: Cash, Johnny, "Ain't No Grave," *American VI: Ain't No Grave*, American Records, 2010.

Chapter 23: Myers, Whiskey, "Stone," *Mud*, Wiggy Thump Records, 2016.

Chapter 24: Keen, Robert Earl, "The Road Goes on Forever," *West Textures*, Sugar Hill, 2006.

ABOUT THE AUTHOR

D. S. Hamilton has spent a lifetime traveling throughout the southern United States, putting a million miles on an already old soul. This debut novel, *The Wicked Twisted Road*, is the culmination of a lifelong love of the region, pop culture, science fiction, military adventure, and crime drama literature, along with great music.

SOMETHING WICKED THIS WAY RIDES

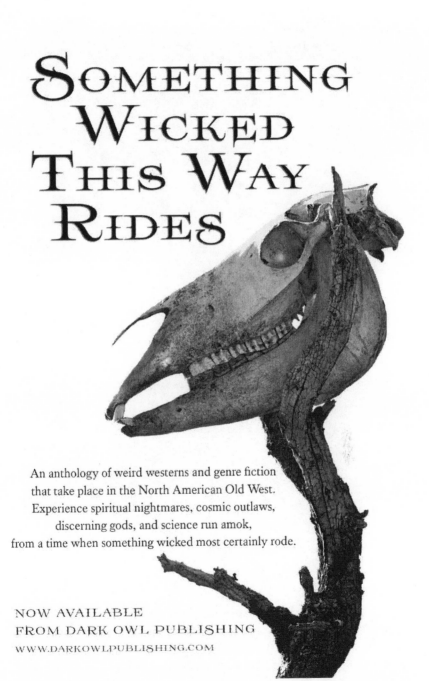

An anthology of weird westerns and genre fiction
that take place in the North American Old West.
Experience spiritual nightmares, cosmic outlaws,
discerning gods, and science run amok,
from a time when something wicked most certainly rode.

THE DARK

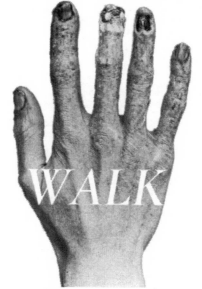

WALK

FORWARD

A HARROWING COLLECTION BY
JOHN S. MCFARLAND

Available in paperback and on Kindle from
DARK OWL PUBLISHING, LLC
www.darkowlpublishing.com

Made in the USA
Columbia, SC
21 July 2022

63793608R00157